To JANÉ HAI --

CW01558948

Peter H

The Clarion Resource

To dear Jane
With my thanks
and best wishes
lots of love
Peter Maines.

First published 2001

© Copyright Peter Haines 2000
The right of Peter Haines to be identified as the author of this work
has been asserted by him in accordance with the
Copyright, Designs and Patents Act 1998.

A CIP catalogue record of this book is available
from the British Library

© ISBN 0-9541431-0-8
Printed in England
Am-Pm Design & Print, Cheltenham

This is a work of fiction. Any similarity with persons
either living or dead is purely coincidental.

ABOUT THE AUTHOR

Peter Haines was born in Gloucestershire in 1952. He enjoyed a fondly remembered childhood in that green, mellow and delicious county.

For most of his working life he has worked in marketing with multi-nationals and advertising agencies. While this is his first attempt at a novel, he has been writing for well over 25 years. He has enjoyed success as an advertising copywriter and still edits three newspapers - each for a charity. His closest friends know him as a cryptic crossword compiler - crosswords of the most heinous kind. For many years he has worked with the Gloucestershire Drug and Alcohol Service, a charity of which he is now Vice Chairman.

After many years away from his home county, Haines now lives once again in his beloved Gloucestershire. Of four children (2 stepsons) only the youngest, Harry, remains at home.

Having entered the world of further education - almost by default - he works at Stroud College as Head of Marketing, a job he loves.

ACKNOWLEDGMENTS

Many have helped me with The Clarion Resource. Inevitably I must miss some, but my special thanks go to Doctors Jane Hawes and George Laverty - the former of medicine, the latter of business administration. It was friend and novelist David Callinan who provided inspiration and encouragement. Debbie Thomas and Chris Mauler who proofed and corrected. (They had much to do.) And a special thanks goes to Doug Garland. When all routes of research had led me to a complete stop, it was Doug who came to the rescue.

My thanks also to editors Edit Ink of New York and to Scorpion Press

For my wife, Jacqui
Who faces the world with fortitude

Phoenix

Heading northwards on Interstate Highway 17, the Lincoln stretch limousine made the miles seep away, fifty-five in every hour. Its destination, Flagstaff, was still some way off. On a long straight the driver, Zach, saw a truck in the far distance. He saw it in the way experienced drivers do, a general awareness of an approaching presence. If Zach had been blindfolded and asked questions about the truck he would not, at this point, have been able to answer any one beyond the fact that the truck was there. Dr Jonjo Grey, Zach's master, now dozing in the back, was not aware of the presence of the truck. As far as he knew he, Zach and the limo were the only occupiers of the highway for a hundred miles in either direction.

When the truck was thirty yards from the car it swerved to its left. At that moment Zach noted it was a White tractor unit liveried in black and gold. It struck the driver's door, spinning the car in a clockwise direction until it was facing the way it had come. As the car spun the lorry scoured its side before returning to its own side of the highway. The combined speed on impact was well over 100 miles an hour. The car bent in the middle to form an L shape. This was possible because of the elongation of the limo allowing weak points in the centre of the chassis. It was this flexibility which probably saved Dr Jonjo Grey's life. The driver's door had taken the initial impact and had absorbed many tons. This door, along with the panel in front and the panel immediately to its rear, had folded inwards, crushing Zach and his seat and compressing both against the floor. The space between the displaced panels and the floor was less than 18 inches.

They had left the city of Phoenix some miles behind and were now well into the desert. Had it not been for the air-conditioning this would have been an uncomfortable place to be. Now, though, the air-conditioning had stopped and there was only silence. Grey was not aware of this as he sat on the thick carpet which covered the floor in the passenger compartment of the Lincoln. He was conscious but in a state of shock. His cigar, contraband Cuban, was burning a hole in the pants of his suit. The flesh on his knee was burning. It was the smell and pain of this that brought him round. As his brain started to function again he became aware of the smell of gasoline. On impulse, without assessing the information, he threw the cigar out of the gap where his offside door had once fitted so neatly.

It was only now Grey started to process information. He knew that Zach, his employee and friend, was dead. He knew that he had been the target and instead of him, his loyal friend and servant had been killed. He knew that he was vulnerable in this place and he knew he had to act quickly. On top of all these things he knew who was responsible. He had expected Ricky Hahn to react, but not quickly and not violently. Grey reached for the car phone. It didn't work. He fumbled around on the floor of the wrecked car, found his briefcase containing his mobile phone and poked the digits.

Now he sat and waited. His mind recalled the last few hours of his life and the last few hours of Zach's life. Just minutes before, Grey had been sprawled in the soft leather of the car. He was feeling the warm glow of well-being, having spent two hours on the tennis court at Phoenix Rackets Club in a resort hotel in Scottsdale. The temperature had been well into the hundreds and he had taken his opponent, Ricky Hahn, twelve years his junior, in straight sets.

Until the crash, this was a day when Dr Jonjo Grey felt he had every right to feel good about the world in general and himself in particular. He had enjoyed his tennis this day. He had been particularly enjoying the trappings of his wealth. The car was good. His suit was good, from one of Italy's finest houses. His shoes were satisfying on this hot, hot day. They came from Lobbs of London and his shirt was from Jermyn Street. Rolex had supplied his watch.

It had been satisfying on this day to sit behind his driver and minder, the loyal and capable Zach Michaels. Zach had served his master for a decade. He had been selected when he had suddenly and unexpectedly found himself unemployed. He had been one of a small and select band whose duty was to protect the life of the incumbent of The White House. There was to be no repeat of 22nd November 1963 when the 35th President of the United States of America had been fatally shot by one or more unknown assassins. The maximum Zach could have served with the unit would have been three years. Zach had not made his first anniversary. He had been carefully chosen, just like each of his colleagues, from candidates from the armed forces, police departments, the C.I.A. or F.B.I.

Zach had been marked for fast track promotion. Most had expected him to reach team leader within eighteen months. This was not to be. It was a surprise to most when he had been asked to leave. Few knew the reason why, although there had been speculation. The First Lady, rumour had it, had been observed paying him a little too much attention. Within four days of his departure and enforced unemployment, Grey's talent scouts had approached Zach and made him an offer he chose not to refuse. Grey and his scouts had been tipped off by Marcus Knox from the State Department.

Zach and Jonjo Grey had become more than just employee and employer over the years. A close bond had developed which was based on trust and mutual regard. Each admired the other's professionalism. Even up until a few minutes ago, Grey had had little fear for his own life, but Zach always played the part of the professional. This used to amuse Grey. Zach's style of dress rarely changed, although colours and patterns changed daily. His shoes were always slip-ons, never lace-ups. His suit jacket was either single vent or ventless. He had explained years ago that double vents had a nasty habit of revealing the hardware beneath. This hardware was attached to a substantial leather belt and included handgun, radio and mobile phone. Zach also wore braces since he could not rely on his belt to keep his pants up. His shirts were never button down. Too easy, Zach reckoned, to get a button pulled off.

And so it was that Dr Jonjo Grey had been feeling good about everything on this day. But there was one thing above all others which provided an intense sensation of satisfaction. He had outnegotiated Ricky Hahn and then shown him the way around a tennis court.

Hahn controlled the leaders of the union. Without union support Grey, president of Ribbon Motor Corporation, knew he had no chance of having ten thousand examples of his new model with his distributors and franchisees by the launch date, or any other date for that matter.

The new model, christened the Yellow Ribbon, had taken 13 years and close to $1 billion to develop. Grey had no intention of allowing Hahn to jeopardise such an investment.

Ricky Hahn was the younger son of a powerful and allegedly commercial dynasty. Grey knew that this was a cover for a crime family of extraordinary size, success, sophistication and organisation. He had tried to pressurise Grey to increase his share from the unions and Ribbon Motor Corporation. Without the increased payoff he had threatened that the Yellow Ribbon would not roll out on schedule. He had the arrogance to believe he could outnegotiate and outmanoeuvre Grey. This was foolish. Grey had been aware from the outset that Hahn would not risk losing his control over the unions by overplaying the greed card. In any case, just for insurance, he had irrefutable proof of the bribes which Hahn had accepted along with video footage of Hahn in a range of the most compromising and indelicate sexual positions with a young woman of impeccable reputation. The relevance of this being not the impeccable reputation but the quality of the stock. She was a cherished angel from an old money family which was well connected, a family which was powerful and unforgiving. Image, honour and reputation were placed above all things. Not a family to go up against when it was not absolutely necessary. In any case the girl was a minor.

All in all this had been a most satisfying day.

Dr Jonjo Grey had taken the Havana cigar from its cedarwood box. He had lit it and savoured the sensation and aroma. All was most definitely right with the world, or at least with his world. Now the Yellow Ribbon would roll out on time. He had smiled as he recalled conversations with his marketing people and the advertising agency. The name was causing concern. Would "yellow" be linked with cowardice or happy, safe homecomings? Eventually it was agreed that it was a safe and comfortable name which fitted with corporate strategy and market positioning. The Blue Ribbon had been, and still was, a great success. General Motors and Ford were watching sales figures with more than a passing interest.

It had been a great day.

At a corner table in a teashop in a small market town in rural England sat a customer. He was alone. He ordered Assam tea and a Danish pastry. At first the waitress had assumed he was a tourist. His Scottish accent had suggested this. Later, she rejected her theory. Tourists dress in a certain, relaxed way. They do not wear dark, chalk-striped city suits, white silk shirts and club ties. While she could see it was a club tie, she had no means of identifying the club. The customer's black Oxford shoes were polished to a mirror finish, not the footwear of a tourist.

The customer was a big man with a broad smile. Every so often his huge head would lift and he would glance, apparently absent-mindedly, over his newspaper and half-moon spectacles and beam at members of staff and, if they were looking in his direction, other customers. When the waitress returned with his order she couldn't help noticing the immaculately manicured nails as his fingers gripped his paper.

Before pouring his tea the big man waited the mandatory four minutes to enable it to brew properly. As he took his first sip, Julie Martin, the teashop owner entered the dining room. A careful observer would have noticed a slight interruption to the rhythm of her walk when she spotted the immaculately presented customer. At the same moment he saw Julie. He slightly tilted his vast head to one side, raised his right eyebrow and grinned. She ignored him, failing to return the grin, and continued about her business.

Minutes later Julie returned to the dining room and recognised the visual message transmitted by the mighty Scot. His smile lessened without disappearing and, almost imperceptibly, he moved his head to the left then the right. He wanted to speak to her but not in the presence of others. In return Julie nodded before disappearing into the kitchen.

As the Scot was about to pop the last morsel of the excellent pastry into his mouth the ringing of his mobile phone shattered the tranquillity of the tearoom. Despite the glares from other customers it was without embarrassment or self-consciousness that he answered the call.

"Right. I'm on my way," he said when the caller had finished talking.

For a moment the smile had evaporated. Sir Harry Buchanan stood, dropped a ten pound note on the table and briskly walked out. While he had wanted a social chat with Julie, when Sir Gordon Melville summoned him, social chats had to take a back seat.

Ricky Hahn sat on the bar stool in Joe's on Chaparral Drive. Not Phoenix's most lively bar but one much favoured by society. It was an interesting bar. The clientele ranged from senior police officers to politicians, industrialists to bigtime criminals. Hahn was drinking imported German beer. He was alone and this was just the way he wanted it for a while.

He was halfway down his third beer when a suited man unobtrusively took up station by his side. As Hahn lifted the glass to his lips the newcomer grabbed his arm with enough force to stop the arm moving in either direction. He bent down to Hahn's right ear.

"That's enough booze. The old man wants to see you."

"The old man can wait. I ain't done here yet."

"He said like now."

There was a tone which suggested to Ricky Hahn that he should comply.

Together the two men left Joe's and stepped into the back door of a black Mercedes which was illegally parked directly outside the door. Noiselessly the big car took its passengers to Phoenix's Sky Harbor International Airport. Here a Bell JetRanger helicopter was waiting on the private apron. The old man kept his helicopter here rather than at the Scottsdale Municipal Airport. It was a matter of convenience. The aircraft was airborne in twenty minutes. The family's ranch was little more than an hour's flight away in Sedona. It was here, some twenty years before, that Ricky's father had set up his ranch to take advantage of the favourable tax concessions allowed to bloodstock ranches. The

I.R.S. had since changed its mind but the old man continued what had become his hobby. He lived in considerable comfort with a sense of security and belonging.

The ranch was quiet, tranquil, green and rural. These were some of the reasons why the senior member of the Hahn family had decided to live there.

The helicopter landed on a metal pad in front of a vast, mock colonial mansion. Its double oak doors matched the house for size. By the time the men had reached the door it had been opened for them by a white coated butler.

"This way please, gentlemen. Your father is anxious to see you, Mister Ricky."

"I just bet he is." Ricky muttered under his breath.

The butler showed them into a vast library. When the escort was satisfied he had safely delivered his charge he turned without a word and left the room. Ricky sat in a leather wing chair.

While he waited he found himself getting increasingly tense. Why had his father summoned him? There could be many reasons. Why was his father keeping him waiting? He stood and started to pace the room. It was called a library simply because it contained thousands of books, most of which had never been touched since they entered the house. It was not a place of study for the Hahn family as far as Ricky knew. His father might use it while alone but somehow he doubted it. He certainly never used it. Ricky was not generally considered to be well read.

As he continued to amble up and down he caught sight of a car rolling up the drive. It was followed by another. Within ten minutes a third luxury car approached the house. He recognised each car as those belonging to chief executives of divisions of the family business. Along with Ricky's father and his older brother, Joseph, these three men comprised what was known in family circles as the management team. They worked closely together and met regularly, yet they lived and had their offices thousands of miles apart. Faxes, electronic mail and modem links made effective communication feasible over large distances. Nevertheless, security was high on the agenda and sensitive material was not sent by these means.

Ricky heard voices outside the library door. They sounded sombre and muted. Was he here to be invited to join the management team? Somehow he doubted that. Surely his father would call him now. How much longer was he expected to wait?

It was close to two hours before the library door opened and Webster Hahn, the old man, walked in. Here was a tall, upright man of 68. His grey hair distinguished him and the impeccable cut of his suit added to an impression of power and authority. Webster Hahn was not a man to tolerate incompetence, disobedience or failure, yet his younger son Ricky was incompetent, disobedient and, very often, a failure. But Ricky was special. He was 33, the baby of the family. Allowances had to be made for him. He wasn't so bright and needed to be helped along. On the other hand his older brother, Joseph, was 42 and he was the smart one. Few allowances were made for him, not that he needed them. There were those who said Joseph was as smart as his father but they wouldn't voice that opinion in front of the old man.

Webster walked to his son and embraced him. He gently pushed him away holding him at arm's length, hands on each shoulder. Quietly and slowly he said, "Don't interrupt me. Don't contradict me. Don't deny this. You tried to whack Jonjo Grey."

Ricky started. He opened his mouth to speak. Webster slapped his son hard on the cheek. Ricky hit the floor. He looked up at his father in absolute amazement. His father hadn't hit him in twenty years. His lower jaw hung down, his eyes were wide in shock and watering.

Softly and in measured tones, the old man continued. "Jonjo Grey is an old and trusted acquaintance of mine. He and I go way back. We have a relationship of trust, respect and considerable mutual benefit. We have value to each other."

"Dad, I -"

Ricky landed on the floor again.

"Shut up. Do you think Grey is stupid? Do you think I'm stupid? I know you've been taking your cut. I know you've been creaming. I know you've put pressure on Grey about his new car launch. No! Grey is not stupid. I am not stupid. You, on the other hand, are very stupid. I don't believe you know what you've done. Grey outplays you so you try to zap him. That's stupid enough, but to do it so soon? Grey has to link the hit with you because you're still fresh in his mind. You're stupid, stupid, stupid. Do you think he's going to let this go? Forget all about it?"

He put his head to one side and held out his hands as if inviting a response.

"What do you think I can do? Talk to him, eh? Tell him it was business, nothing personal, eh?" Webster paused then turned away from his son. He walked towards one of the windows then swung round. "You don't get your way so you try to whack him. You think we got where we are like this? You listen to me good."

For the first time his voice rose. Ricky could not remember the last time he heard his father shout.

"You don't whack no one. You do nothing. You keep your head down. You lose yourself for a while. You check into a hotel, someplace quiet, and you stay there." The man's temper began to subside and his voice returned to its normal volume and pace. "Call me when you've settled in. I need to know where you are and how to get in touch quickly. I don't want to have to send Chip and the boys to find you. You understand me?"

Ricky nodded and said nothing. Now he looked at his shoes.

"One last piece of advice. If I wanted a truck moved would I ask Alvar, Ollie or Michael?" He was referring to the other members of the Management Team, Alvar Knight, Ollie Goldstein and Michael Charlton. Ricky shook his head.

"Right. So you wanted to arrange a hit and you ask a truck driver. Like I said Ricky, sometimes you ain't too smart. Now leave. I have business to attend to. Go see Chip and get yourself lost for a while."

Chip had been Ricky's escort. A man to be trusted and very capable. He obeyed without question and was required to stay close to the family most of the time.

Webster Hahn turned and left the library. He walked with considerable purpose across the marble floor and opened the double doors across the hall. He was met with the gaze of four men all in their forties or early fifties, each immaculately dressed and each waiting for some kind of revelation.

"I'm sorry for the distraction, gentlemen. A piece of family business. It need not concern you further."

Hahn took his chair at the head of the highly polished mahogany table. He appeared calm and most definitely in control. He considered his next words for a moment.

"When my father passed through Ellis Island he was no more than a poor immigrant boy. He came to this country to escape the poverty in his own land. Like millions of others he was attracted by a promise of wealth and power, influence and opportunity. Unlike millions of others his dream did not turn to ashes. His empire, which I inherited, was built on strong foundations. Planning. Responding to needs. Understanding the market and fulfilling it. My father was not frightened of change. Like others his big chance came with the Volstead Act. The Eighteenth Amendment to the Constitution of the United States which prohibited intoxicating liquors. Prohibition was his big break. It elevated him from smalltime protection to bigtime bootlegging. In those days and for many years the women were good. Prostitution paid bigtime and was safe. Now it's a dirty business. Too much scum operating. Drugs was good, fine, profitable business. For many years it was safe.

"It was nearly fifteen years ago I decided to diversify and become legitimate. I knew it would take time. Back then, just like now, we worked with the unions. We developed our transport interests, our building interests, laundry and garbage collection. Gambling has become ever more important to us. But now what's happening?" Hahn sat forward and moved his hands from his lap laying them flat on the table. "New times are with us. New times are here because of casual attitudes and scumbags. Careless people who can't think straight. They're spoiling it for the rest of us.

"Once we only had the cops or the F.B.I. to worry us. They're getting more troublesome. But there are others now. The D.E.A. and Interpol are giving us problems. Not so easy to buy those who can hurt us anymore. Eliot Ness set a bad example." Hahn paused to smile at own wry humour.

"The time has come to change again. Our business is built on respect and reliability. Our friends know they can trust us when they need help. We are admired and feared and that's good. Our friends have turned to us again. They need our help. They're going to war. A drugs war. I don't want to know anything more about their business. What they do is their business and none of our concern."

All eyes in the room were on Webster Hahn. The old man could feel the tension mounting just as he had intended.

"We're going to move out of the front line. Our friends want us to supply arms. We're not talking a case of Saturday Night Specials. We're talking enough arms to supply a small army. Heavy equipment."

Here Hahn paused again, expecting the first interruption. It came from Joseph.

"I assume, Dad, we will not get involved directly?"

"Right. I have a contact in Europe. These people have helped our friends in the past. I'll be meeting with them soon. Let's see what they can do to help us."

For the next hour the management team discussed performances of the divisions of the organisation. They submitted their reports and proposals. They discussed their fears, worries and ideas. Webster Hahn listened to every word. When they had finished they departed, leaving Hahn to ponder.

He retired to his favourite room in the house, his study. He sat behind his vast partner's desk and lit a cigar - a cigar from the private stock of Dr Jonjo Grey. He started to consider Ricky and Dr Jonjo Grey. He had ideas of how to resolve the dispute before major damage was done to anyone. He rejected each idea. Eventually he decided he would call Grey in a couple of days and ask for a meeting. Webster Hahn never made that call.

Erifia

Nestling on the coast between South America's French Guiana and the vast expanse of Brazil is the tiny country of Erifia. The nation lies just north of both the equator and the many mouths of the mighty Amazon. It is low-lying and, by and large, a geographically dull country as countries go. Temperatures are in the high 80s throughout the year and it is wet - very wet. Inhabitants can expect at least 150 inches of precipitation a year. Some years it is much higher.

Information in a gazetteer would tell the casual reader (casual for it is unlikely one would look up Erifia deliberately) that its area is little more than 2000 square miles. The reader would learn that its capital is Erifi, in which 14,000 of its 25,000 people live. There are no other major settlements. The official language is English and its religion is Roman Catholicism. The reader would continue to find that the adult literacy rate is less than 35% and the average life expectancy is 47 years. The unit of currency is the Erifian pound and its per capita gross national product is around US$1470. This figure would surprise an economist as it is remarkably high, not just for this part of the world, but for a country this size. The only exports likely to be listed would be copper and photocopiers.

Just as the Welsh had colonised parts of Patagonia, a few score of Scots had settled in Erifia. Nearly two centuries later their descendants, along with many of their customs, beliefs and culture remained. There was a Princes Street in Erifi just as there was a Sauchiehall Street and a Cowcaddens Road. In the centre of Erifi stood a magnificent statue of a kilted and bonneted Bonnie Prince Charlie waving a mighty claymore. This statue provided a focus for many of the town's and the country's elders, a focus of which they were justifiably proud.

Over the years the Scottish blood had mingled with French, Portuguese and native Indian to produce a rich genetic brew. The Erifians became a resolute and hospitable people, hardworking and cheerful, by and large. There were anomalies which provided specialists with interesting work benches. For example, the per capita consumption of alcohol in Erifia was roughly similar to that of Germany. Despite this, the identifiable level of alcoholism and alcohol related illnesses in Erifia was over 30% lower than could be expected if the rest of the world was used as a benchmark. Statistics also suggested that there should be nearly 40% more alcohol-related accidents than there actually were. Another fact of worldwide significance was that there was no reported domestic violence. So unlikely was this believed to be that the specialists from around the world claimed that families and the state colluded to hide incidents. When these experts were invited to form an independent working party to investigate the cover up along with any domestic violence it could find, the report submitted to the government of Erifia and to the United Nations was very thin and admitted to being unable to find one incidence to investigate.

All in all a small and, on first examination, an insignificant country. However, there are three facts about Erifia which are of very considerable significance. The first being the British Royal Navy base in Erifi. The second, seven miles inland there is a Royal Air Force base and third, and most significant, Erifia had recently been subject to a coup d'etat. It was at this point that the British government suddenly took particular notice of Erifia.

Her Majesty's government took an interest because the mutual benefit, previously taken for granted, was now at risk. The British paid little for the leases on its two bases. And the bases were of some importance. The Royal Navy serviced, refuelled and supplied ships of the Atlantic Fleet in Erifi. The Royal Air Force did much the same for its aeroplanes. But more important than this, the bases provided a presence in South America. Argentina was not so far away and from Erifia, the British could provide at least a token observation on the Falkland Islands, a deterrent rather than a realistic protection support position. From Erifia's point of view, the British presence was highly desirable. At no cost to the Erifian people it appeared to have a friendly naval and air force presence. The Erifians were only required to pay for their small army in their taxes.

L.Y.A Photocopiers was a British government project. Funded by the government, it was an experiment to see if it would provide a real and marketable alternative to relatively inexpensive copiers from the Far East. While taking advantage of the low labour costs in Erifia, the government was aware it could gain a public relations coup at the same time. It provided work for nearly one thousand nationals at the L.Y.A. factory and countless other jobs in services and retailing. All in all most people were very happy with the arrangement.

Components were imported mainly from Britain and the assembled copiers were exported by the container load, principally to Europe. Not only was the quality of the copiers surprisingly high but the price was low. This was due not just to low labour costs but also fairly low transportation costs. Erifia was closer to Europe than the Far East.

The British government commissioned an advertising agency based in London's Soho to handle the advertising and public relations and L.Y.A. Photocopiers was something of a success story. The first job of the agency was to find a name for the company which was acceptable to both the British and the Erifians. Both were happy with Light Years Ahead Photocopiers.

In return for a 49% share in L.Y.A. Photocopiers and a 49% share in Erifian Copper Extraction Limited, the Erifians were required to provide the British with an exclusive option on all copper mined. The price paid by the British was negotiated not just in terms of currency but Erifia's needs at the time. The price would be offset by medical supplies and doctors, foodstuffs and spare parts for Land Rovers.

And so the relationship between Erifia and Britain was mutually beneficial, friendly, harmonious and lucrative. While it proceeded thus there was little need for the people of either country to question the arrangement. However, when the coup came, the relationship between the two countries changed, and this did not suit the British government and the prime minister of Great Britain one bit.

President Jacques Sandriano had enjoyed the function. It had been a fairly lightweight affair in the palace. Several foreign VIPs had been present along with some captains of industry from home. There had been girls, champagne and talk of a great, prosperous and rosy future for the people of Erifia.

After the event President Sandriano and his bodyguard, Sim Campbell, were driven to the president's private villa, which was perched atop one of the very few hills close to Erifi. The driver stopped the old but gleaming Buick outside the front door of the villa and the two men went inside. The president poured himself a whisky and left the main reception room for a shower. Sim took the whisky which had been poured for him, placed his tortoise shell spectacles on his nose, picked up a copy of the previous day's Wall Street Journal and seated himself at one end of a huge settee. This was the first time he had had to himself all day, his first opportunity to unwind.

Sim Campbell's life was, in the main, one of comfort. He lived in relative luxury, ate well and enjoyed many of the better things Erifia could offer. He enjoyed robust health and rarely felt under pressure. He had worked for Jacques Sandriano for many years, since long before Sandriano had taken the Oath of Presidency. He had been at his master's arm during the election campaigning and had rarely left his side at any time since. His view of his president was uncomplicated. He adored him, loved him and saw him as the embodiment of his country, its culture and its future. His trust in President Sandriano was total and unconditional.

While his view of Sandriano was simple he himself was complex. He would gladly use his own body to shield the president from an assassin's bullet. Most evenings saw him working out in the gymnasium at the villa. He pushed himself mercilessly. Every morning, before his boss was awake, he jogged. Come rain or shine, Sim Campbell would be out working off the calories he had enjoyed the previous day. He never started at the same time or took the same route two days in a row. Whichever route he took, however, the run would rarely be less than seven miles. The sight of him trotting around the country could turn a head or two. He was a vast figure of a man and bore little resemblance to most people's view of a jogging stereotype. He didn't enjoy working out but he saw it as his duty to keep himself in trim for the sake of his employer.

On the other hand, Sim Campbell was a gentle giant of a man. He looked, to many, like a favourite uncle. It was this avuncular appearance and attitude along with the quietly spoken voice that made people instinctively like him and trust him. Each Christmas he was much in demand by schools, the hospital and private children's parties to put on the red suit and white beard and hand out the presents with a merry ho-ho.

His sporting interests were not confined to jogging - not that he ever saw jogging as a sport. To Sim jogging was merely a duty. What he really loved was golf. Over the years, however, he had perpetrated a deception which had required vast skill and patience. Amazingly he had never been found out, never exposed. Sim was a brilliant, natural golfer, yet he would not win one round in ten. A drive of 300 yards and more straight down the middle of the fairway was a mere bagatelle to him. Sim was anything but a deceitful man, but he could not tolerate beating his president. For years he had allowed Sandriano to beat him and believe himself to be the superior golfer. In truth, had Sim allowed himself to develop his game he would have played off scratch. But it was not to be; he had to put his master first, above all things. Indeed, it would have been improper and inappropriate to beat President Jacques Sandriano.

Gradually Sim became aware that his president had been a long time in the shower. He had expected him some minutes before for their customary game of backgammon. The president did not take long when backgammon was to be played. Casually Sim got up and walked towards the shower room. He knocked on the door.

"Mr President. Are you okay?"

He could hear running water. There was no reply. He knocked again, louder this time.

"Mr President. Mr President."

Still no reply. Sim, a man of considerable stature, put his left shoulder to the door. There was splintering and part of the door frame came away as the door flew open. As he catapulted into the shower room Sim was immediately aware of the presence of the president and two other men. One was holding his employer in an arm lock, the other was wheeling around to bring his gun to bear on Sim.

Sim was able to change course slightly and his momentum carried his bulk to the gunman at a remarkable rate. He barged into the trespasser who crashed backwards into the wall. An onlooker might have said that what Sim did next was all part of the same move. For a man of his size he moved with grace and agility. While the second intruder was still trying to adjust to the situation in which he now found himself, Sim's fist brushed the president's ear and landed on the nose of the other, sending him off balance. He released his captive.

"Get out!" Sim yelled.

The president ran through the door. The second man had regained his balance and he threw a punch at Sim's head. Sim was much too quick for this amateur pugilist. He punched him three times in quick succession, breaking his jaw in at least one place. He fell to the ground unconscious. Sim turned his attention to the other who, by this time, had gathered his senses. Automatic fire was heard throughout the president's private residence and Sim dropped to the tiled floor, dead.

The gunman staggered to his feet and realised the president was no longer in the shower room. He made for the broken door and into the corridor. The president had disappeared.

Vice President Christian McGregor was waiting impatiently at the palace in the centre of Erifi. Just an hour before, the palace had been the venue for a cordial function. Now it was surrounded by members of Erifia's armed forces. McGregor was smiling and talking to the soldiers, but if his constant pacing was an indication, he was fretting. McGregor was a pompous, strutting man who could, if the occasion demanded, draw on vast reserves of charm. He did not find it easy to be humble.

Yet he was, in many respects, a likeable man. He could amuse and entertain with an ease not found in many. He was well read and could surprise listeners with a deep knowledge of a wide range of subjects, from Scottish and French history to geology.

Soon he was joined by General Francois Gariol, the senior officer of Erifia's army.

"Mr President," said the general, referring to Christian McGregor, "I am pleased to advise you that the palace is now surrounded. There has been very little resistance and no casualties to speak of."

General Gariol was also a strutting man but there the similarity with McGregor ended. He was slim and short and, as is occasionally the case with small men, he carried an attitude which could be extremely unattractive. His finely clipped moustache did nothing to hide the sneer which could cover the lower part of his face. There were those who thought that Gariol grew the moustache to give himself stature. Instead it made him look pretentious, which is exactly what he was. He was a scheming, clever man. When Gariol was appointed head of the armed forces it occurred to Christian McGregor that here was the ideal partner to help him achieve his own objectives. Since Gariol's ego and desire for power were enormous, he jumped at the chance when McGregor, with uncharacteristic timidity, approached him with his idea for national domination. Here was a opportunity far too good to miss, the kind of chance that only comes once in a lifetime.

Gariol's character was further tainted by a streak of cruelty. The army saw him as a despot and senior officers feared him. He occasionally struck his senior officers, who never retaliated but viewed it as a small price to pay for the general's support and patronage.

Gariol seemed to have but one weakness. A few people, a very few, knew of his attraction to young soldiers. Even fewer people knew that, as a young man, Gariol had had an unsuccessful and rather messy relationship with a beautiful woman. She had endured two years of physical, sexual and psychological abuse. The time came when she could take no more of the treatment and she broke off the engagement and later took legal advice. Gariol, who was only concerned about the effect adverse publicity of this kind might have on his career, paid her to keep her mouth shut. Members of his family, which was not rich, clubbed together to bail him out. They threw themselves into a state of hardship because of shame, the desire to protect their family honour and a fear of this violent and ill-tempered little man. Now, though, given a similar set of circumstances, he would have ordered the woman's death and her body to disappear before a whiff of scandal could hit the streets. Some thought that it was this experience which had turned Gariol to seek the pleasures of the young soldiers.

"Good, good, General. Please ensure that the offices of the Examiner are secure and intact. Deploy your men to deliver the leaflets if you would be so kind. Don't miss a single home or office. Is that clear?"

"Very clear, Mr President," replied the general.

There was no radio or television broadcasting on Erifian territory. Satellite broadcasting was available, however the revolutionaries had no access to manipulate this for their propaganda purposes. They intended for every household to have a leaflet delivered during the night. It was then planned that a full explanation should appear in the Examiner the following morning. The copy had been written in advance and was to tell the people of Erifia that President Jacques Sandriano had been deposed. President Christian McGregor was their new leader. It was to announce that ex - President Sandriano was under house arrest and would later be tried for misuse of public funds and various offences against the state. McGregor and Gariol had decided that none of the offences with which Sandriano was to be charged would be serious enough to call for the death penalty. The people of Erifia might react against the next government and McGregor didn't want a martyr.

It went on to say that the new government of President McGregor would examine the economic ties with Great Britain and see if they were in the best interests of the people of Erifia. It doubted at this stage that the ties were of benefit to the people but were, most definitely, of benefit to the last president and his friend, the prime minister of Great Britain. The article said that Erifia was no more than a puppet state. Great Britain pulled the strings.

As of this day, L.Y.A. Photocopiers was wholly owned by the people of Erifia and the leases on the naval and air bases were to be examined. All copper extraction was to cease with immediate effect until further notice.

Later on it was to surprise some that no instructions were issued about sailings of merchant vessels from Erifi. This was also true of the two Royal Navy ships but a close watch was kept at the gates of the naval dock. No persons were allowed to enter or leave until further notice. The R.A.F. base just a few miles away was ignored completely.

In the meantime there was to be no unrest and everything would continue as before but under the government of President Christian McGregor.

An exhausted and battered revolutionary looking very nervous now appeared before Christian McGregor at the palace. Without preamble he addressed McGregor and General Gariol.

"Sandriano escaped. I killed Campbell."

McGregor's smile vanished. He had not worked out the implications of not having the democratically elected president in custody but his instinct told him it was not good. Where would he have gone?

General Gariol took over. He turned to one of his officers. "Take this man out and shoot him. Hang him from a high place where all can see him. This will demonstrate the price of failure. Move. Get him out of my sight. When you have done this thing deploy your men. I want Sandriano's villa searched from top to bottom. I want your men in the homes of every one of Sandriano's relatives. When you have found him bring him to President McGregor."

Erifia's army had no tanks or heavy armoured vehicles. Heavy machine guns mounted on ageing Land Rovers it did have. It was these that General Gariol deployed to patrol the streets and roads of the more highly populated areas. In these early stages of the revolution, the people of Erifia displayed little resistance. They appeared to accept the coup without question. Whether this was due to shock, fear, cowardice or waiting for an opportunity, few people knew or even thought about.

But there was one immediate question asked, and not just on the western shores of the Atlantic. Where was President Sandriano?

Within three hours of the coup, a Westland Wessex, one of the last operational examples of the helicopter anywhere in the world, took off from the R.A.F. base. Within half an hour a line lowered a figure onto the deck of the M.V. *Constancy*. She was bound for Southampton.

President Jacques Sandriano of Erifia and Prime Minister James Bailey of Great Britain were of a similar age and similar politics. While their respective countries enjoyed a harmonious trading and political relationship, the two men enjoyed a harmonious personal relationship.

Not only were there frequent official visits of the leaders, one to the other, there were also frequent unofficial meetings. The purpose of these was purely social. Both men enjoyed the other's company. They enjoyed playing golf and food was a passion for both.

When the news of Sandriano's overthrow arrived, James Bailey took it personally. He demanded more information but, immediately after the coup, there was little more to be acquired. James Bailey had to wait to hear the full story.

Within five hours of the end of the reception at the palace, news reached 10 Downing Street. The prime minister was advised that President Jacques Sandriano was alive and well and making for Southampton on a British owned and registered vessel. Bailey picked up a telephone, pressed the scrambler and issued a series of instructions, the first of which was to contact the master of the M.V. *Constancy*.

Seven days later, President Sandriano was taken ashore unceremoniously packed in a crate. In three hours he was in a comfortable house at a secret location in the English countryside. Here he was the focus of attention for representatives from several government departments, including the Foreign Office. It was several days after Sandriano's arrival that he was visited by his friend James Bailey. This was achieved under the protection of a security fog so dense that the prime minister's whereabouts caused some concern among his closest colleagues and advisers along with senior members of the security services.

As the weeks turned into months, large sections of the population of Erifia began to organise themselves. The quality of life had taken a considerable turn for the worse. L.Y.A. Photocopiers, now known to the government of President Christian McGregor as Erifian Photocopiers, had closed - "temporarily."

Copper remained in the ground. Shops were closed or in the process of closing, even those which had enjoyed considerable profits from the patronage of large numbers of British servicemen and women. Now these were forbidden to leave their bases. Their supplies were airlifted directly to them by helicopters from British Royal Navy vessels which were forming a blockade. Few supplies were reaching shops or the hospital or petrol stations or anywhere else. A black market was operating, but this was supplied by cross border smuggling.

Despite the international condemnation of Prime Minister James Bailey's blockade of Erifia, it continued. Britain's ambassador to the United Nations was being pressed to answer difficult questions, which he had been told to sidestep. Britain's ambassador to Washington was also refusing to answer questions. James Bailey was determined not to lift the blockade. "Let them bluster," he said to his aides. "The ships stay."

While this was going on, some of the people of Erifia were forming themselves in what they chose to call the Erifian Liberation Fighters. But at this time, while the sentiments were applauded by much of the outside world and particularly Prime Minister James Bailey, these liberation fighters had nothing with which to fight. Not yet.

London

Just a short walk from the Cenotaph in Whitehall stands a vast grey building. In another location it would have been imposing but here, in this part of London, it is anonymous. It is surrounded by other buildings, most of which house the departments which are the machinery of government. The particular building in question has the usual mighty double doors immediately next to the pavement. To the right of these doors is a single brass plate which reads, "Rural Development Service, an executive agency of the Department of the Environment."

An observant visitor would notice the closed circuit television cameras at both ends of the building. Each point inwards and slightly downwards and converge at the steps and door. The visitor might see another CCTV camera inside the building pointing directly outwards through the doors. This would be the last camera he would spot, although there are over one hundred others concealed throughout the building.

After entering through the street entrance, it is necessary for the visitor to pass through a second set of double doors which appear to be made of glass. They are exceptionally heavy doors; the glass is over one inch thick. They are easy to open because of a counterweight mechanism concealed in the walls behind the frame. To the left stands a large counter behind which there is a vast array of pamphlets, leaflets and maps. The visitor may make enquiries here about all matters connected with rural Britain. If an audit were to be conducted, it would surprise many that regardless of the nature of the query, the questioner is always referred to another government department or external agency. The glossy brochure handed to the persistent information seeker is little more than a list of organisations dealing with every conceivable aspect of British rural life and rural industry. The addresses and phone numbers are interspersed with colour shots of beauty spots and fields, barns and small manufacturing units in bucolic locations.

This is what the casual information seeker will find in this large grey building in central London. These people never, ever get past the large information desk. Occasionally there are other visitors who visit for altogether different reasons. These people are watched on a series of television monitors before they reach the outer doors. When they enter they are videotaped during the whole time they are in the building. They are carefully watched throughout the visit and a recording is kept in case it is required at a later date.

It is this second type of visitor who will report to the desk, state his name and the name of the person with whom he has an appointment. The person on reception will already be aware that the visitor has an appointment and with whom. Despite this the receptionist will not admit the visitor until a green light appears beneath the reception desk. The visitor will be asked to take a seat. He is watched for several minutes more before a uniformed security guard will approach and ask the visitor to follow him. They will pass through another door and into a room. This room is light and airy. It has marble flooring and oak-panelled walls. There is no furniture here except a visual display unit, a computer keyboard and a printer.

The security escort will ask the visitor to read the instructions on the screen and follow them to the letter. These questions will ask for name, employer, department and who is being visited. The nature of the questions will then change. The screen will ask for home address, security reference code, level and number, name of immediate superior and name of department head. It will then ask for maiden name of maternal grandmother or some other arcane question which is chosen at random by the computer. Finally it will ask for a visit reference number. This is the number provided when the appointment is originally arranged. If the answers given satisfy the computer, a visitor's label is printed, which the security escort takes from the printer, places in a clear plastic envelope, and fastens by means of a metal clip to the visitor's lapel or top pocket.

Another door opens automatically and the two proceed to the next stage. Again the visitor will find himself in another room. Here a third person will ask for his security code number and the visit reference number. With considerable politeness the visitor will be asked to show his security ID pass and finally a random question will be posed. "What was the make and number of the first car ever registered in your name?"

Assuming all the questions have been answered to the satisfaction of the organisation, the visitor will then be asked to take a seat. Without being asked, the visitor will be given a cup of coffee in the morning or tea in the afternoon. The security escort will not have left the visitor's side for one moment thus far. After some little while another person will join the party. The visitor will be asked to follow the newcomer and the security escort will depart, often without the guest's immediate knowledge.

The new escort and guest will pass through yet another heavy door and onto a landing. Immediately facing this door are the doors to a lift. The lift takes the two to the appropriate floor. If the visitor is due to meet the head of the department he will be conducted to the top floor. When the lift doors open the first impression will be one of opulence, Victorian design and decor and silence. There is a long corridor down which the visitor must travel. At the end of the corridor there is another double door, the other side of which lies a comfortable reception room occupied for much of the time by a receptionist. Whoever is on duty, it is likely they will have a degree, a double first not being unusual. The receptionist will welcome the visitor and tell him that Sir Harry is expecting him. The visitor would know this full well since, had Sir Harry not been expecting him, he would not have got any further than the front desk. Had he pretended to have had an appointment when none had been made, he would have been told that there must have been some mistake. One way or another he would have left the building and he would have been followed. Far away from the office of the Rural Development Service he would have been stopped, bundled into a car, and taken to a police station where he would have waited to be questioned by an officer from Special Branch.

The receptionist will wait for a light to appear on her desk and then she will show the visitor into a huge office. At one end of this huge office sits a huge walnut partners desk. Behind this desk sits the colossal figure of Sir Harry Buchanan.

The existence of Sir Harry Buchanan and his department was known to just a very few people. It was financed by a special central government fund. This fund was always available. If a government changed, then the new prime minister would be made aware of the existence of Harry and his team. Occasionally the new incumbent of No 10 would object and talk about "freedom of information," "secret societies" and "responsibilities of high office." Invariably it would not be long before the prime minister or one of his highest ranking colleagues would call upon the services of Sir Harry. It would have been a considerable shock to nearly all of the few people who knew of the existence of Section P if they heard that the department was commissioned for private work as well. For accounting purposes the department was known as Section P. P stood for protector, phantom or some such thing. No one was quite sure.

There had been occasions in the past when the cabinet secretary had been placed in a difficult position when a new prime minister had the intention to sweep out the cupboard. Indignation would be replaced with confusion and occasionally awe when Sir Harry was variously described as a security consultant, risk assessor, risk analyst, damage limitation adviser and an insurance policy against the risk of inappropriate decisions.

Sir Harry Buchanan had very few visitors to his office, but those visitors who came were the good and great of Britain. Harry often amused himself when he recalled that, during the last fourteen years as director of Section P, he had saved the reputation of a prime minister on a number of occasions. But only once had a prime minister visited his office. Harry had no problem with this, it merely amused him. His love for politicians was not great but his love for compromising situations and the search for solutions was.

In order for him to carry out his duties he, along with at least three members of his staff, had a security clearance rating classified as "Cosmic." Very few doors remained closed when either the ID pass was shown or the classification quoted. The door to No 10 would open without hesitation. Armed guards at security installations, even at the most sensitive locations, would stand aside and wave Sir Harry Buchanan through. The Cosmic classification was the most reliable tin opener in Britain.

The gates at the bottom of Downing Street opened to allow a Jaguar to pass into Whitehall. The car was so dark a green it appeared black in some lights. This chauffeur driven car was the government car used by Cabinet Secretary Sir Gordon Melviile. The purpose of a cabinet secretary is to serve the prime minister. He is the highest ranking civil servant in the land. Sir Gordon had remained at the top of the heap for many years due mainly to his uncanny knack of self-preservation, clear thinking and manipulation. There were those who said that he was more interested in his own survival than the interests of his master; many agreed.

The Jaguar took little more than two minutes to roll to a halt directly outside the office of the Rural Development Service. With the gait of a man with a mission Sir Gordon made for the reception desk. The receptionist knew exactly who he was and whom he was scheduled to visit. Despite this, the security procedures were invoked.

It was more than ten minutes later that Melville was greeted by Sir Harry Buchanan's receptionist.

"Good morning, Sir Gordon. Sir Harry is expecting you. May I take your coat? Please come this way."

When Sir Gordon Melville entered the huge office, Sir Harry was already standing. As Melville approached, Harry held out his giant hand. There was a certain mutual warmth in the greeting. Harry turned to the receptionist.

"Bring us some coffee, Margaret." He did not need to add that there should be no calls while Sir Gordon was with him. Margaret would not have interrupted them even had the prime minister telephoned.

"Let's make ourselves comfortable over here." Harry gestured towards two large leather wing chairs positioned each side of a large fireplace.

The coffee arrived quickly. Harry poured and then offered his guest a cigar. Both men lit their cigars and settled themselves into their chairs. Harry knew that this was not an easy meeting for the cabinet secretary. This knowledge gave him some pleasure. Harry inhaled deeply, smiled his broadest smile, which was extremely broad, and picked up his cup of coffee.

"Gordon, you haven't come all this way for a coffee. I'll bet you're here to tell me your master has stepped in something nasty."

Sir Gordon took note of how broad Harry's Scottish accent became at times. This was often when he had mischief in mind. Harry was passionately Scottish. He loved his land and the city in which he grew up. Glasgow, he believed, had provided him with the ideal preparation for his life now. He often visualised himself as the fellow from north of the border who had ventured south to save the English. This was not totally an idle dream. Sir Harry had indeed saved the asses of a good number of politicians regardless of the colour of the government of the day.

"Harry, I believe the prime minister is about to make a blunder which might have the potential to bring down the government. It also has the potential of alienating us from at least one of our most valued allies. My master is about to make the biggest balls up of his career. I want you to look at it for me, Harry. I want you to advise me."

Harry enjoyed the way the cabinet secretary always went to lengths to pronounce his master's title correctly, as "prime minister" rather than "priminister." It amused him the way Gordon had to make an effort to get his teeth around the correct enunciation.

"Before you start, who is in the know?" Harry asked.

"The prime minister has made his decision after consultation with the foreign secretary and the minister of defence. The full cabinet has not been advised. I have been appraised of the decision as has Sir Roger Holbrook, my counterpart at the Foreign and Commonwealth Office.

You are about to become the sixth person who knows anything about our master's intentions."

Harry smiled. "Should I feel honoured or worried?"

"Try worried. What do you know about Erifia?"

Harry placed the side of his thumb against his lips and looked towards the carpet.

"Tinpot democracy. Its President Sandriano has just been kicked out. We've a commercial interest or two in the region. A couple of service bases there. And it's flat, boring, green and bloody wet. Oh, and Sandriano plays golf with the leader. No doubt you have a clue to the whereabouts of Sandriano?"

"That's about what I'd expect. The geographical knowledge of the average secondary school kid. As it happens, I do know the exact whereabouts of President Sandriano."

It was clear that Sir Harry was enjoying the interview so far. A beam had spread across his huge face.

"Surely since he has been ousted, you should now be referring to ex-President Sandriano."

"Hardly. He remains the president since the country is constitutionally a democracy. He has been removed from power by unconstitutional and illegal means. He is the president. While Christian McGregor might choose to call himself president, he is, in the eyes of the world and most of the people of Erifia, a traitor along with that thug, General Francois Gariol. Now here's an interesting point. Gariol is the head of the armed forces. He is obeyed mainly through fear. He is not much loved. Be more at home in a brothel by all accounts. Disgusting table manners too. Sandriano would never be seen close to him at official occasions. Anyway, here's the score. Lots of resentment among the natives. An underground organisation has formed. By some means or other it has managed to find a leader, one Red Pasqualle."

Harry roared with laughter. "Where do they get these names from?"

Melville ignored the interruption. "Sandriano is safe, sound and most irritated, here in England. He knows Pasqualle. Says he's a 'damned good fellow, don't you know?' McGregor, Gariol and company have power at this time. Their arms are limited as is their expertise, training and, by all accounts, the will among the troops is none too resolute. It seems that a counter-revolution is very much on the cards. Pasqualle wants a crack at McGregor.

"Trouble is, Pasqualle has the resolve, the will, the determination, the support of the democratically elected president, the support of the majority of his countrymen. What he doesn't have is the means. He can muster a few fowling pieces, scythes, sickles and a potato peeler. Gariol and his mob don't have very much but they can whip anything that Pasqualle can throw at him."

"The shine is about to disappear from this conversation. I trust you are not about to introduce a note of disquiet into my office? No, don't go on. You are about to tell me that someone has suggested a bit of gunrunning. Tell me I'm wrong."

The cabinet secretary remained silent, as if willing Sir Harry to continue.

"Our priminister," Harry said, deliberately merging the two words of the title, "has decided to help out his old buddy, his golfing pal, his old pen friend. That's why you mentioned the foreign secretary and the minister of defence." Harry paused again, thinking. "The buggers are pulling a number without the cabinet's knowledge since if it had the knowledge it would never, but never, give approval." Harry laughed. "The P.M. has decided to get the minister of defence to smuggle a few container loads of arms out to the region. Silly bugger. However did he get himself elected?"

"I'm glad, Harry, that you find this so amusing. However, it seems you have grasped the plot with your customary speed. The P.M. has charged the minister of defence with the task of putting together an arms consignment list. The minister will be compiling same with his senior defence chiefs, who are, as you know full well, very happy to get involved with such adventures without letting on. They're not renowned for their kiss-and-tell antics.

"My concern is this. Let's imagine, for a moment, that the prime minister sanctions the despatch of arms to Erifia. The danger is not in the world discovering the counter-revolutionaries with arms. If they are successful, then, since the status quo will have been regained, no questions will be asked. If they're unsuccessful, then there will be precious little left to ask questions about. We'll say that the stores on one of our bases was raided or that they were arms previously supplied to the legitimate government of Erifia. No, that's not the worry. What's concerning me is this. What if the arms reach a destination other than that for which they are intended?"

"What do you need from me and my section?"

"Roger Holbrook and I have given this a great deal of thought. We need you to ensure that the consignment arrives in Erifi. We need you to ensure that it is safe. Most of all we need you to ensure that, come what may, the integrity of the prime minister and Her Majesty's government is not called into question."

With that, the cabinet secretary stood and walked towards the door. Before leaving he turned.

"Harry. Whatever you need, eh? And keep me up to speed on this. I don't want any nasty surprises."

Harry's response was little more than a grunt. The huge man stood motionless in front of the leather wing chair for some moments after the cabinet secretary had left. He was looking down at his feet. Close friends would recognise this posture as one which Harry adopted when he was deep in thought. Suddenly his head jerked up and he strode purposefully around his desk. He picked up the phone.

"Margaret, get John and Vanessa in here now."

"Sir, Vanessa is in briefing with Sam and the development team."

"Interrupt her and get her in here now."

While Harry was director of Section P, his work was supported by that of his three deputy directors. John Morgan, 38, was deputy director of operations. Sam Marchant, 41, was deputy director of science and development. The youngest of the senior management team was the 34-year-old Vanessa Stone. She was head of the intelligence division. Moments later Morgan and Stone walked into Harry's office without knocking. Harry gestured towards a refectory table at one end of the room. The two newcomers sat without a word. They knew Harry well enough to wait for him to speak. Harry was well known for his courtesy. They knew well that for him to summon them in this manner all was not well. Harry was looking at his feet again. Eventually he looked up.

"I think it is quite possible we may have a client with a rather disagreeable problem."

Harry fell silent again and resumed the close inspection of his toes. Again this lasted several minutes during which time no one in the room uttered a word. The two younger people hardly breathed. Harry came to life.

He told them a story known only to himself, Sir Gordon Melville, Sir Roger Holbrook at the Foreign and Commonwealth Office and three very senior politicians. This was a limited circulation list indeed. Sir Harry wanted it to remain so. When he had finished he looked at the two deputy directors.

"Questions?"

Both shook their heads. They needed time for the implications of what they had just been told to sort themselves in their minds.

"Seems to me we need a shopping list or two. Concentrate on the lists until 0930 tomorrow. At that time we will discuss how news is likely to leak, who might see the shipment as a viable target, how and where the target could be hit, and then I guess we'd better talk mopping up operations. In the meanwhile I'll get a manifest of the shipment and see if I can get a route when a proposal is submitted by person or persons unknown at the M.o.D. Listen you two. I need hardly tell you ..."

Harry stopped himself, turned from them and returned to his desk. The other two left his office without another word.

Management Consultants

During World War Two there existed an organisation the activities of which were, at the time, secret. Even today little is generally known about it. Historians are now studying the impact MI9 had on the outcome of the war and the effect it had on the morale of Allied servicemen.

This branch of military intelligence concerned itself with escape and evasion under the inspired and inspiring leadership of Major Norman R. Crockatt. Its range of activity was truly remarkable. It maintained the regular exchange of coded letters with prisoner-of-war camps. At the same time it also supplied prisoners with currency, maps, compasses and equipment such as hacksaws which were rarely discovered by the enemy.

At first MI9 worked alone. As the war progressed it was joined by its American counterpart, MIS-X. Working together these two organisations trained servicemen how to evade capture and how to escape once they had been captured. It also established evasion lines in enemy held territory to assist Allied servicemen to return home. So successful were these organisations in this endeavour that by the middle of 1944, if an airman was shot down over France or Belgium the chance of him being brought home was evens.

After the end of the war, some people found the transition back to civilian life extremely difficult. Some had worked in extreme danger for months or years behind enemy lines. The risk of detection and capture was always present. The penalty for capture was often death at the hands of the Gestapo. The pressure was considerable. Living on one's nerves and the thrill of adrenaline could, for some, become a way of life. It was little wonder, then, that a humdrum existence working at a machine in a factory was unsatisfactory. Richard Farmer was such a man.

In the June of 1947, Farmer had been a civilian for 11 months. He had not been finding life at all easy. He still had a circle of acquaintances of his own and of his family. Some of these had offered him work or had at least been able to help him into work. None of these jobs had lasted for more than a few weeks. It was not that Farmer was lazy or incompetent. It was his inability to settle. He became bored quickly and found it difficult to take orders and instruction from people he believed to be less able than himself. Often he was accused of having an attitude problem and very possibly this was correct.

On one blazing June day, Farmer had just heard that his services would no longer be required at the dairy. When he had been told this piece of news at lunch time it had come as no great surprise to him. It had certainly not come as a major disappointment. Operating a machine which squirted milk into a bottle was incredibly dull.

As he left through the dairy gates he counted the money in his pocket. At least he had enough for a couple of pints of bitter and so he made his way to the Prince of Wales off the Barking Road in London's East Ham. His spirits began to lift a little as he made his way down his first pint. After all, he was alive and the matter of his survival had been somewhat less certain just a year or so back. It was a glorious day and he had the rest of his life in front of him. For the last few months he had been going about it all wrong, he told himself. It was high time to rethink his future. He was approaching it from the wrong direction. Yes, that's what he was doing. Change the perspective, old boy, he thought to himself.

"Richard Farmer? By God it is! Dick, 'ow are you?"

Two hands grasped his right hand and shook it vigorously. It was on the third or fourth pump that the light of recognition entered Farmer's eyes. It was the vigorous handshake that gave the first clue. The newcomer was a vigorous man. His fresh face and ruddy complexion gave the appearance of his face being subjected to considerable scrubbing every morning. His clothes were old and wearing a little thin but they were clean and well pressed. Farmer recalled the time when they had first met. At that time he had thought the other to be a little overweight. He had thought that this weight would have made him unfit and possibly a liability. Nothing could have been further from the truth.

"Wynter! Eric Wynter! I never expected to see you again."

"Well, 'ere I am old son, as you live and breath, 'ere I am."

Both men laughed and clapped each other on the shoulders. There was genuine delight for both men.

"There were times I never expected to be in a pub with you," said Richard. "Or anyone else for that matter."

"Well, let's make the most of it, me old China. What'll you have?"

"No let me. It's my shout." Farmer plunged his hand into his pocket and pulled out the remains of his liquid assets. He looked into the palm of his hand rather doubtfully.

Wynter spotted the problem immediately. But then he would. He rarely missed a trick. Quickly he turned to the barman. "Two pints of bitter, mate." He turned back to Farmer. "What 'ave you been doing with yourself then?"

Farmer hesitated. "A bit of this and a bit of that."

"Are you doing this or that at the moment?"

Again Farmer hesitated. "Well.... I'm not really doing anything at the moment. Fact is, Eric, I've just lost my job." He paused, not sure if he should go on. But Wynter waited and he knew he would have to continue. "Hell. I've been doing bugger all since I came back from France. A few jobs. Most didn't last more than a week or two. In fact it would not be entirely inaccurate to say that I have not enjoyed much success since my return, and as of today, no job and no money."

"Best I stand the beer today then," said Wynter.

When the barman called, "Time, ladies and gentlemen, please" and the two men walked into the bright afternoon sunshine, both were smiling and appeared not to have a care in the world.

"I know this little place," said Wynter. "Let's go and have a few more and talk about old times."

They walked for ten minutes or so before they finally turned into a side street that was dark in shadow. At the other end of the street there were steps down in front of the end of the terrace. At the bottom of the stairs was a door. Wynter knocked three times.

A voice said, "Yeah?"

"It's me. Eric Wynter."

The door opened, allowing the two men to enter a dark, smoky and slightly dank room. It took a second or two for Richard Farmer's eyes to adjust but soon he determined he was standing in a private bar. Wynter led him to a table in a corner and disappeared. Within seconds he had returned with two pints.

"Listen, Dick. I'm glad I bumped into you. There's been something on my mind. I've been thinking about you a lot since we left France. I miss those days you know. My bet is you miss them as well. Giving the Krauts the runaround eh?"

Both men laughed. It was evident that the memory pleased them both. Wynter continued.

"I can't settle too well back in civvies but maybe there's a way we can have some fun and have a good little earner at the same time. What do you say?"

Memories of their time behind enemy lines flooded into Farmer's mind. Like Wynter, he had missed much of the excitement. Together they had worked well although they had actually spent very little time in each other's company. Farmer was the planner who rarely, if ever, took an unnecessary risk. His ability to think ahead had saved himself, Wynter and many others. He had the ability to cover the angles. On the other hand, Eric Wynter was a creative cockney. He quickly built a reputation as someone who got things done. He was quick-witted and reliable.

"I haven't got anything to lose Eric. What have you in mind?"

The war may have been over, but Britain in 1947 was, for many, a gloomy place to be. Unemployment was high and rationing was still present. Yet these very conditions presented opportunities for some sectors of the community. There was a thriving black market, and those who were bold enough, dishonest enough and quick-witted enough, discovered that a good living could be made. And so it was that Richard Farmer found himself standing next to Eric Wynter in the dark. Wynter was using bolt cutters to cut the chain that secured a padlock. He swung the gates open to reveal a lorry loaded with coal. It was a simple matter for him to hotwire the Bedford and drive it away. In less than 24 hours they had sold the coal. It took a little longer to sell the Bedford. It had to be repainted before Wynter's buyer was prepared to take delivery. Nevertheless, by the end of their first week together, Farmer found himself with a little over £100 in his pocket.

At the weekend Wynter suggested to his friend that there was to be a dog race, the result of which was already known to him. Farmer knew Wynter much too well to be sceptical. The two men each put all their earnings on a greyhound called Runnymead. The dog came in at 3 to 1.

By New Years Eve the men had invested well over £2,000. Each had a new wardrobe and it seemed entirely fitting that they should enjoy the festivities "up West."

Their reputation in London's underworld blossomed. It was a reputation rather like a guarantee. Whatever needed doing was done, at a price. Since a sort of guarantee came with the commission, the price was always high. In those early days the deal was always the same. Half was payable when a commission was accepted and the second half on completion. For the few who decided not to honour the agreement and chose not to pay the second instalment, the result could be devastating. A sound thrashing was delivered on several occasions, but the punishment could be worse, much worse. If a punishment was called for, then Wynter and Farmer would have cast iron alibis.

They earned the respect of the criminal fraternity but also that of nearly legitimate businessmen who needed their help. A reputation for delivery provided the men with "a good little earner," just as Eric Wynter had predicted. It was not long before they recruited specialist staff. The selection procedure was rigorous and from the day they employed their first employee they insisted on a practice which, while inconvenient at times, paid dividends over the years. They operated a strict "need-to-know" policy. Employees were told only what they needed to know to enable them to achieve their particular task. Never would more than three people ever know about a commission. Much more likely the maximum would be two and sometimes one. Never would one person, other than a senior team leader, know full details of a commission, and even they would not know the name of the client unless the job specifically required that this knowledge was passed on.

Time coupled to skilful management had turned the coal thieves into owners of a large and profitable organisation. Fifty years on, the organisation was called Wynter Farmer Management Consultants. The client base and the portfolio had grown organically so that by this time the range of services offered was vast. It ranged from rebranding of a product range for a reputable company that was a household name to murder for an organisation that was known to few outside of the Metropolitan Police.

There were 48 full-time staff and over 100 specialist consultants. Each was creamed from the top of the heap. They were carefully selected and recruited and each was well rewarded with a salary and commission structure that would have been the envy of the largest of multinationals. The full-time establishment was made up of chartered accountants, an actuary, lawyers, graphic designers, a copywriter, strategic planners and an economist. The information technology department had computer programmers and operators. There was a human resources department, there was a small team of statisticians and there was an operations division. This was made up of investigators, researchers, drivers and murderers.

Most members of the team were highly respectable professionals. They had no idea that W.F.M.C. was anything more than a reputable consultancy house. Had they been told otherwise they would have disbelieved it to the extent of taking legal advice. This was an indication of the success of the cell structure on which Wynter and Farmer insisted from the day they recruited their first employee.

No longer were planning meetings held around tables in smoke filled pubs. Team meetings were now held around a highly polished table in the conference room at the spacious, luxurious, prestigious and well-equipped offices in London's West End. There was every appearance here of the successful management consultancy. To the visitor all would appear perfectly normal. There were indicators, however, that some might have considered abnormal. Employees never wandered through the reception area. Each department or individual was compartmentalised. The client would only ever have one point of contact. He would never meet more than two representatives from W.F.M.C. and much more often only one representative.

Nevertheless, few clients were ever suspicious or dissatisfied with the service they received. On rare occasions when criticisms were made which were considered to be dangerous to the company, then tragedy would hit the client. Fires would break out and a cause would not be found. There was at least one occasion when the chief executive of a client organisation was killed in a flying accident. There had been more than one road traffic accident.

Richard Farmer had died peacefully in his sleep in 1987. Eric Wynter had carried on for some years before handing over to a new chief executive. Wynter had retained his position as chairman and was consulted on a range of matters that were deemed to be of importance. However, the new managing director, Harvey Walsh, did not make a habit of referring to Wynter unless he saw it as critical. In any event he suspected that Wynter had his own spies in the organisation. This gave him no concern whatsoever.

Wynter was now 88 years old. By and large he was enjoying his retirement. He lived in much comfort in his house a few miles from Slough. Until recently he spent his winters at his farm in Provence in the south of France. Now, though, although he was as fit and well as any 88-year-old, it was too much trouble to uproot and bundle himself off each year. He also enjoyed a full social life in England and was seen as a pillar of the community.

Wynter allowed Walsh considerable freedom to run the firm but he did insist that all illegal commissions were referred to him and any commission from certain named clients were also referred. Walsh was trusted, if not totally, then close to it. He was now 45 and had been with W.F.M.C. since leaving university. He had found early promotion because of his remarkable ability to see into the future. He would lay on assets when an opportunity arose. The asset might remain dormant for years but sooner or later Walsh knew that the asset would be useful. In the early days Farmer or Wynter would require Walsh to justify why the firm had suddenly acquired an apartment in Washington, a petrol station at the end of the M4 in London or a new aerospace consultant on a retainer. The need for Walsh to justify his actions had long since disappeared. It was this ability to acquire useful assets which was about to become essential to fulfil a large commission W.F.M.C. was soon to be offered.

In 1979 Margaret Thatcher swept to power with a new and revitalised Conservative government. It swept aside the Labour government of James Callaghan. Thatcher's policy was to remove the stagnation and indolence of the nation and the stranglehold that unions exerted on manufacturers and the public services. When the Falklands conflict landed in her lap, Thatcher could hardly believe her luck. The Argentinean junta could have waited for a Labour government and then invaded with a reasonable expectation that little more would have happened than the exchange of a few words in the United Nations. Galtieri and his henchmen rather missed the point when they invaded the islands. They thought that Prime Minister Thatcher would sit back and do nothing. It was an ideal opportunity for some public relations at home and abroad for the British. The armed forces sailed to the South Atlantic and threw the invaders off the islands. This action further enhanced Thatcher's standing at home and in the international community and allowed her to push through legislation which, under different circumstances, might not have been successful.

A programme of privatisation was embarked upon. Gas, water and electricity utilities were sold off. The railways followed and the process continued under subsequent governments until few assets were in government hands. Clearly this released funds and accountability. The government sold off so many assets that this often caused serious problems when services were required which were unexpected.

From an accountant's or an economist's point of view, the process made sense. What is the point of funding an expensive asset when it is only used 10% of the time? So, by and large, selling off public assets was a sensible concept to reduce waste and release funds to the treasury. It seemed entirely reasonable for the government to commission goods and services from the private sector as and when they were required.

To ensure that the government had ready access to the goods and services it required, it built up a network of approved suppliers. This ensured it could call on the appropriate provider immediately without having to prepare invitations to tender, going through the tender process and the accompanying vetting procedure. Add to this the time it takes to source and negotiate, the process could be long-winded. This was avoided with the Approved Provider List arrangement.

The process considered everything from pencils to missiles. One acknowledged service the government anticipated it would need was marine shipping. Over a period of many months it appointed a number of shipping companies which, the government felt, would be capable of transporting goods around the world if and when the need arose. The name of one such company was Berkeley Marine International Limited.

The terms of the contract between government and the company had been negotiated by the business development manager, Martin Garstang. He was the blue-eyed boy in Berkeley Marine. Unfortunately this was not the case everywhere. In other contexts Garstang was seen as a womaniser despite being married to Naomi and having a six-year-old son called Kent. Others saw him as an unsuccessful gambler and a big drinker.

When news that Berkeley Marine had been awarded the status of Approved Provider reached the desk of Harvey Walsh he immediately tasked a team leader to do some research. Four members of the management team at Berkeley Marine were targeted. As business development manager, it was natural that Garstang would be among the four. The team leader ordered a series of tails, bugged the offices and phones of the four in question and conducted some research in public records. Three of the four were boringly clean, one was not. It took less than a fortnight to discover that Garstang was overdrawn at his bank to the tune of £17,000. His mortgage was high and the equity in his car and that of his wife was low. Nothing too promising here in isolation, but when it was discovered that he also owed £36,000 to a south coast casino, Walsh became aware that it would not be long before he would acquire a new asset. He issued the necessary instructions.

The headteacher looked up as her secretary came in without knocking. She was not surprised when she heard that a representative from Social Services was waiting to see her. She asked her secretary to show the visitor into her office. One minute later a social worker, Miss Emma Johnson, showed her ID card.

"I'm sorry to come at such short notice."

"That's quite all right. Your office telephoned to say you were coming, Miss Johnson. May I offer you a cup of tea?"

Miss Johnson shook her head. "No thank you. Unfortunately the police have advised us that the father of Kent Garstang has been injured in a car accident."

"Oh dear," said the headteacher clasping her hand to her mouth. "Nothing too serious I hope."

"Well, we don't know yet, I'm afraid. The police are trying to contact Kent's mother. Anyway, I would like to take Kent with me until we are clear about Mr Garstang's condition and until we can make contact with the mother."

"Yes, yes. Quite, of course. I'll find Kent."

The head left her office and returned in five minutes with a boy in tow. She introduced Kent to Miss Johnson. Miss Johnson talked to Kent in a kindly, friendly manner. When Miss Johnson and Kent had left, the teacher wondered how and when the boy would be told.

At the time Kent was being introduced to Miss Johnson, two uniformed police officers turned up at the insurance office where Naomi Garstang worked. They asked the manager if they could see Mrs Garstang. When they were alone with her in a meeting room they explained that her husband had been seriously injured in an accident. They offered to take her from her Southampton office to the London hospital where her husband was undergoing life-saving surgery.

At 5.45 that evening Martin Garstang arrived at the family home in Chilworth, a fashionable suburb of Southampton. He was surprised that neither Naomi nor Kent was there. He was surprised there was no note and he was surprised there was no dinner for him ready to stick in the microwave. This had never happened before. Then there was a knock on the door. When Garstang opened it he found a well-dressed and kindly looking man standing in the porch. He was not surprised there was no car on the drive. It didn't occur to him at that time that there was no bus service within a mile and the only feasible way of getting to his front door was by car.

"May I come in, Mr Garstang?"

"What's this all about?"

"If we can just go inside I will explain."

"Who are you?" A note of exasperation was entering Garstang's voice.

"It's about your wife and son, Mr Garstang."

Garstang stepped aside and gestured for the man to enter. He led him to the sitting room and indicated he should sit.

"Thank you," said the newcomer. "It does not matter who I am. What does matter is that it will not have escaped your notice that Mrs Garstang and Kent are not here."

"Where are they? What do you know about this?"

The visitor's tone changed and his smile evaporated. "Sit down, Mr Garstang. If you do exactly as I tell you, your wife and son will be returned to you. At this moment they are fit and well. That happy state will not continue indefinitely. I recommend you listen very carefully. Do I have your undivided attention?"

Garstang nodded. He was becoming frightened and confused.

"The time will come when you will be of help to us. One day we will ask for your help. You will be very pleased to help at that time. We ask nothing more of you. We have temporarily deprived you of the company of your family to demonstrate how easily we can have a negative effect on your life. You will be well advised to heed this warning, Mr Garstang.

When I leave here satisfied that you understand your position, your family will be returned to you. If I am dissatisfied with your level of comprehension, your family will not be returned. Is this still clear to you?"

Garstang was scared. He had entered a world of which he knew nothing and he felt as if he had no control over what was happening to him, as indeed, he did not. Eventually he nodded.

"Good," said the visitor and placed a brown envelope into the trembling hands of Garstang who made no attempt to open it. "In that envelope you will find fifty thousand in cash. Tonight you will use thirty six thousand of it to honour your debt at the casino. The remaining fourteen is to do with as you please. I recommend, however, you bank it. That would reduce your overdraft to three thousand. Your current net monthly salary is two thousand, four hundred and eighty. With careful management you can pay off the overdraft and your car loans in around seventeen months."

Garstang's lower jaw had dropped. He was staring at the visitor with eyes wide. The tremble was still there but he was feeling better.

"Let me remind you of our requirements. We may ask you for a favour at some time in the future. If that time comes you will be required to respond without question. If you can be of help to us and you successfully complete any task or tasks we give you, you will be rewarded financially. Your delightful wife and handsome son will live the rest of their lives without interference from us. If you fail us or if you go to the police regarding this matter either now or in the future, then your life will be in some doubt as will the lives of your wife and son. You would also be well advised not to disclose this meeting to your wife at any time. When I have gone you will find your family will be returned quite soon."

When the stranger left he walked quickly, checking continuously that he was not being followed. He had not expected to be followed. He reached his car in half an hour. He used his mobile phone.

Naomi and Kent Garstang were restored to Martin Garstang just 20 minutes later. They were able to explain to him that social services had met the police car and mother and son were then driven towards London on the M3. Their car received a message and they learned that the person in hospital had been identified as someone other than Mr Garstang. The police car left the M3 at the next exit, turned and rejoined the motorway heading back the way it had just come. Mrs Garstang's relief quashed any anger she may have felt.

Red Pasqualle

Morton Bland Junior drove home in a fit of depression. No matter what he and his management team did, there was always something new to confound them. Just three months previously, Carly Hopkiss Travel was a successful company, the envy of its competitors. Since Bland's father, Morton Senior, had started the coach business many years before, in the days of crossply tyres and Bedford OB coaches, it had always been successful. When coach and bus travel became deregulated in Britain, the company really took off. It now boasted one hundred coaches, most of which were under three years old. It continued to operate its domestic and continental holidays but now it also operated local routes throughout southern England and inter-city routes. It had a fine reputation for service and reliability. Staff turnover was almost zero, which was particularly impressive in an industry renowned for miserable employee relations. This was not the case with the staff of Carly Hopkiss Travel. From drivers to mechanics, the staff was happy, contented, well looked after, well paid. Bonuses were always paid on time. There were four members of staff who were the third generation of their families to work for a Morton Bland.

Now though, things were not going so well and Morton Bland Jnr. was at the end of his tether. So bad had it become that he was thinking the unthinkable. He hated himself for this. He felt at times, usually in the early, still, dark hours of the morning that he should sell to one of the two rival national operators who had made approaches. This would make Morton Senior turn in his grave.

He parked his car in the garage, closed the doors and entered his house by the back door. He looked around him as he entered the luxury kitchen of which he was once so proud. It meant little to him at this moment. Divorced long ago, Morton lived alone. His housekeeper kept the large home spotless while the gardener made the gardens the showplace of the village. All of this he had enjoyed so much, but on this cold, gloomy evening he felt sad, lonely and a little desperate. Slowly he walked through to the sitting room and went straight to the cocktail cabinet as he now did every evening. This was a recent habit he had developed and one that he knew he should lose. He poured a huge whisky and slumped into his favourite chair.

He was just beginning to unwind and, as the whisky began to take effect on his central nervous system, he cheered slightly. Tomorrow is another day, he thought. In any case, would his father have given in? Not likely, he mused. Morton Senior had been a fighter and he, Morton Junior, would be well advised to take a leaf out of his father's book. He owed it to his father. He got up and poured himself another drink. When he sat again he started to wonder about dinner. When he had arrived home he hadn't been hungry but now he realised he was starving. What should he do? He didn't feel like cooking although there was much in the house. His housekeeper always made sure of that. Perhaps he should walk down to the pub where there was a more than adequate restaurant. He dare not drive now but perhaps he could take a taxi into town. A nice Indian curry would be just the job. It wasn't his usual curry night, but what the hell? He had nearly settled upon this as a solution to his catering quandary when he heard a noise. He cocked his head to one side and listened. There it was again. Then he heard the jarring sound of breaking glass.

A second later two men wearing balaclava helmets rushed into the sitting room. One pointed an automatic weapon at Morton. The other walked round the room systematically smashing ornaments. He turned his automatic weapon onto the television. The sound of the gun firing inside the confined space of the room combined with the implosion of the TV's tube was distinctly uncomfortable. Morton dropped his glass. The gunman turned his gun to the state-of-the-art sound system and fired a stream of bullets into it.

Both men aimed their guns at the ceiling and emptied their magazines into it. Then they left. Morton was dumbstruck. He sat in his chair without moving. It was several minutes later that he let out a scream and threw his head forward into his hands. For some time he sobbed bitterly.

Red Pasqualle was the owner of a hotel and restaurant. His hotel overlooked the beach about five miles south of Erifi. There were only 12 letting rooms which, while comfortable, were fairly functional. The restaurant was large, lively and very busy. It was well patronised by tourists and it was a popular haunt for the better off of Erifia. The dishes were based on the local cuisine, which included the famous lobster and clam casserole, but the British influence was apparent. Roast beef and Yorkshire pudding appeared regularly on the Sunday lunchtime menu.

Pasqualle had left school at fifteen to go straight to college in Erifi. This was Erifia's only college and was heavily subsidised by the British. Naturally the main subjects on offer were electrical engineering because of the presence of L.Y.A. Photocopiers and the catering industry. Support and service industries were provided for but there were far less places for these. In fact, 85% of the students were studying the two principle subjects. Red Pasqualle had studied catering, both cookery and management.

When he left college after three years he worked for an ice cream salesman on the sea front of Erifi. His job was to make ice cream starting at 5.00 in the morning. By midday he was required to be on the front selling the confection from a kiosk to tourists. He loved the work although he found it did not satisfy his ambition. Pasqualle had his sights firmly set on becoming a captain of industry in Erifia. He was a lucky man. He always felt lucky. When his boss died, he was amazed to discover that the old man had left his business to Red. He left the kiosk and the small manufacturing unit in the back streets. He left him none of his money however. As Red's luck would have it, he had saved just enough to buy the ingredients and to cover the incidental costs of becoming self-employed. These costs were not high in Erifia.

Within a few months Red had doubled the turnover and reduced his labour costs. This was by the simple expedient of not employing anybody. He did everything himself, including the accounts.

He found that by slightly increasing the quantities served while keeping the price the same and by providing a larger range of flavours, his clientele built. A year after taking over the business his only competitor came to him. He asked Red to buy him out because, he said without a hint of complaint that he could not compete with him. It took Red less than five minutes to answer that he would only buy his competitor out if he agreed to come and work for him. "After all," he said, "you can help me make ice cream at my factory and then you can use my van to deliver to hotels." Red had often been asked to supply hotels and restaurants but had always courteously declined. He did not have the human resources. He sold his new employee's factory for a price greater than he had paid for the entire company.

He kept the kiosk of the other who had once enjoyed a pitch a little further down the coast. When the new employee had completed his delivery rounds his last drop was to the other kiosk. From here he now served Red's famous ice cream.

It took another year for Red to increase his company's turnover tenfold. Ten years later he had twenty kiosks. He delivered to almost every hotel, café and restaurant in the country and he had bought his own hotel and restaurant. He was a well-respected businessman and enjoyed a wide circle of friends. He was a modest man who was happy not to advertise his now, by Erifian standards, considerable wealth. It was true he had a new Land Rover and spent his annual holidays in London. These aside, there was little else to separate him from those who were fortunate enough to work for him.

He counted President Jacques Sandriano among his friends and had been overjoyed when the president had once introduced him to the prime minister of Great Britain. In fact Prime Minister James Bailey had tried some of Red's ice cream and he had said he really enjoyed it. So pleased had Red been that he arranged, at considerable expense, for a consignment to be delivered to Number 10 Downing Street. He would have been devastated had he ever learned that it never reached its destination. Even if it had it would have been destroyed for security reasons. During the Second World War well-wishers sent a previous occupier of Downing Street thousands of Havana cigars. He was not permitted to smoke even one of them. It was felt that the risk of poison was a consideration which could not be ignored.

When Vice President Christian McGregor and the distasteful General Gariol had overthrown his friend, Red had been beside himself with grief and worry. This had eased considerably when he heard that Jacques Sandriano was alive and well in England. But he now had to consider how best he could help his friend.

It was a simple matter to gather together those he trusted. He had little concern that his intentions would become known to McGregor since he knew that each despised the ousting of Sandriano as much as he did. Soon a group of 30 men and women, mainly from the business community, met regularly at his hotel. They simply arrived as diners. Slipping away to the function room was not a complex or even particularly risky business. They all agreed on three points. First, they acknowledged the need to throw McGregor out of office and restore Sandriano, their democratically elected president. Second, they agreed this could and should only be done by force. Third, and here was the major obstacle, they could not hope to achieve this without weapons. They knew they had the will but they also knew they did not have the means. It was unanimously agreed that if they mounted a counterrevolution, most of the army would desert or at least not provide a spirited resistance.

When Red closed his restaurant one Monday evening, the quietest of the week, and cashed his takings he would have been relieved by the knowledge he was about to receive two unexpected visitors.

Fifty miles out in the Atlantic a helicopter took off from the flight deck of H.M.S. Hermes. It took just a few minutes to land at the R.A.F. base where the base commander, Group Captain Colin Wakefield, was waiting. Wakefield briefed the two men who were in khaki and armed. Thirty minutes later the two soldiers, whose uniforms bore no insignia and whose features were obscured by balaclavas, left the base and made for Red Pasqualle's hotel. By the time they reached it, most of the people of Erifia were asleep. The land was quiet apart from the very occasional patrolling Land Rover containing Gariol's men.

The soldiers knew that Pasqualle had his private apartment over the hotel. It was separate from the guests' accommodation. The soldiers had been provided with a layout of the hotel and it took them seconds to locate the private section. Without any apparent communication between the two men they simultaneously threw their grappling hooks, which fixed themselves onto the balcony outside Pasqualle's sitting room. Seconds later they flattened themselves against the balcony wall two storeys up. They waited and listened for thirty seconds. One knocked at the window. The face of a shocked and rather frightened Red Pasqualle appeared at the window. One of the men motioned for him to unlock the balcony door. Without question Pasqualle complied.

The soldiers entered quickly. One stayed with Pasqualle in the sitting room while the other conducted a reconnaissance of the remaining rooms. This survey took only seconds. The second soldier returned to his colleague and nodded. Both soldiers then removed their black masks and smiled.

"Mr Pasqualle, please forgive us for this dramatic arrival. It was not our intention to cause you alarm, however I'm sure you will understand the need for discretion."

Red was immediately at ease. His recognised the two as English.

"May I offer you coffee or perhaps something a little stronger?"

"Thank you, no," said the first soldier. "We bring you President Sandriano's compliments. He wishes you well and wishes he was with you at this time. He knows you are thinking of him and hope for his speedy return. He asked me to tell you something. Clam chowder and stem ginger ice cream. I assume this means something to you?"

Pasqualle laughed out loud. "Yes. Yes. The president's favourite. He often asked me to prepare these things for him myself."

"You will be aware," said the soldier, "that President Sandriano is safe and is the guest of the prime minister of Great Britain. He is in England and he's comfortable. However, he is very worried about the people of Erifia. He is very worried also about what the future holds for his people.

He believes that you will be willing to help his people. Would he be right in his belief?"

"I would do anything to bring back our president. I would do anything to have McGregor and Gariol shot for treason. Tell me what my friend President Sandriano wants me to do. I will do anything."

"President Sandriano hoped you would say that. He has a question for you. What do you need to remove McGregor and Gariol and enable him to return to Erifia?"

Red Pasqualle thought for a moment. His heart was racing and the palms of his hands had become damp. He swallowed hard.

"Give me arms. Give me weapons. We are ready to fight but we have nothing to fight with. Give us the weapons. Ask your prime minister to give us the weapons. There are less than 400 soldiers here. Not many of them have a fight in them. Most are on National Service. I have more than 400 people in the E.P.C. Every one of them is ready to fight and die for our country."

"That's the Erifian Patriotic Cause I assume?" asked the soldier.

"That's what we call ourselves. Can you get us some weapons?"

"What else do you need?"

"Nothing, just weapons and ammunition. We can do the rest and then President Sandriano can come home."

"Thank you, Mr Pasqualle. You will hear from us again soon."

With that the two soldiers pulled their masks back over their faces and left by means of the balcony. They slid down their ropes and disappeared into the darkness. Later that night a coded message was sent from the R.A.F. base. Still later a helicopter took off carrying the two men back to the flight deck of H.M.S. Hermes.

The telephone on Harvey Walsh's desk rang. He picked it up immediately.

"Yes."

"Mr Walsh, a Mr Hahn wants to make an appointment to see you."

"Me personally?"

"He asked for you by name, sir."

52

"Details please, Susan."

"Mr Webster Hahn. President of Hahn Enterprises. He gave me an address in Sedona, Arizona. Apparently it is near to Phoenix. His specific message was he wished to make an appointment to meet with you personally. An acquaintance called Leo Salmon recommended W.F.M.C. Mr Hahn expects you to phone him back when you have done your checking. He also said there would be little point giving you his number because he knew you would get it for yourself. Apparently he's not listed."

"Did he now? Thank you, Susan." Walsh replaced the receiver. He was not quite sure whether he should feel flattered or worried. His first task was to telephone Leo Salmon in San Francisco. The voice at the other end sounded not a bit pleased because, while it was coffee time in London, it was four in the morning on the eastern seaboard of the Pacific Ocean. It thawed a little when Walsh explained the reason for the untimely intrusion. Salmon he knew well. Over the years their two organisations had conducted a number of transactions. After a brief discussion it appeared that Mr Webster Hahn's credentials were impeccable.

Walsh waited until it was four in the afternoon in London. Having obtained the Sedona number of Webster Hahn from Salmon, he made the call. When Hahn came to the phone, Harvey Walsh introduced himself.

"Thank you for returning my call, Mr Walsh. I feel I may have need of your services. I would like to discuss a piece of business with you in London."

"You would be most welcome to visit me in London. May I suggest Thursday the fourteenth?"

"That is very convenient, Mr Walsh. I look forward to meeting you then."

Walsh smiled at the formality of the conversation. Neither man was going to commit on the phone or until each was sitting opposite the other. The problem with telephones is that one never knew who was listening. Hahn would have suspected but not known for certain that the integrity of Walsh's phone was intact. It was. All his offices were swept at least weekly as a further security measure. Walsh had set a date two weeks hence for his meeting with Hahn. In truth Walsh could have met Hahn in four days time but this would not have allowed enough time to conduct an essential piece of research. He looked forward to meeting Hahn but first there was much to be done. He picked up his phone again and dialled an internal number.

The voice at the other end said, "Chris Latcham."

"It's Harvey. Come to my office please, Chris."

Two minutes later Latcham knocked on his chief executive's door. He entered and sat in front of Walsh's desk.

"I want you to produce an insurance policy for me, Chris. You will best achieve this using the services of your old friend at Comint."

Comint or Communications Intelligence was a function within Government Communications Headquarters in Cheltenham. Chris's friend was an employee of G.C.H.Q. and was controlled by Chris. He used his knowledge and technical skills to considerable effect. He was able to secure information that would otherwise have not been available to W.F.M.C.

Walsh explained to Latcham what was required. Chris Latcham was a senior team leader with W.F.M.C. and had served many years with the organisation. Little surprised him these days, but what his employer was asking now was going to be difficult. When he left the offices that day he steered his car to the M4. He exited at Swindon and drove cross country to Cheltenham. It was 6.45 p.m. when he phoned Stephen Wells' home number. He was pleased when Wells answered and not his wife or one of his kids.

"Hello, Steve. Chris Latcham here." He knew that Wells dreaded these calls. He also knew that Wells was trapped. He had been receiving sums of money over a number of years. Any risk of exposure now would mean inevitable imprisonment. It was not the forfeiture of his pension that was his prime concern.

"Don't tell me. You're approaching Cheltenham even as we speak?"

"Right. Meet me in thirty minutes in the wine bar on The Promenade." With that Latcham hung up.

When he had parked his car he walked to the wine bar considering the matter of payment. It was not that he was particularly concerned about his arrangements, but payment in the case of Wells could be risky.

Security at G.C.H.Q. was legendary and did not come to an end with recruitment and the screening process. If an employee appeared to be spending beyond his means, then an investigation would inevitably ensue. Thus the fee in Wells' case was small fry to W.F.M.C. and Wells was extremely careful what he did with it. It was no answer to say he would hide it under his pillow until his retirement. The security people took a continuing interest in ex-employees also. Wells hid the cash and thought he would worry about it at some unspecified time in the future.

Latcham found his man waiting at a corner table on which stood two glasses of claret, a favourite of both. Wells rose and they shook hands.

"Thanks for coming at such short notice. I have a job for you. This job will make everything you have done in the past seem like child's play."

When he had finished explaining the task, he was not surprised to see the poorly concealed look of amazement on Wells' face.

"I understand this is more than we normally expect but you will not need me to tell you I wouldn't ask you to do this if it wasn't important. Because we are asking so much we will double your retainer. I assume you haven't walked here?"

"I drove." Wells sounded depressed.

"Where's your car?"

"It's the white Scorpio parked next to the public lavatories in Royal Well."

"The model I know. It's the location I don't know. When I've gone wait for ten minutes before you leave. There will be a package in your car. In it you'll find a passport which you are to use rather than your own. You'll also find the address of your target. There's a credit card with which to purchase your return air ticket. There's also some cash in sterling and US dollars. The sterling is for you. It's a small token of our gratitude. As you might expect, the US dollars are for your colleague in the States. I've already phoned your man to tell him to expect a call from you. If you phone him tonight you can tell him what you need. Don't get so excited you phone him from your home. Ensure he knows when you expect to land once you've booked your ticket. Oh, and Steve. Remember you only have seven days. I require this information in my office on day eight. Is all this clear?"

Stephen Wells was clear. Booking a holiday at short notice was not a problem. Getting away from his family was easy. He simply told them he was away with his work.

The Commission

From a geographical location remote from the computer it is possible, using sophisticated technology, to read all the information stored. The eventuality of data being stolen by this method is not, as a rule, considered by individuals or even multinational corporations. The hardware necessary to steal files remotely is not available in the average computer store. It is available, however, to the security services and to specialist organisations.

Wells and his American colleague were sitting in a Dodge panel truck just 100 yards from the Hahn ranch. A few minutes before, the Dodge had been travelling down the highway and gradually pulled to a halt. When Wells opened the hood he pulled a tag on a smoke grenade taped to a bulkhead. To an observer it might appear that he was experiencing mechanical trouble. He knew all this would have been captured on the security cameras that surveyed the entire perimeter of the ranch.

He took out a CO2 fire extinguisher and played it over the engine compartment. He then returned to the interior of the Dodge. Within a few minutes his equipment had located a computer inside the ranch and was copying its files. Every so often Wells pulled up a page on a monitor. He made no attempt to conceal his smile. This was precisely the kind of material hoped for by Chris Latcham.

Just half an hour later the Dodge's engine miraculously fired. Five hours later Wells was boarding the 2140 hours British Airways flight, bound nonstop for London's Gatwick Airport. At the check-in Wells was told that his DC10 would land at Gatwick at 1550 local time. The long-haul jet did indeed land at the scheduled hour. A car was waiting to take him to Latcham. It was Chris Latcham who subsequently passed the four disks to Harvey Walsh.

Webster Hahn flew Concorde when he was visiting England. While crossing the Atlantic at twice the speed of sound he would often reflect on what sadness it was that the Anglo-French partnership had stolen the march on the Americans. He would have been much happier had this wonder of technology been made by McDonnell Douglas instead of Sud Aviation and British Aerospace. Nevertheless, he still experienced a thrill whenever he flew in Concorde.

Usually a car was waiting for him at Heathrow to take him into London. On this occasion however he preferred not to draw attention to his visit. He took a black cab through Knightsbridge, left at Hyde Park Corner and into Park Lane. At the top of Park Lane the taxi circled Marble Arch and returned the way it had come to deliver Hahn to his hotel. A uniform opened the taxi's door while another uniform collected the luggage and followed Hahn into the lobby. Hahn checked in. He was looking forward to a shower, a club sandwich in his room and a short nap. He awoke three hours later with the aid of an alarm clock. He shaved, dressed and left his suite.

The same uniform was still on duty. A taxi was hailed for him and within ten minutes he was entering the reception area of Wynter Farmer Management Consultants. Security watched him alight from the taxi and enter the foyer. From now on he would be observed until he entered the office of Harvey Walsh. Once in this office, however, he would not be overheard, filmed, scanned or observed by anyone other than Walsh. Walsh would, however, record the conversation. The main reason for this was to ensure than nothing was missed. Hahn would certainly expect the meeting to be recorded. He would also expect that the security in the office would be of the highest order. In both of these assumptions he was correct. Walsh's office, in common with every other area of the building, was regularly and routinely swept. Once, several years before, a bug had been discovered in an office. It was left there for two or three weeks while misinformation was fed into it. This had caused considerable inconvenience and embarrassment to the party which had ordered the bugging. It had also cost the party a large amount of money. It had cost a fairly junior female employee of W.F.M.C. her life.

Webster Hahn was conducted into the office of Harvey Walsh. He was met in a most affable manner and with a warm handshake. Tea was offered and declined. Both men were happy to dispense with further courtesies. Both were anxious to get down to business.

"Mr Walsh, you will have checked my credentials with Leo Salmon. In turn your own credentials are beyond question. You and I are both aware of the fine reputation of your organisation in certain, shall we say, sensitive areas?"

"It is kind of you to say so."

"I need hardly mention the requirement for absolute security, a concept very well known to you. So sensitive is this that I have flown to London myself. I choose not to trust anyone else with the information I am about to share with you."

Walsh nodded sagely.

"I wish to place an order for arms with you, Mr Walsh. To me it's a matter of insignificance from where these arms come. However, it is of considerable significance that they are not going to bring the wrath of the authorities down on my head. Clear?"

Another nod from Walsh. Walsh was accustomed to conducting business with the heads of organised crime in Europe, The United States and latterly Russia. He was aware, however, that this man was different. Behind the warm, pleasant face there was the promise of a threat. This was a frightening man. Walsh looked forward to doing business with him.

"The exact specification of the weapons is not as important as you might think. What is important is that they are of military origin."

The rather one-sided conversation continued for nearly an hour. It was punctuated from time to time by a pause from Hahn. During these times he required acknowledgement of understanding from Walsh. As the conversation drew to a close Hahn asked, "And now to the matter of your fee. I propose a down payment of one million dollars with a further four million on delivery. I trust this meets with your approval?"

"I regret, Mr Hahn, that it does not."

Hahn raised an eyebrow in mock surprise. In fact he would have been surprised if Walsh had agreed.

"Our fee for this enterprise will be two and a half million pounds payable today. The balance of a further two and a half million to be paid within 24 hours of delivery."

Hahn made the pretence of deliberating. He stood up, holding his right hand out for Walsh. "I agree to your terms, Mr Walsh."

"Thank you, Mr Hahn. There is one further matter we should discuss now."

At this Hahn was taken by surprise. He felt that the initiative had suddenly been taken out of his hands and he liked it not one bit. What was to come appealed to him even less. Walsh handed Hahn four computer disks. Hahn took them and stared into Walsh's eyes without comment.

"When you return to Sedona you might care to read those disks. You will find the information they contain is your information. You will see it includes details of transactions, matters of finance. Of special interest is the information relating to your personal investments. In various forms, letters, memoranda and the like it contains names and addresses of some extremely influential people with whom you conduct business."

"How did you acquire this information, Mr Walsh?" Hahn was trying very hard to appear cool and in control. In reality he was, for one of the very few times in his life, afraid. He was also surprised. He knew full well that Walsh was not bluffing. He thought his own security watertight and he could not imagine how the information was obtained.

Walsh ignored the question. "It goes without saying that the disks in your hand are copies. I have the originals elsewhere. You need not concern yourself regarding their safety. I hope you will understand that I regard the disks as an insurance policy. We have not had the pleasure of conducting business in the past. When our business is concluded and when the balance of two and a half million pounds has been received, the disks will be returned to you."

"Mr Walsh. You play a dangerous game with considerable dash and style. I know now why you were recommended. A banker's draft for two and a half million in sterling will be sent to you later today by messenger."

The two men shook hands. Hahn had come to W.F.M.C. because of its reputation. He should have expected something of this kind but he was still concerned about the nature of the insurance taken out by Walsh. The matter would be looked into promptly on his return to Sedona.

A messenger did arrive later in the day bearing the draft for £2,500,000. Another messenger carried the paper to W.F.M.C's bank. While he did so Harvey Walsh was speaking on the internal phone.

"Mel. How's your desk looking?"

"You may well ask," returned Melanie Coleman-Burns. Like Chris Latcham, Melanie was a much trusted team leader although she was his junior. A classics graduate, she had joined the organisation when Eric Wynter was still very much in control. She had fast tracked through the company at such a rate, questions were occasionally asked how she had achieved such a meteoric rise. In truth her progression was due entirely to her ability to deliver. She possessed the unusual ability for both convergent and divergent thought. She was often able to see a way when others could not. Of all his staff, Walsh thought of Melanie as his own, his own special star performer. This had its downside however. Because so much was expected of her it never occurred to Walsh that she might be fallible. For Melanie, then, there was an additional pressure. She knew what was expected of her. Thus far Walsh's confidence had not been misplaced, but Melanie was only too well aware that there was always a first time. In this business a first time always ran the risk of being the last time.

"I am asking. Tell me about Culver Joyce Materials Dynamics."

"Bland's nerve has nearly cracked. We invaded his personal space a couple of days ago. My guess is he's about ready to reconsider. In fact, he might soon be pleased to sell at any price."

"Right, bring the C.J.M.D. contract to a conclusion now. Use whatever it takes. Fetch your other outstanding files to my office when you get here in thirty seconds. We'll look at reassigning them."

When Melanie Coleman-Burns entered the office, Walsh was struck yet again with her beauty. Walsh knew that she knew she was beautiful and was quite prepared to use this to further her career and achieve her objectives. Tall, slim, confident, she walked to a chair in front of the desk and sat. She appeared to her boss rather like a barrister. She would look at home at the Old Bailey in her cream silk blouse and navy suit. At 36 she would seem a most eligible spinster. Sadly for the male population of London this particular female was far more interested in her work than in sharing her life with another person. Too many ties, restraints and explanations. One-night stands and sex was fine. Commitment was not fine.

"Your files, please." Walsh held out his hand.

He thumbed through them and placed them to one side.

"Leave these to me. I have a new job for you. Sort out Culver Joyce now and then I would like you to devote your life to the new job until it is complete. You will ask me for any help you feel you need. The entire resources of our firm will be placed at your disposal. You are to use whatever means you feel appropriate. Keep me up to pace each day, please. I'm going to see Eric about this one."

For the next ninety minutes Walsh gave Melanie the background and the requirements of the commission. He omitted to tell her about the scanning operation at the Sedona ranch.

When the woman left his office, Walsh picked up his phone. He made just one call, after which he left.

The late poet laureate, Sir John Betjeman, irritated one or two people when he suggested that Slough should be bombed out of existence. Slough lies to the west of London and just to the north of the M4. It boasts a huge industrial estate, and is probably best known as the home of a famous chocolate bar manufacturer. Much of its housing is drab, homogeneous and rather depressing. Yet, just a few miles outside lies a different world. In semi-rural seclusion lies a commuter belt with its fine and expensive housing, where every car is a Rolls Royce or Mercedes. Out of sight behind mature trees can be found mansions, often pseudoTudor. One such house was the retirement home of Eric Wynter.

Harvey Walsh used the heavy brass, foxhead knocker to summon the butler, who escorted him through the house and into the extensive gardens behind. Eric Wynter enjoyed many luxuries and one of these was to employ three full-time gardeners. The quality of the gardens reflected this. They were breathtaking. Had they been open to the public a busy turnstile would have been inevitable. As it was, the public was the last thing required by the old man. Walsh was one of the few visitors welcomed at the house.

Eric Wynter was well wrapped against the chill and sitting on a cedarwood garden seat staring at the massive koi carp in the garden pond. "Pond" was a misnomer. "Lake" would have been a much more appropriate word. As Walsh approached, the old man smiled. He was always genuinely pleased to see his protégé. Walsh shook Wynter's hand and sat in the wooden chair next to him.

"Eric, something's come up."

For the next few minutes Wynter listened to Walsh. His facial expression gave away nothing of what he was thinking. It was only when Wynter was sure the younger man had finished that he spoke, and when he spoke Walsh listened, returning the courtesy of not interrupting.

"There will be elements at play here of which you will have no knowledge. To deliver your commission you will have to go to the military. This is always a risky enterprise. Be very sure you are covered. Don't allow yourself or the firm to get too close. It is good you have entrusted Miss Coleman-Burns with this. She stands a chance of making it work. Don't cover her pretty little ass too much. You might get hit by the fallout if she is compromised, and a very messy business it would be too.

"I like the insurance policy you took out against the Americans. Very wise. Yet I feel it is not likely to be them you will have to worry about. You will find yourself confronting even more dangerous people."

Wynter paused and gave Walsh the opportunity to comment.

"It appears to me that you have something in mind." Walsh's face showed nothing other than respect. He was in the presence of a man for whom he had only respect. He knew that if the old man decided to give him advice, something he did rarely, then it would be advice worth listening to and considering favourably. Walsh waited patiently for Wynter to speak again.

"There may be a relatively easy, realistic and inexpensive way forward for you. This is just an idea. You will have read in your Daily Telegraph that Erifia's president has been ousted. His name is Sandriano. He is a close personal friend of James Bailey. I suspect Sandriano is in England even as we speak. He will have Bailey's protection. Bailey finds British friendship with, or perhaps control over, Erifia most accommodating. He will want his friend back in his rightful position in Erifia.

"A friend tells me that there is a counterrevolutionary. Chap called Pasqualle. He enjoys some local support and is apparently ready to bear arms against the gentleman who has declared himself president. I think his name is McGregor. He used to be vice president. Trouble is, Pasqualle hasn't any guns. It would not surprise me if our prime minister found him a gun or two.

"A year or two ago there would have been a problem getting the ordnance out to South America. Seems to me that it would no longer be an insurmountable problem. Check out Berkeley Marine International and Pickering Navigation. They are, as I am sure you are aware, on the approved provider list of Her Majesty's government.

"On second thoughts drop Pickering Navigation. It's controlled to the nth degree. Tighter than a crab's ass. Berkeley is not as well managed, organised or controlled. If I remember correctly you have an asset at Berkeley Marine."

Walsh smiled inwardly. He knew that Wynter was well aware of the position.

"I suggest you might like a word or two with your asset." Eric Wynter paused again. He appeared deep in thought. "Remember my words, Harvey. Keep clear of this. Use your pawns. Get your hands dirty and germs get into the cuts and abrasions. Might give you blood poisoning. If you think you are at risk then drop the contract. I like the style of this idea but that's what's worrying me. Is style taking precedence over common sense? Don't forget we always have our Czech contacts.

You might want to get the hardware from them. It would eat into your margin, but it would be easier, and safer."

Walsh's eyes opened wide. He had never heard his chairman talk like this before. Wynter noticed the reaction.

"I mean it, Harvey. Stay distant but keep a watching brief. I don't like this. Too much to go wrong. Too many people involved. Too many important people who need to protect their reputations. Too many big egos. You could end up the fall guy. If you are in any doubt give the Americans their money back. You are in a position to insist they take their money back; you have your insurance policy."

Sir Harry Plans

Morton Bland dined out at his favourite Indian restaurant at least once a week. Whatever other days he chose to eat his curry, there would have had to be a very important reason for him not to be eating Indian on a Wednesday. Bland was, by and large, a creature of habit. Habit he interpreted as structure and organisation, and these made him feel comfortable. On this occasion it was not Wednesday and, despite his troubles and tribulations, Bland was looking forward to the chicken tikka dish he was about to order from the dark-skinned waiter. He was puzzling over the starter, should he go for the lamb shaslick or the shish kebab? He was dragged from his dreams by a woman's voice.

"May I join you, Mr Bland?"

The woman was young, beautiful and sounded cultured. She appeared to Bland to be well dressed but he would be the first to admit that he had little idea about dress. The woman sat without waiting for Bland to reply.

"Right," she said, "I'll have the same as you. Whatever you're having is good enough for me."

Bland was beginning to recover his senses. It had started to dawn on him that he was in the midst of a bizarre situation.

"Pleasant though it is to be dining with such an attractive companion, who are you and what do you want?"

"Oh, let's not spoil our meal by discussing vulgar business," the woman replied with a charming smile.

The waiter brought the meal and they ate, mainly in silence. The silence was broken occasionally when the woman asked some inconsequential questions or passed comments about the weather, holidays, the quality of the food or the value of first class raw ingredients. She smiled a good deal.

"I really don't like this time of year," she said, almost to herself. "You know - the dark evenings, dark mornings. So depressing, don't you think, Morton? You don't mind if I call you Morton, do you?"

"What may I call you?" asked Bland uncertainly.

His companion thought before replying. Suddenly a smile came across her face.

"You may call me F.G."

"F.G?" Bland retorted.

"Yep. F.G. as in fairy godmother."

"You are my fairy godmother?" Bland was confused and unsettled.

"Absolutely. That's what I am. I'm going to put an end to all your troubles."

"What troubles?" said Bland rather too defensively.

"No. No. All in good time. Let's eat. I always think that business talk spoils a good meal. Eat, Morton dear, eat."

It seemed to Bland an age before the meal was finished and the waiter had cleared the table replacing the dirty cutlery and crockery with coffee cups. He was intrigued by this woman and wanted to know just what was coming next. His curiosity was getting the better of him. Eventually she spoke.

"Now, let's see." She paused as if toying with Bland. She furrowed her brow pretending to be deep in thought. Suddenly she smiled in glee, rather as a child does. "Oh yes. I remember. You've had some problems lately, haven't you, Morton? Let's think what's happened. Some of your best drivers resigned or went ill. Then there were those ads you placed in the local press to recruit new drivers. They failed to appear, didn't they? Wonder what happened to them? What was next? Oh yes, I remember. Trainee drivers and mechanics failed to complete their training and then there were those Public Service Vehicle licences that failed to appear. All this is having a bad effect on you and Carly Hopkiss Travel, isn't it? I hear tell that because of your chronic staff shortage you can't operate some of your routes at the moment. That true?"

Bland did not reply to this question.

"Course it is," the woman said. "Anyone can see the buses lying idle in your garage. Not making any money while they're in the garage, are they? Expensive machinery needs to work to pay for itself, Morton. You should know that.

"Then there was that Customs and Excise investigation. It was disruptive wasn't it? V.A.T. irregularities and your people using that red agricultural fuel the V.A.T. man found in your buses. All most embarrassing and expensive and very bad for your reputation. The local papers loved it, didn't they? Mind you, they're bastards like that, don't you think? They love to have a go at important people. And what about the Health and Safety people? They gave you a right going over too, so I'm told."

It was at this point in the odd, one-sided and rather unbalanced communication that the woman placed her elbow on the table and, with her index finger, tapped her lips as if in deep thought. When she spoke again it was with a cheerful lilt in her voice.

"There's been so much it's difficult to remember it all. There have been your vandalism problems. Course, vandalism is on the increase. All those young sods with nothing better to do with their time. I blame the government and parents myself. What these little buggers need is a bit more control. How many thousands of damage did they do to your buses?" Bland did not reply so the woman continued. "Well, it was lots, wasn't it? Food poisoning traced back to the staff canteen. That was a nasty business and, as if that wasn't enough, your computers crashed. You lost all that data. You really should be more careful with your backing up, shouldn't you?"

Finally Bland spoke.

"How do you know all this?" Bland said.

"Fairy godmothers know everything. Then to cap it all, you were attacked in your own home, weren't you? That must have been really frightening. That was too bad." The woman shook her head and pursed her lips.

Bland froze and his eyes widened. "It's you, isn't it? That's how you know all this. You're doing this to me."

Melanie Coleman-Burns stood. "Steady, Morton. You'll have a seizure if you're not careful. When you've calmed down we'll talk again. Now don't forget to pay for the meal. See you."

That night it took Bland a long time to fall asleep. Eventually he did with the help of an unhealthy quantity of whisky. He was awoken by being roughly shaken.

"Wake up, Morton. Come on, stir yourself."

With that, Bland sat up quickly. Coleman-Burns pushed him back onto the bed. She used a remarkable amount of force and inwardly smiled as she thought how unladylike it was. In fear, Morton Bland pulled the bedclothes up to his neck. The sight of him peering up at her over the bedclothes was comical.

"What do you want?" stammered Bland. "Please, won't you tell me what you want?"

"Shut up and listen to me. Listen to me very carefully. You will sell Carly Hopkiss Travel immediately. If you refuse then your problems will increase and the business will end up being worth not a tinker's spit. Life will become unbearable, although I should think it's close to that now. Sell now, Morton, while you still have something to sell. Now then, what's your decision?"

It was all too much for Bland. The pressure and uncertainty of the last few weeks and now this intrusion into his home in the middle of the night. His space had been violated as had his home and the whole of his life. He started to sob and Coleman-Burns allowed him to do this for a couple of minutes.

"There, there, Morton dear. It's not as bad as all that. Sell now and you will be free of troubles and worries and you can enjoy a comfortable retirement. So what's the decision going to be?"

"Who do I sell to? Two offers have been made."

"Now, Morton," replied the woman with a big smile all over her face, "I just know you're going to make the right decision."

The next day, South East Travel Services, one of the two major operators who had made an offer for Carly Hopkiss Travel, withdrew, leaving Culver Joyce Materials Dynamics as the only interested party.

Because of the troubles that had beset Carly Hopkiss, the original offer was reduced by 25%. A beaten Morton Bland sold at the new price.

The director of Section P and his senior staff team had achieved little in the last few weeks. They had tried their conventional or immediately apparent sources and come up with absolutely nothing. The delicacy of the situation made their investigations more sensitive than even they were accustomed to. The fact remained that up to this point they had achieved little. Sir Harry remained outwardly jovial yet he was becoming increasingly concerned. This concern he was keeping to himself for the time being.

On this particular morning he was sitting round the vast refectory table in his office with Deputy Director Operations John Morgan and Deputy Director Intelligence Vanessa Stone. Harry turned to Vanessa Stone.

"What have you got for us this bright morning?"

"Nothing, Harry."

"Nothing, Vanessa? Surely you have something we can discuss. If not we may as well all bugger off home."

Clearly Vanessa was uncomfortable. She looked coy and stared at the pad on the table in front of her. "Well, you recall we were to see if we could come up with a list of possible destinations for the arms? The list of potentials is not short. We might choose to include terrorist organisations, organised crime, other states, particularly those which are suffering instability at this time. Think of Albania. Think of the Serbs. What about a member of the Confederation of Independent States? What about the Irish? How do you feel about the Chechens? This conversation could go on forever. Our friends at Special Branch have a lead. Unfortunately I can hardly tell them just what we are looking for, but they have their eyes on the Sons of Glyndwr."

"Who?" said John Morgan.

"The Sons of Glyndwr. A group of Welsh nationalists. They want a Welsh assembly. They feel they have been let down by successive governments, both left and right. They think that the democratic process is getting them nowhere. Membership is primarily young and middle class. Many appear to be well educated. Seems they started by resurrecting the practice of burning down English owned holiday cottages in Wales. They derailed that train recently, the one that was taking nuclear waste to Snowdonia for safe disposal. They attacked and stoned the coach taking the Japanese businessmen to Swansea. The Japs were considering a massive investment programme for the automotive industry and computer hardware in the area. A press release issued by the Sons of Glyndwr claimed the Japs were the accomplices of Westminster and the English and their trip to Swansea was a government PR exercise. The press releases they issue contain no address for the organisation. Every one bears a different postmark."

"Why are you mentioning this outfit now?" Sir Harry said.

For her life Vanessa could have sworn that Harry was fighting to keep a straight face. "Special Branch has infiltrated the organisation. Apparently the Sons of Glyndwr are planning something bigger. Quotes like 'armed struggle,' and 'English oppression' are coming our way. They feel they are being ignored and want to do something which will make Westminster take notice."

"Okay, Vanessa. What do we know for sure about Sons of Glyndwr?"

"We know that it is a compartmentalised organisation. We know that one regional compartment is centred on a seaside café in Barmouth in Mid Wales. We know the owner lives in a large farmhouse inland, or rather a little way up the estuary."

Vanessa paused. The two men in the room were looking at her. Her discomfort intensified. "Sorry, Harry. Best I've got at the moment." She smiled and the smile turned to a giggle. Sir Harry and John Morgan laughed with her.

"Are we to believe this outfit has the organisation and planning capability of pulling off a major heist? Are we also to believe it has access to the intelligence material? Of course it could buy these essential ingredients if it had the odd million or two. Always assuming it had access to the right contractor." Harry stopped. "Bugger me! That's it! Well done, Vanessa. The right contractor.

"Enough of this nonsense about Sons of Glyndwr. As far as I'm concerned they can have the bloody place anyway. We need to approach this problem from a different angle. We have tried the proactive approach, and with our hands tied. Now we try the reactive approach. If the shipment is to be lifted then we'll make sure we know who is doing it. Perhaps more important, we'll find out who is doing it for whom.

"The game has now moved to another stage, folks. The cabinet secretary has given me a copy of the shopping list with which the P.M. has been provided by the military. Much of this stuff was changed and updated in the mid-eighties. It was stored just in case. Probably very easy to have it removed by someone at a high level. A question of 'who knows, who cares?' Here goes." Harry referred to the typewritten sheet of A4 paper in front of him. Apart from the type there was no heading, no logo, in fact no indication of its origin.

"Self-loading rifles, known to every soldier in the British Army as the SLR, 7.62-millimetre. This rifle is now obsolete. GPMG's. Also 7.62-millimetre. Stands for general purpose machine gun. This is a heavier piece of ordnance and capable of considerable damage. Plus the good old 66-millimetre. Just the ticket for knocking out Land Rovers and light armoured vehicles. To round it all off there's also the 84-millimetre anti-tank weapon. Obsolete yes. Deadly yes. The weapons are wrapped in canvas and boxed in wood. The ammunition is in metal boxes. Gordon Melville tells me that the consignment will fill six containers when it is transported."

"Sounds like enough to start a minor war," said Morgan.

"That's just the intention. Pasqualle and his people could very likely achieve their objectives with this little present. What concerns us here is what it could do in the wrong hands. Gordon also tells me that our masters have chosen Berkeley Marine International to ship the stuff to Erifia." Harry turned to Morgan. "Over to you, John. Now maybe we'll get somewhere."

That afternoon Martin Garstang had endured a contingency planning meeting at Berkeley Marine International's office off Piccadilly. He had performed well even though his mind had been dealing with issues other than eventualities that were unlikely to occur. He found contingency planning rather dull. He failed to see why it was necessary to plan for events that were beyond any reasonable expectation of occurring. Garstang could understand why they should consider the strength of the pound and its performance against other major currencies. He could understand carrying insurance against loss. He could even understand the need to consider what they would do if a ship was lost. But why on earth were they required to consider the effect a European war would have on the business or what would be the first ten action points if the chief executive died unexpectedly?

He was relieved then to find himself on the underground platform waiting for the train to carry him to Waterloo Station. It was here he would catch his train home. Not long now until he could have a drink in the buffet car. Even had he been more aware of his surroundings he would not have been aware that he had grown a tail.

The tube ride was uneventful. It was crowded and he was jostled but he arrived at Waterloo without interruption or too much discomfort. He took his seat in a first class carriage and was delighted to feel the motion of the train as it pulled out exactly on time. In an effort to demonstrate to himself that he was in control, he resisted the temptation to move straight to the buffet car. Instead he opened his Financial Times. He was able to finish the crossword he had already started in a few minutes. In truth the reason he bought the Financial Times was the crossword. He could usually complete it - well fifty per cent of the time. Unfortunately he could not say the same about the Daily Telegraph or the Times. The crossword in both of these broadsheets he found beyond him.

When he had finished he folded the paper and, as he stood bowing his head under the luggage rack, he dropped it into his seat. He made his way back to the buffet car, which was already beginning to fill. It was with growing anticipation he awaited his turn in the queue. When it came to his turn to be served he ordered two miniatures of whisky, taking the bottles and the glass to the shelf in the corner of the carriage. Here he could stand and enjoy his drinks. He poured the first and drank it in one swallow. It was while he was unscrewing the cap on the second he had the uncomfortable feeling that he was not alone. Garstang became aware that he was the object of attention of the person standing next to him. Turning, he found himself facing an attractive woman. He felt a thrill when he realised that she was indeed watching him closely. The woman smiled.

"Good evening, Mr Garstang. Please listen to me very carefully. Not long ago you discovered you had a guardian angel. This guardian angel provided you with money that helped you during a personal cash crisis. In return you were made aware that one day a favour would be asked. You were also told that you would be provided with further funds. My friends have asked me to give you this."

The woman handed Garstang a fat envelope. Garstang put out his hand automatically.

"Place that in your pocket. When you are alone you will find it contains £10,000 in cash. You may do with this as you please." The woman paused. "I suggest you pay some of the debt you have managed to run up again at your casino. Mr Garstang, not that it's any of my business, but I think you may have a problem. Have you ever tried Gamblers Anonymous? No, I don't suppose you have. Still, that's your affair."

Garstang's discomfort had returned. "May I offer you a drink, Miss ... ? I don't think I know your name."

"That's right. You don't know my name. At this point you don't need to know my name. However, you may buy me a drink. Gin and tonic, please."

When Garstang went to the bar it gave the woman chance to look around the buffet car. She knew that the possibility of her being followed was so remote as to be unworthy of consideration. Yet her training and her instinct impelled her to survey the other occupants of the carriage. It took her a matter of seconds to take in the entire scene. She saw a range of people, mainly males, each of which was in a suit. There were three or four females, also dressed in suits. This was a scene that was repeated on hundreds of trains which left London during every weekday afternoon every week of the year. There was nothing she saw that gave her any concern. Garstang returned with two miniatures of gin, two of whisky and a bottle of tonic. He also carried a fresh glass for his guest. The woman smiled at how clumsy and ill at ease he appeared. He had not found carrying all these objects to be a simple matter. Garstang misinterpreted the smile as one of friendliness. It would have been difficult to have been more wrong.

"Thank you," said the woman. "If you do exactly as I say you will find that my friends are extremely generous. On the other hand, if you do not or if you tell anyone of our arrangement or this conversation you will most certainly be killed. You know this is a simple matter for my friends. Do not put it to the test. You have seen what they can do. Are you now ready for your instructions?"

Garstang swallowed hard. He found her words totally compelling. He knew she was not joking and she had his undivided attention. He had an odd sensation that he was part of something big. More interesting, he was also aware that he was important in some way. Somehow he was most definitely important to this woman and her friends. It was clear he was essential to their plans. This helped him to recover some of his confidence. In fact, with a little effort and imagination he could believe he was in control.

"Your threats are not necessary. I understand the nature of our arrangement and I have no intention of dying yet. What do you need from me?"

"There is a possibility that your employer, Berkeley Marine International, will be contracted to transport a consignment to a little known country in South America. Erifia. It is possible the shipment will be containerised. In fact, it is likely to be containerised. It is not certain that the port of entry will be Erifi but it is likely. It is unlikely the port will be in another South American country, but not impossible. The paperwork will show that the shipment is something quite harmless. It might be electrical or electronic components being sent to a company called L.Y.A. It might be ingredients for the manufacture of ice cream or components for ice cream manufacturing machinery. Mining equipment is just conceivable. When information of this nature comes to your attention you will contact me immediately."

"I don't know your name or your telephone number."

Something in his manner alerted the woman. She knew Garstang had something on his mind. She took a risk.

"You know something, don't you?"

Garstang gave a smug grin. The woman found this man to be revolting. Her eyes narrowed almost imperceptibly.

"Mr Garstang, you don't get too many warnings. Tell me what is on your mind. It would be a bad idea to make me think you are not to be trusted. Naomi could find herself a widow. Worse, Kent could find himself an orphan." She paused and smiled seductively. "Don't fuck with me, Mr Garstang."

Garstang's confidence evaporated. He was scared again. This attractive woman was very scary indeed.

"Well, I might be able to help."

"Then do so quickly." The smile had gone.

"We have an order to take six containers to Erifi. They're listed as nonperishable foodstuffs. It's milk powder."

"Details, Mr. Garstang, if you please."

"I didn't take much notice. The paperwork hit my desk yesterday. I haven't costed it yet."

"Be sure you are in your office at 1600 hours tomorrow. You will be contacted on your direct line. Good afternoon."

The woman left without further conversation. Garstang decided to stay where he was and finish his drink. He returned to his seat as the train started to slow as it approached Southampton. Still shaken by his conversation with the beautiful but unnamed woman, he collected his paper and briefcase and stood next to the door until the train grated to a halt. The door opened. As Garstang stepped out and quickly walked down the platform, Melanie Coleman-Burns watched him.

In his office the following day, Martin Garstang read details from the shipping department. He made notes. At lunchtime he went to the pub and drank rather more than he usually did at this time of the day. He felt nervous and slightly nauseous and he was dismayed to note he had developed a slight tremor. By the time his direct line phone rang at four o'clock in the afternoon he was sweating and had an obvious tremble. When he picked up his phone he recognised the female voice immediately.

"Hello, Martin. What do you have for me?"

"Milk powder bound for Erifi. There are six containers. They will be inspected and sealed by Customs and Excise at the container depot in Gloucester. They will then come by road to our depot in Southampton. They will be shipped on the Nellie May and will arrive in Erifi nine days after sailing."

"Very well," said the woman at the other end of the line. "Who will drive the containers to Southampton?"

"They will driven down by our haulage contractors."

"Which route?"

"From Gloucester to Stroud. Then to Tetbury, Malmesbury, Devizes, Salisbury and finally Southampton."

"How long will that journey take?"

"No more than three hours."

There was a delay before Melanie Coleman-Burns asked her next question.

"When is the collection at Gloucester scheduled?"

"The twenty-seventh. Thursday fortnight."

"The containers. How do you identify the correct ones?"

"The containers are owned by a division of our company. It's called Merritime. The containers are lime green with black lettering. On the two sides you will see the logo and 'Merritime, a division of Berkeley Marine International.' On the two ends and on the sides you will see a container number. In each case the data is high up on the right. There is a block of information. It will say "Cubic Capacity" or rather "Cu. Cap. 33.2 metres." Then it might give tare details. They're all a bit different, you see? But certainly at the bottom of this information it will give a number."

"When will you know the serial numbers of the containers?"

"We know now. The milk powder is packed and ready for collection."

This took Coleman-Burns by surprise. Naturally she didn't show this.

"Give me the numbers, please."

"What are you going to do?"

"The numbers, please."

"All right. But I didn't tell you this. It would cost me my job."

Coleman-Burns thought of saying that it would cost him a bloody sight more than his job if he didn't. She decided to keep this to herself.

"The numbers, please," she repeated.

"84137, 99421, 99422, 99423, 80445, 80089."

"There are three consecutive numbers. Why is that?"

"The first two digits relate to the year of manufacture. The last three simply to the order in which we take delivery. The three consecutive containers must be brand new and not separated yet."

"What time will the lorries leave the depot?"

"They have to arrive here before 1400 hours on the twenty-seventh. Normally I would expect them to leave at around 1000 hours."

"Thank you, Mr Garstang. Get me the plans of the Gloucester depot. Make sure the plans clearly indicate the location of closed circuit TV cameras and any other security measures and equipment that are present. I want the staff shift patterns also. When you have this information or you need to contact me this is how you will do it. There is the free-standing postbox at the end of your road in Chilworth. When you need to talk to us, chalk a cross on the back of it. If it is raining use a child's yellow wax crayon. I'm sure Kent will have just the thing."

The phone went dead. Garstang found the last comment sinister and threatening. He was sure it was meant to sound just so.

Melanie Coleman-Burns rang through to Harvey Walsh on the internal phone.

"Got a minute, Harvey?"

Within 30 seconds she was sitting in front of her boss's desk. She took her time relating the details of the shipment of powder to Erifi. When she had gone he called Eric Wynter and congratulated him on his instinct. Even while he was saying the words, he questioned whether this was a matter of instinct, chance, luck or guesswork. Did the old man know something? It was difficult for Harvey to imagine a scenario whereby Wynter could have been made aware of the shipment. Never mind. The project was rolling. His next call was to Webster Hahn in Sedona.

Hahn's reaction had been predictable. He told Walsh to arrange for the consignment to be shipped, in the original containers, to New York. His people would be waiting for the cargo to land. There would be no trouble from the Coast Guard. He would make the necessary arrangements with the longshoremen's union. His relaxed attitude and the apparent ease with which the American could make these arrangements came as no surprise to Walsh.

Relaxation

The director of Section P worked hard. Rarely were the results of his hard work publicly acknowledged as they would have been had he worked for other organisations in other fields. However, being director of Section P had its advantages. Sir Harry Buchanan preferred the considerable freedom that came with his job. The nature of his particular line of work made this essential. He also enjoyed a considerable salary and, often viewed by Harry as being more important, he had access to expenses and perks only dreamed of by even the most successful captains of British industry.

Harry made use of two of these perks whenever possible. By necessity he took several long weekends off every year. He often made use of them by escaping to his hunting lodge not far from Oban in the Strathclyde region of Scotland. Oban is situated on the west coast and it relies, by and large, on tourism, ferries and the sea for its relative prosperity. To reach it by road from London would take the motorist two days. It can be achieved in one, but few try this a second time. For Harry this was not an issue. Some twenty miles inland from Oban on the shores of Loch Etive lies the village of Taynuilt. A short distance from this village there is a tiny airfield.

Harry's second perk necessary for his long weekends away was the unlimited access to an aeroplane. The aeroplane he favoured for his trips to Oban was a Handley Page Jetstream, a training and light transport. With a two-man crew the Jetstream could carry up to 12 troops. The aeroplane used by Harry, however, had only two seats. Troops were not invited to board this plane.

As the crow or the Jetstream fly, it is almost exactly 400 miles from R.A.F. Northolt on the western outskirts of London, to Taynuilt. If the pilot was allowed a direct flight at a cruising speed of 280 m.p.h. Harry could be in his hunting lodge inside two hours. On the other hand, there were occasions when the route required the Jetstream to fly northwest from London, changing course to north only when it was over the Irish Sea. This route could take an hour off Harry's weekend.

These weekends were intended to recharge Harry's batteries. He always intended to spend most of the daylight hours walking around the shores of Loch Etive. Etive was said by many to be Scotland's most beautiful loch. Harry found nothing to argue with on that point. He loved to watch the grey seals basking on the rocks in the loch and the deer grazing around its shores. Most thrilling of all were the golden eagles he had seen so often gliding around the peaks of the surrounding mountains.

There had been no hunters telling their tall stories, drinking and dining in Harry's lodge for many years, not since Harry had bought it nearly twenty years before. For most of this time Mr and Mrs Fraser had been paid a generous retainer. This ensured Harry's comfort. They kept the lodge spotlessly clean. They ensured the larder and freezer were well provisioned. They maintained and cleaned the long-wheelbase Land Rover. The gardens were immaculate if a little uninspiring. When Harry was due to land at Taynuilt, a phone call to Mr Fraser would make sure he would be waiting with the Land Rover.

Harry's other home was a mile or so outside of Marlow. From here he could drive to his office and be seated behind his desk in an hour and a few minutes. Harry had never married although he had enjoyed many relationships, some of which had been extremely rewarding. Others he preferred to forget. Although he lived alone in Marlow he was never lonely. He was a genial and generous host. He entertained regularly and lavishly. The good and great visited the house often. His office and his clients knew his home phone number and his home fax number. He could also be contacted by electronic mail.

In Scotland, however, things were very different. Harry had many luxuries in the lodge including satellite television. What Harry did not have there was a listed telephone. His number was known to only a few privileged people. He zealously guarded his peace and quiet when he was at the lodge. None of his neighbours knew when he was due to arrive or leave, apart from the Frasers. More important, they did not know what Harry did for a living, and that included the Frasers. Apart from long walks around the loch, Harry often drove into Oban to sample a whisky or two in the bars and hotels of the town. He was known here as Roly Poly although this name was never mentioned within his hearing. More often he would be addressed as Mr Buchanan. He did not advertise the fact that he was a knight. This was Harry's time to himself. He had reduced any connection to his other life to an absolute minimum. In fact he would not have had a phone had it been possible. Unfortunately, life without a phone was merely a dream, it was simply impossible. Occasionally he was required at short notice. On more than one occasion the Jetstream had left London to collect him even before he had been contacted to be told to return to the capital. On other occasions the aeroplane had turned back to Northolt before it had entered Scottish airspace.

A favourite trip that Harry took several times a year was on the Caledonian MacBrayne ferry from Oban. It would sail round the Island of Mull, pause to show tourists Fingal's Cave on a rock in the sea called Staffa and then on to Iona.

All these were the reasons why Harry loved to return to the land of his forefathers.

He had just entered the lodge after a long walk around the shores of Loch Etive when the phone rang in his study. This did not please him one bit. He had planned to spend another 48 hours north of the border. The sound of the phone usually meant he was required back in London and quickly. For just a moment Harry was tempted to allow the phone to continue ringing. The irresponsibility of that was appealing but inappropriate. Harry was a professional and he owed all the good things he enjoyed in life to his work. He picked up the phone.

"Buchanan."

"Harry. It's Gordon. The painting leaves on the twenty-seventh."

"Shit," replied Harry. "No good asking you if you can stop it, I suppose?"

"Nothing I can do, old boy. The P.M. is adamant."

"Today's the thirteenth. Where is the package now?" Both men knew that they were not talking on a secure line. Their use of the cryptic English was therefore a little bizarre.

"It's with the auctioneers ready to be taken to the buyer's agent."

"Okay. I'll get the plane and be in my office as soon as I can."

"That's the other thing, Harry. Your plane will touch down in about 15 minutes. Sorry and all that, but I've been trying to call you for hours."

The combined services of the Jetstream and car which was waiting for him at Northolt allowed Harry to be in his office in a little over three hours. Having not smoked this day he found he was in need of nicotine. His first job was to light a cigar. He inhaled deeply instantly feeling the familiar buzz. His next task was to talk to his deputy director of operations. He stabbed a button on his hands-free phone. A woman answered.

"DDOps there?"

"No, Sir Harry. Mr Morgan has an appointment out of the building. I understand he will be back in about thirty minutes."

"Please be sure to ask him to come to my office immediately he returns." Without waiting for an answer Harry clicked the button again.

Impatiently he paced his office, pulling on his cigar with considerable vigour. He didn't feel in the mood to be kept waiting. He returned to the phone on his desk. It took him less than 30 seconds to track down his deputy director of intelligence. In a further 30 seconds Vanessa Stone was standing in front of his desk.

"Where the bloody hell is John? When I need the bugger I can't find him. Why can't I find the sod when I need him, eh? Tell me that!"

Stone smiled. "I rather think it might be his mum's birthday."

"Great. The government is in danger of tumbling. We run the risk of being censured by our global allies. The cabinet secretary is on the verge of a coronary. We are possibly in a position of losing enough arms to start a crime war the like of which the world hasn't witnessed since Chicago in the thirties and my DDOps is out buying flowers."

Harry's big smile returned to his big face. Vanessa knew that the little outburst she had just witnessed would have the effect of restoring her boss to his customary good natured and affable self.

"Berkeley Marine International," he said. "Let's have a sitrep."

Stone knew that since Berkeley Marine International had landed the contract to ship the containers to Erifi, her boss would, at some time or other, require a situation report, or sitrep. She and her team had done their homework. She was able to provide details of the company in rather more depth and detail than a mere company search would have achieved. She provided Harry with trading details, staff, contracts and operations throughout the world. She told him about the areas of risk she had identified. One of these risks was one Martin Garstang, B.M.I.'s business development manager. The ever widening beam on Harry's face told Stone that she was probably giving him what he sought. Harry waited until he was sure she had finished before he spoke.

"Good. Thank you. Let us consider this for a moment. If a big league contractor is planning to lift the arms, then how would it obtain the intelligence it would need to be successful? If an organisation had commissioned a contractor to lift the arms, how do we find out who that is? Ideas?"

"Easy. Lift them in transit. Get the transit details from the shipping company. Find the weakest link in that organisation. Ask 'Who can I bribe?' Threaten someone or get that certain someone pissed. Who has an embarrassing secret or two? Garstang looks like a soft touch. How do we find out if there is a contractor and client? If there is, who are they? Also easy. Watch Berkeley Marine in general and one Martin Garstang in particular. Between them they should answer all the questions."

At this moment the door opened and in walked John Morgan.

"Sorry, Harry. Important meeting. How can I help."

Harry ignored the newcomer. "Good thinking, Vanessa. So watch them well." He turned to face Morgan. "Important meeting be buggered. You up to pace on Berkeley Marine?" Morgan nodded. "You know the stuff leaves Gloucester on the twenty-seventh?" Morgan nodded again. "Good. Keep in close touch with Vanessa. Now what's your next step?"

"Well, it seems likely that a thief would wish to check out the cargo before taking unnecessary risks. I'll mount a watch over the consignment and see what crawls out of the woodwork."

Morgan's response seemed to satisfy the director. His smile reappeared even wider than before. "Make it so."

The two realised that the interview was over. They both turned to leave the office. As Morgan was about to leave, Harry called to him.

"Oh, and John? Wish your mum a very happy birthday from me."

Stephen Wells had provided W.F.M.C. with the information it required. Chris Latcham was delighted with the disks and the data gathered from the computer at the Hahn ranch in Sedona. Harvey Walsh had been pleased. It had furnished him with a hold over his client, Webster Hahn, and it had provided a lesson. The lesson had not been lost on Hahn. Latcham was content in the knowledge that the operation had been an unqualified success.

In reality, however, had the staff with W.F.M.C. been aware of the whole story they would not have been quite as satisfied with the operation. Wells and his American colleague had been totally engrossed in gathering the information. They had failed to notice a Chrysler New Yorker parked half a mile down the road. Sitting quietly, unspeaking, unmoving in the car were two men. They simply sat and watched. They saw the smoke billowing from the engine compartment of the Dodge van. They saw the CO_2 fire extinguisher being used. They saw the apparent lack of activity. They watched the Dodge move off and, as it did so, the New Yorker followed.

The two men in the Dodge failed to notice the car following them. Had they been looking for a tail it is possible they would still not have spotted it. The car remained at a distance throughout the journey. It never approached closer than a block. When Wells was dropped off at Sky Harbor International Airport, a man left the Chrysler and followed the Englishman into the terminal. He watched him check in.

When the pursuer had checked if he could have a seat on the same 2140 flight to Gatwick he used his mobile phone. In less than half an hour a woman arrived and handed him an overnight case and a briefcase. His passport was in the briefcase along with other items that might be required. Secretly the American was pleased. Surveillance was invariably boring. Tails rarely led him out of state. Here was a real bonus. An expenses paid trip to London was decidedly different. While training covered such an operation it was a boon when the opportunity arose to put the training into practice.

When Wells emerged from the terminal at Gatwick he had no idea he was being followed by the American who had been behind him all the way from Sedona. He didn't notice the American get into a taxi and he failed to notice the taxi slowing as he got out of his car outside the West End offices of W.F.M.C.

Thirty-six hours later the American was back in his native land relating every detail of his trip to Dr Jonjo Grey. Grey had never heard of Wynter Farmer Management Consultants. He had no idea what business W.F.M.C. had with the Hahn family but he wanted to know. When Grey had dismissed the very tired, red eyed employee he entered his password to access the personal computer that sat on his desk. A company search was easy. The public information required by statute for a limited liability company were there for him to see. He was not sure why he was surprised. He scribbled some notes on a pad as he read from the screen. He noted the nature of W.F.M.C's business, which included consultancy, accountancy and legal services. He wrote down the names of the directors and the company's bankers. He was interested in turnover, the value of the fixed assets and the pre-tax profits. He was surprised at the low level of hire purchase commitments, the low level owed to creditors and the remarkably low borrowings at the bank. For a company of this size, creditors were unusually low. He was staggered to discover a notation at the bottom of the comments page which read, "We would suggest a credit limit on monthly terms of £1,500,000."

Wynter Farmer Management Consultants. Grey turned the name over in his mind. He hadn't reached the position of president of Ribbon Motor Corporation by chance. Now his formidable brain was considering what he had just read. He quickly arrived at a hypothesis. He based this on the declared financial position of W.F.M.C. Tiny borrowing requirement; huge assets; and yet the apparent relatively low turnover could not explain this wealth. Maybe this organisation had additional, undeclared forms of income. Cash deals perhaps, or payment in kind. If these people were involved with the Hahn family then there was more than a passing chance they were less than legitimate.

Placing a transatlantic call, Dr Jonjo Grey had words with a contact in London. His order was simple. "Find out all you can about W.F.M.C."

The night of Thursday 20th was moonlit and warm for the time of year. A great night for lovers. Love was not the first thing on the mind of Melanie Coleman-Burns this night. Tonight was the night she had chosen to visit Gloucester.

On the previous Monday a chalk cross on the pillar box had been spotted by an observer. The observer had contacted Coleman-Burns, who then arranged to meet Garstang after work. The venue was a pub in the centre of Southampton. This particular pub had been chosen because it was always crowded between 5.30 and 7.00. Tired executives and managers enjoyed their gin and tonics here before returning to their homes. No one would notice Garstang talking to a smartly dressed woman here. With the crowds came the hubbub of conversation. It would be extremely difficult, even impossible to overhear what they were saying to each other. Coleman-Burns left the pub with the plans and other information she had demanded.

The two men she had dropped off in central Gloucester had been well briefed. They had memorised the layout of the depot. They knew where the CCTV cameras were located and how to avoid being picked up by them. They also knew that all the staff had gone home. There was only a security guard, more like a uniformed night watchman, left on site. If anyone had remained on site to catch up on work, they were well prepared to deal with this. They also knew they had at least two hours before the early shift of packers and transport administrators clocked on.

It was the job of the security guard to remain in his booth close to the front gates. Every half hour he was required to walk around the outside of the distribution and storage building. The building itself was securely locked and alarmed and he was not required to go inside. At seven points around the outside there were time clocks into which the guard inserted his card for punching. In this way his supervisor could check that the guard had done his rounds and not spent the entire night in his booth watching the portable television, smoking and drinking tea.

Coleman-Burns and a small group of colleagues from the operations division had carefully analysed the timings and the routine. It was evident that her people could not get through the wire, open the containers, check the contents and get out in the time it took the guard to walk around the other side of the depot building. A role play staged on a disused wartime airfield, miles away from prying eyes, confirmed this. It was regrettable but necessary to take the guard out.

The two men walked from the city centre towards the Gloucester docks. It took them less than ten minutes to cover the distance and find the Merritime distribution depot. They saw the guard in his booth. One of the men in a dark, formal suit walked to the main gate and showed his identity card through the wire. The card proclaimed him to be a Customs and Excise officer. The pressure such a card could exert on a security guard usually achieved results nothing short of miraculous. In his effort to please, the guard rushed from his booth and unlocked the huge steel gates. He failed to check with anyone or notify head office where there was a voice mail facility for just such an eventuality.

"Good evening. I want to check your manifests for all containers leaving tomorrow. Can you provide the journey sheets or do you have to call in a senior manager?"

These words were carefully scripted. They were chosen in such a way as to make it difficult for the guard to call anyone. After all he, the night security operative, was important, wasn't he? He could sort this out without bothering a senior manager. He could show them in the morning that he had used his initiative.

"Follow me," said the guard in his best self-important voice. He kept a very straight face, rather like the police officers he'd seen on television, the face that said, "This is important. I am taking this very seriously indeed and I'm important too."

The two men entered the small booth, the guard first. Before he had a chance to turn around, a length of hose pipe, one end of which was loaded with lead shot, thudded down on the top of his skull. He dropped to the floor without a sound. The man in the suit went to the gate, checked there were no unwelcome passersby and signalled to his companion. When the two men were reunited, they pushed the steel gates together. All this had been easy so far. Now they needed to be more careful. They could see the first infrared camera mounted high on the depot wall. They knew that it could pick them up when they had moved to the other side of the booth.

Fortunately it swivelled, scanning through 120 degrees in order to view a large area of the yard. They waited until it was pointing away from them and dashed to the diesel pumps. They hid, one behind each of the two pumps. This gave them time to spot the second camera. This was situated on a pylon and scanned down one side of the building and the trailers that were backed up to the loading ramps at the front of the depot. When the camera moved towards the side they made a second sprint and ducked between the loading ramps and the trailers. They were safe from the camera here.

The moon was bright and by the ambient light they were able to read the container numbers. They quickly found two of the six numbers they had been given by Coleman-Burns. At the first container, the wire cutters on the pliers removed the Customs and Excise lead seal. The double doors were opened and one of the men jumped inside. With a jemmy he opened three wooden boxes, checked inside and then, with a hammer, sealed them again. When he jumped down the doors were shut and a fresh Customs and Excise seal pinched into place with the pliers.

They repeated this exercise with the second container they had identified. They watched the cameras and left the yard by the route they had entered. They walked back towards the centre of the city throwing the jemmy, hammer and pliers into a dock as they passed.

Melanie Coleman-Burns was waiting and they settled themselves into the back seat of the car. Their report was good. Two of the containers contained arms, and if two did then so did the other four.

John Morgan and his team had spent the last three nights on top of the distribution depot's roof. This they had enjoyed not one bit. They watched the entire operation. They were sorry for the guard. Unfortunately there was nothing they could do to help him. They could certainly not have warned him of the likelihood of intruders. Morgan used his mobile phone to alert a car outside the depot. Ten minutes after the intruders had left the yard, he and his men removed themselves from the roof and went to their car. Morgan made a second call, this time to Sir Harry Buchanan.

The first car located the two intruders as they walked towards the city centre. The driver parked and followed on foot. When he saw them getting into the back seat of a BMW, his sophisticated photographic equipment was able to take studio quality shots of the men and the female driver.

Decay

Erifia's President Christian McGregor had moved into ex President Sandriano's villa outside of the capital, Erifi. General Gariol had taken up residence in the palace in the centre of Erifi. He had explained to McGregor that if there were to be counter-revolution, then it would most likely start in the capital. He should therefore be in situ should such an unlikely situation arise. In reality, Gariol rather fancied the idea of living in Erifia's grandest building. This, he felt, was his rightful place as head of the armed forces.

Life for the new president and the general had, by and large, been pleasant and fun since they had taken power. They enjoyed their status and the control they had over the people of Erifia. They considered there was not too much to worry about. Industry was gradually getting back to work. Hunger made that inevitable. Unfortunately L.Y.A. Photocopiers was still silent. McGregor knew this was because the workers there earned far more than the country's average. Their reserves could enable them to stay out for longer than most other people. Still, it would not be long before they too would become hungry. They would resent the decrease in their hitherto high standard of living.

Tourism would soon resume. Things were going as well as could be expected. But all was not well in the gardens of McGregor and Gariol. They were aware that there was not as much shipping in the commercial port of Erifi. The wretched Royal Navy was still there. Seven miles inland the R.A.F. still had its presence. Neither service, however, was spending any money. Both had provided a considerable income for the bars, brothels, shops, restaurants, taxis and other services in the country. The servicemen and women were compelled to stay on base.

There was another and more immediate problem. Gariol had been unable to pay his army for three months now. There were definite signs of restlessness and dissatisfaction. McGregor had spoken to the Russians and the Japanese about the possibility of aid. He had been snubbed.

Next he had tried the Argentineans. He was amazed when they had told him he was an illegal president. As if they had room to be moralistic, he thought, as a wave of righteous indignation washed over him. Some of the smaller countries in South America had pledged halfhearted support on the grounds of continental solidarity, but as yet nothing had materialised. Perhaps even worse, both of Erifia's banks had locked their doors. McGregor found he had no access to senior managers. When he sent a representative to London to meet the head of one of the banks, his agent had been told that no funds would be available until further notice. All accounts had been frozen and no trading would take place until sanction had been received from President Sandriano or the British government. This was a major worry for McGregor.

He was even more angry when he found he could not contact the governor or the directors of the People's Bank of Erifia. Gariol had instructed his soldiers to blast their way into the bank and its vault. They found nothing until, in a frenzy of anger and frustration, the soldiers broke open all the safe deposit boxes. Here they found cash, share certificates, jewellery. Little of this reached either Gariol or McGregor.

Never mind, all this would be sorted soon. Copper was on the move at last. Thailand had bought a large quantity at a special price. Payment was to be received in dollars the moment the copper arrived.

Gariol had taken an extremely strong line with looters and thieves, both civilians and soldiers. Public floggings were a common sight outside the palace. It seemed odd to the general that these public displays of discipline didn't seem to be reducing crime. Two sergeants and a corporal had been publicly shot for losing control over a group of soldiers who had gone on a drunken rampage one Saturday night. It had all started in a bar by a garrison close to the border with French Guiana. When the owner had asked them to leave in the early hours of the morning, they had shot him dead. All the liquor that could be found was taken and the bar smashed. Not a single window remained unbroken. Every table, chair, gaming machine and light was smashed. Having had their hunger for carnage heightened, the soldiers left in four army Land Rovers and made their way to Erifi. One crashed into a drainage ditch, spilling its occupiers into the filthy water. The other three arrived more or less intact.

They broke into a closed bar and started drinking from the stock. When the owner, obviously a brave man, came down to investigate the noise, his head was smashed in with the butt of a rifle. Groups headed to the residential districts. Houses were broken into and there were three reported cases of rape. By morning all had quietened down. When Gariol toured the damaged areas he was genuinely shocked by what he saw. The three NCOs were executed. There were floggings and many soldiers were confined to barracks.

The Examiner, presses now back in operation on some days at least, said it was the work of soldiers loyal to ex-President Sandriano. The paper made it clear that the criminals had been severely dealt with. Money was given to the families of the injured civilians. It was explained to the families that nothing could compensate them for the raping, looting and damage to their property, but it was hoped the money would made it all easier to bear. If they required further help then President McGregor wanted to hear from them in person.

Journalists had been expelled from Erifia. The People's Government of Erifia made it clear that it knew that the foreign journalists were all spies. They were to consider themselves fortunate that because of the good nature of President McGregor they were being allowed to leave. A less compassionate president would undoubtedly have had them all executed. McGregor and Gariol had thought it a PR coup when they had had their picture on the front page of The Examiner watching the plane carrying the journalists take off.

McGregor had now reached a decision. He would make his peace with some of the more influential people of Erifia. He would hold a banquet for invited guests. A sumptuous feast would be held in the palace. He would ensure that selected representatives of the foreign press heard about this. These would be the more desirable members of the press, the quality press. Not the tabloid riffraff. He issued a special invitation to Richard Warren of the London Times and Dave Newbeck of the Washington Post. Guy Ammann of Le Figaro was invited along with

Walter Teishal representing Die Zeitung. Each was offered a suite at the palace and free air tickets.

The following day, during a meeting with Gariol, McGregor made the decision to invite CBS and the BBC. In front of these guests he would put his point and lay out his vision of the future. He would bring the rest of the world round to his way of thinking. It was settled then. This seemed like a good time for McGregor and Gariol to share a bottle of champagne. Things were definitely looking up. The press circus was set for the following Saturday.

Several thousand miles away, Harry Buchanan picked up his telephone.

"Okay. Move them out."

This simple message triggered a complex series of operations. It had been set up by Vanessa Stone and John Morgan under the guidance and watchful eye of Harry. Harry's main concern was that they had needed to involve people outside Section P. Those who had to be involved were only told what was required of them. The reasons for the operation and the individual tasks were not disclosed. The stories contrived by Harry and his team gave Harry to believe that security needs were met. Two of the directors of Merritime were involved. They would keep very quiet. After all, it was the activities of an employee of Merritime's sister company which were the cause of the danger and inconvenience. Customs and Excise was involved. Harry knew from experience that there was absolutely no security risk there.

To keep the risk to a minimum, it was department staff who were to tranship the arms into other containers and to drive the six new containers to Harwich. It was here the 20,000-ton Skanda Containerway was waiting to take the consignment to Erifi. This was the only cargo.

The operation started at 0200 hours the following day. By midday the arms were aboard the Skanda Containerway, which then sailed at 1600 hours.

When, at 10 a.m. on Thursday 27th, the six containers numbered 84137, 99421, 99422, 99423, 80445 and 80089 rolled out of the yard in Gloucester, the Skanda Containerway was in mid Atlantic. It was a fine, sunny morning. With hardly a cloud in the sky the drivers looked forward to a pleasant journey to Southampton. Their big Volvo tractor units were a joy to drive and this was a day to make use of the air-conditioning.

The convoy made good time with just the shortest holdup for road works in Devizes. Each driver felt mild irritation, however, when a police officer pulled the lorries over into a large lay by between Devizes and Salisbury. A Vehicle Inspectorate spot check was not a new experience for any of the drivers. They knew that the check could take 15 minutes or an hour. They were confident, however, that the excellent maintenance and monitoring programmes would ensure that tractors and trailers alike would pass with flying colours.

Each driver knew that the Vehicle Inspectorate officers along with the police officers would check the tachographs and journey sheets before they conducted a physical check on the vehicles. They also knew that the delay would be minimal because of the Customs and Excise documentation and seals on the containers.

As each lorry pulled to a halt there was the hiss of the air brakes followed by the silence when the engine was turned off. Automatically the drivers reached for their clipboards and jumped down from the cabs. Each was greeted by a smiling police officer and conducted to a mobile Vehicle Inspectorate control van. Only when the drivers stepped into the van did they realise that this was no ordinary, routine spot check. The smiles on the faces of the policemen had disappeared and the drivers were unceremoniously bundled onto seats. Each driver had his right hand shoved between his legs and handcuffed to the tubular steel frame of the bench seat.

There were no windows in the van and there was also no way they could see into the driver's cab. They were provided with chocolate and cans of soft drinks during their long journey. Twice the van stopped and one at a time the drivers were escorted into woods to relieve themselves. It was a full 24 hours later that the van stopped for the last time and the policemen disappeared. No one had spoken to the captives during the entire journey. It was a further two hours before one of the drivers saw a key on the floor of the van. The key unlocked the handcuffs. When the men emerged into the daylight they were surprised to find themselves in a country lane in the Cotswolds less than ten miles from Gloucester. They had expected to have been stranded in the north of Scotland, not within walking distance of their homes.

By the time their situation had become clear to the drivers, their tractor units were parked up in a lorry park in Felixstowe and the containers were aboard a container vessel already two hours out and heading for New York.

It gave Harvey Walsh some pleasure when he spoke to Webster Hahn in Arizona. He conveyed details of the containers, the ship and the estimated time of arrival in New York. Hahn assured Walsh that he would do the rest. He congratulated Walsh on a job well done and assured him that as soon as the consignment arrived and had been checked, Walsh would receive the balance of the agreed fee.

Counterrevolution

On Friday 28th, the Skanda Containerway steamed into the port of Erifi. Waiting to meet it was a team of well-briefed dockworkers. Two hours after tying up, the lime green and black containers were being lifted by the single large crane. One by one they were dropped onto a battered yellow shunter and taken into one of the cargo sheds. Watching from a discrete distance was a group of observers. The group was made up of people who would not normally be found hanging around the port.

It took just a further two hours for the contents of the six containers to disappear.

The evening of the 28th saw much activity in Erifi's palace, now the home of General Francois Gariol. The main reception hall was being converted to present the appropriate atmosphere for the forthcoming press conference and banquet. The menu had been agreed and local fish featured. Ice cream and sorbets from the factory of Red Pasqualle were to be laid on. A Hereford steer had been slaughtered and hung. Roast ribs were designed to impress the foreign press. French wines had been purchased across the border.

Locals had been bribed into service with the promise of fat pay packets. Little did they know that the coffers were empty and the president had no means with which to pay them. Because of the presence of the press they had also been carefully briefed. They had been told to whom they might speak and what they might say. They had also been told what they might not say. They had been warned that if anyone was indiscreet they and their families could expect a visit from Gariol's soldiers. No trouble was expected.

That night McGregor and Gariol met with the senior army officers. They drank champagne and discussed the security arrangements. McGregor was insistent that there should be no trouble while the foreign journalists were in the country. Army posts were to be set up at strategic positions around the capital, the villages and throughout the countryside. Any unrest was to be dealt with swiftly and quietly. Those soldiers not deployed at these posts were to be positioned in and around the palace. The better trained were to be in plain clothes and instructed to mingle with the guests.

McGregor proposed a toast. They drank to the people of Erifia. May they prosper. Let there be peace.

The following day saw McGregor and Gariol up earlier than usual. Each man was determined to be seen by as many of the Erifians as possible and by the press. During the morning representatives arrived from the London Times, Washington Post and Le Figaro. When McGregor was told that a crew from the BBC had also booked into the Palace he was overjoyed. He felt he was now onto a winner. He was being taken seriously. He ordered that champagne should be taken to the rooms of each press representative immediately with his compliments.

At five o'clock in the afternoon McGregor met Gariol at his villa. The new president demanded a report. Were Gariol's soldiers deployed? Were the journalists comfortable? Were the caterers on top of their work? Was the wine being chilled? Were tables laid correctly? Had the cutlery been polished? Which of the invited guests had said they would not be attending? He would deal with them after the reception. Where were the members of his bodyguards to be situated?

On each point Gariol assured his president that all was in order. In fact, he explained to McGregor how peaceful everything was, more so than usual. He suggested that the people of Erifi were obviously coming to terms with the new regime. He said that they clearly realised that there was absolutely no point in resistance or unrest. Everyone, he expected, would soon be back at work and the country would be back to normal. What a wonderful stroke of luck that all this should happen when the foreign press was here. McGregor stood and shook the General's hand.

"You have done well, my friend. And now it is time to prepare ourselves for the reception."

Gariol left. He knew he had to meet his master at the palace at 7.30. There was to be a cocktail reception before taking seats for dinner.

While President McGregor and General Gariol were being presented to members of the press and the invited guests, both were experiencing a feeling of well being. There was also a sense of excitement. Everyone was courteous to the hosts. Not a discordant note sounded. When the master of ceremonies asked the guests to take their places as dinner was about to be served, McGregor was conscious of the noise of talk and laughter. This was better than he had dared to expect. All tension had evaporated and this was now certain to be a happy and positive occasion.

The meal was a success also. The waiters and waitresses had been well trained for this special event. They were quick and efficient. There were no disasters. No spoons were dropped noisily. No soup was spilled down low-cut evening dresses or on pristine tuxedos. The good-natured and relaxed talk continued. It didn't stop until the master of ceremonies banged a serving spoon onto the table.

"Ladies and gentlemen, your attention please. Please be silent for President McGregor."

Ten minutes prior to this announcement, the MC had warned the people from the BBC. This had given them time to man their cameras and sound equipment. It was important that the cameras caught the moment when President McGregor rose to address the people of Erifia and the world.

"Ladies, gentlemen and members of the press," McGregor began. "It gives me great pleasure to receive you all here this evening. This is a moment for which I have waited many years. This is a proud moment when the people of Erifi are free again, when they can hold their heads high once more. Never again will we be the servants of a foreign power.

"Now is the time for all of us to look to the future, a time to rebuild. To rebuild our industry, our tourism, our homes, sewers, schools. To rebuild our fine college and our roads. But most of all to rebuild our sense of pride in our country and in ourselves."

He waited here expecting a round of ecstatic applause. Instead there was only silence. He moved on quickly.

"You will all know that I decided it was time to regain our wonderful and beautiful country for ourselves. It was time to take back what is rightfully ours. Ex-President Sandriano had sold us out to foreign powers, especially the British. In fact I understand that he is now the honoured guest of Prime Minister Bailey. Where else would he be, I ask you?"

He paused again. It was at this point he had expected laughter. There was none.

"Now you have a president of the people for the people. Now you are all free."

A voice from the floor yelled, "When will there be elections?"

"A good question and I am very pleased you asked me that. As you know we are proud of our democracy. Before we can consider elections we must rebuild."

The reporter from the Times stood. "You say you are proud of your democracy. President Sandriano was democratically elected, yet you overthrew him and his government by force. There are those who might say this was not an act of democracy. Some might even say this was an illegal act of treason. How do you square this with your claim to democracy?"

McGregor was red-faced and sweating. He was becoming angry. How dare the foreigner ask him a question like this? The British bastard hadn't even addressed him correctly, he was the president after all. He was especially angry that he could not show his displeasure with the camera on him and with pencils poised over the note pads.

"Some may view it as such. They would be fools. I had to act to restore our country to the people. We were being sold out to you Brits." He tried to laugh in the vain hope that others would laugh with him.

"Mister McGregor," said the man from the Washington Post. "When you overthrew President Sandriano most everyone in Erifia was employed. You were exporting copper and photocopiers. You enjoyed cordial relations with the rest of the world and you enjoyed aid from the rest of the world. Your tourism industry brought you wealth. Your schools were open, as was your college. From what I have seen here today there now exists a very different picture."

"This is temporary. Soon we will be back on our feet. This disruption is due to Sandriano and his friend James Bailey of Great Britain. They are sabotaging our economy."

"How?" replied the *Post's* Dave Newbeck.

"I am sorry, I can't disclose that at this time. It might compromise our internal security. But," McGregor's voice rose to almost a shout, "the time will come when the world will know what those bastards are doing to us."

Richard Warren from the *Times* rose again. "Tell us, please, about the murders and criminal damage caused by your soldiers on innocent civilians."

"That's it," yelled McGregor. "This press conference is over. You were invited here as our guests and in friendship. You show us discourtesy and contempt. You are not welcome here anymore. Pack your bags and go home."

With that McGregor turned to walk from the top table. Gariol rose to join him. When they reached the edge of the slightly raised platform they were prevented from stepping down. Two men pointing SLRs at them stopped them in their tracks. They turned and looked around the room. They were surprised to see that guests were pointing similar weapons at them and their own security people.

Most of the remaining guests were amazed by this turn of events. The journalists were delighted. Cameras rolled but pencils did not touch notepads. These members of the press didn't intend to miss anything. They would never again have such a chance. They were not reporting the news here, they were part of it. They were actually watching international news take place.

Red Pasqualle slowly stood. He had been a guest. Now he was centre stage. He approached the raised top table. In a calm and clear voice which everyone in the room heard he said, "General Gariol, remove your gun from its holster and place it on the table. You are relieved of your command. You will be taken into custody."

"On what charge, Pasqualle?" said Gariol.

"The charge is treason, General. Now place your weapon on the table."

It was no surprise to Red or any of his men who were spread throughout the room when Gariol drew his automatic and tried to aim it at Pasqualle. Before the movement could be completed several shots rang out. Gariol dropped to the floor, dead.

"That was unnecessary. McGregor, please go with these men." Pasqualle pointed towards the two men at the side of the stage. "You are also under arrest for treason. Further charges will follow, which will include murder and fraud." He turned to the two men. "Take him away."

Red Pasqualle mounted the stage and turned to address his audience, for his it was. All eyes were now on him. "I am sorry if any of you have been frightened by what you have just witnessed. I am sorry Gariol did not live to stand trial. I am sorry I have spoiled your evening. Members of the press, please report to the world what you have witnessed tonight. Erifia is, as of now, back in the hands of the people. Our democratically elected President Sandriano is on his way here. The army has put down its weapons. We were ready to take our land back by force if it was required. I am delighted to tell you that not a shot has been fired. Not one life has been lost. Except this one." Pasqualle pointed to the lifeless figure of General Gariol. "It seems that Erifia's army was not altogether behind McGregor and Gariol. It hadn't been paid for weeks. It was hungry. It was abused. That goes for many of the other people of Erifia."

Pasqualle paused and smiled. "I guess McGregor was right about one thing. Now is the time to rebuild."

The journalists thronged forward and surrounded Pasqualle. A flood of questions overwhelmed him. It was impossible to respond to all the questions but he was able to select questions he felt might help. He heard one journalist ask what would happen to McGregor.

"It is not for me to determine McGregor's future. That is a question for the courts."

"What is the next step for you and the people of Erifia?"

"We must prepare to welcome President Sandriano, our democratically elected president."

"What will be President Sandriano's first step?"

"I am sure he will wish to reassure our people. There is much lost ground to be made up. There is much damage and hurt to be put right. In any case, I suggest that your question should be addressed to him when he arrives."

Eventually Red Pasqualle was ushered out of the hall. The people of Erifia crowded round him making it difficult for the journalists to follow. Red Pasqualle's place in history had been assured. He would now return to his business.

Vanessa Stone had an appointment with Chief Inspector Roger Court. Court was aware that Stone worked for a government department and carried considerable clout. In the past he had been required to provide Section P with information and this was another of those occasions. He complied with requests for assistance without question. This time Stone asked him to provide the name and address of the owner of a BMW. The police officer looked at the slip of paper showing a vehicle registration number. He turned to his computer terminal. This offered him access to the Police National Computer. In turn this linked him with the computer at the DVLA in Swansea, South Wales.

Seconds later he wrote down the name of Melanie Coleman-Burns and her address. She was the registered owner of the BMW. Thanking him, Stone left for her next appointment at the Jobcentre. Here she made her presence known at the reception desk. Her Security Service ID card ensured that an executive officer was soon at her side leading her to her desk. Vanessa Stone explained that she wanted the National Insurance number of Melanie Coleman-Burns of the address shown on the slip of paper she handed over. With some pride the executive officer said it would take just a moment.

This had been no exaggeration. Within seconds Stone was holding a printout containing further details on Coleman-Burns. These details included the fact she had never made a claim for benefit and had no recorded periods of unemployment. It gave her date of birth and, most important to Stone, her National Insurance number.

She took the National Insurance number to a local tax office. Again her ID card ensured that a tax supervisor saw her quickly. Using the NI number the supervisor was able to identify the employer of Melanie Coleman-Burns as Wynter Farmer Management Consultants. It provided a London address.

Vanessa Stone, while pleased with her work of the last two hours, was a little uneasy. Would this woman use her own car? Would she drive it to Gloucester to assist in an illegal act? Maybe she would, but it was careless. She had not expected carelessness. Perhaps she should check that it was indeed Melanie Coleman-Burns driving the BMW.

Stone returned to her office and collected her car. It took her two hours to travel west on the M4 to Newport in South Wales. Newport is the home of the Passport Office. The magic ID card provided access to the office of a rather formal, spinster-like woman. Stone gave the woman the name, address and date of birth of Melanie Coleman-Burns. She said she wanted details of her latest passport application and to see a copy of the photograph which accompanied the application.

The woman left the room for a long fifteen minutes. Stone was struck by the impersonal nature of the office. There was nothing here to give any indication of the personality or interests of the occupier. No photographs, calendars or potted plants. It was extremely dull. When the woman returned she handed Stone a copy of the passport application and the application photograph. This photograph Stone compared to the photographs of the driver of the BMW. There was no doubt. This was the same person.

Stone enjoyed her drive back up the M4. She now felt confident she had something concrete to share with her boss. Harry appeared pleased to see her and used his internal phone to ask John Morgan to join them. The two men listened to Stone as she brought them up to date.

"Well done," said Harry. "Seems to me then we have a positive on Wynter Farmer Management Consultants. Your findings confirm our initial belief. We tracked the bogus Department of Transport officials and the sham police officers who lifted the containers. Time we made our move on Misters Wynter and Farmer. I suspect that by this time they may be aware that things are not going their way. Have you seen the papers today?"

He threw a copy of the Times across his desk to Stone. There was an excellent photograph of Red Pasqualle alongside another of President Sandriano. Stone smiled.

Dr Grey's Research

Dr Jonjo Grey replaced his telephone handset. After the conversation with his contact in London he had heard nothing he didn't already know about Wynter Farmer Management Consultants. The absence of new information caused him some irritation and considerable frustration. Paradoxically, the difficulty in uncovering further details about the organisation was in itself suggestive. Grey asked himself why information was so difficult to collect. Obviously these people had something to hide.

Grey had already planned a contingency for the eventuality of his London people failing. It was a last resort because it would alert the Hahn family that all was not as it might be. He would have to have a word with Chip, the Hahn family's functionary. He knew that Chip's loyalty to the Hahns was not in question. He had weighed the use of subterfuge against bribery, threats against violence. No matter from which angle he viewed it, violence always came out on top. Grey was not a particularly violent man, but he was not above such action when circumstances required or a lack of options was presented. So violence it was then.

Grey picked up his phone again. "Get me Mr Rocchiciolli, please."

It was two hours later that Grey received the news from his personal assistant. Mr Rocchiciolli would meet him in the morning. They were to meet in Grey's office. This Grey did not like but he knew from experience that there was little point arguing. In any event he knew the other man would be careful he was not followed and he would certainly not tell anyone where he was going or what he was doing. And so it was that Grey had to wait until the next day.

When the next day came, the meeting was short and the instructions conveyed were unambiguous. A fee was agreed and Rocchiciolli left. Grey knew it would take the other a day or two to survey, plan and equip himself to carry out the commission.

Albert Rocchiciolli was an Italian American. Short, dark and a little overweight, he was a man with an awesome reputation. He was a freelancer providing a service to a number of rich clients. Above all things, he was an assassin. No one knew how many people he had killed; a lot was the closest figure that could be arrived at. His activities had inevitably come to the attention of the F.B.I. Unfortunately for the fibbies, while they were aware of his activities, they had no information which would help them identify him as the killer. They had witness reports from Miami to Portland and the only vague constant was that the target was less than average height and was a shade overweight, probably. Rarely did any other confirmable details match. In any case, almost all the evidence amassed so far was anecdotal.

Albert was a stylish man. His appearance was a matter of importance to him. He usually wore a dark suit, white silk shirt and dark tie. He resisted diamond tie pins and cuff links. He viewed accessories like these as a cliché. He saw them as badges invented by Hollywood to label the bad guys. His shoes always shone, as did his car. He saw it as being entirely appropriate that he should drive a Jaguar. Jonjo Grey thought this odd. Top of the range Jaguars did not ensure anonymity. Grey also found Albert's habit of chewing gum a distasteful practice.

Albert Rocchiciolli rarely accepted more than two jobs a year. Too much activity might provide the F.B.I. with a trail leading straight to him. Just two jobs a year would ensure that any trail was dusted over. Identifying any links was difficult without consistent and regular activity. In any case, Albert was now a rich man. To maintain his lifestyle he did not need more work. Interest on his investments provided a substantial income but, as with many people of means, there was always the temptation to increase his wealth. He would never know when he might need extra funds.

Now here he was again. He had accepted a job from Dr Jonjo Grey. This was not the first time, but this time it was different. His targets now were members of the Hahn family and organisation and it was this that confused him. Surely Grey must know that Albert and Webster Hahn were old acquaintances. Hahn had once been his single biggest client.

Now he was being asked to hit the family. If Grey knew this, why was he asking Albert to do this job? What was Grey up to?

That evening Albert Rocchiciolli sat at his home and puzzled. He was tasked to abduct Chip and, by using any means at his disposal, extract information from him. Albert had never liked Chip. He thought him uncouth and a thug, but he admired his unerring loyalty to the Hahn family. He was not to kill Chip. That was odd and dangerous. Leaving Chip alive provided Webster Hahn with a route to Albert. Next he was to hit Ricky. Grey had said that while Ricky lived, his own life was at risk. Albert knew a great deal about Ricky Hahn. He was the idiot of the family. A real smartass. Albert was surprised Webster had not sorted the kid years ago.

So what was Grey planning? None of this made sense, unless Grey didn't know of Albert's connection with the Hahns. Was this possible? Surely not. What if Grey did know of the connection? Was he expecting Albert to go to the Hahns and if so, to what purpose? All very confusing. Had Grey underestimated him, or maybe he had overestimated him? Albert Rocchiciolli didn't like the situation.

Later in the evening Albert reached a decision. Dr Jonjo Grey and Webster Hahn were both powerful men. Each had considerable resources and now Albert was caught between the two. On balance, however, he thought Hahn was probably the most dangerous. If Grey was setting Albert up, what did he have to lose by talking to Hahn? In any case he and Hahn went back a long way. He would speak to Webster Hahn the next morning. That night Albert did not sleep well. In the early hours of the morning he changed his mind.

Dr Jonjo Grey had commissioned him to do a job. He had accepted the assignment. If he went back on his word his name would not be worth a whole hill of beans. He would never be trusted again. He couldn't go to Webster Hahn. He had to complete the assignment regardless of his personal relationship with the Hahn family. This was business.

Chip usually kept Sundays to himself. Sundays were designed for indulgence and enjoyment. Webster Hahn went to church and later played golf with his friends. Joseph Hahn spent the day with his wife and kids. The divisional chief executives, Knight, Goldstein and Charlton, were rarely seen in Sedona on Sundays. Ricky Hahn would be away drinking or womanising or both. The only people at the ranch on a Sunday would be Chip and the household staff. The gardeners and ranch hands would all be enjoying time away with their own families. This was Sunday for this community.

Not far from the Arizona State University in the Tempe district of Phoenix was a small, private club. It was not cheap to become a member, but money alone was not enough. Few prospective members who had to be proposed and seconded by existing members, survived blackballing. Membership was a question of money, a close personal relationship with at least two senior club members and a talent or influence that could be of use to others. Chip had been a member of the club for a quarter of a century. He had secured membership with ease. First, he worked for Webster Hahn, and second, he had been prepared to provide to senior club members the sort of services that were not listed in the yellow pages. Now a club elder himself, he was able to enjoy his membership to the full. No one ever whispered in his ear that some small service was required. Much more likely he would be whispering in a younger member's ear.

Chip was not a big drinker. He took his duties to the Hahn family seriously and so he rarely touched alcohol during the week. But he was known to enjoy his bourbon on Sundays. In fact he often overindulged during the afternoon and early evening at the club. He did not take the drive north back to Sedona on a Sunday. He stayed over in Phoenix in a small apartment and drove back on Monday morning.

On this Sunday he left the club at 7.15 in the evening. He had enjoyed several hours drinking with his acquaintances. He was therefore not entirely in control when he swayed towards the black Mercedes. He fumbled for his keys and pressed the remote button on the car key as he approached the car. Opening the door he sat behind the wheel. In this position he remained for a moment to gather his thoughts and his breath. He inserted the key into the ignition and the big engine came to life. It was at this point he felt a gun thrust into the back of his neck. He froze. Albert Rocchiciolli had been lying on the floor in the back.

"Drive nice and careful. I'll tell you where to go."

Chip's pulse quickened but there was no external sign of this. His fuzzy mind started to consider the alternatives. He had no idea what was planned for him. He didn't know who was behind him holding the gun although the voice was familiar. He couldn't reach backwards over the seat back. It was too high in the Mercedes and in any event he was sober enough to realise that if it was a professional holding the gun, then he would be allowed no time at all. There was only one thing he could do at this time. He had to do exactly as he was told.

"Okay. Now you know what's going on. Do what you are told or you'll die real quick. No second chances, Chip. Now pull away."

"Where we going?" Chip didn't expect an answer.

"You'll find out soon enough. Just drive."

The car rolled forwards. Chip drove slowly because he had been drinking and he wanted to play for some time. He didn't expect to be killed. That could have been achieved without all this drama. They passed through Sunflower and into the Mazatzal Mountains. Obeying the directions from the back seat, Chip steered the car off the highway and onto a side track. Soon they reached trees well away from the highway. Reacting to Rocchiciolli's instructions, Chip pulled off the track and guided the car between the trees. He stopped when told to do so. He turned the engine off and was about to turn to view the man in the rear seat. Before he could do so, the barrel of the Browning automatic hit him on the side of the head an inch above this right ear. Chip saw flashing lights and was vaguely aware that he had been hit before unconsciousness overwhelmed him and he slumped across the two front seats.

When he regained consciousness Chip's first thought was the searing pain around the site of the impact and the intense ache inside his head. He ventured to open his eyes. This made the ache worse. The light inflicted a moment of searing pain. His vision was blurred. The fuzziness gradually cleared and he could make out the blue of the sky and the green of the canopy of the woodland. Chip had difficulty understanding what had happened and why he was looking up at the sky and trees. Then it came back to him. There was no sight of or sound from Rocchiciolli. Chip tried to get up but failed. His arms and legs wouldn't move.

"Welcome back," said Rocchiciolli. "Don't try to move. It won't help you none. I need some information. Give it to me now and I won't have to hurt you. What business does Webster have with Wynter Farmer Management Consultants in England? Next, where will I find that shit Ricky Hahn?"

Chip was still trying to marshal his thoughts. Why couldn't he get up? Why wouldn't his arms and legs move?

"I guess you're confused. Well, it's like this, Chip. Your feet are tied to that great big tree there. Your arms are tied to the towing hook underneath the front fender on your big, powerful car. Now if you don't tell me what I want to know I'm going to have to start that big, powerful car and reverse it a piece. Never experienced it myself but I guess for someone in your position it could be painful."

Chip's eyes were now focused, as was his mind. He was not a coward, in fact there had been times in his eventful life when he had displayed great courage. He was not especially afraid of death, but death by this method was not something he had previously considered. For what was perhaps the first time in his life, he was frightened. He didn't mind dying for his boss; that was what he was paid for. But to die like this, well, this was different. No amount of money was worth this and he felt his loyalty evaporating.

"Okay, Okay. I'll tell you." Chip was trembling as much as his bonds would allow. Sweat had broken out all over his body. "Hahn is tying up a deal to buy arms from the limeys. I don't got any more details. Webster is doing it all himself. He ain't told me no more than I told you. Ricky is at his apartment in Sedona. The Old Man told him to stay out of sight for a while. I've been looking after him. He's at his place in town."

"Are you sure he's not at the ranch?"

Now Chip recognised the voice. Now he knew it was Albert Rocchiciolli. But why was Rocchiciolli doing this? He and Webster Hahn went way back.

"Yeah. Yeah. I'm sure. The Old Man don't want him there for a while. Honest. It's the truth."

Chip knew enough to know he was placing Ricky's life in jeopardy. The only reason the question had been asked was for Rocchiciolli to get to him. Chip didn't mind this so much. Like most people, he despised Ricky. He had been an embarrassment to the family for years. He was a waster. He knew that one day Ricky would get what was coming to him. Maybe this was the day. He felt worse about divulging Webster Hahn's plans.

"Okay, Chip. Thanks for your help."

Chip relaxed. He waited to be released. Although he fully expected a long walk, he hadn't expected what happened next. He heard Albert walk away behind his head. He heard the car engine start. Albert put the car into reverse and slammed his foot onto the accelerator. A grotesque chain of events followed. Chip's body jerked away from the woodland floor and rose above the bonnet of the Mercedes. As it reached the top of its trajectory his back snapped. The body sagged and the bonds which tied his wrists to the towing loop dragged themselves away over his hands and flew back slapping against the radiator grill. The knots pulled away much of the hands at the same time.

Rocchiciolli stopped the car and walked round to the front. He removed the rope from the car and dropped it onto the ground.

Albert Rocchiciolli leaned against a wall. On the other side of the street he could see Ricky Hahn's apartment, from which there were no signs of life. At two a.m. very little was moving in Sedona. A few delivery trucks were out and about. He had seen the odd car and an old man walking his dog. So Ricky is at his apartment, eh? thought Albert. But he was a patient man. He had been engaged in his craft for many years and he was accustomed to waiting. Experience had taught him that a plan was all very well until you came to put it into action. In the world of reality anything could happen. It was no surprise to him that there was no sign of Ricky Hahn. He felt vague sense of disappointment and frustration, but this would pass.

At 2.20 he saw a car at the end of the street. It was coming in his direction. As it drew closer he recognised it as a Mercedes. It crossed the street and pulled up outside Hahn's building. Out reeled Ricky. Albert wondered how many Mercedes cars the Hahn family possessed. It was a further ten minutes before the apartment light went on. Albert lit a cigarette and waited another twenty minutes. It was clear that Ricky was drunk; no surprises there either. Albert figured that by the end of twenty minutes the youngest Hahn would be asleep or well relaxed. It was unlikely Ricky would present him with resistance.

Albert threw the butt of another cigarette into the street as he crossed it. Entering the building he walked up to the top floor and listened at the door. There was sound of movement from inside. Ricky was still awake. Albert tapped the door gently. No loud sudden raps to alarm or agitate. A dishevelled Ricky Hahn opened the door.

"Yeah. What do you want?"

Albert could see that the younger man was having difficulty focusing. Without a word he grabbed Hahn's neck with his left hand and walked him back into the apartment. He kicked the door shut as he entered without pausing. The momentum ensured that Hahn was in no position to resist him. The backs of his knees caught the seat edge of an easy chair and he sat. Reaching behind his back, Albert Rocchiciolli pulled his Browning from its belt holster.

"Good night, Ricky."

Still grasping Ricky's neck with his left hand, Albert shot him through the forehead. He died instantly.

Grief

The following morning Webster Hahn was surprised that Chip was not at the ranch. Chip was generally extremely reliable although there had been infrequent occasions in the past when he had slept in, having overdone the bourbon the previous night. So when Webster realised that Chip was not around, he left it an hour and, suspecting that Chip was probably at Ricky's apartment in town, he phoned his son. No reply. That didn't surprise him either. Today was Monday. Ricky usually went on the town on Sundays. He would be hung over and sleeping through the ringing of the phone.

By lunchtime Hahn had not heard from Chip or Ricky. Now he was becoming angry, not anxious. He had no reason to fear for their safety and in any case they could look after themselves. But this day their absence was inconvenient. At least Chip's absence was inconvenient. An important shipment was arriving today. Another hour wore on and Webster Hahn could wait no longer. Six containers were scheduled to arrive at one of his warehouses in Phoenix at 5.30 that afternoon. He needed to be there to meet them.

Hahn strode through the mansion yelling at his staff. Within ten minutes, eight men including the Old Man were seated in two black Mercedes and heading in the direction of Phoenix. When they arrived at the warehouse Hahn was told that the containers had been slightly delayed in New York but had caught up and were now on schedule. Hahn sat in the back of his car and lit a cigar. He picked up the car phone and called the ranch. He learned nothing about the whereabouts of Chip and Ricky. Hahn could think of a number of reasons for Ricky's absence, most of which were linked to drink and women. But Chip was different. He was reliable and had never, in all their years together, failed to show. Slight tardiness was one thing. Failing to show was quite another. Hahn started to worry. There could be only a handful of reasons for Chip's absence. One reason was that he could be dead. Hahn dismissed this thought. If Chip were dead he would know by now. Maybe he had had a heart attack last night. Maybe he was unconscious now in a hospital. He would check these possibilities later. Meanwhile six Peterbilt 379 Big Rig tractors hauling containers had arrived and were driving into the vast warehouse. Chains were pulled and heavy doors rolled down into place, hiding the vehicles from prying eyes. The drivers were dismissed and told to book into a local motel. They were to return the following morning to pick up their rigs.

Seals were broken and the rear doors of the containers were swung open. A man jumped up into each of the containers. One by one the men emerged and each appeared puzzled. Hahn noticed their faces. He stubbed his cigar into the ashtray and got out of the Mercedes.

"What? What is it?" he yelled.

"Milk powder, boss?" queried one of the men.

"Milk powder. What do you mean, milk powder?"

"It's milk powder, sir. Milk powder in every container."

Webster Hahn didn't bother to check for himself. First Chip, then Ricky and now this. He shouted to his driver to take him home. As they pulled up the long drive to the ranch, Hahn recognised the car of Lieutenant Greaves. What could he want? Deep down Hahn knew it was news of Chip or Ricky.

Greaves was waiting in the study for Hahn to arrive. As Hahn entered the room Greaves offered his hand.

"Evening, Pete," said Hahn.

"Mr Hahn, it's bad news, I'm afraid." He paused.

"Get on with it, Pete."

"It's Ricky, Mr Hahn. He's dead."

Webster Hahn placed his two hands on the back of a chair to steady himself. "What can you tell me?"

"Ricky was found in his apartment this afternoon by a woman called Megan Coates. Real looker. Think she had something going with Ricky. Coates called us. Lieutenant Murray from homicide went over. His preliminary report says that Ricky was shot through the head from close range. Died straight away, Mr Hahn. He wouldn't have felt a thing. I'm real sorry Ricky's dead."

Webster Hahn showed no emotion now. He stared straight ahead. Gradually he became aware that Pete Greaves was not talking. He turned to face him.

"What, Pete? What's on your mind?"

"There's more. Chip. He's dead too. He was found the other side of Sunflower. Couple of kids in a Piper spotted his body from the air. If they hadn't it might have taken weeks to find him. Can't tell you how he died yet."

"What do you mean? Could it have been an accident?" Webster knew that it had not been an accident.

"No, sir. No accident. Chip was pulled apart."

"Pete, I'm grateful to you for coming up here to tell me this news yourself. I'll not forget your kindness. Permit me to impose upon our friendship once more." Pete nodded. "If you hear anything else, any clues, any leads, any suspects, then you let me know, okay?"

"Yeah, sure, Mr Hahn. And, well, like I said, I'm real sorry."

The lieutenant left. Hahn locked his study door and sat behind his desk. Then he cried. He cried until the early hours of Tuesday morning. This was only the second time in his adult life he had cried. The first time was when Ricky's mother had died of cancer twenty years earlier. And now this was the first time Hahn was glad Ricky's mother was dead. No mother should have to hear of the death of a son.

When he stopped crying he went into the bathroom adjacent to the study and washed his face in cold water. He unlocked the study door and went through to the kitchen. He had expected that there would be no one around. It was late and time for all good people to be in a bed but Sally, the cook, was still in the kitchen.

"What you doing here?" asked Webster roughly.

"I thought you might need some company or maybe something to eat or some coffee maybe."

Hahn smiled. "Thanks, Sally. Yeah. Bring some coffee into my study, will you?"

Webster Hahn returned to his study and the chair behind his desk. He lit a cigar. It was now he wished he had made the phone call to Jonjo Grey. Ricky had tried to whack Grey. What could Grey do? He would not have felt safe with Ricky still around. Grey obviously wanted to teach the Hahn family a lesson. It would have been Grey who had hit Chip. It would have been Grey who had tampered with the containers. Webster didn't know how he had done it, but somehow he had. Webster was not yet sure of all the details but he was sure of one thing. The bad blood between him and Jonjo Grey had to stop, here and now. They were both powerful men and each had the power to inflict considerable damage on the other. Ricky had started all this and it must finish now, with Ricky's death.

That same evening Albert Rocchiciolli arranged to meet Dr Jonjo Grey. At an anonymous diner several miles from town, Grey's limousine waited in a far corner of the car park. He sat there with patience while he awaited the arrival of Rocchiciolli's Jaguar. When he saw the Jag arrive and its driver enter the diner, Grey left his car. His driver remained behind the wheel. Grey walked to the diner and glanced through the window. Rocchiciolli was seated in a corner seat facing the door. In front of him was a coffee.

Grey walked confidently to the other's table and sat. He said nothing until the waitress arrived and asked for his order.

"Same as him please," said Grey, pointing towards the coffee.

This did not satisfy the waitress, who tried to sell him food. Grey refused burgers, steaks, ham and eggs, apple pie and cherry pie graciously. When she moved to a club sandwich Grey turned to face the young, over-keen waitress.

"Get the coffee and then get lost." There was little the woman could do other than to follow this instruction. Grey now turned to Rocchiciolli. "Since you have invited me here at this late and inconvenient hour, I have to assume you have some news for me."

"Yeah. Ricky's dead. Problem with Chip, though. He's dead too. He kinda met with an accident."

"I told you to ensure that Chip stayed alive. It was important that Chip stayed alive. That's why I made a point of telling you to keep him alive." Grey stopped as the waitress arrived with the coffee. "You have not done well, have you?"

"Look, it was just an accident. I'm sorry to piss in your ear but Chip got a bit rough."

"Mr Rocchiciolli. You are a professional. You don't have accidents. I assume you were able to get the information from Chip before his accident?"

"He said Webster Hahn was buying guns from these English guys. He said he didn't know no more. I believed him."

Grey stood without having touched his coffee. He reached into an inside pocket and withdrew a large envelope. He threw it onto the table in front of the other man. Without another word he turned and left the diner.

The dark green Jaguar of Sir Gordon Melville took him down Whitehall, past the Cenotaph and on to the offices of the Rural Development Service. Melville timed how long it took him to negotiate all the obstacles placed in his path before he could enter Harry Buchanan's office. It was 14 minutes and 32 seconds. He had done worse but he'd done a lot better too.

The two knights shook hands. Margaret brought them glasses, ice and two bottles, one containing gin, the other tonic. The cherubic, smiling face of Harry looked up at her.

"Thank you, Margaret. No calls now. No interruptions. If we need anything we'll shout."

The cabinet secretary smiled as he offered Harry a Havana from a leather case.

"The P.M. is mightily pleased. Sir Roger Holbrook at the Foreign Office is mightily pleased. And me, here and now? Well, I'm at once relieved and worried.

"Erifia got its guns. These so-called management consultants got bugger all. No news is out. No irritating journalists chasing the press office. So perhaps one might think that the matter is over, and so it might be. But me, well, I don't think so.

"The P.M. called Roger Holbrook and me in this morning. He thinks there are too many people in the know. He's right, isn't he? Trouble is, Harry, we don't know who is in the know and who is not. My instruction from the P.M. is clear. I am to ensure that no leaks occur by whatever lawful means I have at my disposal. He knows full well that the prevention of leaks in a situation like this cannot be done within the law. Nevertheless his instruction to me is clear. What he is saying is locate and make safe any potential leak before it occurs. Use any means at your disposal, legal or otherwise, but keep my name out of it. Now then, Harry, do you think I have grasped the situation correctly?"

Harry drew deeply on his cigar. His face was a picture of benign good humour.

"It seems to me, Gordon, that you have grasped the situation with your usual skill. I think you are all correct to be concerned about leaks. We don't know how many people know enough to enable a sharp investigator to piece together enough of the story to make things difficult. Excluding my staff, I can think of several people who might conceivably know enough. Inevitably at least a couple will have enough dangerous knowledge. Can't think of any reason at the moment, though, why any of them should talk. Probably not be in their best interests to talk. Rather the opposite, I think.

"Something else worries me a little. I can do some more digging and find a knowledge audit trail. There is a danger with that, though. The trail may alert someone else who has no direct involvement. That someone could then blow the whistle with minimum personal danger. "

"I have to agree," said the cabinet secretary. "Not sure, though, if we have any choice. Best go to it, Harry. Find out who knows enough to be a risk and take whatever steps you consider appropriate. I don't need to remind you to retain your usual, discrete distance from the prime minister, the government, my office, the Foreign and Commonwealth Office and Sir Roger Holbrook. And good luck."

Sir Gordon stubbed out his unfinished cigar. Took a large swallow to finish the last of his gin and tonic, stood and left the office. Harry sat motionless for several minutes. He stared at his shoes. Then he stood, walked to his desk and spoke into the intercom on his desk.

"Margaret, ask Vanessa Stone and John Morgan to join me now, please."

Harry crossed his office and sat at the highly polished conference table to await his guests. They arrived at the same time and Harry gestured, inviting them to sit at the table.

"I smell trouble, good people. Before you do anything else, do these things for me, please." Harry paused and appeared reflective. "No. Rather more, do these things for yourselves, I think. Destroy all references to your involvement with the arms scam and Wynter Farmer Management Consultants. You know how difficult these cover-ups are? First your meeting logs and your diaries. Don't forget the mirror diaries held by your administrators. Destroy the computer file, the hard drive, the disks and the tape streamer. Don't forget hard copy in the registry. The archive files next. Change your telephone logs. Booking in and out is okay, but make sure fictitious trips are planned around the security log." Harry paused again. "For Christ's sake don't forget your expense claim forms. Falsify those. Show me how good you are at creative writing. No doubt you have had plenty of practice. Now, have we forgotten anything?"

The lack of response from the two deputy directors confirmed Harry's thoughts. When the two left his office, Harry returned to his desk. He used the intercom to tell Margaret he was leaving the office for 30 minutes.

He hailed a black taxi outside the front door of the Rural Development Service. It deposited him outside Harrods in London's Knightsbridge. Harry strolled towards the Natural History Museum where he found a bank of public telephones. He waited until a cash phone became vacant. He punched in a series of numbers which began with 010 33. An answering machine clicked. *"Vous etes actuellement en contact avec un repondeur automatique. Vous pouvez laisser votre nom, votre numero et un message apres le bip sonore."*

Harry's message was simple. "It's Uncle. Meet me this Sunday. Usual time. Usual place."

The answering machine was located on a table in an apartment that was situated under the shadow of Sacre Coeur Cathedral in Paris. There was nothing else in the apartment. The rent was always paid on the apartment on the appointed date. It was the only apartment in the building to which the concierge had no access. This provided no difficulties because of a premium paid on top of the normal rent.

In the shadowy world of security, things rarely appear as they are. Sir Harry Buchanan had total faith in his three deputy directors and the carefully selected staff which, in the main, were identified at university and recruited there. Occasionally people with special skills and knowledge were recruited from the armed forces or the police, some even from industry. There were times, however, to protect staff or indeed to protect Harry himself, when he drew upon resources outside Section P. There were a number of resources, some of which were known to and available to the deputy directors. A few were known only to Harry. One such facility Harry called the Clarion Resource. He had now started the procedure required to invoke the services of the Clarion Resource.

Meetings

On the same day at around the same time on different sides of the Atlantic Ocean, two meetings took place. The first happened in the early morning in Arizona. It had been set up the previous evening when Dr Jonjo Grey had telephoned Webster Hahn at the ranch. Feeling wary, Hahn had agreed to meet Grey on his own territory. Hahn had little idea that Grey shared the wariness. And so it was that the following day Grey's limousine was waved through the gates and up the drive to the mansion. When it drew to a halt under the portico, one of Hahn's staff was there to open the car door. Another opened the front doors and led the visitor to the door of Hahn's library. The door was knocked and Hahn's voice told them to enter.

The two men faced each other. Both were immaculately presented. Both normally radiated an air of confidence but now both were unsure of the ground on which they stood and of the outcome of the difficult and uncomfortable meeting that was to come. For several seconds the men faced each other. Hahn broke the spell.

"Fetch Dr Grey some coffee. Coffee for me too."

The other man departed and for the first time in years the two men of power and influence were alone. Webster Hahn approached Grey and offered him his hand. Grey was grateful to accept it. Hahn placed a hand gently on the other's shoulder and led him to an easy chair. When Hahn had seated his guest and was sure he was comfortable, he took another easy chair opposite. To Grey, his host seemed very close. It felt as if his space were being invaded given the circumstances. Under more normal conditions there would have been no such uncomfortable sensation at this range.

"Let's wait until the coffee has arrived," said Hahn. "How are you, Jonjo?"

This appeared rather like a conciliatory signal to Grey and the question seemed to be genuine. Hahn could be a man of great charm.

Grey knew that there were occasions when the charm evaporated to be replaced with a coldness and ruthlessness. He knew Hahn possessed a calculating singlemindedness unequalled by anyone he had ever met. He also knew that Hahn could become a cold-blooded murderer who would let nothing stand in his way. These unsettling properties, however, appeared to be absent at this moment. Grey could only see the charm, and it was easy to see why Hahn was so admired in quarters where admiration was inappropriate.

"I'm well, Webster. I trust I find you well."

The coffee arrived. When the butler had left the library, Grey opened his mouth as if to speak. Hahn held up his hand to prevent him.

"I'm grateful you asked to see me. It could not have been easy for you. I thank you for this opportunity to talk with you. We need to talk with confidence and in trust. We will not be disturbed and I hope you will believe me when I tell you this is not being recorded. It's my only hope that we can reach an understanding, you and me." He paused as if waiting for a sign of agreement from Grey.

"We share that hope, Webster. This matter has got all out of control."

Hahn smiled and slowly nodded. "Sometimes these things happen. Now is the time to put a stop to the madness. I know why you killed Ricky. I can understand why you did it. I understand the trouble my boy was causing you. He didn't know his limitations. He didn't understand business the way we do. I'm sorry he caused you trouble with your new car. I guess his interference cost you plenty. I think the unions will cause you no more trouble and I wish you well with the launch of your car. I don't say I'll buy one, I'll continue with my German cars."

Another slight smile from Hahn. It was appreciated by Grey.

"I also know Ricky tried to hit you. That was unforgivable and very foolish. I know you felt you had no alternative. Ricky would have tried again and who knows? He may have succeeded. I don't hold you responsible for Ricky's death. I hold myself responsible for two reasons. I did my best for the boy after his mother died. I tried to raise him, educate him. I know I failed. He was always wild. He could be impetuous. There were times when he was real stupid. I did a bad job for the boy and I guess I always knew he would end up dead. Some will say he had it coming but, Jonjo, I loved him. He was my son and I loved him. He didn't have a mother to care for him, just me."

Tears welled up in Hahn's eyes again. He made no attempt to hide the tears or to wipe them away. To Grey, Hahn now looked several years older than when he had first arrived. Grey felt grief for his host and this surprised him. He waited in silence as Hahn composed himself.

"Yeah. I take responsibility. Not just because of the lousy way I brought him up but also because I failed to make a call. I was going to make a call when I heard that Ricky had tried to whack you. I wanted to keep you away from my boy. I was going to tell you that I'd keep him out of your face. I didn't make the call. I guess I was too busy running my business and I guess that's been the problem all along. If I hadn't always put my business first Ricky would be alive today. So I hold myself responsible, Jonjo. I don't want to hear anything more about it. You had no choice."

Again Hahn paused. Now the tears had gone and Grey could feel a change in the temperature.

"What I don't understand though is Chip. Why did Chip have to die? What had he done to you? He wasn't involved with Ricky's dumbass schemes. Tell me why, Jonjo?"

Grey now sensed danger. This was the question he had been dreading. He knew that he had no reasonable explanation for Hahn. This was the moment when he would either buy his life or condemn himself.

"Webster, I regret Chip's death more than you can know or more than you will believe. It was an accident. Chip was meant to live. He was a good and loyal man. I'm very sorry. I want to make it up to you for Chip's death. Tell me how."

"I'll tell you how. Who did you give the contract to? Who?"

Grey knew that there was a grave danger in passing on this information but at this moment he saw no alternative. He swallowed hard and hoped the host would not see his discomfort.

"Albert Rocchiciolli. I told him not to hurt Chip."

Grey saw Hahn turning red. His breathing was deepening and he was clenching both fists. After a moment Hahn regained control. His next words were so quiet Grey had difficulty hearing them.

"Albert Rocchiciolli. Albert Rocchiciolli. That no-good bastard. He's been a fucking guest in my home. That fucking bastard has worked for me." Hahn took a deep breath and his shoulders relaxed. Grey was surprised at Hahn's profanity. He had never heard him talk in that way before. "Thank you, Jonjo. I won't refer to this matter again. Neither will you. This matter is closed. Mister Rocchiciolli has made an enemy. He will not be forgiven. There is a final matter Jonjo. What about my shipment? Your vengeance seems endless. My son is killed. Chip dies and then you lay a heist on my consignment. When will it end Jonjo? When?" The last word was louder.

For a moment Grey was confused. His mind quickly processed the snippets of information he had gathered. When he was ready he spoke.

"You're talking about the ordnance from the guys in London?"

"Of course I am. I don't know how you found out and I guess I don't need a discussion on why. What I do want is my guns."

"Webster, I don't know where your guns are. I don't know who lifted them. What I do know is that you intended to buy guns from an organisation in England called Wynter Farmer Management Consultants. I also know they were watching the ranch. They had their surveillance equipment in a Dodge van. Looked like it had caught fire outside your place. It hadn't. My people followed a guy from the van to London. I know this because I was watching you. I ended up watching them watching you."

Grey permitted himself a smile. "I didn't take your guns, Webster. I don't know who did. Maybe a good place to start looking would be with the London guys."

Hahn was thoughtful. He rose from his chair, turned and walked away from Grey. He gazed through a window overlooking his parkland. Eventually he turned to face Grey once again.

"Okay, Jonjo. I believe you. Thank you for your honesty with the other matters. I believe the time will soon come when we will have learned to trust each other again. Now if you'll excuse me I have calls to make."

Grey rose and the two men shook hands. When the visitor had left, Hahn walked through to his study. There he made two phone calls. The first was short and simple. When he was connected he said, "Find out where Albert Rocchiciolli is. When you find him you will tell only me."

His second call was to London, where it was mid afternoon. He asked to speak to Harvey Walsh. After several minutes he heard Walsh's voice.

"Mr Hahn. How are you?"

"The state of my health is of no concern, Mr Walsh. I came to you because my good friend Leo Salmon told me good things about you. In return for you delivering my arms into my warehouse in the United States I agreed to pay you five million. I've given you half of that already. When I go to collect my guns what do I find? I'll tell you what I found Mr Walsh. Milk powder. That's what I found. Milk powder. What do you say to that, Mr Walsh?"

There were few times when Harvey Walsh was at a loss for words, but this was one of them. When he had heard that Christian McGregor had been thrown into jail, Gariol had been killed and Jacques Sandriano restored to power, he had started to worry. Despite his best efforts he had been unable to discover if the arms had reached Erifia. Indeed, if they had, how would he have known if they were the consignment he was shipping to America? Now Walsh knew he was in trouble. He had kept himself distanced from the exercise. He could not distance himself from the client, however. He was now very pleased he had taken the insurance policy.

"As far as I am concerned, Mr Hahn, the consignment was shipped to the United States as agreed with you. If they have been lifted, then it happened your side of the Atlantic. I really feel that -" He was cut short.

"I don't give one damn what you really feel. All I know is that I've paid you two and a half million sterling and I've seen nothing for it except milk powder. What do you propose I do with six container loads of milk powder? On second thought, don't tell me. Instead tell me what you propose to do about my guns?"

"I find it difficult to make any sensible or realistic suggestions at this time, Mr Hahn. Please leave it with me for a few days. I need to investigate. Good afternoon." Walsh replaced his handset. He knew that this would not satisfy Hahn for long. What was worse was that he had told the truth. At the moment he had not a single proposal to make.

The second meeting that day took place near Slough, England. It was at the home of Eric Wynter. There was a loud knock on the front door that summoned the butler. Wynter did not hear it. He was seated in his orangery enjoying the dying warmth of the late autumn sun. His butler coughed as he approached. Wynter always enjoyed this affectation. He viewed it as a cliché and recalled P.G. Wodehouse's Jeeves. He refused to view himself as Bertie Wooster however.

"A Sir Harry Buchanan is here to speak to you, sir. He says he doesn't have an appointment but feels sure you will see him."

Wynter sat bolt upright. Harry Buchanan, the prime minister's hatchet man. He had never met Harry, in fact he had never read about him or seen photographs of him. He knew he existed though. Very occasionally his name was used in connection with some of W.F.M.C.'s more powerful clients. Wynter knew that to receive a visit from Harry Buchanan there must be a very special reason. He knew full well that this visit was caused by Harvey Walsh's decision to lift the P.M's arms for the American client. He had warned his man to drop the commission if it looked like going bad. He had even suggested using the Czech contacts for the arms but no, this was presumably not exciting enough for Walsh. He had told him it was too dangerous, but Walsh had assured him all would be well. He said he had it all "under control." Having Sir Harry Buchanan on your doorstep was not suggestive of control. Buchanan had more clout than the P.M. himself. Democratically elected politicians think it is they who have the clout. The reality is different. Wynter knew it was the senior civil servants and government employees who had the real power. The politicians merely pursued their political dreams and enacted cosmetic and superficial legislation, little of which made lasting, fundamental or deep impressions on the lives of the people. Harry Buchanan could make a lasting, fundamental and deep impression on him and W.F.M.C. however. At this point Wynter wanted to instruct his butler to inform Buchanan that Wynter was not in.

"Show Sir Harry out here," said Wynter, pointing to a seat next to his own. It had been placed there not for Buchanan but for Harvey Walsh, whom he had been expecting.

The mighty figure of Harry moved across the lawns in the direction of the older man. His hand was outstretched. "Mr Wynter. How kind of you to see me without an appointment. I appreciate your courtesy."

Harry's face was the picture of affability. It smiled and beamed. Wynter was not taken in. Little did he know that this was no act presented for his benefit. This was the real Sir Harry Buchanan.

"Won't you take a seat please?" Eric Wynter had been around for a long time. It was not so easy to intimidate him and now he was putting on a brave face. The truth was that he personally had little to worry about. He couldn't say the same for Walsh. "May I offer you tea or perhaps something a little stronger?"

"I think tea would do very nicely," replied Harry.

Wynter nodded to the butler, who turned and left the huge conservatory.

"And now, Sir Harry, what brings you to my house?"

Harry smiled. "It seems that your organisation has been a wee bit naughty. Shall we say, a little indiscreet?"

"In what way, Sir Harry?"

"I wonder, Mr Wynter, how much Harvey Walsh confides in you? Well, that doesn't matter just now. I will assume that, since he is now the managing director of Wynter Farmer Management Consultants, and since you have now retired to enjoy your most beautiful home, orangery and gardens..." Harry turned his neck, surveying the immaculately tended grounds. "What was I saying? Oh yes. Retired now. Well, I will assume that Mr Walsh acts on his own judgment. I will assume he does not involve you."

The butler interrupted with the tea. Neither man spoke while he was within earshot.

"Do continue Sir Harry."

"However, to avoid wasting my time since, unlike you, I am not retired and am a very busy man, I will get straight to the point." Harry's affability had disappeared along with his smile. "Your man and his scum bag operation have involved themselves in areas which may shortly become the concern of a large number of government agencies. It would not be inappropriate to mention Customs and Excise, Inland Revenue, the Health and Safety Executive, Environmental Health, the police in general and Special Branch in particular, Interpol, most certainly the director of Public Prosecutions and, oh yes, I nearly forgot the Serious Fraud Office and I'm confident a few of the D.T.I's executive agencies. That's the local people. I shouldn't be surprised if the F.B.I. didn't want a piece. Shall I go on?"

"You have the stage, Sir Harry."

"Good. What are we looking at here? How's about theft, murder, fraud? Might even have a case for treason." Harry thought he may have gone over the top here but he was on a roll.

"Sir Harry, you wouldn't be telling me all this if you didn't see a solution, a way out of this little um... predicament. Perhaps you will share it with me?"

"I'm coming to it, my dear Wynter. There may be a way out. Her Majesty's government would rather like to avoid unnecessary publicity and the expense of an investigation and trial. The prime minister certainly wants no embarrassment and I have his authority to discuss these matters with you. If you doubt my word, I will not feel offended if you choose to ring the cabinet secretary, Sir Gordon Melville, for confirmation. You will find him at Number 10 even as we speak."

"Thank you, that won't be necessary."

Harry was banking on Wynter refusing this offer. Melville was nowhere near Number 10 and certainly had no idea Harry was negotiating with Wynter.

"I want the names and full details of Walsh's clients in the U.S. Further, I want the names of employees of W.F.M.C. who were involved in the operation. I also require the details of any freelancers and subcontractors used. I require you, Mr Wynter, and that means you personally, to assist me in any way possible to cover up this most regrettable situation."

"What do I get in return, Sir Harry?"

"My dear fellow." Harry's most affable expression was back and his smile was as broad as ever. "You get to keep the remains of W.F.M.C after we have conducted some surgery on it, and you remain free from the worry of late night knocks on the door from overzealous public servants. There will be no prosecutions, publicity, fines, imprisonments and, above all Mr Wynter, you get to keep your life. Now what do you say, man?"

"You leave me little choice, Sir Harry. I agree to your terms. Your list will be available by this time tomorrow."

"Good. I'll send a courier to collect it. You will not, of course, alert any of your people to this discussion. You will ensure Harvey Walsh knows nothing of this discussion."

Wynter nodded. Harry rose and Wynter offered his hand. Ignoring it, Harry left without another word. Both men had an odd sensation that each had liked the other. Under different circumstances they might have been friends and allies.

As Harry drove out of Wynter's drive he passed a car going in. He immediately recognised the driver as Harvey Walsh. He was almost sorry he had missed him.

"An unfamiliar face," said Harvey Walsh when he had installed himself on the garden chair next to his mentor.

"Suspicious, aren't we?" replied Wynter, smiling.

"Maybe. Just someone I didn't recognise."

"A very old friend of mine. Served with the S.O.E. in the war."

"He's worn well. I assume you mean the Special Operations Executive?"

"I do and you're right. Cushy life has kept him looking so young I shouldn't wonder. Now, to what do I owe this pleasure?"

"I come for advice. I would prefer it if you didn't tell me 'told you so' but there has been a little hiccup. The commission for the Americans; it's gone pear-shaped."

Walsh explained about the phone conversation with Hahn and his own suspicion that somewhere at sometime after he had hijacked the convoy, the containers had been switched. He explained about the £2,500,000 deposit. When he had finished Wynter was silent while he marshalled his thoughts.

"When I warned you off, I asked you to distance yourself from the project. I assume you listened to my advice?"

"Yes. Apart from my contact with Webster Hahn I am whiter than white. Melanie has been lead on this one."

"Good. I want a full report on the operation. Tell it as it is. I don't want speculation or solutions at this stage. I also want a carefully compiled list of all those who were involved and all those who might be aware of the heist and the contract with Mr Hahn. I will forgo my copy of the Times and use your material to entertain me with my breakfast. I suggest you prepare a bankers draft for two and a half million pounds from an off shore account and get it to Mr Hahn very quickly. He will not want the matter to rest there. To ensure there are no repercussions remind him about your disks. That should keep him quiet." Somehow Wynter didn't believe this. When things had cooled down he would have a word with Leo Salmon.

"I've rather messed this up. I'm sorry. I hope your confidence in me isn't entirely destroyed."

"Not at all, my dear boy. Not at all. You took a risk. You gambled. Without taking a risk occasionally, life would be boring. When dear old Richard, God rest his soul, and I started in the business, we took risks. Most paid off. Some didn't. Without those risks none of us would be where we are today. If you get it wrong you have to limit the damage. No, my confidence in you is not entirely destroyed. I put you in the job because you were the best man for it. You remain the best man for it. All you have done is made a miscalculation. Now go home and start on your report." Throughout this, Wynter maintained an expression of benevolence and understanding.

When Wynter heard the sound of Walsh's car on the drive, his facial expression changed.

"Damn and blast you," he muttered to himself.

The Teashop

The historic market town of Tewkesbury lies at the foot of the Cotswold Hills at the confluence of the rivers Severn and Avon. Tourists flock in the summer to this town with its ancient buildings and magnificent abbey. Because of high tech industry it is, by and large, a fairly prosperous area. Tewkesbury is surrounded by many villages where much of the housing is expensive. For many, it is a good area in which to live and work.

Because of the high discretionary spending capability in the area, easy access to the motorway system and the volume of tourist business, Julie Martin opened her now famous delicatessen and tea shop in Tewkesbury. Situated in a double-fronted shop, Martin's was undeniably a successful, small business. One side of the premises contained the large deli to which, because of its vast range of quality products, shoppers flocked from miles around. The other side housed the intimate tea shop renowned for its home baked bread, cakes and gateaux.

Julie Martin ran the operation with a military precision. Her team of twenty-five staff was led by a delicatessen manager and a tea shop manager via a structure of supervisors. While Martin allowed each a degree of authority and decision-making responsibility, it was Martin herself who retained the authority for staff selection, purchasing and quality control. Because of the fine reputation of Martin's and the relatively high wages, there was never any problem with recruiting. If ever an advertisement was placed for a vacancy, Julie could expect fifty or more applicants. Some new staff were unable to work in what seemed to be a restrictive environment with its rigid structures. On the other hand, many found the structure comfortable. They also knew that the owner could be extremely generous. There was a bonus system that appealed greatly and staff knew that if they had problems of a personal nature, they could turn to Julie for help. This help could take many forms, from interest free loans to time off to sort family matters. Yet sometimes new members of staff might fail to turn up on time or take suspect sick leave. This was not tolerated. Staff turnover was low.

Julie Martin was, to those locals who cared to think about it, an enigmatic character. None had ever seen inside her home in an extremely pretty cottage in the Cotswolds a few miles from Tewkesbury. While she was undoubtedly a successful business woman, she did not take part in local business matters. She had never been seen at a Chamber of Commerce meeting. She did not involve herself in anything outside of the business. Apparently she had no close friends. This was seen by some as odd. Julie Martin was strikingly beautiful, tall, slim and elegant. She was acknowledged as one of the best dressers for miles around. She seemed self-assured and in control. She was also articulate, charming and courteous. Yet, when she ate in any one of the many restaurants in the area or called in to the more up-market watering holes for a gin and tonic, she was invariably alone. On the rare occasions she was seen out with anyone, it would be with men much older than she. It had been noted that these men were always well dressed and not local.

Often local men and women had tried to befriend Julie for a variety of reasons. Such advances were always rejected with courtesy. So it was that Julie Martin appeared to be lonely.

No one knew much about her. Clearly she had money. She bought the freehold of her shop without a mortgage. Those who knew where she lived would have placed a high value on her home. It was not widely known that this, too, had been bought with cash. She drove an MGF and a high specification Range Rover. Most people assumed she had inherited her money.

The few who knew her superficially and members of her staff would have been amazed had they read her curriculum vitae, not that she had ever compiled one. Oxford had provided her with a first class honours degree. It was while she was still at Oxford she had been approached by the Foreign Office. On graduating she had accepted their offer. After an extensive induction period and 18 months working in London, she had moved to Virginia for two years. Based in Langley, her job title was liaison officer. This suggested she liaised between the intelligence divisions of the CIA and MI6 in London and in part this was the case.

From Virginia she returned to London and from thence to Paris. There she worked with the DST, Direction de la Surveillance du Territoire, again as a liaison officer. After Paris it was back to England, but not London this time. She went to Hereford, the home of the world famous Special Air Service. A few miles outside Hereford, the S.A.S. operates a counterterrorist training school. Contrary to popular belief, women are recruited and have been involved in intelligence gathering operations in Northern Ireland, Bosnia, Central America and the Middle East.

Here Julie Martin stood out, although this was not her name at that time. The S.A.S made her eat to put on weight. She was too conspicuous in most environments and so her missions were those where her looks would be accepted and indeed would help her. Two and half years later, Julie Martin resigned from the Foreign Office, which was still her employer. Throughout her time with the F.O. and since, she had but one friend, the overweight, jovial Scot she had met in her first week at Langley. Harry Buchanan had been her mentor and guardian angel since before she left university, although she didn't know it. It had been no accident she had met him at Langley. It was difficult for Harry to gauge what her reaction might have been if Julie had known the truth. Julie's father and Harry had served together in Her Majesty's Secret Intelligence Service. Harry had first met Julie when she was a baby but, because of the nature of his work, he only made his existence known to her years later.

Julie had fallen for Harry. She viewed him as a father. Her father had died in Prague many years before and Harry had adopted his role. It was Harry who had inspired her to leave the service and Harry who had provided her with her new identity. Harry had chosen the name Julie Martin and the location of Tewkesbury for her business and home. Harry was one of the very few people who knew the number of her answering service in Paris. It was also Harry who paid for the Paris apartment, the answering service and the table.

Harry only called her Julie when they were in each other's company. On the very few occasions he referred to her elsewhere, he called her the Clarion Resource.

Once every week, Julie took a day off work and drove to wherever the mood took her. She might go shopping in Cheltenham, Worcester or possibly Bath. On this occasion the weather was fine and she fancied a trip down the A46 passing through rich, green arable countryside to Bath. She arrived at the Francis Hotel in Bath's centre in time for morning coffee. This gave her the opportunity to unwind after struggling with the usual parking problem. She unfolded her copy of the Daily Telegraph, going straight to the back page for the cryptic crossword. It was not easy on this sunny morning and it took her nearly twenty minutes to solve.

When she had finished her coffee and the crossword, she left. Window-shopping was a great pleasure for her, an activity for which Bath provided much scope. After a couple of hours she found a public telephone. Julie fed the coin box with a series of £1 coins and dialled a long number. When she heard the answering machine responding, she held a small black box to the mouthpiece. This sent a series of pulses that instructed the machine to replay any recorded messages and then wipe itself. Messages were rare but on this occasion there was one. It said, "It's Uncle. Meet me this Sunday. Usual time. Usual place."

Julie replaced the handset. She instantly recognised the voice. It was Harry's and this thrilled her. It was always good to hear from Harry but she knew this was not social. Social for Harry was calling in unexpectedly at Martin's or the cottage. No, this was official. And official with Harry meant fun and reward. In her excitement the lure of the shops disappeared. She returned to her car and headed straight back to Tewkesbury.

The following Sunday Julie's MGF left Tewkesbury early in the morning. She avoided the motorways, instead going cross country. During the drive she encountered few delays in Devizes and Salisbury.

Before reaching Ringwood she turned off across the New Forest, a drive she particularly enjoyed. The first major delay was trying to enter Lyndhurst. She cleared the tailback when she entered the town itself and the remaining few miles to Lymington were clear. She parked the MG in a lane into which she was directed. Now she had time for a coffee before driving onto the ferry which was to take her to Yarmouth on the Isle of Wight.

That same Sunday Harry's car left Marlow. He took a motorway, the M3. Within 80 minutes this car was parked in a lane waiting for the Southampton to Cowes ferry. Both drivers caught a late morning ferry to the island. After disembarkation the travellers made for Shanklin which, for both, was on the other side of the island. Harry parked his car on the east side of the town close to Sandown while Julie parked on the west side. Each then walked towards the other along the seafront promenade. This well rehearsed procedure ensured they met at exactly four in the afternoon by the cliff lift. When the attendant opened the lift doors, seven passengers entered. Harry and Julie were amongst them. At no time did they acknowledge each other. In fact Harry was the only male in the vicinity who did not spare Julie a second glance.

When the doors at the top of the cliff lift opened, the passengers stepped out. Julie turned to the right and continued her walk eastwards. Harry, on the other hand, turned left and headed west. This operation allowed one to offer the other a double-check for tails. Neither had grown one. After each had walked for 30 minutes they turned and headed back towards the other. As Julie approached the centre of the town she saw Harry entering the main foyer of the Ashleigh Hotel. He entered the lounge and ordered cream tea for two. An elderly waitress asked what blend of tea he would like with the scones, jam and clotted cream. He settled for Assam.

Ten minutes later Julie entered. As she approached, Harry stood. They embraced warmly. Harry's smile was enormous. Julie felt tiny tears in her eyes. They were both pleased to see each other. Harry guided her gently towards an easy chair. Through the huge panoramic windows there was a fine view of the seafront, the sea and the bathers having fun.

"You're looking well, my dear." Harry beamed at the one person he really cared for.

In turn Julie smiled back at the only person who meant anything to her. "I'm good, Harry. You wouldn't be putting on a bit more weight, would you?"

Harry knew this was a tease. But at this moment he couldn't help thinking about his doctor's warnings, which had been coming more often and more severely lately. He really was a very big man. On the other hand Julie looked like the kind of woman every man would be proud to be seen with. Despite the heat of the day and the long journey, she appeared totally fresh.

When the waitress had managed to serve the cream teas, Harry watched her disappear. He asked Julie about her business and her home. He talked about the takings and the requirements of the VAT man. In turn Julie wanted to know what time off Harry had had away from the office and where he had gone. She wanted to know about the home in Scotland and the house in Marlow. An hour was pleasantly whiled away. Suddenly Harry's expression changed; a different sort of smile crossed his face. Julie knew that Harry was ready to come to the point.

"I have a job for the Clarion Resource. This is the most complex job yet. I will not fill you in with the details." Harry laughed. "Well, you wouldn't expect me to, would you? This is a real bitch of a job. I need you to ensure that some potential leaks are plugged.

"This goes right to the top, Julie. The greatest in the land are implicated. Probably worse, some very dangerous people are involved. It's all so bloody complicated now I don't know who to advise you to look out for. To make matters worse, you're on a time scale. The sands in the hourglass are already trickling. If you're very careful you'll get away with it. If you use your wit, training, sixth sense, you just might come through. You will not have the time to plan as you usually do. You don't have the luxury of time.

"Some of your targets will expect nothing. They'll be easy. Some will expect something unpleasant but not be in a position to do anything about it. Others will be accustomed to living on the edge. They may be protected by professionals." There was a long pause here. "Look, Julie. I know you're the best. Hell, I taught you. You were trained by others, some of whom were the very best in the game. This job is different though. This job is likely to get you killed. This time the choice is all yours. No one knows we're talking. If you say no I'll respect that. There will be no repercussions. It's entirely up to you."

"Harry, you are the most frightful old bastard at times, aren't you? You know I can't resist the big one. Do you think for one moment I'll say no. If I said no I would spend the rest of my life regretting it. The answer is yes. What's the fee?"

"A quarter million, plus twenty-five thousand per hit. Plus expenses of course."

"Harry, I'm thrilled. The way you say twenty-five thousand per hit suggests to me that there are a fair few candidates for the removal men."

Harry grunted. He opened the bag he was carrying and took out a plain buff folder.

"You'll find details of each target in there." He handed the folder to Julie. "Keep it safe, won't you?"

She giggled. "Piss off, Harry."

"Names, addresses, families, hangouts, employment, idiosyncrasies, vehicles, mug shots, hobbies, associates. If you need anything else you'll have to find it out for yourself. I doubt you and I will speak again until this is over."

"You're all heart, Harry."

"Yeah, yeah, I know. Since I presumed you would accept this little job offer I arranged for the quarter million to be deposited in your remarkably secure account. It's sitting there now."

Julie grinned again. "Like I said, Harry, you really are an old bastard at times."

"When news reaches me that the job is complete, I'll contact you and we'll meet again. Remember, don't contact me. Don't contact anyone at the department. No one there knows a thing. They're still not one hundred per cent sure that you really exist, or rather they're not one hundred per cent sure the Clarion Resource exists. Those who think they know that Clarion exists think its an organisation or perhaps a man. Keep well clear Julie. As they say in all the best films, 'you're on your own.'"

"Okay, Harry. I'll leave first and start the ball rolling. You finish your tea and don't forget the last of that cream. Looks like you need it. Build yourself up a bit."

The two friends kissed and hugged again.

Harry took the advice and stayed for some while. He finished the cream tea and ordered another pot of Assam. When he had finished he went to the reception, paid the bill and ordered a taxi.

In the back of the taxi, Harry pondered. He recalled Julie's words to him some years before. She had once lectured him on the law of lethal intimacy, the concept of proximity to a victim. Professionals, she had said, got close to the target. The closest was when the body of the assassin came into contact with that of the victim. Strangulation was the example she had used to highlight her point. There was a certain primitive sensation, almost primeval, when killing with her own hands. It required confidence, technique or in some cases desperation.

Next came killing with a knife. This required skill, accuracy, knowledge and nerve. There was still considerable intimacy with the victim. When the blade penetrated the body there could be a sense of satisfaction. Next was shooting from close range with a handgun. When this close, it was possible to see features on the victim's face, what the victim was wearing and the expression of fear, shock, surprise, amazement and pain. Long range shooting with a telescopic-sighted, high-powered rifle was, she felt, much less intimate. From this distance it was possible to view the target as an inanimate object.

Murder by poison was very different. So much could go wrong with poison. Since poison was readily available and required little nerve, this was often the choice of the amateur. The jealous wife might choose poison for a wayward, unfaithful husband. For the professional, though, there was the risk of the wrong person dying in agony. It was also remote. There was no need for contact of any kind. It was not even necessary to see the target. Clarion did not favour poison because she said there were too many variables, too much to go wrong. Worst of all, she claimed, was bombing. The murderer required luck. There was a big risk of the target being missed altogether while others could be killed or maimed. This method was for cowards and amateurs. The chance of being caught was low but the chance of achieving the objective was also low.

Sometimes Harry worried about what he had created.

He shuddered.

Clarion At Work

Martin Garstang had not been able to get away from the Piccadilly office as early as he had intended. Now he was caught in the rush hour. As his train pulled out of Waterloo he made his way to the buffet car, queued and eventually ordered his two miniatures of whisky. He found a shelf in the corner of the car and contemplated his lot. It was an uncomfortable exercise. His gambling debts were mounting again. But having said this, his credibility had improved somewhat with his recent affluence and his credit limits had risen. He had made full use of them. The stresses he was under were making him taciturn, moody and remote. Naomi and Kent were both reacting to his humour and appeared to him to be ever more distant. There were times when Naomi was downright off hand with him. When on the rare occasions his guilt inspired him to ask Kent to play football or engage in some other father-son activity, he had been rejected. Kent seemed to prefer a video to quality time with his dad. Well damn them both, he thought. They can't say I haven't tried.

A couple of weeks previously, Garstang had enjoyed some success at the tables. He had been on a winning streak. He had thought his luck was changing. He responded to this newfound luck by increasing his stakes, but it had all gone pear-shaped. Despite net winnings of £4,500 in one week, he was now down by a similar amount. And then there was the drinking. The more he gambled, the more he drank and the more he drank, the more he gambled, or so it seemed. Tonight I'll go straight home, he said to himself, all the time knowing full well he wouldn't.

It was at this point Garstang became aware of the presence of a woman standing close to his side. She was grasping a drink and appeared to be having difficulty standing upright. The crowds and the movement of the train could make things difficult at times. Despite his mood, Garstang managed a smile. The woman turned to face him fully and returned his smile. Garstang's heart stopped. This woman was a vision of loveliness. She was nearly as tall as him. Blond with brown eyes.

Unusual, he thought. She was dressed by one of the more expensive haute-couturiers and it showed. That smile was enough to die for.

"Crowded tonight," said Garstang rather lamely.

The woman didn't reply, she just smiled. Garstang took this as a signal to stay away. He felt the mildest twinge of embarrassment. What would a creature like her be doing talking to a guy like me? He returned to his contemplations. The thought of this woman, still close to his elbow, was difficult to keep from his mind. Thinking about her was easier than thinking about the state of his world at the moment. He finished the second miniature. He needed a couple more. He tried again.

"Look. I'm going to try to get another drink if I can fight my way through this lot. Can I get you a refill at the same time?"

Again the smile and a polite shake of the head, but still not a word.

On his return Garstang was very surprised to discover that there was still a space next to her. He was surprised she was still there. But then again, why shouldn't she be?

He resumed his station and started the first of the two small bottles. Now he became aware of the woman's perfume. It was faint but he could definitely smell it. Then he remembered the last beautiful woman he had met in the buffet car. This brought him up with a jolt. That had not been a happy occasion. He shuddered. Although, he thought, the first woman would be handy now. Perhaps he could pass her a little more harmless information in return for cash. That would get him out of the hole he was in. He heard a crack. The woman by his side had dropped her glass. It had smashed on the ledge. Garstang swung round.

The woman smiled again. "Sorry," she said. "Didn't mean to startle you. Very clumsy of me."

Odd, he thought. The sight of this woman didn't suggest anything of clumsiness. The thought passed from his mind.

"That's quite all right. Will you allow me to get you another drink now?" Without waiting for a response he continued. "Vodka and tonic, was it?"

"Gin and tonic, please."

As he made his way to the bar he felt an odd sensation of elation. He had been engaged in conversation by the kind of girl he didn't come across every day. He returned with the drink.

"Thank you."

"Not at all. Do you catch this train often?" The moment he said it he regretted it. Such a corny line.

"Hardly ever. You?"

"Oh, quite often. My head office is in the West End but I'm based in Southampton. Shipping. Well, it pays the bills, you know. And you, what do you do?"

"Well, not too much really. I'm lucky. I've got a rich uncle, you see. He tends to look after me. He gives me the odd job or two to keep me out of mischief. Married?" she enquired in a nonchalant way, as if she couldn't care one jot if he were married or not.

"Nope," he lied. He wondered then why he had lied. He did not come up with an answer.

The train swayed rather more violently than usual. The woman bumped into him, her breast prodding his upper arm. Garstang enjoyed this especially since he was aware she could have stopped the contact had she so wished. He swallowed hard.

"You married?" He tried to sound as nonchalant as he could. He was not at all sure he sounded convincing.

His companion merely smiled the smile that so captivated him. There was another lull in their conversation. Garstang was surprised when the woman said, "Do you know Southampton well?"

"Yes. Fairly. I live on the outskirts."

She nodded and fell silent.

"Why do you ask?"

"I was just thinking. Silly idea really. It doesn't matter."

"No. Go on."

"Well, I'm going to be at a bit of a loose end tonight. I had thought I might stay the night in Southampton but now I'm on my way there, to a strange town, it doesn't seem such a good idea. I'm going to pick up a friend's doctoral thesis. She wants me to read it for her. She's at

Southampton University. It's all about the theory of reality, whatever that might be. Then I was going to find a hotel and stay over." The woman paused. "I was going to ask what you would recommend I should see and where I might find a good hotel. By good I mean comfortable and quiet and where the food is very good."

Garstang held his breath. Then he blurted, "Well, I've got nothing planned tonight. Why don't you let me show you round a bit? I know some places you'll like."

"Oh, I couldn't impose upon you. But it was a very kind offer. Thank you."

"Not at all. It would be my pleasure. Why not let me buy you dinner? I know just the place."

The woman visibly relaxed and there was that smile again. "Yes, all right then. That would be really good. Thank you. I need to see my friend first but that won't take long. Well, I don't want to stay long. Can't stand her bloke and I want to get out before he comes home. Perhaps we could meet somewhere at, say, seven o'clock? "

"That sounds great," Garstang said, and he meant it. "Let's meet at seven at Gino's Trattoria. Great Italian food. Great atmosphere. My treat."

"I'd like that very much. Where do I find Gino's?"

"Ask any taxi driver."

It was settled then. When the train stopped and the two people stepped onto the platform, they reaffirmed their agreement and went their separate ways. Garstang was beside himself with anticipation. For her part, the young woman now had two hours to kill. She found a small pub close to the station. This was not the sort of pub in which she would usually be found. She attracted suspicious looks from the landlord and the few old and rather scruffy drinkers who were spaced apart in the one and only bar. She ordered a gin and tonic and by the response it seemed as if this was the first time the landlord had been asked for such a bizarre concoction.

The woman sat at a corner table and stared back at the old men. They quickly averted their eyes and stared at their pints instead. The woman allowed herself a smile. At ten minutes to seven she stood and walked to the bar.

"Will you order me a taxi, please? Right away."

The landlord was surprised at this request. This was the first time he had been asked to perform this service.

"Where do you want to go, love?"

She glared at him. It didn't occur to him that the use of "love" might cause offence.

"Local."

The taxi driver took her to Gino's. She was not at all surprised to discover Garstang waiting by the bar. She was laughing as she approached him.

"What's the joke?" he said.

"I've just realised I don't know your name. A man is going to buy me dinner and I don't even know his name. Now what does that make me, I wonder?"

"Martin," he replied, relaxing. "Martin Garstang. And yours, what's your name?" They both laughed.

"Helen Smith."

"Very pleased to meet you, Helen." He offered his hand.

They engaged in small talk until the waiter conducted them to an intimate table in a corner of the rapidly filling restaurant. When the waiter brought their first course of spaghetti carbonara their conversation stopped. It was at about this time that Garstang became aware that some of the other diners were looking at his companion. It made him feel rather proud. Men were wondering what he had that made him attractive to this gorgeous female, while women were wondering something quite different. This was a sensation he intended to enjoy to the full.

The spaghetti was followed by pan fried veal, a speciality of the house, with seasonal vegetables. It was excellent, they agreed. This was washed down with the contents of a bottle of a better Chianti. Syllabubs completed the food and the meal was completed with coffee and Strega. Garstang was thinking about his next move. He had no wish to break the spell of this near perfect evening, but how could he progress without frightening Helen off?

As if Julie had been reading his thoughts, she said, "How far away is your home?"

"About four miles. Why?"

"I thought you might like to invite me home for coffee."

Cracked it, thought Garstang. But there was a problem. He had said he was single. He could hardly say that his wife was at home.

"My company has a waterside house about ten minutes walk from here. We keep it for visitors and senior managers. It's very comfortable." As Berkeley Marine International's business development manager, he had a key to the company house. It overlooked Southampton's marina and was, because of its function, very well furnished. "Why don't we go back there for coffee and drinks? I can call you a cab when you want to go back to your hotel."

Julie smiled. "I have a confession to make. I haven't booked into a hotel. I thought I might play things by ear."

"You don't plan very well, do you?" said Garstang, teasing her.

A taxi took the couple to the marina. The taxi driver was struck by his attractive blonde fare. He expected a good tip and was not disappointed. Garstang fumbled for the key, unlocked the door and went straight to a closet to deactivate the alarm.

"Take your coat off and make yourself comfortable through there." He pointed to the sitting room. "I'll fix us some coffee."

From the kitchen he shouted, "Help yourself to a drink. There's lots in the cabinet. I'll bring you some ice in a minute."

Julie walked around the room. It was pleasant but, she thought, a little plain, sterile and maybe a bit unloved. It needed a woman's touch. When she heard his footsteps as he left the kitchen, she sat in the middle of the sofa rather than an easy chair. Seeing her placed on the sofa pleased him as he entered the sitting room. He placed the cups on a coffee table in front of the sofa.

"I've helped myself to a gin and tonic and I chose whisky for you. Hope that's all right."

"Perfectly," Garstang replied.

They sipped their drinks and chatted. It was easy small talk and the time flew. Garstang was waiting for the right moment. Then it arrived. Julie had finished her coffee and her gin. There was a lull in the conversation. He put his arm around her shoulder and gently drew her to him. He kissed her and she responded. Her total lack of resistance encouraged him. He moved his right hand to her breast. She allowed this for a moment. As he became more passionate she took his hand away.

"Not here. Wouldn't it be more comfortable in bed?"

"Yes. Come on."

He held her hand and led her to the stairs. His anticipation was exquisite now. He led her up the stairs, his right hand holding her left. She was two stairs below him. Two stairs from the top she paused.

"Martin, darling."

He turned with an expression of expectation on his face. The palm of her right hand was flattened away from her and her right arm shot forward and upwards. There was little more than a slight slapping noise as the base of her palm struck just below Garstang's nose. Almost all the force was going upwards. Before he fell backwards, she grabbed the front of his shirt, carefully missing his tie, and pulled him forwards. In this way she ensured he fell down the stairs. He came to a rest when his face and upper shoulders hit the floor at the bottom. It was necessary for him to fall down the stairs so there would be bruising consistent with such a fall.

Julie untied his left shoe lace and adjusted it so that one end was longer than the other. There would be no lengthy police investigation here. The post mortem would show a high blood alcohol level. This was clearly an accident. She went back to the sitting room and collected her coffee cup and glass, placing them in her handbag next to the flask into which she had been pouring her drinks throughout the evening.

The night air was colder when she left and she walked quickly towards the centre of town where she knew she would find a taxi. The taxi took her to the Avenue, which led northwards, away from the town centre. Down a side road she found the hired Ford Escort, an inconspicuous car that she had rented in London two days previously using false documents. Unlocking it, she got in. She took off the blonde wig and looked into the rearview mirror. She preferred the brunette Julie Martin to the blonde Helen Smith. Into a thick, plastic, supermarket carrier bag she placed the wig, the coffee cup and saucer, the glass and the flask. Sealing the bag, she stuffed it into the glove compartment.

Within ten minutes she had left Southampton behind and was on her way to London.

Wynter Comes Out Of Retirement

Eric Wynter was an old man. He had handed his organisation to the one man he really trusted; Harvey Walsh. He had thought that this decision would be the one most likely to ensure he would enjoy his retirement with the minimum of fuss, disruption and inconvenience. It had been many months since he had been obliged to take a close personal interest in the running of W.F.M.C. Now, for the first time since his retirement, he felt that the organisation was faced with a problem so great it could mean its end. He considered Webster Hahn to be a major risk. Even more dangerous, W.F.M.C. had made an adversary of Sir Harry Buchanan. Wynter knew that there were many people in high places he could bribe, blackmail or threaten, but he viewed Buchanan as being untouchable. He also knew that Walsh's fate was sealed. One way or another, Walsh had to go. In the light of this, Wynter knew he had to use Walsh as a bargaining point. This he would now do with regret and not a little embarrassment.

He waited until it was breakfast time in San Francisco and, using a mobile phone, put a call though to Leo Salmon. Salmon did not sound pleased to hear from his old acquaintance.

"You know how it goes, Eric. You were tops when you and Richard were running the show. You assured us that Walsh could take over where you guys left off. And now this."

Wynter had expected this reaction. He felt a mixture of shame and anger.

"Okay, Leo. What's done is done. I can't change what's happened but maybe I can put it right. You and me, Leo, we go back a long way. I have never let you down, have I? How often have I and my associates helped you? How many times have we saved your ass? Well the time has come for payback. I have never asked for your help before. Now you can help me. I do hope you're not going to turn your back on me now."

There was a long pause.

"Ah shit, Eric. I owe you plenty. What do you need from me?"

Wynter had been almost certain he would be able to rely on Salmon. Despite this, he was relieved to hear these words.

"I need to talk to Webster Hahn."

"You given him his money back?"

"Yes, we have."

"Hahn is feeling pretty sore about you people. He didn't get his delivery, or rather not the delivery he was expecting. There's another thing. Apparently Walsh got some stuff on Hahn and his business. One way or another he'll get that back. I don't know what you got on him but it sure has made Hahn sore."

"Get me a meet, will you, Leo?"

"I'll see what I can do."

Wynter was anxious. If Hahn wouldn't see him he knew he had problems like never before. His next problem was to contact Sir Harry Buchanan. He had no contact number and no address. It would have surprised him had he known that he and Buchanan were practically neighbours. He hadn't bothered looking for a number in the directories. He knew Buchanan's number would not be listed and even if it was, what was he to look under? However, he reasoned, there could well be an easy way. He picked up the handset on his landline and dialled 123 for the Timeline. While the disembodied voice repeated the time, Wynter spoke.

"Eric Wynter would value a discussion with Sir Harry Buchanan." He replaced the handset and waited.

It was not until the following day, by which time he was beginning to doubt he would be able to contact Buchanan, that his phone rang. His butler went to answer but Wynter shouted to leave it alone.

"Hello," Wynter said.

"Ah, Mr Wynter! Harry Buchanan here. I understand you wish to talk to me?" Harry sound like a good-natured, kindly, country vicar phoning his favourite parishioner.

"How kind of you to contact me, Sir Harry. Yes, I do indeed wish to speak with you. Perhaps we can meet somewhere appropriate?"

"Your own house is appropriate enough, Mr Wynter. I'll be there at 6.30 this evening. I will not want to see anyone else while I'm your guest. Ensure there are no other guests and be very sure that you do not receive any unexpected visitors."

"Be assured we will be alone, Sir Harry."

"I am assured, Mr Wynter." Buchanan put his phone down without another word.

When Harry knocked on Wynter's front door at precisely 6.30, it was Wynter himself who opened the door. The two men shook hands and Sir Harry was led through to the study.

"A drink, Sir Harry?"

"A single malt would be very pleasant."

Wynter poured two malts and the two men sat facing each other with the drinks between them.

"I have to take it on trust that you are not recording this conversation," said Wynter.

"My dear Mr Wynter, I have to return the compliment. You and I both know that neither wants a record of this conversation. I am entirely satisfied you are not recording us. Now, how may I be of service?"

"I am aware you have the power to invoke all the agencies with which you threatened me."

"No threat, Mr Wynter," said Harry. Both men smiled affably.

"No quite, Sir Harry, quite. However, I believe I still have a little room to bargain. Not much, I grant, but a little."

"How so?"

"You have the power to wind up my organisation and me along with it. That would still leave a slight risk in your mind of an unfortunate and embarrassing leak, wouldn't it? My proposal is this. I will guarantee to work with you to assist you to achieve all your objectives. In return, you leave W.F.M.C. alone and you leave me to enjoy the remainder of my retirement."

Wynter waited for a response as he watched Harry ponder this. He could not resist a slight smile. He knew that Harry had his answer ready before they had met this evening. He already knew what Harry would say and, oddest of all, he knew that Harry knew he knew. Yet the game had to be played to the full.

"I think you may have something there, Mr Wynter. Your proposition has some merit. I am in a position to ensure your organisation and you are left alone. The price may be higher than you are prepared to pay however."

"Go on, please."

"I require that every record relating to this little adventure is delivered to me. That will include every piece of documentary evidence including reports, expense claims, restaurant receipts, diary entries, ledger entries, minutes of meetings and whatever else you will find. It will include computer records and hard copies. Every last reference will be removed and delivered to me. Agreed?"

"Agreed," replied Wynter.

"Next. You are aware, I am sure, that Mr Walsh has dues to pay now. Agreed?"

"Agreed." Wynter had been waiting for this.

"You and W.F.M.C. will need to distance yourselves from Mr Walsh. You will need to do this very quickly. I suggest a dismissal with an acceptable settlement. I'll leave that to you."

"Sir Harry, that's not enough, is it? What more do you want regarding this matter?"

"My dear Mr Wynter, absolutely nothing from you. Any further arrangements will be administered by others. I'm sure you will understand that I couldn't possibly rely upon you to make the arrangements and conclude the business. I need Mr Walsh's home address."

"Anything else?" asked Wynter.

"At this time, no. Deliver the documents and Walsh's details and I will be satisfied for now. You and your organisation will remain in my debt. In return for the survival of W.F.M.C. and your own survival, I may call upon you in future for your help, but for now this will conclude our business together." Sir Harry rose from his chair and held out his hand.

"Thank you, Sir Harry," said Wynter, shaking Harry's hand.

"I will personally make sure you receive all the material." Wynter walked to his desk and scribbled notes onto a sheet of paper. He returned and handed it to Harry. "Here is the information you require. Walsh has two homes. These are the addresses of his London flat and his cottage in the Cotswolds."

Harry smiled, nodded and left.

At eight o'clock that evening the phone rang. This time, Wynter's butler answered it and announced to his master that a Mr Salmon wished to speak to him.

"Hello, Leo. I do hope you have some news for me."

"Eric, you're going to owe me big time for this one. Webster Hahn will meet you to see if an accommodation can be arranged."

"Good. Thank you, Leo."

"Wait. There's more. He requires a gesture of good faith first. He wants Harvey Walsh's head on a plate before he'll meet you."

"He wants Harvey's what?" replied Wynter, feigning shock.

"You heard, Eric. Walsh in return for talks. I've gotta go now. Playing golf with a certain senator with a problem. He wants my help as well. Do you people think I work for the Samaritans? Goodbye, Eric, and good luck."

Wynter knew that he could never trust Walsh's judgment again. He also knew that by handing Walsh over he might go some way to restoring the credibility of W.F.M.C. All in all, he reasoned, this was the best he could expect. Perhaps it was even better than he had a right to expect. Buchanan gets what he wants and hits Walsh. This would be something Buchanan would never advertise. Hahn would see his condition fulfilled and assume Wynter had made this great sacrifice. Maybe this was not too bad at all.

That evening Eric Wynter phoned Harvey Walsh at home. He requested that Walsh should call in to see him first thing in the morning, before he went into the office. Walsh was surprised and asked what this was all about. Wynter told him to have a good night and said it would wait till morning. He made a second call and booked another appointment for the morning.

Early mornings were no novelty for Wynter. At five o'clock he was up, showered and dressed. At 5.30 there was a knock at the door. Wynter invited Melanie Coleman-Burns in. Fresh ground, filtered coffee was waiting in the study. Wynter could see that she was on edge but that was to be expected. Melanie had met Wynter infrequently and she had never been invited to his home. She found the experience unnerving.

"Sit down," said Wynter, pointing to a chair. "I am sorry to have to bring you here at such an unholy hour. I do hope it hasn't inconvenienced you too much."

"No, sir, not at all," she lied.

Wynter smiled, recognising the lie. "Good," he said. "Now, young lady, we have a problem. It is a problem you are in a position to help me with. I have to rely on your absolute discretion. Can I assume that your loyalty is absolute?"

"Of course, sir."

Wynter smiled again. "You may live to regret that." Melanie wriggled in discomfort. "I have some tasks for you. You will do them without reference to anyone, for any reason, other than myself. You will report to me and to me alone."

"What about Harvey?" asked Coleman-Burns with some concern.

"I am sorry to tell you that our problems have been brought about by Mr Walsh. Now, drink your coffee while I explain what I want." The old man watched the young woman as she sipped her coffee. He noticed the slight quiver of her hand. "Place all of Mr Walsh's personal belongings into a box and bring them here when I tell you. Wait in the office until I phone you and tell no one what you are doing. If you are subjected to any pressure refer them to me. Take this letter to Mr Latcham." Wynter handed her a sealed letter addressed to Chris Latcham, a team leader. "It tells him to work with you to collect certain items. When they have been collected, box them also and deliver them to me when I tell you.

"I am relying on you totally. Your work for W.F.M.C. has always been of the highest order. If you are able to complete all of my requests in the manner in which I expect you to, then I wouldn't be at all surprised if a sudden promotion didn't come your way. Off you go now and I'll talk to you later."

At eight o'clock the same morning, there was another knock at the door. This time it was Harvey Walsh. He too appeared nervous. Wynter ushered him to the study where there was more fresh coffee. He gestured to a chair and Walsh sat. Without speaking, Wynter slowly poured two coffees, placed them on the coffee table and seated himself.

"We have a problem, Harvey. I have reason to fear for your life. Hahn isn't going to let us get away with this."

"You want me to resign?"

"No. I'm going to sack you." Wynter held up his hand to quell Walsh's shock. "It would make sense if you took a long holiday. Go to your cottage for a while. When all this is sorted I'll bring you back. Harvey, I still respect you and still need you."

"When do you want me to go?"

"Now."

Walsh's shoulders visibly sank. Some poker face this guy, some professional, thought Wynter.

"I'll go and clear out my office."

"No. I'll arrange that. Now to business. Where are the disks?"

"The disks?" said Walsh.

Wynter struggled to hide his irritation. "The Hahn insurance disks. Are they in your safe?"

"They're in the safe at my flat."

"Are they the only ones or do you have copies?"

"They're the only ones."

I'll bet, thought Wynter. "Good. Excuse me for a moment please."

Wynter got up and left the study leaving Walsh alone to his thoughts. In the kitchen the old man picked up a phone and called Melanie. He had no fear of Walsh picking up the extension in the study. The kitchen phone was intentionally a separate line.

"Melanie, take a team round to Harvey's Knightsbridge apartment. A thorough search for any interesting material. Get into his safe and empty

156

it. You'll find some computer disks in there. Box everything again and bring it all here when I give you the word. Also pack a couple of suitcases with Mr Walsh's clothes."

"Do you have the combination to his safe, sir?"

"Melanie, please. Just open it."

"Sorry, sir. Of course."

"Take everything back to the office. Change all the locks and combinations at the office. Tell security that Mr Walsh no longer has access to the building. Should Mr Walsh turn up, they are to disregard anything he may tell them. He no longer works for W.F.M.C. When you have the disks from the safe and all security arrangements have been made, call me back here."

Wynter returned to the study. Walsh was looking not a bit like the successful and powerful man of business.

"Look, I'm sorry about this, Harvey. I know this is really tough for you. But it's not so easy for me either. We always look after our own and you're no exception. I want you to go directly to your cottage when you leave here. Anything you want from Knightsbridge, just tell me and I'll get it for you. Whatever you do, don't go there. It's being watched. Can I assume I'm the only person who knows about the cottage?"

"Yes."

"Good. I want your company car back. We'll sell it. Get yourself something less conspicuous. I'll get you some cash to tide you over, one hundred thousand. That should do for a bit. Now, what about some breakfast?" said Wynter, rubbing his hands together with apparent glee.

"I don't feel too hungry."

Wynter ignored this and called to his butler. He ordered two English breakfasts, big ones. He was starving. It was only a few minutes later that the butler entered the study to announce that breakfast was served in the dining room.

Despite his feelings for Walsh at the moment, Wynter was able to amuse him convincingly while he waited for Coleman-Burns to phone. The call came at ten minutes to midday. He took the call in his study.

"I have what you asked for, sir."

"Good. Listen carefully. Get someone to hire a car in Mr Walsh's name using his spare documentation. A Scorpio will do nicely. Put Mr Walsh's cases in the boot. Get someone to drive it here with you. You drive your car with all the boxes I asked for in the boot. When you get here get the Scorpio to my front door. You wait in your car in the rear car park of the King's Head pub until I call you."

He replaced the handset as the letterbox rattled with the morning papers being delivered. Wynter gathered the broadsheets from the doormat and took them to Walsh.

"Amuse yourself with these for a while."

With that, he left Walsh with the papers and his thoughts. Wynter knew that his action of placing the papers in front of Walsh and leaving him to contemplate his future would be an uncomfortable experience.

The Scorpio pulled into Eric Wynter's drive at one thirty. The driver knocked the door and was asked by the butler to sit in the hall.

"Harvey, there's a car for you outside," said Wynter speaking for the first time since giving him the papers. "It's hired. Keep it until you find yourself another car. In the boot there's some of your clothes. They'll do for a while. Tell me what else you want and I'll collect it for you in a day or two. Now off you go to your cottage on the hill and don't stay too far from your phone for too long. I'll talk to you soon. Now remember, don't ring me here. The line's tapped and, at the moment I prefer it that way, it suits my purposes. I'll let on to the Home Secretary when it doesn't suit me any longer."

Wynter took Walsh's hand and shook it warmly. "Try not to worry too much. We'll all get out of this and return to normal as soon as possible."

When Walsh had left, Wynter phoned Melanie in her car. She drove round to his home in five minutes.

"Get your colleague to take Mr Walsh's car. Sell it please. Before he goes however, get him to bring the boxes in from your car."

Sir Harry Buchanan and Clarion met for afternoon tea at the Ashleigh Hotel in Shanklin on the Isle of Wight. As usual, Julie entered the hotel a few minutes after Harry and by the time she found Harry at a table by a window, he had ordered the tea and sandwiches. Harry kissed her and in return she gave him a big hug.

"Progress then?"

"Target one down."

Harry smiled and handed her a brown envelope.

"In that you will find the first instalment. It's a banker's draft as usual. As usual it is untraceable. You will also find the address of Harvey Walsh's cottage. Would you believe it's on Tall Boys Hill?"

"Shit," said Julie, "that's too close to home."

"Don't swear. In all the years I knew your father, I never once heard him swear."

"Harry, don't be a boring old fart. It's like you never swear. Tall Boys Hill is too close. I'll have to hit him somewhere else."

"No can do. He has been instructed to go there and stay there. Likelihood is, he will do that for a day or two but within a few days my guess is he will be out and about setting up the odd intrigue or two of his own. He'll feel he has a couple of scores to settle. It has to be in the next two or three days."

"Harry, you're asking too much. There's a chance I'll compromise myself. I reduce risks to a minimum. You know that. That's why you use me and that's why I'm alive today. Tall Boys Hill is fifteen miles from my home. It's just the other side of Cheltenham. To set up a realistic hit, I need several weeks. To get me to hit this target within fifteen miles of home and in three days is a bit unfair."

"I know, poppet. I know it's unfair and I feel bad about it. However, as our friends the Americans say, there is zero option. It's got to be done and it's got to be done quickly. I told you this job was going to be a bitch. There's more. I need a photograph of the target when its dead. I also need the local press report when it appears. A clipping won't do. I need the whole paper. You will also need to search the place for some floppy disks. Do your best."

"Harry, you really are an angel. You don't need me, you want Merlin the Magician."

A Bad Week For Harry

Not far from the northern edge of London's Hyde Park and a few yards off the Bayswater Road lies a small private hospital. The knowledge of its existence is restricted to a few and the patient lists are made up of politicians, diplomats, senior civil servants and favoured foreign dignitaries. Despite strangled funding in National Health Service hospitals in Britain, this hospital is unencumbered by such worries as money. If the great British public was made aware of the resources enjoyed by this hospital, there would be a scandal. Petitions would be delivered to Number 10. There would be marches and demonstrations. This hospital was equipped in a way that would have made any major hospital in any major city green with envy. Labour shortages were never a problem since staff were well paid and enjoyed benefits unheard of in the public sector.

The week had not started well for Sir Harry Buchanan. The ache in his lower back and the throbbing lump in his tummy had got the better of him and he had seen his G.P. The good doctor had sent Harry to his local hospital for an ultrasound scan that same afternoon. Now here he was, sitting in a plush waiting room in this private hospital north of the Thames. Harry, always a busy man, turned up just three minutes before his appointment time. He did not have to wait long, not that anyone ever waited for long at this hospital. A middle-aged, rather plump, immaculately uniformed nurse walked across the deep carpet.

"Sir Harry. Mr Craig will see you now. Will you follow me, please?"

The nurse led Harry into a large office. Behind the desk sat a young man who, Harry thought, could not be more than thirty-five. The man rose and shook Harry by the hand.

"Please take a seat, Sir Harry." Craig pointed to the chair in front of the desk. He then dragged a matching chair to Harry's side so that they were both sitting on the same side of the desk. Craig sat and Harry was vaguely amused to see he was not clutching a clipboard.

"My name is Robert Craig. I'm a vascular surgeon. I have spoken to your G.P. and I have seen the results of your ultrasound scan." Craig was calm and spoke slowly and softly. Harry would have commended him for his bedside manner in different circumstances. "You saw your G.P. and discussed with him your back ache and the throbbing lump in your tummy?"

"Yes."

"The ultrasound was to confirm your G.P.'s suspicions. It has done that. I am sorry to tell you, you have an aortic aneurysm. What do you know about aortic aneurysms?"

"Nothing. It sounds exotic," replied Harry.

Robert Craig smiled in a kindly manner. "Imagine an aneurysm as a balloon. The aorta, which supplies the blood to your legs, is ballooning. The reason you have back pain is because the aneurysm is pressing on nerves affecting your back. The lump in your tummy is the balloon itself and the throbbing you feel is your heart beat."

"Bottom line, please, Mr Craig. What does the future hold?"

"When the balloon bursts, blood will flow into your body. You will notice I said 'when' and not 'if,' for burst it surely will, one day. When that day comes, the aneurysm will kill you. However, there is every chance we will be able to operate. The chances of a full recovery are also very good. I would like to arrange for you to be admitted to this hospital immediately."

"I am afraid that is out of the question. If I ignore this what is the risk?"

"That's very difficult to say."

"Oh come now, doctor. Give it a try."

"Without an operation, the aneurysm will, without doubt, kill you."

"How long have I got?" said Harry.

"That is impossible to say. It could be a month, a year or longer. It could also be as you walk out of this building. Sir Harry, I must urge you to reconsider. It is vital we operate without delay."

"What has caused this?" Harry changed the subject to give himself a little thinking time.

"You have a history of high blood pressure. You smoke cigars, and quite a few I suspect. You drink alcohol. Your family has a history of high blood pressure and heart disease. Any or all of these may have contributed."

"Assuming I had your operation, how long would I be out of circulation?"

"Again difficult to say, but it would be a matter of months rather than weeks."

"To subject myself to an operation and long convalescence is out of the question at the moment. I need time to think. I'll get back to you."

"That is, of course, your choice, Sir Harry. But I must repeat that any delay, any delay at all, is most inadvisable. Your life is at risk. You may reconsider when you have come to terms with the seriousness of this. Without an operation your life will constantly be at risk. You may have important matters to deal with now but I suggest you consider what contribution you can make when it is too late."

Harry rose. "Thank you for your time, Mr Craig. I will give your words very careful consideration. How may I contact you?"

Craig gave Harry a card. As he made for the door Craig spoke again. "Sir Harry. While you are considering your condition I recommend minimum exercise and no stress. Watch your smoking, drinking and eating. I'll be here when you want me. Good afternoon."

Harry smiled, nodded and left. He returned to his office, poured a large drink, lit a cigar and pondered. It had been a bad week.

This was also a bad week for Julie Martin. Love Harry though she did, she resented the unreasonable pressure he had now exerted on her. He was asking her to compromise her standards, which in turn could jeopardise her freedom or even her life. Her anger with Harry was not diminishing. In the peace and tranquillity of her cottage she thought back over her life. She wondered to what extent she had chosen her life and the way she made her living. She considered what might happen to her if she resigned, or rather refused to be the Clarion Resource. Maybe she could stop playing this game? On the other hand, she was trained for it, she had made sacrifices for it and she enjoyed it immensely. This was her identity and familiar territory. She was also extraordinarily good at it and that knowledge was something she needed, probably for her ego.

As the day wore on her anger subsided. In reality she knew that Harry would not have asked her to place herself in additional danger had it not been absolutely necessary. Her problem now was a question of logistics and research. The issue of logistics could not be sorted within Harry's deadline. Possibly, however, there was a little time for some fundamental research. Just maybe, in the light of the urgency, the proximity of the target would work in her favour.

Late that afternoon, Julie walked into Martin's. She called the two duty supervisors into her office. She explained to them that she was going to take some time off. She would spend most of it at home, but would prefer it if they didn't bother her. In emergencies they were to ring her and if she wasn't in, leave a message on her answering service. She promised she would go through the stock reports and leave stock orders and any other instructions before she left that evening.

Both members of staff were secretly pleased that Julie had decided to trust them. They were devoted to their boss but it would be nice not to have the pressure of her presence for a few days.

It was after eight that evening when Julie had finished in her office. It was dark and there was a chill in the air when she left her warm premises and joined the shadows of the night. She experienced an involuntary shudder. She had checked the alarm before locking up and was confident she could leave her business to her staff. Instead of going home she drove the few miles to the top of Tall Boys Hill. The road up the hill was bordered by high quality housing, hotels, a couple of pubs and a rest home or two. Close to the top on the right she found the house she was looking for. It was not as big as many on the hill but it was obviously expensive. On the drive, in front of the garage, was a blue Scorpio. She wondered why it wasn't in the garage. She thought it was a bit untidy leaving it out. She saw a light in a front window as she drove past.

She didn't slow but continued to the top of the hill. On the left she found a lay-by and pulled over. Leaving the car she walked back down the hill. When she reached the house she looked up and down the road. There was the occasional car and the odd lorry labouring up the gradient. When she reached the house, a last look convinced her that the road was clear and there were no pedestrians in sight. She trotted up the driveway and flattened herself against the side of the house. She could not be seen from the road. Listening for any noise from the house or the drive, she carefully made her way round to the back of the house. As she rounded the corner she was aware of a lawn and summer house. There were shrubberies but she could make out little else.

Again she flattened herself to the wall and listened. There were no lights shining at the back and so, with great care, she peeped through the windows. The first room was a kitchen. She made out a sink under the window and the fitted units around and behind. There was an open door and light was shining through it from another room or passageway. Passing a back door she looked into another window. It appeared to be a study. There was no light shining into this room and it was difficult to make anything out, but she fancied there was a desk facing the window upon which there was a personal computer.

Her next task was to take a look through the front windows, one of which was likely to be occupied, the light suggested so. She crept round to the front of the house, listening all the way. It was never a good idea to look into a lighted room at night, especially when she could be seen from the road or pavement. Before she took this risk, she sought an escape route. It was imperative that if she was spotted she get away before her face and shape could register. She also knew she would run down the road away from her car if she were spotted. A little way down the hill and across the road there was a lane. She could lose herself down there. Now she cursed. She had brought her own car, the MGF, because of the time pressure. She knew that this was not something she would normally have done and it was careless. This was an example of what could happen when undue demands were placed upon her.

There was no sound of vehicles on the hill. There was no sign of pedestrians, people taking their dogs for a last walk. Quickly she moved herself underneath the window, which was a protruding bay variety. It was likely any occupier would be watching television. Julie could now hear a television. Most likely it would be in a corner either opposite or adjacent to the door into the room. It was unlikely that, with these magnificent views over the River Severn floodplain, the TV would be in a corner away from the windows. The odds were then, that she could peep through the bay side closest to the centre of the house without being seen, and this she did.

With a slight smile she found she had been right about the television. She could see it clearly, even what programme was on, a western. She could also see the occupant of the room. He was facing the TV but was reading a newspaper. The side of his head was very clear and Julie saw him to be Harvey Walsh, her target.

She picked her way back to the drive and to the road. She relaxed slightly as she walked up the hill back to her MG. When she reached the car she sat in it for another hour. From this place the front garden of the house could be seen, just. During this hour she saw Walsh walk up the road to the last building at the top of the hill on the right. It was a pub and the time was 10 p.m.

When she arrived home that night, Julie went to her bookshelf and grabbed a British Airways timetable. She checked the internal flight times from Birmingham Airport. She found a departure time that suited her purpose. Although she was tired and would have preferred to go to bed, she drove instead to Birmingham Airport. There she parked her MG in the long stay and hired another Ford Escort using a false identity and false papers that were indistinguishable from genuine articles, even to an expert. Before she set off home she phoned David Ginsberg in London from a public callbox. It was late and Ginsberg was not at all pleased to have to answer the phone. When he heard it was Julie his manner changed.

"Julie, my flower. How nice to hear from you! How are you?"

"Good, David. How about you and the family?"

"Also good. Goodness me, it has been a long time. Whatever can I do for you at this hour?"

"I need to see you soon. How about your workshop on Sunday? Four o'clock Okay?"

"Of course, of course. A pleasure, flower, a pleasure. I look forward to it."

Seventy-five minutes later, Julie was in bed.

For the next two evenings she parked the Escort in public places at the foot of Tall Boys Hill and walked to the top. On both evenings she watched from the shadows as Walsh went to the pub at ten o'clock. Julie found this odd. This guy was showing few signs of security awareness. It was as if he didn't care or had no idea that he was at risk. She knew she didn't have time to research intrusion systems and so the job would have to be done outside. This she liked not one bit. A small consolation was that when he returned from the pub at eleven each evening, he entered his house by the back door and therefore was out of sight of the road. This man's actions suggested to Julie that he was an unsuspecting amateur. Unfortunately she could not treat him as such. While she had been given little information about him, she knew that there was a good chance that he was professionally trained.

She had spent the morning in her workshop at the end of her garage at the cottage. She drilled out the centre of a piece of wooden doweling. She used a hacksaw to cut off the boss at the top of a knitting needle and about three inches off its length. Into the hole in the doweling she inserted the needle, fixing it with contact adhesive. Placing the handle in a vice she sawed halfway through the needle about an inch from the handle. She now had a homemade stiletto. Using white spirit she carefully wiped the needle to remove any traces of sweat, fingerprints and anything else. She knew she had little to fear, yet it made her feel better to reduce any risk to a minimum.

The next evening she parked the hire car at the bottom of the hill and walked again to the top. From the lane on the opposite side of the road she watched Walsh leave his house for the pub. It came as no surprise to her that the time was ten o'clock. She remained in the shadows of the lane until 10.50. There were no vehicles coming from either direction and, walking across the road, she checked again for cars and pedestrians. Since she was still not aware of external security arrangements, she made her way to the back of the house with care. She thought it unlikely that there were any concealed infrared TV cameras for two reasons. Firstly they are not easy to conceal. Second, if there were, she would have been recorded on her first visit and Walsh would have changed his patterns. Well, she thought, that's the theory.

In any case, she was not going to take this risk either. She wore jeans that would normally have been too big for her. She had carefully fashioned foam rubber to make her hips appear much bigger than they actually were. She had stuffed an oversized bra with foam rubber. She wore a ginger wig and make-up that aged her considerably. She knew that she would not be identified if she were caught on camera, particularly at night, or if she were seen by passersby. This gave her confidence.

Julie waited in the shadows of the summer house which was within 15 feet of the back door. She knew Walsh did not carry a torch and so she would not be seen as he rounded the corner. The minutes ticked away and by two minutes after eleven, the target had not returned. He had broken his routine, the dread of every assassin. Julie cursed Harry again. By ten past he had still not shown. She had been set up. The next arrival at the house would be the police or, more likely, Walsh's colleagues. Julie was tempted to run but her training prevented her. Instead she peered to the back of the garden to locate an escape route. God, she thought, I'm getting sloppy. She would normally have had this sorted. Then she heard it.

"Night then, Harvey. Nice to have met you."

"Yes. You too. See you tomorrow night and we'll have another session."

So that was it. Walsh had met someone, a neighbour by the sound of it, in the pub. Julie flattened herself against the wooden wall of the summer house and watched as Walsh came round the side of the house and made for the back door. He swayed slightly. He had had one or two too many. This was good. Each time she had observed Walsh she had checked his height. She was tall enough for this. She knew she could do this and a sensation of detachment came over her. It was based on confidence, experience and training.

As Walsh fumbled in his pocket for his keys, Julie came up behind him. She held the point of the homemade weapon between her thumb and next two fingers of her right hand. Her right arm wrapped around his neck. In an instant her thumb and fingers guided the tip of the needle to a point just behind and beneath Walsh's left ear. Holding the tip in position with the fingers of her right hand, she struck the handle with the flat of her left hand. So quick was the operation that Walsh had not even moved his head by the time the needle entered his neck. One strike was enough to drive the needle in four inches. Julie pulled back her left hand and struck the handle again, this time on the side. Where she had sawed halfway through the needle, it snapped and the handle fell to the ground.

The lifeless body of Walsh fell towards the still locked door. He started to slither down it and before he slumped to the ground, Julie had found the handle and stuffed it into her pocket. She found the keys in the dead man's pocket. Fishing out a camera from a pouch strapped to her back, she popped up the flash and photographed the corpse. Using the keys, she unlocked the door and entered the house. There was no sound of an alarm although she took no consolation in this. There was every chance there was a silent alarm. A bell could now be ringing at a local police station or private security company. She allowed herself 90 seconds to find computer disks.

Human nature being what it is, Julie reckoned that the disks Harry wanted would be hidden among the rest of Walsh's disks. She went to his desk in the study, the one she had already identified, and rifled it, starting with the bottom drawers. By starting with those at the bottom she did not have to shut them to reach the next drawers. She found a disk box in the right hand drawer second from top. She stuffed this into the pouch. Checking the rest of the drawers she found no more disks. Next she went to the bookshelf and pulled all the books to the floor. There was nothing behind them. The black enamel log burning stove fixed to the back wall was different. She opened the doors and found an envelope lying inside. Ripping it open she discovered four disks. This guy was an amateur, she thought. Or is this a smoke screen? If these aren't the disks then, tough. Ninety seconds are up. Julie left.

Two days later, a piece appeared on page three of the local press. The headline read, "Murder mystery. Police seek killer of businessman."

No Lie In

Julie came round and looked at her bedside clock. Through her blurred vision she made out 6.53 on the digital display. Bugger it, she thought. Some lie in this is going to be. Then she heard a hard rap on her front door. She realised that this was not the first knock. It was a knock that had awoken her in the first place. Slowly she dragged herself out of bed and wrapped a silk dressing gown around her naked body. She made no effort to rush downstairs even when the rapping was repeated. Eventually she reached the door, peeped through the spy hole and opened the door to reveal a smiling Harry Buchanan.

"Christ, Harry! Do you know what time it is?"

"Morning, poppet."

"It's bloody not seven o'clock yet. It's still bloody dark nearly."

"Nonsense, sweet thing. Best time of the day. Lovely and fresh. You can breathe the air no one else has breathed. Now what about breakfast?"

"You want breakfast, you bloody make it."

"Poppet, I do wish you'd watch your profanity."

"Just go and make the breakfast. If you're cooking, cook for me too. I like a cooked breakfast on a Sunday."

"Quite, poppet. It's what made the Empire great. I am a firm believer that the Empire crumbled when we Brits stopped eating a proper breakfast. All this foreign stuff is no good to man nor beast. Croissants and jam and honey and muck. No, it's eggs, bacon, mushrooms and tomatoes for me. That's what we need."

"You'll find everything in the kitchen. I'm going to shower."

It was forty minutes before Julie came down. She had showered, dressed in tight jeans and a jumper and applied some makeup. She looked a little less grumpy. The table in her dining room was set with the best silver, toast and marmalade was there. From the kitchen she could smell the breakfast. She could also hear Harry singing.

"Harry."

"Uh-huh?"

"I like to have a lie-in on a Sunday. What's the point of keeping the place in Paris when you just turn up here? Anyway, what's so important you have to come and disturb my peace?"

"Things have changed now. We know who the enemy is. Battle lines are drawn, targets identified. We're in control now. And I just wanted to see that you're looking after yourself."

"That was on your mind when you got me to whack target two with ten minutes notice, was it? There must be something on your twisted mind to get you down to Gloucestershire at this time on a Sunday. Bloody hell, it's not even eight o'clock yet."

Harry came through carrying two plates laden with traditional breakfasts.

"Now you tuck into this, poppet. It'll improve your disposition."

They ate while Harry whittered on about inconsequentials. When he finished he pushed the plate away.

"That was excellent although I say so myself. Of course you're right, poppet. There are things to talk about. Now, you have some odds and ends for me?"

Julie disappeared for several minutes and returned carrying an attaché case.

"Is this what you mean?" said Julie, knowing full well it was.

Harry removed a newspaper, a Polaroid shot of Walsh's corpse and a number of floppy disks. His smile broadened.

"Thank you so much. I see that despite your protestations you managed to eat your breakfast. Now don't you feel better?"

"No." Julie pouted.

Harry reached into his jacket pocket and withdrew a brown envelope.

"Some spends for you."

"Look, Harry, if this is so hush-hush, how come you're here? Isn't it a bit risky?"

"Not at all. Not at all. What are your plans today?"

"I'm going to London."

"That's nice. What for?"

"Mind your own bloody business." Julie softened. "You don't want to know Harry, dear. Trust me, you really don't want to know."

Harry laughed. "Then I'll press you no further. I suppose you have read these disks?"

"Actually I haven't. Do you want me to?"

"Not particularly. I want to use your computer to have a little look myself. I suggest you go about your business and leave me in peace. I'll help myself to coffee and things."

"Why don't you do that, Harry?"

For the remainder of the morning Julie busied herself with household chores. It was just before midday when she bent over Harry, who was still at her computer, and kissed him on the forehead.

"I'm off now. Set the alarm and pull the door to when you leave."

"Yes, my dear. You take good care of yourself."

Julie smiled. "And you. See you."

There is much misunderstanding about handguns, due at least in part to Hollywood. It is not possible to silence a gun by screwing a tiny silencer into the muzzle. The noise is due to the explosion of gases which exit the weapon, not just from the muzzle, but also from around the chamber. It is possible to reduce this noise to a pop in a bespoke, single-shot handgun where there are no points of emission from a chamber. The silencer, about the size of a can of hair spray, deadens the rest of the noise. The next problem with noise reduction is rather more complex to rectify. When a bullet passes through the sound barrier it creates a loud crack. To avoid this the bullet velocity must be below 1080 feet per second.

This creates another problem. Bullets kill in two ways. First, by shock and trauma to the nervous system. Second, and probably more important, by destroying a vital organ. Low velocity, lightweight bullets do not have a good chance of shocking to death. High velocity, heavy calibre bullets will do the job much better, but the problem of noise remains.

To increase the chance of killing by trauma and the destruction of a vital organ, simple measures can be taken. Hollow point bullets allow for mercury to be poured into them. The end can be sealed with solder to keep the mercury in. In this way, when a bullet hits its target, it expands on entry, making a terrible mess of the victim's insides.

Julie was sensitive to these matters and about the ammunition she chose to use. She preferred to make her own ammunition to ensure all the criteria she required were fulfilled. She could measure the quantity of powder to ensure the bullet would travel at below the speed of sound. She had a handmade, bespoke, single-shot handgun on her shopping list and she wanted another weapon. She wanted the nine shot Type 67, a particularly effective gun made in the People's Republic of China. This gun, a 7.65-millimetre, has an effective moderator or silencer which can make it virtually impossible to hear from the side or rear. The Type 67 requires a special and unique rimless 7.65 x 17-millimetre low power cartridge. To increase effectiveness, the bullets need the judicious insertion of mercury.

Julie parked her car a mile from David Ginsberg's workshop in London's East End. She walked the rest of the way and knocked at his door at exactly 4.00 p.m. Ginsberg answered her knock and shook her firmly by the hand. The old man was, to Julie, a cliché. He was short, wrinkled, none too well dressed, wore gold rimmed, half-moon spectacles over which he stared, and he spoke with an East European accent. Most striking of all were his eyes. They sparkled with what Julie interpreted to be mirth, a zest for life and a sense of humour. While Ginsberg's body was old and bent, his eyes were full of life.

"Julie, how nice to see you again. It's been so long."

"Good to see you too, David."

"Come on through the back. May I offer you some tea?"

"No. I'd rather get down to business. I have a shopping list for you."

"Of course. Why else would you come to see me?" Ginsberg said this in such a way as to imply criticism. "You young people are too busy for the likes of us old people. You only come to see us when you need something."

"Don't go on so," said Julie with an affectionate smile. "Rachel and your boys, how are they?"

"Rachel, she is very well. But my sons. They are just like you. They only come to see me when they want something. But they're good boys. And doing so well too. To business then."

"As always, David, there is no rush for the things I want. Today will do nicely." Julie smiled at her rather thin joke.

"You are teasing me, I think?"

"Only a little. I want you to make me a gun, a special gun like this." Julie handed Ginsberg a sheet of paper. The old man took it and peered through his spectacles at the sheet.

"I think I can make this in a week. What else?"

"I want a Type 67 and let's say 50 rounds. Can you also find me a Glock?"

"A Glock? Nothing easier. It will take me two hours. Type 67, that might be a problem. I need to talk to an old friend of mine. He might be able to help us. Go on."

The Austrian manufacturer, Glock, makes a range of semi-automatic pistols. What is different is that they are made almost entirely of plastic. More precisely, they are primarily constructed of polymer developed for the space industry. The polymer is stronger than steel and is able to withstand temperatures up to 200 degrees centigrade. The polymer weighs around 14% of steel. The construction of Glock pistols makes them incredibly reliable, but this in itself was not the reason Julie wanted one. Because they are made of plastic, they do not show on X-ray equipment at airports. The few metal components are easy to hide, say, in a purse. Even a zealous customs official would be unlikely to correctly identify the little pieces. The plastic body of the gun can be concealed in the base of an aerosol hair spray can.

Julie handed him another sheet of paper. "This completes my shopping list."

Ginsberg took the paper and went into an office. Julie heard rustling and grunting. She also heard the old man talking and grumbling to himself. Ten minutes later he emerged from his office carrying a duffel bag. Oh hell, she thought. I haven't got to carry that through the streets, have I?'

"This is all you want. Call me in a week or two about the guns."

"No, David. I'll call you in a few days. Tell your friend whatever it costs, he can have it."

Ginsberg laughed. "Always the eye for the practicalities of life. I'm certain he can find a Type 67. Leave it to me. I have a Welrod here. Only a single-shot. Can you use it?"

"If I need it, I'll get back to you."

When Julie arrived home it had been dark for some time. She found that Harry had locked up and set the alarm. He had left the place as if no one had been there. She made herself a cup of tea, sat in an easy chair and kicked her shoes off. When the tea had started to revive her she got up, gathered the unbecoming duffel bag and went to the bench in her workshop. Emptying the bag she laid its contents along the bench. Standing on a stool she reached a box from a high shelf. It contained a loading press that she clamped to the bench. Next she emptied one of Ginsberg's brown packages which contained already fired nine millimeter shell cases. One by one she reformed the cases back to size using a swage. This is necessary because they were used cases that had swollen slightly under the pressure of gas when they were originally fired. She knocked out the old fired primers and pressed in new primers from another of Ginsberg's packages. At the same time she slightly bellmouthed the top of the cases to enable her to more easily insert the bullets.

From the box she had collected from her shelf she lifted a small set of handheld scales, dropping a small brass weight onto one of the pans. She opened yet another of the packages and with a small scoop placed small piles of powder onto the other scale pan. When the scales balanced, she poured the powder onto a sheet of paper, folded the paper and tipped powder into each of the cases. She placed the bullets onto the cases and pressed them down. Finally she crimped the cases into the circular groove around the bullets.

With great care each bullet was placed back into the loading press. Into their hollow points she used a syringe to insert mercury and sealed each with melted solder. For the first time since she had entered her garage she glanced at her watch. It was nearly midnight and she was cold. She tidied and went back into her house. Here she kicked off her shoes again, poured a large drink and settled into her favourite chair. The warmth, silence and sensation of a job well done soon combined and Julie nodded off to sleep.

The atmosphere in the offices of W.F.M.C. was strained. Harvey Walsh, the leader who was generally thought of as all powerful and unassailable, had been sacked. This caused considerable uncertainty and discomfort. Because of the cell structure within the organisation, the reasons for his demise were not known to anyone. He had just gone and the chairman, Eric Wynter, had let it be known that it had not been Walsh's decision, but his. He had asked that no one should consider that their job was at risk. There had been no euphemisms like "difference of opinion" or "he wished to spend more time with his family" or "that his other interests required more of his time." These lies were left for politicians. Instead the statement had been clear and unambiguous. Walsh had gone because his judgment in an important matter had been flawed. He no longer had the full confidence of Wynter and it was felt that, in the best interests of the organisation, he should leave. All staff were warned that Walsh should no longer be allowed on company premises. No one in the organisation should talk to him, meet him or write to him. In fact, there must be no communication whatsoever. If Walsh made any attempt to contact any member of staff, then they must inform Melanie Coleman-Burns and she would pass the information to the chairman.

The nature of the dismissal and the subsequent statement were bound to cause concern. Wynter's attitude was that it would keep the others on their toes. The atmosphere had not improved when the news of Walsh's death reached the office. Most members of the workforce saw it as being unfortunate and failed to link the death with recent events. A few others thought it was probably suicide because Walsh could not stand being deposed from his important position of power and influence. Clearly he had been unable to cope with the ignominy of it all. In any event, he would never have been able to get another job like it, managing director of a multi-million pound company. No, for sure he had topped himself.

There were just two people who had a different view of the death. These two knew that it was linked to a recent commission that had gone belly up. Chris Latcham and Melanie Coleman-Burns met away from work. At the moment they didn't feel too confident about the internal security. They met in a crowded pub at lunchtime. They eventually found a corner table when the occupants got up to return to their boring office routines. It was only when they were seated that Melanie spoke of her concerns.

Latcham put on a reassuring tone. "It's clear. Walsh's pet project went up in smoke. His clients were powerful people. Walsh hit the weakest link in the chain, Garstang. When that was done, his disappointed clients hit him. Probably revenge or to send out the message that failure would not be tolerated."

"I wish I could be so sure," said Coleman-Burns. "I set much of this up. I controlled Garstang."

"You did indeed. Only Walsh and I knew that though. Mel, you're safe. There is no value, nothing to be gained, by hitting you. In fact, I was involved with Wells and I'm your boss. If there was any threat to you I guess I would feature above you on the list."

"Nice try, Chris, but I'm still not happy. When this job went tits up I reckon we all got caught with our hands in the proverbial jar of cookies."

"Look at it this way. Walsh was hit by his customer. His customer would have no knowledge of you, me or anyone else. Walsh was the only person to have any contact with the customer. He was their only interest.

The alternative is that we hit him. That isn't likely, is it? There would have been no point. The trail might lead back to his employers. If we did it, we would have left a decent time. There certainly wouldn't have been a body left hanging around. If you're worried, why not have a word with Wynter? You seem to have his ear at the moment."

"I think I'll watch my back for a bit," she said. In truth, Latcham's optimistic opinion reflected her own. She had wanted confirmation and this she had now obtained. She did not feel she was at risk especially because Wynter seemed to be trusting her at the moment. She certainly had no idea who Walsh's clients had been. But, just to be on the safe side, she would be extra vigilant for the next week or two.

The Tsars Meet

It was some years since Eric Wynter had visited the United States of America. His visit on this occasion was inspired by his fear of the damage that could be inflicted on W.F.M.C. by Webster Hahn. Wynter was aware that either he or the world was changing. It would not have been so many years ago when, faced with a potential risk like Hahn, he would have destroyed that risk. He spent much of the flight wondering just what it was that had changed. He did not feel he had lost his nerve, neither did he feel that he had gone soft. Compassion was no more in his make-up now than it was back in 1947 when he and Richard Farmer had stolen a Bedford lorry. He recalled just how rich he and Farmer had felt each with £100 in their pockets. More than half a century later and the old man was worth millions. All these millions, however, gave him nothing like the pleasure that that £100 had.

Now he was faced with what was potentially the greatest threat the organisation had ever faced and all because of that bastard Walsh. In the old days when he and Farmer were in complete control, the company would never had got in this mess. In the old days he had his dear friend Farmer to help, support and advise. Now Farmer was gone and he was alone. He had no one to trust. Maybe it was that which was different.

What could he offer Hahn? Possibly nothing. But he still held some of the cards, or more precisely four floppy disks. As the British Airways aircraft commenced its descent to Phoenix's Sky Harbor International Airport, Wynter's spirits rose. He sensed the chase was soon to be on. He felt that old familiar thrill and soon, much to his surprise, he began to enjoy it. It had been many years since he had felt the effects of adrenaline. Hahn had not invited him to the Sedona ranch, instead he had insisted they meet at the hotel at which Wynter was staying. Wynter had told him he was booked into the Lancaster on Hayden Road in Scottsdale. He had used his charm and urbanity to the full when he invited Hahn to dinner. It had seemed as if Hahn had agreed before thinking the implications through. But then again, they were civilised men, not at all like the younger generation. Experience and sophistication inspired these old men to talk, negotiate and reach an accommodation without resorting to vulgar methods.

A hotel car took Wynter to the Lancaster. He went straight to his room where he rested. At seven he took a shower, dressed in a Prince of Wales check, three piece suit, and made his way to the bar. The appointment was scheduled for eight and he had every intention of being in the bar before Hahn arrived. It was no surprise to him that Hahn did not appear until eight precisely. The large hotel bar was not quite empty, and it would have been possible for Hahn to have selected the wrong man, but when he entered the bar he made straight for Wynter. As he approached, Wynter raised himself from his bar stool and held out his hand. The two men shook.

Wynter knew that control would be gained by one of the men in the first few minutes. Before Hahn could speak, Wynter said, "I have taken the liberty of ordering champagne. I do hope you don't object but I always think that great occasions call for a great champagne. Perhaps we can sit at that table over there in the corner." Without waiting for a reply the Englishman led the way to the table. He sat in an easy chair and waited for the American to sit in the other. "I'm so pleased you felt you could meet me, Mr Hahn, and I'm also pleased you chose to come alone."

"My people are outside, Mr Wynter."

"Of course. Naturally. Ah, here's the champagne. Jolly good."

"You have something for me, Mr Wynter." This was a statement rather than a question.

"That remains to be seen, Mr Hahn." The tension mounted and this was not what Wynter wanted at this stage. He went on quickly. "Allow me to be blunt. My organisation must take much of the responsibility for failing you. However, you too must take some responsibility. You made no mention to Mr Walsh that you had an influential enemy. Perhaps enemy is not the right word. Perhaps competitor or contestant would be more appropriate. You chose not to inform Mr Walsh that there might be people, other than those already identified by Walsh, against whom he should have taken precautions."

"So this is my fault, Mr Wynter? You are suggesting this is my fault?"

"No, sir, I'm not. I'm suggesting there are other factors in this whole sorry story which should be taken into account. Walsh should have taken precautions against all comers. He didn't. He failed and as a result he has paid the ultimate price. I cannot forgive him for that and I know you cannot either."

A waiter came to the table to advise them that their table in the restaurant was ready. They followed him and sat. No further words were mentioned regarding the Walsh issue until their first course had been served and the wine ordered.

"How do you propose to settle this matter?" asked Hahn.

"What I propose is this. We are each at the head of large and vulnerable organisations. We are faced with threats that other, shall we say more conventional organisations, do not have to face? We are each in a position to do the other considerable and very possibly permanent harm."

"Agreed," said Hahn.

Wynter continued as if he had heard nothing. "What would be the point? There would be only losers and possibly no winners if you and I declared war on each other. My proposals, I hope you will agree, will go a very long way to putting everything right between us."

Wynter stopped talking as the waiter removed their plates and served the next course. When he had gone it was Hahn's turn to gain some control. He caught Wynter off guard.

"I wait to hear your proposals with some interest. However, you don't get a chance to tell me about them unless you have what I asked for."

"I have the items you requested. They're in my room."

"Go get them now. We don't talk until I see them."

Wynter could see that Hahn was serious but he felt it was rude of Hahn to interrupt the meal. Nevertheless, he realised that he had no choice. He rose without another word and returned in a few minutes clutching a leather briefcase. He sat, opened the case and retrieved a brown envelope, a newspaper and a smaller white envelope. He pushed them across the table to Hahn. Hahn stopped eating. He opened the brown envelope first, then the white one. He left the newspaper till last.

"You'll find what you're looking for on page three," said Wynter.

Hahn laid out the newspaper, the shots of Walsh's dead body and the four floppy disks on the table. For a moment this surprised Wynter, who felt this somewhat indiscreet. It wasn't until this moment that he realised that they were almost alone. All the other diners were seated at the far side of the restaurant. The waiters kept a discrete distance but didn't take their eyes off the two men in case one wanted something. It became obvious to Wynter that this particular stage had been set by Hahn. But of course it would be. This was Hahn's territory and Wynter was the stranger.

"Thank you Mr Wynter. Please tell me about your ideas."

"Your two and a half million pounds deposit has been returned to you along with the interest you would have earned had the money been in your bank rather than mine."

Hahn nodded in what appeared to be appreciation at this small courtesy. Wynter went on.

"I have arranged for an old friend of mine to expect a call from you. He operates an organisation in Czechoslovakia. On your word he will arrange to transport the arms you require."

"The cost?" said Hahn.

"I am aware that the loss of the arms as promised by Mr Walsh may have caused you some inconvenience and embarrassment. My friend will send his account to me. There will be no charge to you. Please view this as a gesture of good faith."

"Now why would you want to do that, Mr Wynter?" said Hahn with poorly hidden suspicion.

"I and my organisation have an enviable reputation. This reputation we have guarded zealously over many years. You have it in your power to damage our reputation considerably. I would not like that, Mr Hahn. Furthermore I will not allow it." At this point the charm and smile evaporated. His tone became grave. "I will do whatever it takes to ensure our reputation remains intact. Whatever it takes, Mr Hahn, whatever it takes. Now you choose which way you want it played." Wynter's smile returned. "Your American steaks really are very good. I sometimes find it quite difficult to get the steaks I want in England." From the corner of his eye Wynter could see the American smile.

"Leo Salmon said you had style. I accept your proposals. I do, however, have one last question. I have here four disks. Are these the only disks?" He paused and smiled again. "I guess that was a stupid question." Wynter's face was expressionless except for his right eyebrow, which raised slightly. "Well, Mr Wynter, you take real good care of my disks."

The two men finished their meal with hardly another word. Oddly, each was enjoying the other's company. At the end of the meal they walked to a lounge where they ordered coffee and cigars and the rest of the evening was spent in cordial conversation.

Finally Hahn rose. "It's been a pleasure meeting you, Mr Wynter." He held out his hand. "I consider the matter closed. However, I would like to think that we may find we can help each other in the future. Perhaps there will be opportunities of mutual interest and benefit."

"Mr Hahn, I wouldn't want it any other way. Good day to you."

Hahn smiled and nodded. He turned to leave but before taking a step he seemed to have an afterthought. "One more question, please."

Wynter nodded.

"Something puzzles me. Why did your people go to the trouble of trying to lift the Erifian hardware? It now seems you could have sourced them in Czechoslovakia from the outset. I don't understand."

Wynter didn't answer at once. He knew Hahn's question was reasonable and obvious. Eventually he said, "Walsh wanted to make a name for himself. His choice was consistent with his cavalier self image. I let him have his head to demonstrate my trust in him and in his judgment." Wynter paused and shook his head slowly. "I was in error."

Hahn nodded again and left.

Ron Markham was based in a series of dreary offices in Basingstoke in Hampshire. On a dull, cold and overcast morning, his office seemed even less appealing than usual. Personal touches were kept to a minimum since most expressions of personal taste or interests were frowned upon. Creative instincts and energies were channelled in altogether a different direction. Markham was a senior case officer with the Investigation Department of the Security Directorate with special responsibilities for G.C.H.Q. On this particular morning even his strong coffee and cigarette were having little success in cheering him up. He was rather glad when there was a knock on his door, a knock that might just bring the promise of a diversion. He raised his voice to indicate that the person standing outside should enter.

Liam Harris, a young case officer attached to security, entered.

"Morning, guv," said Harris in a much too cheery way for Markham. However, Markham was not, by nature, a miserable man and with a little effort he managed a smile.

"Come on in and help yourself to a coffee."

The newcomer did as he was invited. He sat down. "We got us a potential situation, guv."

"Oh? Do tell, Liam." Now Markham's spirits were most definitely rising.

"I've been looking at a guy called Stephen Wells in Cheltenham."

"Routine or instigated?"

"Instigated. It appears Wells has been having an unusual number of overseas trips over the last few years."

"So?"

"Not holiday fortnights. The odd couple of days here and three days there."

"Okay," said Markham as he sat forward in his chair.

"His last short trip was to the States. That in itself might be suggestive but there's more. He bought his ticket with a cloned credit card. He has two credit cards of his own, yet didn't use them. When he has a break, it tends to be at very short notice. Wells' salary is forty-seven thousand a year. He lives in a fairly fashionable area, has lots of holidays, and a recent house extension. He runs a Scorpio at the moment but he's had three fairly high quality cars in the last seven years. His wife runs a two year old Golf. Now I reckon he could just about afford it, but there'd be precious little to spare. His missus only works part time. All in all, I think we have enough to dig a bit deeper, especially because our colleagues at Gatwick clocked Wells. I've seen the video and I'd swear it's him. Funny thing, though. We tracked his journey and the passport of Stephen Wells didn't show anywhere. What do you reckon?"

"What do you need, Liam?"

"I don't want to go overboard yet. I'd like a little look inside his home."

"Well, you know the rules. You take great care. Let me know what you find."

Gaining entry to Wells' home was simplicity itself. The front door was not visible from the road. When Wells was at work, Harris merely watched and waited until his wife left. He followed her and saw her enter an out-of-town superstore. He watched her collect a trolley that indicated she had popped in for more than a tin of beans. Harris then doubled back and gained entry by the simple expedient of buckling one of the doors of the French windows at the rear of the house. By inserting a jemmy or the blade of a spade it is an easy matter to buckle one of the windows so that it pops open. He was relieved but not surprised that the alarm didn't sound. Even when burglar alarms are fitted, women, Mrs Wells included, rarely activate them when they go shopping. This omission is a matter of some concern to insurance companies the world over.

With great dexterity Harris searched the house in a well-practised and systematic way. The desk took less than forty seconds and he missed nothing of interest. The sitting room took a similar time. The kitchen, as always, took slightly longer. Then to the master bedroom where Harris found a tin in less than ten seconds. It took him seven minutes to count £19,600 in £50, £20 and £10 notes. In Wells' sock drawer he found his passport. Stamps contained within confirmed the trips already identified.

"Got you," muttered Harris, wondering why Wells had not used this passport on his latest trip.

Back at Markham's office, Harris and his boss pored over a sheet of calculations.

"Well, in theory it's possible, I suppose," mused Markham.

"Oh come on," Liam said. He's on forty-seven thousand a year. We've checked with probate. No inheritances for him or his wife. The cars! I wish I could afford flash motors like him. And holidays, I'm lucky if I get a week away and the best I can manage is the Costa Del Lager. That bastard's on the take. I'm sure of it."

"I think there's every chance you're right, but remember, proof you don't have. I'll have a word with Cheltenham and ask them to filter his workload, while you, my dear friend, watch him. Don't let him out of your sight for a minute. Your report will be required to account for his every movement. I don't want him to fart without you knowing about it. Don't forget he's careless. He doesn't know you're onto him. The cash filled biscuit tin tells us that. Keep it that way for now. Remember also that careless people usually live unstructured lives. That could well be his downfall but there is a downside to it. Unstructured people can also be unpredictable. This thing could come back and bite you on your ass. You and I can both do without an investigation on us. Questions?" Harris shook his head. "Okay, let's go for it, condition amber."

"Thanks, guv." This last piece of information pleased Harris. It was the first time he had been given operational control of a condition amber. The colour denoted the level of priority and the level of resources in terms of man hours, equipment and expenses. It also told him what level of intervention was permitted without seeking authority from above. Amber was good, it enabled him a certain latitude, and this was something Harris was going to enjoy.

The young case officer was able to assemble a team of eight staff officers and four cars within thirty minutes. He sat the eight round a table and started his briefing.

Clifford Morley Hospital

On Thursday morning Julie telephoned David Ginsberg.

"A result for me?" was all she said after having introduced herself.

"Ready for collection and complete."

She took the train from Tewkesbury's new station to Paddington. By lunchtime she was at Ginsberg's workshop. First he showed her the Type 67, for which he had also been able to acquire 30 rounds. These, Julie knew, would need the insertion of mercury she had given the other bullets not so many days before. Next he handed her a nine-millimetre Glock 19. It was obvious however, he was keeping the best till last.

Finally, Ginsberg said, "And what do you think of this?"

He opened a box and removed a hand-machined, single shot handgun. It was sealed to prevent the emission of sound from around a chamber. On the workbench next to the gun he laid a silencer. It was the size of an aerosol can of hair spray. He stood back to admire his work and, at the same time, to ensure that Julie was also admiring it. He picked up the gun and the silencer and carefully inserted the muzzle into the base of the silencer.

"Now don't forget. This will be as close to silent as technology will allow. The bad news is that you will have to be close to your target. There is no sight, no real way to aim it. Just point in the general direction of your target and hope for the best. I expect you will convert the bullets?" The old man looked at Julie with a serious expression. She nodded.

"Good." His sombre mood changed abruptly. "Now go and try it. Go on!" He was excited.

Julie allowed herself to be led by Ginsberg to a range at the back of the workshop. He closed the door behind them. Julie did not need instruction to load the gun. To her it came as second nature. At the far end of the range was a railway sleeper on which Ginsberg had erected a line of grapefruit. Julie aimed. Despite her specification and Ginsberg's promise of silence, she was amazed. The sound was less than she would have expected from an air gun. She missed the first grapefruit but noted, from the hole which had appeared in the sheet hanging behind the targets, that the bullet had been left and low. Julie made a mental adjustment. The next three grapefruit she killed.

It was rare for a hospital in a small town to have an accident and emergency unit. The Clifford Morley Hospital was an exception. During the cuts of the 80's and 90's the hospital continued to find funding support for its accident and emergency department because it was situated in a small but busy market town - busy, that is, on market days and at weekends. The town supported many pubs, a feature of small, country, market towns. The pubs ensured that on market day and at weekends the A & E department was busy. In any case, the distance between the town and major hospitals in Swindon or Bristol was much too far for the available ambulance cover.

So it was that the Clifford Morley Hospital retained its A & E department. Known locally as Cliffs, the hospital was highly regarded by the community.

It was because it was so busy during certain times of the week that Julie chose it. She knew that there are more incidents of violence when drinkers leave pubs than when they are inside the premises. She waited, on this Saturday night, until 11 o'clock. It was no accident she also chose an evening when England's soccer team was playing Germany's national side at Wembley. She was delighted to learn that Germany beat England by three goals to one. Her joy at this news was not based on any particular love for Germans or any particular anti-English feeling. She knew that there would be many soccer supporters who would be drowning their sorrows. To start drinking when in a negative frame of mind would likely produce aggression. Had England won, then the drinking would have been in celebration and bonhomie would be the more likely outcome. The general mood around town was very much in her favour.

She was sitting in a lay-by a few yards from the hospital's main entrance waiting for yet another ambulance. She had expected a large police presence on the streets that evening and so she was not in the least ruffled to see police vehicles on many of the town's intersections. At ten minutes past eleven she saw an ambulance. She followed it up the drive of the hospital and parked her hire car, this time a Vauxhall Astra, in the doctor's car park. She quickly put on a white coat to which was pinned an official looking name badge. A stethoscope around her neck completed the illusion that Julie was a doctor.

As the paramedics were unloading their patient to be wheeled into A & E, Julie walked briskly around the back of the ambulance and straight into the casualty department. As she had expected, the department was bedlam. Every bed was occupied as the staff tended the wounded. The waiting room was full and two patients were lying on trolleys in a corridor. Julie read the names on the green plastic panels screwed to the doors. Soon she found what she was looking for, "Resuscitation Room." She walked in and, somewhat to her relief, found that not a single person gave her more than a first glance.

Scanning the wall cupboards she saw the second sign she was after. It read "Intravenous."

"Doctor. Over here, please."

Julie turned to find a doctor calling to her. He was bent over a still body lying on a table. "I'll be right with you."

"Now, Doctor!"

Julie ignored this instruction. She opened the cupboard, which, during times of intense activity, she knew would be unlocked. Her eyes scanned the boxes until she found a brown, square box marked KCl. This was the potassium chloride she needed. She grabbed the box, which contained ten vials. Two shelves down in the same cupboard she found a transparent plastic box containing ten-millimeter hypodermic needles and two plastic boxes further along she found the needles with the orange, plastic collars. The colour told her that these were a fine calibre.

"Doctor!" yelled the angry voice from behind. "I've got a bleeder here."

"You certainly have, Doctor."

With that Julie walked briskly to the exit door. As she passed through it she heard the doctor say, "Find out who that is, will you?" But it was much too late. By the time anyone had been able to extricate themselves from their cases, Julie was in her car and driving too quickly out of the hospital.

At an informal, internal enquiry held later that night, the doctor was able to describe the mystery doctor. She had ginger hair, green eyes and was overweight. What he actually said was, "bloody rude and had a fat ass." Nothing was thought to be missing and no patients had been exposed to the intruder and so it was decided to let the matter drop. To pursue it would inevitably mean the mystery would become public.

By the time all this was considered, Julie had arrived in London. To start and finish a specific operation in London gave her a sense of cover and security. She always felt she could lose herself there and the capital provided her with a cloak of invisibility. On this occasion, however, she had a purpose other than returning the hired Astra.

After handing the car back, she found a public lavatory that was still open despite the late hour. Unsavoury though she found this, it provided an opportunity for her to change her identity. She locked herself in a cubicle and removed the oversized shirt and bra and the packs of foam rubber. These she replaced with a bra that fitted and a cream silk blouse. She was grateful to take off the huge jeans and the padding that made her very hot. Apart from the temperature, they were uncomfortable and inconvenient. She changed into French knickers and tight Armani jeans. The sensible flat shoes she replaced with brown Chelsea boots. Off came the ginger wig and she shook her own dark hair to loosen it before brushing it vigorously. All this was stuffed into a suitcase. Finally she put on a sheepskin lined flying jacket and then listened at the cubicle door. There were no sounds so she took a minor chance and left the cubicle going to the washbasins over which were screwed mirrors.

She placed a makeup bag on the vanity unit next to a wash basin. Bending over the basin, she removed first one green contact lens then the other. Quickly adjusting her makeup she hurried to leave this sordid place. She would have a long bath and put her makeup on properly when she found a hotel.

It took her thirty minutes or more to find the small, inconspicuous sort of hotel she was looking for. She booked in, signing the register in the name of Helen Smith. Her room was comfortable enough, although not to the standard to which she was used. Never mind, it would do nicely for now. The bath was her next task and then to bed. It was late now and it had been a long day.

She slept until eleven the next morning. She felt refreshed but ravenous. As soon as she had bathed, applied her makeup and dressed, she left the hotel. She bought the Sunday Times and soon found herself a greasy spoon which she thought would be sure to serve the kind of breakfast that dieticians and health bores warned about. She was used to being the centre of attraction in places like this and this morning was no exception. She sat at a table that had a view of the window, ate a wonderful breakfast and read her newspaper. She drank several mugs of tea, after all of which she felt thoroughly indulged.

Julie spent the remainder of the day reading, relaxing and drinking in the hotel bar in the evening. The restaurant provided little promise but she decided to give it a go rather than take the trouble to go out. It was a decision she soon regretted. The food was something less than average and there was no one else in the restaurant. It was as if the chef was getting his own back for being made to cook this Sunday evening. After eating very little, Julie went to the bar again. This too was uninspiring and she retired early.

She awoke to a fine morning. The sun was shining through a cloudless sky and it was cold. Breakfast at the hotel was a much more fulfilling experience than the previous evening's dinner. But then, she thought, they probably had more practice at breakfasts. This was, after all, a down-market, commercial hotel. But it was clean, quiet and warm and that was exactly what she was looking for on this occasion. After the third slice of toast she went to her room and packed. She now had several hours to kill.

Her first stop was Euston Station, where she was able to hire another car. The choice was not great but she was able to rent a Renault Clio, admirable for her purposes. Her papers indicated that her name was Helen Smith and she paid with a credit card in the name of Helen Smith. Leaving her luggage in the car, she walked away from the station. She could now indulge herself in one of her favourite pastimes, shopping. It was three in the afternoon by the time she returned to the Clio. By ten past she was heading westward towards the M40.

She wanted to reach the Vine Tree Inn in Little Appleton by 5.30 that afternoon. Little Appleton is a village some fifteen miles from Oxford. It is off the beaten track and exclusive. There is no local authority housing in Little Appleton. Most of the residents commute to London, Oxford or Birmingham, while some work from their homes. The village, surrounded by fields, boasts one church, one pub, the Vine Tree Inn and a well-patronised restaurant specialising in foods of Olde England. She found the pub within seven minutes of her anticipated arrival time. As she drove through the village the pub lay to her right. She drove straight past and found a gateway in which to turn. She returned the way she had come until she found the lay-by she had spotted earlier. In here she parked facing back towards Little Appleton. This was the kind of lay-by created when corners on old roads are straightened, leaving a kind of oxbow. There were trees on the reservation between the road and the lay-by that provided adequate cover.

Now all she had to do was wait. She smiled to herself as she considered her current position. At the moment Julie appeared as herself but her name on this occasion was Claire Noble. In her handbag she carried a selection of credit and charge cards in the name of Claire Noble. Her Dunhill cigarette lighter was engraved with the name Claire Noble. The initials CN appeared on the leather purse that contained a large amount of cash and Claire Noble's driving licence. She liked the name Claire, it suited her, she thought. This was not a busy road and Julie knew she would not miss the car she was looking for. Despite it now being dark, she could see the rear of cars as they passed the village end of the lay-by. There was a slight bend at this point and a rural road light which conveniently illuminated index numbers. It didn't pass her until 6.57 p.m. The Clio left the lay-by and followed the big BMW. She remained out of sight of the car and breathed a sigh of relief when she saw it parked in the car park at the front of the Vine Tree. As she pulled in, the tall, athletic and bronzed Chris Latcham was getting out. Cool, she thought.

She followed him into the pub and when it was her turn to be served, she asked for a tomato juice. She knew she had about half an hour in which to drink it. Twenty five minutes later she drained the remnants of the drink and left. Five minutes later, the BMW driver came out. Without hesitation he approached her when he saw a beautiful woman struggling with her broken car. Julie had been pleased to notice that this man had been eyeing her up in the pub. She knew he had an impressive record of womanising and he would not be able to resist her charms. Or at least that was the plan.

The Clio's bonnet was up and Julie was peering into the engine compartment.

"Hello. Can I help you?"

Julie smiled. "I don't know. It won't start. Do you know anything about cars?"

"Just a little perhaps. Let's have a look." Now there were two people peering under the bonnet.

"I just drove it here and it was fine. Now it just won't start."

"Try now," said the tall man in the expensive suit. Latcham had fiddled with some wires. When she tried the ignition there was still no life.

Latcham went to the passenger door, opened it and felt under the glove box where he found the fuse box. Julie watched him fiddle around some more.

Five minutes later he looked up at her. "A fuse. That was all. Try her now."

The Clio fired first time.

"What a relief. I'm so grateful. Thank you so much. I don't know what I would have done if you hadn't come by. Look, can I buy you a drink?

It's the least I can do." Julie gave the smile which was, to most, utterly irresistible.

"I've got a better idea. Let me buy you a drink."

Her intelligence had been accurate. This guy was a sucker for a pretty girl. The two were well matched, both being taller than average, both well dressed and both well tanned. They went back into the pub.

A week and a half earlier, Claire Noble had walked into an estate agency in Bristol. Filton was an area renown throughout the world for its aviation heritage. It was not a district which, under normal circumstances, would have attracted her. However, quality of life was not the first item on her agenda now. More important was anonymity and access. Filton was close to the M4, the main artery running from South Wales to London. A little further to the west was the access to the M5 that could take her to the north or the far West Country. For the purpose of quick transportation, Filton was ideal.

The agent Charles Weaver, a man in his late forties, fell over himself to assist this beautiful and charming woman. He was immediately able to clear a window in his diary and show her around three apartments that were available to let at that very moment. Julie turned down the first two. The third was a spacious furnished flat which, Julie explained, was exactly what she was looking for. In response to the agent's request, Julie provided references. It took a week for the agreement to be signed and the first three months rent and a rather weighty deposit was settled with her credit card. The keys became available two days later. Julie collected them from the agent.

She returned to the flat, opened the door and shuddered. This was not at all her style. Still, it would suit the needs of the next week or two admirably. When she entered the sitting room she noticed a bottle of champagne on the coffee table against which was propped an envelope. It contained a welcome card from Weaver wishing her happiness in her new home. Julie wondered how many of his clients received similar treatment.

Chris Latcham was a perfect gentleman. He was charming and urbane. He treated her to wine and when he suggested they should have dinner together at the Mill House restaurant in the village, she protested not at all. Unlike previous occasions she was enjoying the drink and felt no need to pour it into the flask she often carried in her bag when she was working. In any event, the flask was not accompanying her to Little Appleton. They agreed to have one more drink before going to the restaurant. A previous phone call had ensured that a table was reserved in two hours time. They still had thirty minutes.

In response to Latcham's courteous questions, Julie had told him she was not working at the moment. She was financially well placed, having a modest private income and a rich uncle. Her uncle was pleased to provide her with work when she needed it, but she was not specific about the nature of this work. And where did she live? Well at the moment she had a flat in Filton. It wasn't ideal but she was trying to decide what to do with the next few years of her life and it would do for the time being. Maybe she would move to the sun.

She found that when she had questioned Latcham, his answers were ambiguous. He worked for a management consultancy. He helped major companies to put their commercial problems on an even keel. His areas of interest were financial, marketing and legal. When Julie pushed him for further explanation he equated his work to Newton's Third Law.

"To every action there is an equal and opposite reaction," said Julie with some pride.

Latcham laughed. "You've got it. That's what I do. In the world of commerce it is very similar. My job is to find reactions that will return things to the status quo. It's a question of balance really."

"It sounds fun," said Julie.

"It can be," he replied. "Shall we go to eat?"

Julie excused herself telling Latcham she needed the ladies room. It was intentional that she left her handbag open and next to his chair. It would be a simple matter for him to have a rummage in it without drawing attention to himself. Julie knew full well that at least Latcham would try to satisfy himself as to her identity. She knew she had provided plenty of evidence to satisfy his curiosity.

When she returned she was able to tell at a glance that her purse was a good two inches away from the location at which she had left it. Careless, she thought. She put this down to too much drink, too much excitement and very little time available in which to check her bag and identity.

The Mill House restaurant did not disappoint either Latcham or Julie. The crowning glory was the steak, kidney and oyster pie. The English wine was delightful and the company better.

They both knew that each had drunk far too much to drive. Julie knew that Latcham would have no alternative but to invite her back to his home for the night. She could not possibly drive to Bristol and he would not be able to suggest she booked into a hotel. That was her theory. If she had miscalculated she would find herself in an embarrassing situation. This she would like not one bit. As the meal neared its end, she was relieved when Latcham addressed the subject of the rest of the evening.

"Look," he said, "I live just around the corner. My house is big, my hospitality famous and you've had a little too much to drink. May I respectfully suggest you stay at my home this evening? If that sounds a little presumptuous you have the choice of three guest bedrooms." Latcham laughed again. His smile appeared genuine and good-natured.

Julie was pleased to accept his offer of hospitality. They left both cars in the Vine Tree car park and walked the short way to Latcham's house after first collecting a small valise from the Clio. It was warm and comfortable inside the house. It was also obvious to Julie that someone else did Chris Latcham's housework. The place was spotless. A busy working man like Latcham would not have the time to keep such a large home in this order. Julie surprised herself when she agreed to more wine. On the other hand, she was not surprised to find herself responding when Latcham kissed her. It was but a short step to the bedroom. The sex was good and the sleep was satisfying.

When Julie awoke the following morning, Latcham was not beside her. She knew that he would have been up before her to give himself the opportunity to check out her handbag properly along with her valise and possibly her car as well. This she had intended. It wasn't long before she heard footsteps on the stairs. As he entered the bedroom he smiled.

"I assume it must be tea for an English rose?"

"You assume right," she replied.

"I've got to get off to work soon. But I really want to see you again. Last night was special and you are special, and I don't say this to every woman I meet. I really do want to see you again. What do you think?"

"I want to see you again too." Julie flashed her eyes and followed this with the demure look.

The two agreed that they should meet again on Friday. Despite her professional requirements, Julie felt the butterflies in her stomach. This job really has its good points, she thought. She was going to look forward to the weekend.

Pay Back Time

Frank Miles was typical of farmers in the west of England. He had inherited more than 1000 acres when his mother died. She had inherited it, in her time, from her father. In fact the land had been in the family for more generations than Frank knew. He was born to the land, knew little else and cared to do nothing else. Despite many of the pressures exerted on farmers by the general economic climate in recent years and in particular the Common Agricultural Policy, Frank was doing as well as he always had. He and his wife, Trudy, knew little of hardship and they lived the lives of relatively prosperous farmers. Beef scares and the occasional, inevitable blips that affected the livestock markets affected Frank not at all. He concentrated his efforts on arable farming. He avoided tying himself into contracts with large supermarkets. He avoided monopsony markets like the plague. He had seen his peers tied into these contracts where they had had to cut their prices to the bone after they had turned their backs on their traditional outlets. They could not regain their old customers and found themselves stuck with the supermarkets. Often the quality, size and delivery contract requirements along with the prices imposed on them took these farmers to the wall or close to it. Once or twice Frank had been courted by the corporate buyers. They approached with attractive offers, which at the time seemed like madness to reject. Frank was able to resist.

He diversified his crops from artichokes to barley. Half of his land was turned over to soft fruits and he found the concept of "pick your own" to be extremely profitable. He liked the idea of customers picking their own strawberries, tayberries and raspberries because his harvesting labour costs were next to nothing. In addition he enjoyed arrangements with several market traders who bought vegetables and fruit from him. He even exported artichokes to France, which seemed paradoxical to him. Nevertheless, he was never able to fulfil all the enquiries he received each season. Brand or supplier loyalty and the laws of supply and demand were instinctive for him. He had not studied such matters at college. His judgment, which he often described as luck, always ensured that his farm did well.

In fact, had it not been for one small matter, Frank's life would have been perfect. For all the blessings bestowed on him, he had a cross to bear. Trudy, his wife of over forty years, was a bad-tempered, interfering and rarely satisfied harpy. She nagged him from breakfast to bedtime. In order to survive in this atmosphere of constant harassment he had evolved a series of coping strategies. Mainly these involved staying out of his wife's way. Market days were easy to arrange. The company of other farmers was easy. Then there was the pub. He spent as much time in a pub as possible. He rarely appeared drunk, but at any time of the day or night he would have been unlikely to pass a breath test.

Frank's problem was compounded because the farm, Jollies Farm, was some seven miles from Cheltenham. By Cotswold standards it was isolated and some way from a bus route. Having said this, however, it is unlikely that Frank would have taken a bus even had one been available. He drove himself to the various pubs he patronised in his old and battered Land Rover. It was a miracle in the eyes of some that he had not had an accident or been breathalized, until recently. Six months previously he had been stopped by the police while driving home from the pub. He had been three times over the limit. His solicitor had told the court that he needed to drive in order to conduct his business. The magistrates had been unimpressed and imposed a two year driving ban along with a fine of £400.

At the head of the huge table at the Sedona ranch sat Webster Hahn. Also seated were Hahn's remaining son Joseph, Ollie Goldstein and Michael Charlton. Each man had updated Webster and the performance reports were encouraging. They reached the point on the agenda when any other business was addressed.

"All matters relating to the late delivery of our arms have now been concluded." Webster Hahn turned to Michael Charlton, the oldest of his management team. "Michael, tell your West Coast contacts that their merchandise is now in the country. Ollie, you do the same with your people. Make no apologies for the delay. Make no mention of our problems. It's enough to tell them their guns are here. Do the business, gentlemen.

"And now to another matter. Ricky's death was a great sadness for me, as I know it was for you. But Ricky was impetuous. He didn't think. One day someone was going to hit him. Chip was different. Chip didn't hurt anyone. If he iced someone it was for legitimate business reasons. He was almost a civilian and was of great value to me and our organisation. Now he too is dead. It was unnecessary. It was vindictive and it was not business."

Hahn waited for his words to sink in. He watched Joseph, who was looking at his lap.

"Chip and Ricky," he continued, "were killed by Albert Rocchiciolli."

At first there was the silence of disbelief. Then a murmur of anger and surprise started. Hahn held up his hand to restore the silence.

"He killed Chip through vicious vindictiveness. I want the son of a bitch. I want his stinking head on a plate."

"Who was Rocchiciolli working for?" asked Joseph.

"That doesn't matter," replied Hahn.

"It matters to me. Who was he working for?"

"Joseph, I understand your anger and grief. He was working for someone who had no choice in the case of Ricky. I'm satisfied it was business. Ricky left him no choice. Joseph, you will not interfere. Is that understood?" When there was no response from Joseph, he raised his voice further and slammed his hand on the table. "Is that understood?"

"No, Father. Ricky was my brother. He was family, one of us. Someone has to pay. Our people will expect it. If we fail to respond to this, we'll lose our credibility and strength."

Hahn could feel that control was slipping away from him. Joseph was known for levelheadedness and objectivity and his behaviour now seemed out of character. But Hahn knew he had a point. Hahn's temper subsided and he spoke quietly.

"Joseph, I know that you're right. I know who commissioned Rocchiciolli and I know why. It was business. Unfortunately Rocchiciolli acted on his own when he killed Chip. Chip was not a target. He was not a hit."

Hahn paused here to gather his thoughts. He felt he needed to regain control. "Soon, Joseph, you will become head of our organisation. I'm getting old and you're getting wiser. You have the trust of our people and the people we do business with. Everyone trusts you and respects your judgment. I want you to trust my judgment now. I've spoken to the man who ordered Ricky's death. I believe he had no choice in this matter. I also believe that, if we go to war with this man, we may destroy ourselves and all we've worked for. This would not be a war with another family. This would be a war with an empire with resources greater even than our own. At best, a war would be wasteful. At worst, it could destroy us all. Now, Joseph, I beg you to trust me this one time."

Joseph's eyes were wild and he held his head high in a gesture of defiance. Gradually his father's words had their effect and his shoulders dropped. For a moment he stared at the floor as if in shame. "Father I'm sorry to offend you this way. I know you know best and of course I trust your judgment. I will accept your decision and I will not ask you again for the name of this man. If, however, I ever find that he has damaged our interests in any other way, I tell you now, I will take matters into my own hands."

Joseph was behaving himself much to Hahn's relief.

"Thank you, Joseph. You're a man of stature and sense. I'll feel easy when you take the head of our organisation. When the day comes for you to take over, I will tell you who ordered Ricky's hit. I believe this man will become a help to you. There will be much you can do together. But the choice will be yours. Now, that scum Rocchiciolli. I want him dead. I want him dead now."

"He's doing a small job for me right now," said Joseph. He looked embarrassed and fidgeted with his discomfort.

"I know. It's reasonable you use him, he's always been professional and reliable. Now I want him dead. Let him complete his work for you. He won't expect a hit. Let him finish and then you dust him. Make sure that everyone knows he's been killed. People will draw their own conclusions. They'll believe we've done this thing but you will ensure there is nothing to bring the police to our door. I want that scum-sucking bastard dead."

It took Sir Gordon Melville seventeen minutes and fourteen seconds from entering the Rural Development Service building to being conducted into Sir Harry Buchanan's office by Margaret. The two knights shook hands and Margaret departed to make the coffee.

"The P.M. is a mite fretful," Sir Gordon said. "He wants to know how we're getting on. Harry, forgive the intrusion, but I need to take something back. Perhaps you can give me something to put his mind at rest?"

Harry laughed. "I love to see others under pressure. It was the P.M. himself who dropped himself into something nasty. That point will not have missed him, I suspect." The big man paused to give himself time to compose an appropriate response to Melville's question. "Tell him that stage one is complete and successful. The next stage requires some setting up. It needs to be coordinated. The timing has to be right or it could set off a chain reaction leading right back to Downing Street. I'm confident, however, that all will be in place within the next few weeks."

"Who are you using, Harry? Our people or contractors?"

"Oh come on, Gordon. You know better than that. I'm using appropriate resources. Appropriate in as much as the assets I am using stand the greatest chance of getting this very complex job done. Appropriate in as much as the assets are the most likely to keep the P.M. in the clear. That's as much as you get."

This appeared to satisfy the cabinet secretary. He drank his coffee and returned to his office. Harry was left slumped in his chair. He was not feeling well. The ache in his back had returned and he was beginning to think he would not last the course. This gave him concern, not so much for his own life but because he had no idea who could take over the operation and who would look after the Clarion Resource. He had toyed with the idea of telling Clarion but had rejected this, for the time being at least. If he left the picture she would be on her own. Harry knew that she, of all people, was well able to look after her own back. Inevitably she would hear of Harry's death and would be able to take whatever steps she saw appropriate at that time.

"Yes, poppet. You'd be on your own," Harry said aloud.

Two days later, Joseph Hahn was eating a solitary dinner at Monty's, his favourite downtown restaurant. It was uncharacteristically quiet this evening and Joseph wondered if it might be the big ball game on television. In any case he was happy not to be exposed to the trials of others talking and laughing. He was pensive. He felt uneasy about the way the Old Man was handling the family affairs. He also missed his kid brother, which was something he could not have said often during Ricky's life time. Joseph yearned for the day when his father handed the business to him. While the Old Man had been a great leader and organiser, building the business into an empire, Joseph felt he was softening now. Maybe he was too old. Maybe he couldn't take the pressure anymore. It was surely time for him to retire and take things easy. Great men knew the right time to quit.

The maitre d'hotel approached Joseph. He bent low and whispered into Joseph's ear. Joseph looked around at the other diners enjoying Monty's excellent food. He cleared his throat and said to the waiter, "Show him over."

Two minutes later the maitre d' walked back to the table followed by Albert Rocchiciolli. Rocchiciolli looked uneasy.

"Sit down, Albert."

The waiter pulled a chair out for the newcomer.

"How'd you find me here?" Joseph knew that Albert would be wary. He would not expect the family to be aware that he had killed Ricky and Chip. But he would be wary just in case. He would be looking for any sign of danger and Joseph was not going to give away anything that might rattle him. Joseph also suspected that Albert had been trailing him for an hour or two, just as a precaution.

"Your boys told me you were here," said Albert.

Liar, thought Joseph. The only people who knew he was at Monty's were two of his bodyguards, one of which was out in the car. The other was eating alone at a table close to the door. Joseph was not surprised to find that both his men were now inside the restaurant watching Albert closely. Joseph raised a finger to suggest to his two men that they could stand down, but not too much.

"What do you want, Albert? You got something for me?"

A brown envelope crossed the table. Joseph put down his fork and opened the envelope.

"What's the story?"

"You were right about the kid. He was passing information to the cops in return for favours and dope. That picture you got there is Sergeant MacCarthy handing the kid some crack. Seems the kid told MacCarthy that you were having problems with your San Francisco operations. He also told them that you and Leo Salmon worked together." Rocchiciolli paused to see if this news caused Joseph to look up. There was no reaction at all and Albert relaxed a little. "You want me to fix the kid?"

"No. Leave him to me." Joseph smiled at Albert. "Thanks for getting this so quick."

Joseph picked up his fork again and started to eat. Rocchiciolli knew this was a sign for him to leave. As he left the restaurant, Joseph gave a single nod to the suit at the table by the door. The suit rose, whispered to the maitre d', who in turn looked at Joseph. Joseph nodded to indicate he would pay for the meal.

Albert's Jaguar was not difficult to follow. To ensure that the same car stayed behind him for only a short distance, a carefully practised routine came into operation. The routine was only feasible since the advent of the mobile phone. Thirty years previously, a coordinated relay tail was not possible. Albert went straight to a health club. He took a steam bath and then a swim in the large but nearly unused swimming pool. With a slow, rhythmical, powerful stroke, Albert swam length after length. As he was completing his swim, the one Hahn car outside the health club was joined by three others. Two men entered the reception area. One went to talk to the receptionist, a young woman who quickly appeared agitated. The other entered the health complex. He looked into the gym, stream room and sauna before he saw Albert walking to a changing cubicle. When Albert had shut the door, the man walked briskly towards it. He kicked the door open. Albert was naked and partly turned to see what had happened.

"Nah, don't turn round. You got a cute ass, Al. Got a message for you from Mr Joseph Hahn. He says you got a choice. Who got you to ice Ricky? Your choice is this. If you don't tell, then, well, I got to lower you into an acid tank, feet first. You'll disappear real slow. They tell me people don't die until the acid reaches their balls. Guess you won't be doing much kicking by then." The suit laughed at his own wit. "Or you can tell me now who ordered the contract. Who wanted Ricky out of the way? Tell me now and you might get to walk."

Albert Rocchiciolli was not a coward. He had never expected to die peacefully in his sleep. But now he was scared. He knew that this guy would not let him walk even if he told him about Grey. He felt vulnerable. He was a yard from his gun and he felt claustrophobic. The walls of the cubicle pressed in on him and there was nowhere to hide and nowhere to run. And his nakedness - that was it, it was his nakedness. He looked down at his body and tried to imagine it dissolving in acid. His only chance, no matter how slight, was to tell.

"It was a guy called Jonjo Grey. Big shot at Ribbon Motor Corporation. Ricky tried to hit Grey. Grey knew he would keep on till he got him. You satisfied now? Do I get to walk?" Rocchiciolli tried to turn enough to see the assailant.

"You wish."

Three bullets fired in quick succession thudded into Rocchiciolli's body. The assassin showed no sign of panic or rush. He closed the cubicle door, turned and walked back to the reception. The few people who were around took pains to be minding their own business as he passed. He collected his colleague in the reception area, and without a word they left the building.

It was a regular source of tension and frustration within the police department that when homicide officers came to take statements no one was able to give precise descriptions of the men. In fact, no two descriptions matched. There was no one who could remember a licence plate number and no one could say in which direction the men had left. The lieutenant knew that this file would remain open indefinitely. He was able to identify Albert Rocchiciolli from his possessions and he despatched two officers to his home address. By the time they reached it, they found a scene of devastation. The furniture had been ripped to pieces, every drawer was open and the contents strewn about the rooms. The desk had been ransacked and the computer disembowelled. It came as no surprise that no witnesses could be found.

The Tail

Sir Harry Buchanan had collated the information from the disks he had started reading in Julie's home. He had passed them to his lawyers and accountants. Sir Harry now had a use for them. He ensured that copies were properly stored in the registry and then made an appointment with his friends at Special Branch. It was this department within the Metropolitan Police Force that had sleepless nights worrying about the arrival of American organised crime in Britain. As far as Harry knew, things were quiet at the moment, but you could never be too careful. He had passed the disks to Special Branch and the commander had been grateful. If the Hahn family ever tried to gain a foothold in Britain, the authorities now had material that could be used to discourage the Americans. In any case, one never knew when one might require an edge. This kind of intelligence could be beyond price.

Julie Martin returned to her flat in Filton. She parked the hired Clio outside. She unlocked the flat door and opened it with great care. Before closing it behind her, she ran her hand along its top. Finding nothing, she knelt down to examine the carpet. It took her less than fifteen seconds to find what she had been looking for. There on the carpet, was the tiny red pebble she had placed on the door. This ploy told her that someone had been in the flat while she had been out.

When she checked the drawers in the single chest allowed by the landlord, she was not surprised to find that her clothes were not exactly as she had left them. Had Latcham moved this quickly? Julie was impressed. She was glad she had set the scene for him. She wanted a shower now above all things but resisted the temptation. She went back to the Clio and drove to Temple Meads Station. She went straight to the left luggage lockers and opened hers. She wanted to check, just to make sure, that the black holdall was still there. She did not dare hide her guns in the flat. She knew that no matter how creative she was in finding   a hiding place, it would be just a few minutes work for a professional to find the hardware. This was a risk she could not take even if it was inconvenient to keep them at the station.

She could now enjoy her shower. On her return she found there were no parking spaces. She cursed. It took her over twenty minutes of circling the block before a space became available. This was a good way to draw attention to herself. However, this was no bad thing considering the circumstances at the moment. She was, after all, a new resident. Eventually she unlocked her door again. This time the pebble was resting on the door where she had left it.

Julie enjoyed her hot shower and she returned to the sitting room. She still felt cold and turned on the gas fire. Just as she dropped the ice into the gin and tonic she had poured for herself, the phone rang. She had been hoping for this and she knew who it must be. Only one person knew of her location and her telephone number.

"Hello, Claire," Chris said. "I've been trying to call you all day."

Questions already, thought Julie.

"Hi, Chris. I've been out. How are you?"

"Good. I'm missing you."

Julie laughed. "You say the nicest things. I do hope you're not going to call Friday off."

"Not at all. I was just checking that you're still on for it?"

"Oh, you bet. Looking forward to it."

"Well, what do you think if I come to Bristol?"

As if you haven't been already, she thought. "Oh. I'd rather come to you. My flat isn't like your house, you know?"

"Okay. Suits me," replied Latcham.

"What do you want me to bring?"

"Just yourself and the clothes you stand in."

"I'm only coming if you let me take you out for dinner," she teased.

"You've got yourself a deal. See you Friday then."

Julie put the phone down. This was turning into fun.

The agenda for the following day, Thursday, was for Julie to establish her presence in the community. At least she thought it was a good excuse for a leisurely day and a browse. She took her morning coffee in the best café she could find, although she found it dreary and lacking in character. At least the coffee was fresh ground and high roast. She ordered a second cup that would accompany her to the end of the crossword. The rest of the morning, before finding a suitable venue for lunch, would be spent wandering the streets. There was little she could find to gladden her heart. Expectations for the following day became heightened. She would be pleased to run away from Filton.

As she walked past a cycle shop, she turned to her right and saw a man keeping pace with her on the other side of the road. This in itself was little to worry about but this man had been sitting in the corner of the coffee shop, she was sure of it. She hadn't been able to see his face in the café. It had been obscured by a tabloid newspaper. Even now she could see none of the features because the man's head was turned to his right, away from Julie. Further on she found a passageway on her left. She quickly turned down it. The walled passage was some two hundred yards long. Not a good place to find oneself at night, thought Julie. It was strewn with litter, empty cans, newspapers and the garbage of today's disposable society. She was struck by how sordid she found the path. It crossed her mind that this was a dreadful place in which to die.

Parked at the end of the passage was a Volvo estate car. Julie believed that there was one use for a Volvo. When clean, the slab sides provided a mirror. When she reached the car she bent down abruptly and feigned to tie a shoe lace. She was wearing Chelsea boots, but who cared? By lifting her eyes slightly she could she the reflection of the alley in the polished paintwork of the car. The alley was empty. All she could see was the rubbish. The council should clean that up, she said to herself. Perhaps the pressure of the last couple of weeks was getting to her. Now she was imagining things. Paranoia was setting in. She made a mental note to take a real holiday when this thing was over.

Half an hour later, she was sitting in a steak house. Passé though they were believed to be in some circles, Julie liked nothing more than a grilled steak and fries. She ordered a sirloin medium and a carafe of house red. She had a good idea what the wine would be like before it arrived. When it finally appeared she found her preconception had not been misplaced. But she enjoyed the sensation of straining the wine through her teeth. After paying for the lunch, she passed the payphone in the lobby. There was a taxi card pinned next to the phone, and on impulse she called the number.

The taxi arrived within ten minutes. It was the driver's lucky day. Julie ordered to be taken for a two-hour tour of Bristol, particularly the city centre. She promised him £50 and this was music to the ears of the driver. It was Thursday afternoon. The chances of getting another fare until the school runs was remote. The only fare he might pick up in this time would most likely be some old dear going shopping. Instead of a dull and profitless afternoon, he had this beauty in the back of his car for two whole hours. He was even getting paid for the privilege and, to cap it all, he would be back in time for the school runs.

Julie was going to break a golden rule. On this occasion she asked the driver to drop her off at the flat. This was a departure from the usual modus operandi, but her needs on this occasion were different. As they approached the flat, Julie spotted someone bending next to the Clio. From the distance she could see the man's hands pressed up against the front, passenger side window and forming a canopy over his eyes. By the time the taxi drew close, the man had started to walk away. The driver hesitated as he looked for somewhere to pull in.

"Just stop anywhere," said Julie with total calm. She fished in her pocket and pulled out five £10 notes. "Thanks for the ride."

"You're welcome, miss," replied the driver as he grabbed for the money. "Any time, love."

When Julie had straightened after leaving the taxi she looked towards her car. The man was nowhere to be seen. She flung her head high and quickened her pace. This paranoia would have to stop. She hummed to herself. The humming stopped when she found the pebble on the carpet again. She locked the door, changed into jeans and T-shirt, poured a gin and tonic and sat on the settee. She began to consider the options.

Chris Latcham was a busy man. His boss was dead and presumably some of his work load and responsibility would fall on Latcham's shoulders. Would he really go to the time and expense of checking out this casual relationship to this extent? Surely, after having checked her personal effects in Little Appleton and checking out her flat, that would have been enough. Maybe not. Maybe he was running scared. Or maybe she was flattering herself too much. Had Harry sent one of his own spooks to keep an eye on her? That was unlikely. The power of the Clarion Resource was that no one knew for sure of its existence. Harry would hardly risk exposing or compromising her.

Perhaps it was the police. Julie began to retrace her steps. She thought about her hire cars and false identities. She considered her disguises. Had she been traced back to her shop? No. If that was the case she would have known by now. There was her first visit to Tall Boys Hill. She had gone in her own car. Had someone linked her car to Walsh's murder? She had been parked at the top of the hill for some time. Could that be it? If it was, how then had they linked Julie Martin of Tewkesbury to Claire Noble of Filton? No, that wasn't it. Had she been followed from David Ginberg's? Was that the link? Not a chance.

Harry was playing with some very big boys here. Julie knew that much. Somehow they were onto her. Had Harry been made to expose her? He would never do that. But then Harry was capable of anything. Had she left clues at the hospital? No. It had to be Latcham. It could be no one else. Well, he would find nothing to hurt her in Filton. But if he was prepared to dig this deep at this early stage in their relationship, where would he stop? He would try to find a history and that would be difficult. This was getting messy.

Julie's instinct told her to go home. She might find a link there. Had she left something around that was enough to lead someone to Filton? But, with one or two exceptions, she kept her home and private life well away from her life as Clarion. The only thing she could think of was her equipment in the workshop in the garage. But in the unlikely event someone found that, she would argue that it was left over from her days as a member of a gun club before all handguns were outlawed in Britain. Ownership of the equipment she held in her garage was entirely legal but she made a mental note to remove it. She changed her mind; rushing off to the cottage was not a good idea. She could not take the Clio since she didn't want it linked to her or her home. Public transport would take hours to get her home. She would stay put. She was overreacting. Latcham was merely making sure of her bone fides and the truth was, that was good news. It meant he was really interested and that was just what she wanted. Clearly, because it was personal and not business, he was using a local man to check her out. Equally clearly the local man was not a professional. He was an amateur.

Next she wondered why the man who had been peering so intently into her car had disappeared so quickly. He must have realised that he had been seen. If that was the case, he would have had to have known that she was the driver of that particular car. That presupposed he had prior knowledge. That being the case, Julie must act as if she had seen nothing; she must act normally. What would be more normal than casually going out to dinner? She still didn't know the area and so it seemed natural to go to the steak house again. Julie changed and went out again after first putting her pebble on the door and checking the exact position of her clothes in the drawers.

As she ate her second steak of the day she began to relax. She decided she had been overreacting. But just in case she would be especially vigilant the next day. The evening passed without further sightings and Julie went to bed at peace with the world. Tomorrow was another day and she was looking forward to it. It was going to be a great weekend. What more could a girl ask for, sharing a weekend with an unattached and urbane guy like Latcham? It seemed almost a shame it was destined not to last.

At around the time that Julie was dropping off to sleep, Liam Harris knocked on the window of a Security Directorate car. The two men inside were not fully alert. They had been on shift for seven hours, five of which had been spent sitting in the car watching the front of Stephen Wells' house. One of the men pressed the central locking release and Harris climbed into the back seat.

"Anything?" asked Harris.

"Not a bloody thing. Quiet as the grave. Wells came home at 1800 hours. Hasn't been out since. His missus went out at 1945. The other car is watching her. Probably gone to W.I. Kids are out. You can see the target in the upstairs right window from time to time. He's in there all right."

"Jesus, you two. This is like a pigsty," said Harris in exasperation.

The man behind the steering wheel turned round to face Harris. "What?"

"I'll tell you what. Look at the fucking mess in here. Chip papers all over the floor, and what's this crap on the seat?" Harris gingerly lifted something. "Bloody hell. What is it?"

"Oh sorry, guv. Piece of fish. I chucked it there when Mrs Wells left. Forgot all about it."

"I bet you don't treat your own cars like this. It's bloody disgusting."

"Yeah. Sorry, guv. Anything on the line tap?"

"No. One outgoing call to his golfing mate. One incoming from his office. Routine call." Harris paused. "We think it was routine. Markham's checking it out now."

"How are we going to watch Wells at work?"

"I wanted to go in and baby-sit him. The powers that be said no. They reckon that any cover we come up with would be blown and scare Wells off. I expect they're right. Still, he can't do much without them knowing about it. His workload is screened and his phone is monitored."

"That's all well and good but his controller isn't going to contact him at work. Hello! What's this?"

Mrs Wells' Golf turned into the drive. There was a passenger in the front seat. As the car decanted its contents, the watchers could clearly see that the passenger was the daughter. The watchers made a note of the time of their return. It was 2216.

Julie arose early the following morning. It was dark and cold. Some people find the cold invigorating. Julie did not share this. She did not like winter and would have been very happy to remain out of the country every year until about May. California would be nice. She was meeting Latcham at seven that evening and so she had a day to kill. She left the flat at five. Traffic at that time was still light. The rush hour would not start for another two hours. She drove northwards up the M5 towards Cheltenham, where she exited the motorway. The road outside Stephen Wells' house was quiet at five past six. Despite being unremarkable it would have been difficult to miss the family saloon parked opposite the Wells' drive and fifty yards down. It contained two men who both looked bored. Julie dared not slow for a closer look so she simply drove by without adjusting her speed. It was evident that these guys were not there for the purpose of taking the cold morning air. So who was watching Wells? Harry's was the first name that came to her. But Harry had completed his researches and would have withdrawn by now. Watching briefs were not his thing. Still, as far as she could see at the moment, it didn't matter who was watching Wells. It would not immediately affect her plans. Just in case, however, she would do a bit more research of her own after the weekend. In fact, there was time now for a look around.

She parked the Clio in a multi-storey car park in the centre of town. It was a short walk to the taxi rank, and even at this early hour there were two cars available. She issued instructions to the driver, making sure that the route to her stated destination would take her down Wells' road. At 6.35 the car and its occupants were still there and Wells' house was quiet. Two corners further on, Julie was dropped off. She walked back and found herself a bus stop. From this point she had a clear view of the waiting car and the house. She knew from the local press that bus operators were experiencing difficulties recruiting drivers. It followed that, with a bit of luck, there wouldn't be a bus along for some while. It turned out that there wasn't a bus along at all. At 8.15 she saw Wells' Scorpio leave the driveway. There was only one occupant. As it turned the corner at the bottom of the road, the watchers' car pulled away from the kerb and turned in the same direction as Wells. This rather confirmed Julie's suspicions.

To appear enthusiastic, Julie made sure she arrived a little ahead of time. Not so early she caused inconvenience but just enough to seem keen. She knocked on Latcham's door at ten minutes to seven. When he answered the knock he looked fresh and relaxed. When she entered the hallway, they embraced. When the kissing was over they exchanged pleasantries. Latcham picked up her case and led her through to the sitting room. On the coffee table sat a wine cooler containing a bottle of champagne.

"Setting the scene for the weekend?" asked Julie.

"That's it," he replied. "Start as we mean to go on." They both laughed and Julie felt like a naughty schoolgirl. "I thought we might stay in tonight. I want to cook for us. Hope that's all right?"

Julie remembered that she had offered to treat them to dinner and Latcham had agreed, yet here he was taking control. She went along with his manipulation. "Perfect. Have you had a good week?"

"Not the best. Let me take this up to the room and I'll be right back with you. Why don't you open the bubbly?"

Julie removed the gold foil and wire from around the cork and waited for Latcham to return before decorking the bottle. She smiled to herself when he took just a little longer than was absolutely necessary to take the case up to his bedroom. He would be having a little look at its contents. To make this easier for him, the case was not locked. It contained only clothes and a leather accessory case for makeup and perfume. It was embossed with the initials C.N.

"How's the car?" he said when he returned to the room.

"Fine." She smiled. "Have you ever thought of taking up a career as a mechanic?"

"I sometimes think that would be infinitely preferable to the one I have at the moment. Now I've cooked us something to keep the cold out. It's -" He was cut short by the telephone. "Oh, sorry. Please excuse me." Latcham left the room and didn't return for some ten minutes. "Sorry again."

"Tough at the top, eh?"

"Wouldn't know. Never been there," he replied in good humour.

Dinner was pleasant. Julie decided that Latcham was a good cook, which was contrary to her expectations. Perhaps he was also a good housekeeper and gardener. So far she had only seen the gardens in the dark. What little she had seen suggested that they were well tended. After they had finished, Latcham rose and started stacking the dishes into a dishwasher.

"Here," Julie said, "let me do that. Thank you for dinner. I'm impressed with your culinary expertise."

"Why, thank you ma'am. I get it all from watching television. You stack then and I'll go and pour us something."

When Julie entered the sitting room, Latcham was pouring brandy into two huge balloon glasses. They sat, talked, giggled and drank. Eventually Latcham said, "Look at the time. I think it's time for bed don't you?"

Julie smiled and without another word took his hand and led him to the bedroom.

"Hello, guv. Didn't expect to find you in on a Saturday morning," said Harris.

"Don't be so bloody cheeky," replied Markham with a smile. "What do you have on Wells?"

"Nothing. The model employee and husband. He hasn't spent an evening away from his house so far. Mrs Wells goes out most evenings. Wells seems like a creature of habit. Leaves for work at about 8.15. Gets home around 6 or 6.30 and then stays in. Mrs Wells goes out later to night school. She does a quilting course at college and she also teaches French at the same college. Kids go out every night, usually to meet friends at a pub. They went clubbing last night. The researchers have nothing new for us and the lads in communications haven't intercepted anything interesting. Suburban bliss. They seem a totally normal, middle class family."

"Don't look so disappointed," said Markham. "What did you expect? Visitors in homburgs and dark glasses arriving in the small hours? The odd Zil pulling up the drive."

"We're friends with those Zil guys now, boss," said Harris. He had clearly lost his sense of humour.

"Thank you for telling me. What's your next step?"

"We're not getting anywhere like this. It could be months before anything happens."

"Years possibly," said Markham. "Okay. Tell me, if you had a free hand, what would you like to do next?"

"Pull him in. Have a little talk."

"You're probably right. He doesn't have access to anything sensitive now. He has been positioned to lead a project team. Internal work practices or something. Well, it's your show, but a word of advice. If we have a rotten apple here I don't want him panicking. Routine security monitoring exercise, I suggest. Wells has been through three of these before when they were exactly what they claimed to be. Routine security monitoring. If you decide to pull him in, let me know."

Melanie

Julie and Latcham stayed in bed late. They had enjoyed a rather energetic night and needed the rest. When Julie opened her eyes she found Latcham watching her. She smiled.

"Don't stare. It's rude," she said with a bleary-eyed smile.

"Sorry. Breakfast?"

Julie turned her nose up. "I think I overdid it last night. Just tea I think."

After she had drunk her cup of tea in bed she got up. She took a shower and while she was putting on her face she heard voices downstairs. She had not heard a knock at the door. Whoever Latcham was talking to must have knocked the door while she was in the shower. She finished making up and then quietly went downstairs. She stood by the kitchen door and saw Latcham in conversation with a strikingly attractive and tall woman in her mid thirties. Julie made a fake coughing noise. The two people turned to face her.

"Mel, this is Claire. Claire, this is Melanie, Mel to her friends. We work together."

Melanie gave a genuine smile and walked towards Julie with her hand outstretched. "How very nice to meet you, Claire."

"Likewise," replied Julie.

"I'm so sorry to interrupt your weekend. I needed to have a word with Chris and Monday morning wouldn't do."

"Not at all. I'll tell you what. Why don't I grab a coffee and take it into the sitting room. I'll leave you in peace and you can talk away then."

Julie poured herself coffee from the filter jug. She simply could not believe her luck. Her next task was to have manoeuvred an introduction to Melanie. She had expected to fail in this endeavour but now here she was, in the same house. Things were going very well. Half an hour later Latcham and Melanie joined Julie in the sitting room where she had been relaxing with *Country Life.*

"Sorry, Claire. It was just too bad of me. Chris, I hope you will buy Claire a very expensive dinner this evening to say sorry."

"Please don't give it another thought. You work for the same company as Chris then?"

"Yes. It usually doesn't involve our weekends but occasionally there is a panic on. When you dance to the tune of international, corporate paymasters it's inevitable sometimes. You staying for the whole weekend?"

"It depends when he kicks me out," said Julie.

"Well, you make sure he spoils you. I must be off. Nice to have met you, Claire." Melanie turned.

"Don't go," said Julie. "Have a coffee and tell me all about this man."

Melanie looked towards Latcham, who shrugged and smiled.

"You two girls carry on. Have a little natter while I have a shower and tidy myself up."

What a great act, Julie thought. Now Melanie could probe and ask her questions. These two had obviously been practising this for years. Latcham left them and Melanie went to fetch herself a coffee. She returned to the room with a coffee for herself and a fresh one for Julie. She sat next to Julie on the settee.

"Now what do you want to know about Chris?"

"Oh, nothing really. I was more interested in checking out the other women in his life."

Both laughed.

"Smart move. Actually, I've known Chris for a fair few years now and he rarely has a woman in his life. You're the first I've known about for a very long time. He must think a lot of you. He told us about you in the office. That's something I've never known him to do. How did you two meet?"

Julie knew that Melanie knew exactly how they had met. "He was my knight in shining armour. Well, my mechanic at least. He came to my rescue when my car broke down."

"Do you like the Clio?" asked Melanie casually.

Clever, thought Julie. By now she knows damn well it's not my car. Best I watch myself.

"It's not mine. I haven't got a car at the moment. It's a hire car." That'll give the bitch something to check out. "I don't really like driving and I sure don't intend to have an expensive car hanging around my neck like a millstone. I hire one when the mood takes me."

"Sounds sensible. We're lucky, we get company cars. We have a generous employer. Do you work?"

"As little as possible. I'm taking some time out while I decide what to do with the rest of my life. I've got a little money put by and I'm lucky enough to have a small private income. It keeps the wolf from the door."

Melanie tutted. "And here's me, a poor working girl. Want some more coffee?"

"Yes, please." Julie watched her as she walked to the kitchen. She could feel the tension mounting. She knew that Melanie was not comfortable with her presence although she was being friendly and pleasant. By the time Melanie had returned, Julie had decided to up the stakes. It was legitimate, she felt, and it might diffuse her doubts. Melanie sat next to her again.

"Look, Melanie, what's with all the questions? I know it's none of my business, I've only just met Chris, but have you and he got something going?"

Immediately she knew she stood a chance of blowing it. There was a short silence. Julie was not going to back down. She faced Melanie with a straight expression with both eyebrows slightly raised. Melanie broke the uncomfortable silence.

"I'm sorry." Melanie squeezed Julie's forearm. "You're quite right. I'm a nosy cow. No, Chris and I don't have something going. It's very much against the rules anyway. But we are good friends. We've known each other for a long time. Maybe it's like a brother and sister thing. You must think me a perfect bitch but it's like I said, Chris hasn't talked about anyone like he has about you. It looks like you've knocked him off his feet. And good for you."

"You two getting on?" said Latcham as he rejoined the women.

"Like a house on fire. I'll leave you two lovebirds now," Melanie teased. "I hope to see you again soon, Claire."

With that Melanie left. Julie was impressed by the way she happened to be there when, according to Melanie, they rarely worked at weekends. She was impressed by the way the subtle inquisition had been staged. As far as she could tell she had favourably impressed Latcham's colleague. If she hadn't then it would mean changing her plans and adopting a rather less structured approach to her commission. The scene was set now and she would have to play her part as it was presented to her. She knew she was playing a dangerous game. Assassins stayed remote from their targets until the very last moment. But here she was, well trained and experienced as she was, actually socialising with her targets. There would be scores of ways of linking her with these people. She was still confident that to make the link investigators would have to know what they were looking for and where.

As the weekend wore on, Julie's mind was put at rest. Latcham was attentive, courteous and affectionate. They ate out for the remaining meals and enjoyed sex several times, the last occasion being shortly after they had returned to the house after Sunday lunch at the Mill House. They lay side by side, staring up at the ceiling.

"Chris, I've got to go soon."

"Why?" he answered.

"It's been a fabulous weekend. I've really enjoyed it. But I have to get back to Bristol."

"Okay. I'll miss you though."

Julie detected the faintest hint of a sulk.

"I'll miss you too. When can we see each other again? Please make it soon."

"Sadly my diary is always full during the week. Next weekend would be great. That okay with you? I'd like to come and stay with you."

Julie had been waiting for this. She didn't want him in Bristol but knew it was almost inevitable. In any case, why had she gone to all that trouble to set up the Filton connection? It was for this very reason.

"Oh, I don't think you'd like my place. It's not like this." Julie waved her hand around to indicate Latcham's house. "I can't spoil you like you spoil me."

"Do you think that's important to me? Filton it is then."

As Julie drove westwards she was not looking forward to the flat. Even though she had been working, she had genuinely enjoyed the weekend. Now she had to go back to the drab and uninspiring flat. She was not going directly back to Filton however. First she had a visit to make. She entered Cheltenham and made for the road in which Wells' house stood. The car she had seen on her way to Latcham's was not there. Instead, parked in just the same place, was a similar model but of a different colour. Inside she saw a man and a woman. Julie was surprised at the lack of discretion. This was no sophisticated, covert observation exercise. It would have been impossible to miss these people. So who was taking such an interest in Wells? Julie thought of contacting Harry, then decided against it. Apart from making Harry cross, the deal was that she was on her own. If Harry had anything to tell her, he would contact her in the normal way.

When she arrived back at her flat, she was irritated at not being able to find a convenient parking slot. She opened the flat door and discovered that the pebble was on the carpet again. Her drawers had been tampered with as had the bottles and aerosols in the bathroom. When she checked her kitchen cupboards, which contained little, she found that the tins and packets had been slightly rearranged.

Dropping the catch on the door, she went to bed still considering the options and questioning whether she had been careless. The first job in the morning would be to get rid of the Clio. She had no need of it for some days now, and in any case if it was parked in the area it gave her tail a clue that she was in the flat. If the car disappeared the tail might make a mistake.

At the same time as Julie put her head upon her pillow, Latcham's phone rang.

"I don't like it, Chris," said Melanie Coleman-Burns. "She's lovely, totally beautiful. She's got a bob or two if her clothes are anything to go by. She's quick-witted, smart. In fact she's too smart, too smart by far."

"What are you getting at, Mel?"

"Why has this perfect woman turned up now? It's all too pat and she's too bloody perfect."

"I believe the term is paranoia, or are we talking a bit of female jealousy here? Chill out, Mel. Thanks for your concern but I think you're getting a bit oversensitive."

"Yeah, maybe. Like I said, why now? And how come she's so perfect and just what exactly do you know about her? Tell me that!"

"Leave me to worry about Claire. Good night, Mel."

Gala Night

The hotel dining room was packed. Not a single seat was left unoccupied and at $2000 a ticket that was no mean feat. For this price, those attending could enjoy a nine course banquet and listen to a series of boring speeches designed by the speakers for self aggrandisement rather than the interest or education of listeners. Nevertheless, this was the place to be and the place to be seen. Anyone who was anyone was there. The men were courteous and friendly, which was a painful experience for some. The women competed in the best bejewelled and most expensively gowned stakes. The tables on the floor were round while behind the long top table sat a glittering register of the good and the great. There were politicians, captains of industry, doctors and high-fliers and the odd tinseltown starlet or two.

Joseph Hahn sat at his table smiling when it seemed appropriate. He was not accompanied by a stunning woman. Instead, on each side of him sat a colleague. He had spent $6000 for his places and he and his companions were getting bored. It was the third speech and he had been compelled to hear how well the speakers had done in raising this "outstanding contribution for our community." The gala evening was an annual event and was but one item in a programme of fund-raising events during the year to raise money for local charities. Joseph, ever the man to want to get to the point, wanted the talk to finish and, as a matter of academic interest, to find out how much had been raised so far this year.

The third speaker sat to rapturous applause and the master of ceremonies stood.

"Ladies and gentlemen, your chairman, William Grant the Third."

More applause. Grant's speech was short and to the point.

"Well, ladies and gentlemen, here we all are again. It is good to see the faces of so many old friends. You are the supporters who have been with us for many years and without whom we could never do such good work for our less fortunate brothers and sisters. It is also good to see some new faces. It is you who, I hope, will pick up where we old ones have left off. You who will carry the torch onwards and ever upwards to new heights. Each year our fund-raising activities raise more than the previous year and this year is no exception. This is thanks in no small measure to our good friend here on my right, Dr Jonjo Grey. Dr Grey, president of Ribbon Motor Corporation has seen fit to honour us by a most generous contribution to our funds. Yes, ladies and gentlemen. I have a cheque here for two hundred and fifty thousand dollars signed by Dr Grey. This will enable us to offer..."

Joseph Hahn leaned towards the man on his left. "How much longer do I have to listen to this bullshit?"

"You wanted to come, Joseph. You know what these things are like."

"Yeah, yeah. Make yourself useful. Go and order us some more champagne. At five hundred bucks a bottle it's difficult to say no. Jesus. I could buy a vineyard in France for that."

Joseph was faced with a dilemma. His instinct and sense of revenge demanded that he kill Dr Jonjo Grey, the murderer of his younger brother. He needed to show he was in charge and was still credible. On the other hand his father, whom he loved and respected and even feared, had made his requirements quite clear. Joseph was not to touch this murdering bastard. Joseph did not dare cross his father. He needed to stay in his good books because it would not be long before the old man would pass on the family empire to him. Despite all this, Joseph's ego and his arrogance would not let the matter pass. It was for this reason he was now at the gala occasion, the sort of event he would normally avoid. He was totally committed to running his divisions of the empire and not at all given to small talk and sociability. He found the posturing and cant to be distasteful.

He wanted to have a word with the great Dr Grey. He had an overwhelming desire to prevent the man feeling he had escaped the wrath of the Hahns. Joseph had considerable faith in his father's judgment but he believed that on this one occasion the Old Man's judgment was flawed.

Grey stood. "I have long been associated with the aims of our organisation. It is all too easy for some of us to sit back and allow the injustices of the world to prevail. Some people are less fortunate and less able than us to..."

"Oh, do me a favour," whispered Hahn, to no one in particular.

When Grey had finished, the master of ceremonies announced that the dancing would begin. Joseph knew that it would be incumbent on Grey, the great benefactor, to circulate to receive the praise and accolades he was most surely due. Joseph watched as an entire wall silently slid away to reveal a vast dance floor. At one end was a band. The music started.

Joseph's eyes rarely left Grey. They followed him around the room. When he left the room to visit the lavatory, Hahn rose.

"Watch my back," he said to one of his suits.

Hahn entered the gents to find Grey standing at the urinal. Hahn stood at the stall next to Grey. "Dr Grey?"

"Yes." Grey's smiling face turned to look at the newcomer.

"My name is Joseph Hahn. I wonder if you can spare me a moment of your time? Perhaps we can take a walk?"

There was menace in his voice that did not pass Grey by. They washed their hands and emerged from the toilets together. They found a quiet table in the hotel lobby.

"What can I do for you, Mr Hahn?" asked Grey.

"I think you've done enough for my family. You issued the order to have my brother, Ricky, wiped out. I understand it was business. For reasons best known to himself, my father wants you left alone. I'm not interested in those reasons."

Grey was not an easy man to intimidate. But here he was with a tsar of organised crime. He was close to the top of a family that had a formidable reputation. Grey knew that Webster Hahn was a man with whom he could reason. He was a man who saw the big picture and was not given to hasty reactions. He had heard that Joseph was very like his father and not at all like his younger brother. But this was only hearsay. In truth, he had no firsthand knowledge of Joseph. He had no real idea how Joseph would react. But the burning question on Grey's mind was, if Joseph knew he was responsible for Ricky's death, why were they talking now? Why wasn't Grey lying in a pool of blood?

"The day will come when I take my father's place. That will be a black day for you, Dr Grey. That's the day when I'll come looking for you. That's the day you will die. We're talking like this because I want you to spend your life looking over your shoulder. I want you scared. I want you to stop trusting anyone. From now on you won't know who you can trust."

A lesser man would have been unable to conceal his fear. Grey looked down his nose at Hahn and appeared to be in control. His tone was hostile and defiant. "Mr Hahn, I think it's unclear to you who I am. I have considerable resources at my disposal. It would be unwise to incur my displeasure, or you may discover just how powerful I am."

"I know you're a powerful man, Dr Grey. I also know you don't want a war. It would not be beyond my capability to stop production. What's the use of a car manufacturer that can't make cars? It would not be beyond my capability to ensure you are removed from the board. The publicity that you involved yourself in murder would ensure that. Furthermore, I'm equipped to go to war. You, on the other hand, are merely an industrialist. Few of your mighty resources would be of concern to me.

"One more thing, Doctor. Your foot soldier, Albert Rocchiciolli, is dead. Take care you're not next. Good evening."

Hahn walked back to the banquet suite and summoned his employees. The cloakroom attendant returned their coats and they left the hotel.

On a cold and wet evening, Stephen Wells answered the knock at his door. Standing on his step were three men, one in police uniform. The two men in plain-clothes held up their ID cards.

"Good evening, Mr Wells, I am Liam Harris and this is David Mears, Security Directorate, Investigations Branch. This is Sergeant Jones, Gloucestershire Constabulary."

"Yes?" said Wells uncertainly.

"We would like a word with you, please. Just routine, you understand."

Wells was not at all sure he did understand. "You'd better come in."

"I would rather talk at the police station, Mr Wells. It's always a bit embarrassing to talk in someone's home. Perhaps you'd be good enough to come with us."

"Uh, well there's, ah, no one here at the moment. Other members of my family are out. Let's see, can I leave a note for them? They'd be worried if they came back and I was gone."

Harris gave him a friendly smile. "Not at all, Mr Wells. Please bring your bank statements for the last twelve months and any documentation relating to your savings - building society pass books and the like. I also want to see your credit card statements."

When Wells had finished scribbling his note, the four men got into an unmarked car. It was a three mile journey to county headquarters. It was evident that the officers at the reception desk were expecting the visitors. There was a buzzing sound as the reception officer pushed the button to electronically release the lock to the door that led to the main body of the building. The men walked in silence to an interview room. Sergeant Jones opened the door and stood aside to allow the other three to pass. Wells sat on one side of the table and Harris and Mears sat side by side on the other. Harris took a packet of cigarettes from his pocket and offered the pack to Wells, who shook his head. Harris lit his cigarette.

"Sorry to drag you away like this. This is just an interview, informal if you like, as part of the routine security monitoring process. You know the score. I expect you've had them before, haven't you?"

"You would know that, wouldn't you?" replied Wells.

Harris smiled. "As a matter of fact, yes. You've been through three of these before, Mr Wells. May I call you Stephen?" Harris didn't wait for the permission. "Just a few questions. It shouldn't take us too long and then you can get back to your family. Now then, when was the last time you had a family holiday?"

"June this year."

"Where did you go?"

"Tenerife."

"During your time in Tenerife did you go anywhere else which required the use of your passport?"

"No."

"You've gone abroad fairly regularly during the last few years, haven't you?"

"Yes, I have. I'm a twitcher, you see."

"What's a twitcher, Stephen?" asked Mears.

Harris gave him a mock disparaging look.

"Bird-watcher, Mr Mears. I like to watch birds."

"Please write down your foreign trips during the last two years." Harris said. "Rough dates are good enough. Next to the dates and destinations write down the purpose of the trip. If it was to watch birds then best you write down bird-watching. Twitching seems to throw my colleague here and it might confuse our less well educated people." Harris handed Wells an A4 sheet of paper and a pen. "When you've finished, please write something like this. I certify that this is an accurate record of my overseas trips in the last two years. Sign it and date it please." Harris then turned to Mears. "Where are your manners? I'm sure Stephen would like some coffee and I know I would."

Mears left the interview room. In his absence Wells fluctuated between rapid writing and apparent deep thought. As Mears came back into the room, Wells put his pen down and pushed the sheet of paper across to Harris. For some moments Harris looked at the sheet. Then with a smile he looked up at Wells again.

"Thank you. That's clear. Very helpful. Here, have your coffee. Now just a few more points. Your car, a Scorpio, I understand. How long have you had it?"

"Oh, about eighteen months I think."

"How did you pay for it?"

"Bank loan. You'll see the debits in my bank statement, where it says personal loan."

A small bead of sweat had broken out on Wells' right temple. This in itself meant nothing. It was by no means unusual that this happened during questioning, but neither Harris nor Mears missed it.

"Your wife drives a Golf?"

"Yes. We bought that for cash. My wife is a part-time language lecturer at college. She works for some of the little luxuries in life, like her car."

"I see. Your salary is nearly £50,000 a year isn't it?"

"Forty-seven actually."

"Yes, quite. Do you keep any cash anywhere?"

"No. Chance would be a fine thing."

Wells answered this very quickly. Harris was now interested in the way that Wells held his stare. During normal conversation, Harris knew that it is usual for eye contact to be intermittent. People who are lying assume that liars fail to achieve eye contact. In order to make the questioner believe the interrogated is telling the truth, he overcompensates by staring right into the face of the interrogator. Harris found Wells' staring to be suggestive. He was behaving like a liar.

"I don't suppose Mrs Wells earns much and what with two kids living at home and your foreign trips, things must be quite difficult at times." There was no apparent threat in the way Harris spoke these words. It sounded as if he was being sympathetic. "Money'll be tight, I expect."

"It's not so bad. We have simple tastes by and large and we can cope quite well. Anyway my wife earns about fourteen seventy-five an hour. She can bring home about a hundred pounds a week after deductions."

"Okay. Good." Harris started to sort the credit card statements into chronological order. "Thank you, Stephen. You can have these back now." He pushed the statements towards Wells. Wells straightened them in front of him. The next moment he picked up his coffee.

"You went to the United States recently. There is no mention of that on the itinerary you just wrote down and I don't see, according to your card statements, that you bought your ticket with credit card."

The coffee in the cup in Wells' hand started to drip onto the statements in front of him. His hand was shaking violently and Wells started to chew his bottom lip.

It was Mears who spoke now. "So how did you pay for your air tickets, Stephen?"

"I...I can't quite remember. How silly. Uh, it must have been cash."

"I don't think so, Stephen," Harris took over again. "You paid by credit card, but not your own."

"Did I? No, surely not? There must be some mistake."

This was a sentence much loved by Harris and his colleagues. Markham used to say that if he had a pound for every time he heard that, he would be able to retire. The other phrases which regularly popped up when the screws were on were "it's all been a big misunderstanding" and "it must have been a breakdown in communications."

"Well no," said Harris gently, "I don't think so. You used a cloned card. Do you want to tell me where you got it? More important, what was the purpose of your trip to the States and why didn't you record it just now?"

Wells had managed to return the cup to the table but not before spilling more coffee. Both Harris and Mears could see that Wells had "lost the plot." They knew his mind was desperately darting from one lie to another in the vain search for an answer which would seem plausible. Harris gathered the papers in front of him, tapped them on the table, bottom and side, to align them and placed them in a buff folder.

"Thank you, Stephen. That's all for now. I expect we'll be in touch. David will show you out." Harris left the room.

At eight the following morning, Harris knocked on Wells' door again. This time he was accompanied by his senior officer, Ron Markham. When Wells opened the door Harris was surprised at the way he looked. He was pale and had developed a tremor. He looked a very sick man indeed. He was unshaven and wore the same clothes he had on the previous evening. There were bags under his eyes and he seemed to be having difficulty focusing his eyes. One answer could be tiredness, although there were other possibilities.

Harris noted that Wells seemed pleased to see them, it appeared almost like relief. Harris smiled.

"Good morning, Stephen. This is my boss, Ron Markham. We think we need to talk to you. May we come in?"

Wells stepped back to allow them to enter. He closed the door and led them through to the sitting room. When they had seated themselves, Wells left the room and the two visitors could hear him talking to his wife. He returned to the room, closing the door behind him.

"My wife and the children will be going out soon. Then we'll be alone."

"Fine," replied Harris, who then turned to Markham as if in invitation for him to speak.

Markham smiled, paused and then spoke in quiet, measured tones. "It seems to me, Stephen, there are some issues we need to talk to you about. Before we do, however, I must tell you that you are hereby suspended from duties pending a full investigation into your affairs and activities. I will require your passport and it would be very helpful if you would allow my colleague, Liam here, to search your house."

Markham waited for a response. There was absolute silence while Wells seemed to be considering the request. The sound of voices in the hall and the thud of the front door closing brought him out of his daydream.

"Yes, all right. Help yourself."

"Thank you," said Markham. "May I have your passport please?"

Wells rose and walked towards the bureau in the corner of the room. He returned with the passport and handed it to Markham.

"We have a problem with this trip to America, don't we? Why did you go, Stephen?" There was no response. "Okay. How did you pay for it?" Still nothing.

Harris returned with a tin, the contents of which he emptied onto the floor. There was a pile of high denomination notes in front of them.

"Where has all this come from, Stephen?" asked Markham. "That looks like a lot of money. Where did it come from?"

There was another very long pause and not the slightest hint of impatience or exasperation was shown by the two security people.

"Okay," said Harris. "That was a difficult one. Let's try something a bit easier. Tell us about the trip. Why did you go to America, Stephen?" Still there was no answer. "Look. It's like this. Sooner or later you will tell us. I think I can promise you that when you do tell us you'll feel much better. We can then sort this thing out together."

"You're putting yourself under too much pressure, Stephen." Markham said. "You are not a superspy. You're not trained to take this pressure, and in any case you're not the type. Help us to help you. Why did you go to America?"

"Do you love your family, Stephen?" Harris knew that this new tactic could turn Wells. In this belief he was not disappointed. Wells slumped forward in the chair. He cupped his head in his hands and started to sob. Harris went on. "It's going to be difficult for them, whatever happens, isn't it? Let's try to make it as easy as possible for all of you."

They then left Wells to his tears and trembling. Eventually he stopped and looked at Markham.

"I'm sorry about that. I, well, ah, what do you want to know?"

With great serenity Markham said, "Why did you go to America?"

Wells told the two men about the purpose of the trip to Sedona. He explained the technical details of the operation and how the Dodge van had been rigged. In fact, as far as the visitors could tell, the only thing he left out was on whose behalf he had gone. When he was pressed on this point, his resistance had evaporated. He told them about Chris Latcham and Wynter Farmer Management Consultants. He told them how he had bought the ticket and how much he had been paid. They believed him when he said he had no idea why the information he had collected on the disks was required.

When Wells had finished his story, Markham said in a kindly way, "Okay, Stephen. Thanks for your co-operation. I don't know what will happen next, but you'll be hearing from us soon. In the meantime stay in the house. Don't go out for any reason. If something happens and you feel you have no choice but to go out, ring me on this number, day or night, just ring." Markham handed Wells a card. "Your telephone line is tapped and your house is being watched. Make no attempt to get in touch with Mr Latcham. Do not contact your work. You will not be allowed to speak to anyone. The only person you are to call is me." Markham paused. "Try to take things easy for a while. Why don't you go and have a bath and try to get a bit of sleep?"

"Aren't you going to arrest me?" asked Wells with some surprise.

"No. What for? I'm not sure you have broken any laws yet. It may be you've done nothing illegal. No, you just stay here and try not to worry too much. We'll let ourselves out. Now don't forget, ring me on that number if you need anything."

The two men rose and left Wells to his thoughts. When they were sitting in their car Harris said, "Well, what do you think?"

"I think that Wells is a prat," Markham said. "I think he's got himself in over his head. I also think we'll need to watch him. He may just decide he can't face what he knows must be coming. He may not be able to face the shame, the ignominy of it all. He's the type who considers what his family and friends think comes above all things. I think he might decide to do away with himself."

"What? You mean top himself?"

"That's about it. So watch him. We don't want to lose him yet."

Julie was surprised to hear Harry's voice on her answering service that evening. As a rule, while she was working, there would be no contact between them. Harry seemed happy to break the rule with the commission she was currently working on. She heard Harry say that Auntie was unwell. This told Julie she was to call Harry at his home during the evening. When she heard this she realised something had gone wrong and her first thought was for the man she had seen following her and the intruder in her flat. She fished in her bag to find some more coins for the public telephone.

Harry answered his phone after just three rings.

"Hello, Uncle. I hope I haven't disturbed you?"

"Not at all, poppet. Thank you for phoning. Name a motorway service area you can reach in one hour."

"No can do. No car."

"Stand by. I'll call you on your mobile in ten minutes."

Without another word the line went dead. Harry had hung up. Julie knew he would now leave his home to find a public telephone. While Harry's domestic line was checked regularly and his home was swept, he was not prepared to take risks beyond that which he had already taken. When Julie's mobile phone trilled, she answered it immediately.

"Yeah."

"Need to meet now. Give me a point we can both reach in one hour."

"Ramsey's Steak House, Gloucester Road, Filton, Bristol."

Julie was at a table close to the door of the bar a little before the hour was up. While she loved Harry dearly she was not looking forward to meeting him. There could only be bad news if Harry was prepared to break every rule in the book. Nevertheless, when she saw his great frame filling the door she got up and hugged him.

"What are you drinking, Harry?"

"Sit. I'll get a bottle of plonk to share. I don't want to be here any longer than necessary so I'll not be treating us to dinner." Harry went to the bar and returned with a bottle and two glasses.

"What's up, Harry?"

"Little problem you need to know about. The security people have got Wells."

"I know they've been watching him for a day or two."

"Well, they've now interrogated him. He's under house arrest. Our problem is this. I don't know if he's let on about W.F.M.C. or our friend Latcham. My guess is that he has. He's weak and the pressure of being questioned by the security guys would be too much. He's not a pro. My guess is, he would have fallen apart in a very short time.

"Here's the problem for us. If he's talked about Latcham, W.F.M.C. and company, this thing could break open at any time. That means we've run out of time. How close are you?"

"I'm not ready to make my move. You want me to get what I can from Latcham and the girl and to hit them at once. You then want me to hit Wells before anything appears in the press to warn him. Well, I'm close but I'm not there yet."

"I've asked Special Branch to put a security curtain around the Wells business. The effectiveness of that will be doubtful though. Bloody nosy neighbours and the like. There's every chance Latcham will know about Wells soon. If he does, then our birds will fly. Our problem then will be twofold. First, they might choose to do a deal with our people. They might tell all in return for immunity and guaranteed safety. Second, these people have access to resources. They might get lost only to resurface again when they have set up a deal. The deal would most likely be with the press. We're then up Cack Strasse without a paddle. Poppet. We have no time left. You've got to act now."

"I'm not ready. I've taken enough risks on this show already."

"No choice. You have to strike now."

Julie knew Harry was right. She resented it and felt some anger that Harry had placed her in this position. After a few moments and two or three swallows of the rough house wine, which she still rather enjoyed, she calmed down and started to look at the situation more objectively. She knew it was not Harry's fault. It was certainly not Harry's intention to place her at risk and, at the end of the day, this is what she was paid large sums for.

"Okay. I'll move. One question. How did they get onto Wells? Coleman-Burns I can understand, but Wells?"

"I don't have many details. As far as I can tell, Wells had one too many overseas trips. They got suspicious and checked him out. I think that's how it started."

"Well, that doesn't lead to us, does it? Wells is being watched. I think I'll assume that Latcham is as well."

"What a sensible girl you are." Harry stood up and pulled his coat around himself. "By the way, poppet, you've grown a tail. Best you sort that first. See you." With that Harry left.

"Oh thanks, Harry dear," muttered Julie.

She stood and put her coat on. This gave her a moment or two to think. As she walked from the bar, instead of turning right, she turned left through a door marked "Private." The sounds of clattering pans and utensils enabled her to find the kitchen. Looks of surprise came from the chefs.

"Sorry, gentlemen," she said in answer to their questioning stares. "Think I must be lost. Is that the way out?"

"You can't go through there, love."

"Oh, surely I can." Julie went to the door that opened into a yard stacked with boxes, empty vegetable crates and oil cans. It was surrounded by a wooden fence with a single door which led to the car park. Once out, Julie stood still in the shadows while she got her bearings. In a far corner of the car park she saw the figure of a man leaning against a large refuse container. From where he was standing he had a clear view of the steak house's front door. She approached the man from behind and as she neared she recognised him. With the recognition came annoyance. She could now identify the person who had been following her. Quietly she neared him until she was right behind him when she spoke.

"Good evening, Mr Weaver." The estate agent jumped with shock or fright or both.

"Oh! Oh! Good evening to you, Miss Noble."

Julie was innocence itself. "Taking the night air, Mr Weaver?"

"Yes, yes. I like to take some fresh air this time of night. And you?"

"I've just had dinner in there. Being a stranger it's difficult to know where to go or what to do. Truth is, Mr Weaver, I'm feeling a bit lonely. I'm not used to having no company. Tell you what. How would you like to come round for coffee on Saturday morning. It would be really good to see a friendly face. Still, I expect you have family commitments. Never mind."

"No, no. Not at all. I would love to join you for coffee on Saturday.

That's very kind of you. Yes, I'll look forward to that."

"Good," said Julie. "I'll expect you around eleven then. Bye." Julie walked home without a backward glance. She felt confident she would not be followed.

Dr Jonjo Grey pressed a button on his intercom and spoke into it. "Find me the W.F.M.C. file, will you?"

Within two minutes, his secretary entered the office and handed him a thin red wallet file. He took it without acknowledgment.

Thursday night of that week was, according to the weather reports, the coldest December evening for over a hundred years. Julie had been cold when she had collected another hire car, a blue Mondeo, in Bristol using the documentary identity of Helen Smith. Her ginger wig failed to keep her head warm and the polystyrene padding seemed not to help her body temperature. After collecting the car she did not return to the flat. Instead she drove to Cheltenham. There was only one car parked in Wells' road. She had seen this car before. She did not slow as she drove past but she fancied she had seen the two male occupants before.

Julie found a pull-in and parked the car. It was 9.17 p.m. Taking a parcel from the glove compartment, she got out of the car and locked it carefully. She pressed the button on the little black box attached to the key ring to activate the alarm.

While studying a large-scale map she had discovered there was a road behind the Wells residence that ran parallel to the road in front. It showed that Wells had a back garden that abutted the back garden of the house behind. It was to this house that Julie now made her way. The pavements were deserted, probably because of the cold. The large detached house was not difficult to find. Its curtains were drawn but she could clearly see a light shining through the slits where the curtains had been carelessly pulled. There was no gate across the end of the drive, which suggested to her that there was no dog living at this house.

Carefully she walked up the drive, having first checked there were no other pedestrians out for a constitutional. There was a gap between the garage and the hedge that marked the edge of the property. Squeezing down the gap, she found herself in the back garden. Staying close to the hedge with her back to it, she watched the back windows of the house. Each was in darkness. When she reached the end of the garden she found that the two back gardens were separated by a thick hedge of leylandii trees. As was so often the case she found that low down the trees were dying back a little. This gave her just enough room to crawl under the boundary, although her artificial bulk was not helpful. Slowly she stood upright and stock-still.

She could see inside the sitting room, the lights of which flooded out into the garden. Inside she could see Stephen Wells, who was not alone. There was a woman with him who Julie assumed was the wife. Julie hesitated to get closer because the back lawn was bathed in light. Her movement might be enough to attract their attention and if they looked out of their windows there was every chance they would see her. She had little option but to wait and this, in the intense cold, was a most unattractive proposition. Fortunately she did not have to wait long. It was clear from the rapid and jerky movements of Wells and his wife, both standing, that they were arguing. Mrs Wells appeared to storm out of the room and a light went on in the kitchen. Julie saw the kitchen door open and the woman walked briskly between the house and the garage, towards the drive. Seconds later she heard a car engine start and the sound of the car pulling away.

Julie waited for five more minutes, by which time she deemed it safe to proceed. With great care she picked her way to the kitchen door. It was a relief to find it unlocked, but then Julie was sure it would be since the woman had left in a hurry. Julie went in. By what she had observed already she knew the way to the sitting room in which Wells was located. She opened the door and walked into the room. Wells looked up and it was clear to Julie he expected his wife. His first expression was one of sadness, which quickly turned to panic when he realised that this was not Mrs Wells. In her right hand Julie was holding the single-shot handgun so carefully made by David Ginsberg. She quickly raised her arm, aimed and squeezed the trigger. There was a faint pop and Wells was thrown backwards across his sitting room. The wallpaper behind him was splattered with blood, bone and brain. There was a small hole in his forehead but the back of his head was elsewhere.

In silence, Julie made her way back taking the same route by which she had arrived. She was not pleased to find that the windscreen of her car was iced and it took her two minutes to scrape off the ice with the tool so thoughtfully provided by the hire company. No matter how experienced the assassin, there was always the time immediately after the hit when the adrenaline and the thrill of the adventure caused at least the slightest change in response times, focus and clarity of thought. Julie drove too quickly now to put distance between herself and the Wells' house. This was a mistake and she knew it, but still she did it.

The Red Lion was a popular pub on the outskirts of Cheltenham. Its prime clientele was business types at lunchtime and similar in the evening. It was also the pub much favoured by the farming community. A little way down the road from the Red Lion was a side road leading to a residential area. On this Thursday night, a police patrol car was parked. It was not inconspicuous in its white livery with the florescent yellow and blue pattern. From this vantage point, the two male officers inside the car had a clear view of the car park of the Red Lion. Their interest was particularly taken by Frank Miles' old and battered Land Rover. The officers knew Miles well; after all he was a pillar of the community and was renowned for his drinking habits. It was also well known that Miles had lost his licence and so, asked the officers, what was his motor doing in the car park of the Red Lion? It was well worth waiting to see who drove it away.

At a little before 10.30 the policemen found their answer. Frank Miles tottered out of the pub and found his way to the car. He got in and pulled into the road. His driving showed no sign of incapacity through drink, his lights were on and all appeared well. Yet Miles had had his licence pulled. The patrol car pulled onto the road some 200 yards behind the Land Rover. The policemen were just about to switch on the siren and blue lights when a blue Mondeo pulled into the road between them and

Miles.

The officer in the front passenger seat reported to the control room that they were about to pull Frank Miles over and he gave the location. He leaned forward and flicked two rocker switches. The blue lights came on as did the wailing sound of the new sirens which were designed not to give sudden shocks to motorists. An extensive research programme had shown that the new sirens reduced the risk of road traffic accidents. Drivers were startled by the old sirens with their sudden harsh tones. Neither officer relished the idea of pulling Miles over. He was well connected and was an extremely pleasant man, but driving while serving a ban was not sensible and, in any case, he would most certainly be over the drink and drive limit.

At the sound of the sirens, the Mondeo which was travelling close to Miles' rear bumper suddenly swung around the Land Rover to overtake. It crossed a double white line and faced a car coming in the opposite direction. It narrowly missed a head-on collision by returning to its own lane, cutting in front of Miles. The Land Rover mounted the pavement and came to a rest. The Mondeo was leaving the scene at a pace. The police officers radioed their control to advise of the changed plan. This was Frank Miles' lucky night. The colourful patrol car roared straight past him in pursuit of the Mondeo.

Within three minutes the speeding cars had left the built-up area of the town and were in countryside. Fortunately the roads were quiet because the driver of the Mondeo was causing a hazard at this speed. The police officers were pleased to see the car pull into a lay-by. A potentially dangerous chase had been averted.

The police driver got out of his car and approached the Mondeo. By the time he reached the driver's side window it was opening.

"Good evening, Madam."

Those were his last words. Julie trained the Type 67 on him and shot him twice in the chest. The impact propelled him backwards and before he had stopped moving, Julie got out of the car. In one, well practised movement she raised her gun and fired twice through the windscreen of the patrol car. The bullets killed the other officer before he had time to report the first death to his control room.

Julie looked up and down the road. Her luck was still holding, nothing was coming. She blessed the cold night and returned to her car.

The rules of the game had just changed. The stakes had been raised. Killing hoods was one thing, but killing police officers was quite another. When working for Harry, Julie had always been led to understand that she was on her own. Regardless of this, she always felt that, in time of real need, Harry would pull some strings. He would help in time of dire need. Now, though, she would be truly on her own. Public outcry and pressure would ensure that Harry could not be seen to associate with her in any way. So what's new? she thought sulkily. She had placed herself at risk. Harry might find himself faced with no alternative but to silence her. He could not allow the police to find her and charge her with the murder of their colleagues. They might find a clear trail back to Harry and those he was working for.

It was definitely time for Helen Smith to disappear for ever. This was inconvenient. Julie had one further use for Helen but it was not to be. Her immediate problem was how much had the police told their control. She would have liked to have got as far back to Bristol as possible. It was sensible, though, to assume that the officers had transmitted the index number of the Mondeo. She could not take the risk that they had not. The first job was to hide the car. During daylight hours she would have favoured taking it to an isolated spot, of which there were many in the area, and burning it. At night though, this expedient might attract attention too quickly and not give her the time she needed to clear out of the county. This left her with the River Severn.

Taking the lanes through woods and only crossing major roads instead of using them, she made for an isolated spot on the left riverbank where the river wound to the right. The faster flowing river on the outside of the bend ensured that the water was deepest at that spot. She could not risk a shelf where the top of the car might be visible. She reversed the car to the bank. Getting out, she checked the road both ways and found it empty. Quickly she removed the outsized clothes and the padding. She stood on the bank in just her bra and pants feeling exposed and cold. She pulled on a pullover, her jeans and the flying jacket. Throwing the discarded clothes into the back seat she set fire to them. Within seconds they were ablaze and the upholstery with them. Leaving them as long as she dared, she waited until there was little of her clothes remaining apart from charred remains. By this time, however, the front seats were catching alight. She leaned over the driver's seat, released the hand brake and placed the gear lever into the neutral position. With a great effort she pushed the car backwards until its momentum carried it over the edge of the bank.

It was essential to push the car in backwards. Had she pushed in frontwards, the extra weight of the engine at the front could so easily have made the car nose-dive. There was a real danger then, that the back of the car would have remained visible above the water line while the front was buried in the mud at the bottom of the river. As it was, the Mondeo hit the water more or less level. To her delight, it was taken by the flow of the river and it moved away from the bank and downstream. This she had intended and hoped for. She knew that by leaving the windows closed and with the strong current of the Severn, there stood a chance that the car would not sink immediately. In the moonlight she watched with satisfaction as the roof disappeared beneath the water many yards from the bank. Julie pulled the strap of her bag over her shoulder and gave the hardware within a reassuring tap. Despite the fact she now had the prospect of a long walk to Gloucester, her confidence was returning. She could still not risk being seen at this time of the night. Single females most certainly did not walk around at this hour. If she was spotted she would inevitably arouse suspicion. She knew that by staying in the lanes and avoiding the main arteries to the city, the chances of being seen were remote.

She walked into the train station in the early hours of the morning. While waiting for the cafeteria to open she freshened up in the toilet. A hot coffee helped her to regain the feelings in her extremities. An hour later she stepped onto the express to Bristol, Temple Meads.

Grey Talks to Salmon

San Francisco was Dr Jonjo Grey's favourite place on earth. As he walked towards Fisherman's Wharf old memories came flooding back. He breathed in that unique air and dreamed of the time he could retire and move his home to California. He reckoned that everyone should enjoy clam chowder and fresh lobster salad on Fisherman's Wharf at least once before they died. It was for this reason he arranged to meet Salmon there. He would have preferred to keep distasteful business and the extraordinary seafood separate, but on this occasion that was a luxury he could not afford.

As he approached the restaurant he saw Leo Salmon's large frame sitting at an outside table. It was a little cold for this but it made sense. There was always a feeling that one could be overheard at a table inside a restaurant, although in reality it was highly unlikely and if a casual listener heard what they were going to talk about, it was improbable they would have understood what they heard. Even if they did, it was even more unlikely they would know what to do with the information.

Salmon made no effort to raise himself from the table. He was in the process of lighting a large Cuban cigar with a petrol Zippo lighter.

"They tell me I shouldn't light a good cigar with this." Salmon waved the Zippo in the air. "Say it spoils the taste. Never appreciated that myself. Sit down, Jonjo. Take the weight off your legs."

"Looks to me as if it's your legs which are under the greater strain."

Salmon laughed. "Yeah. You got a point there. Too much good food and not enough exercise. Maybe age has something to do with it?"

The waiter arrived quickly and placed menus before each of the men. Grey didn't look at his and immediately ordered chowder and lobster. Salmon followed suit. Grey glanced at the wine list and selected a Chablis.

"They tell me your new car is shaping up to be a success."

"So it should with the kind of investment we made," replied Grey with a slight grimace.

"A cool billion they tell me."

"Who are 'they,' Leo?" asked Grey with a smile.

"Ah, you know. It's the kind of thing I heard around. I also hear that that little shit Ricky tried to put the screws on you. That true?"

"Yes."

"That why you hit him?"

"Yes."

"Well, the little bastard had it coming. Webster should have kept him locked in a padded cell. It was sure to happen sooner or later. If it hadn't been you it would have been someone else. Me, for example. The old man was too soft on him."

"Leo." Grey paused while he selected the right words. "I need your help. It regards the Hahn family."

Salmon raised his hand as if to silence Grey. "Careful, Jonjo. Webster has been a good friend to me for more years than I care to remember. Known him a good deal longer than I've known you."

"I know," said Grey. "We have a mess. You put Webster onto the guys in London. It's all gone bad." Grey grunted. "But then, I guess you've been told as much. We got to sort this. It's like when a pebble is dropped into a pool. The ripples go outwards and touch everything on the edge."

"What do you need?"

"I need to avoid a war between me and Webster's family. That's a war I might just win but it would cost. On the other hand I might not be able to win and that I don't intend to happen."

"Why are you talking to me?" Salmon stopped as the waiter placed two steaming bowls on the table. "Webster is a reasonable man. You should be talking to him."

"I'll do that, but not just yet. If we go to war you'll be drawn in Leo."

"You mean you'll draw me in. Let's eat."

The two men enjoyed their chowders without speaking. Only when the waiter had cleared away and returned with the lobster salads did they speak. Salmon re-opened the conversation.

"Like I said, Jonjo, what do you need?"

"Joseph knows he'll inherit. Who knows when? I hope never, but who knows? He says that when the day comes he'll even the score."

"Even the score?" Salmon raised an eyebrow to indicate a question.

"I gave the order on Ricky. Joseph is threatening revenge. It's like this Leo. I hit Joseph now. My self-preservation instinct is strong. Or I talk to Webster and get this thing done with. If I hit Joseph then where will it all end? I would rather settle matters with Webster. But what do I have to take? I need something to put on the table." Grey looked Salmon right in the eyes. "What have I got to put on the table?"

There was another long pause. Grey seemed to have lost his appetite and he watched Salmon eat. Salmon had definitely not lost his. Grey wanted to push his guest but he knew it would be unwise. Instead he allowed him to finish. Eventually Salmon picked up his napkin and dabbed his mouth. He refolded it and placed it by the side of the plate which only held the shell of the half lobster.

"It appears you aren't too hungry, Jonjo. It was very good. Now order us some coffee."

Grey raised his arm to attract the waiter's attention.

"Something wrong with the lobster, sir?" asked the waiter.

"Nothing wrong with the lobster. Fetch us some coffee, please," replied Grey. The waiter cleared the table and disappeared.

"You're right," Salmon said at last. "You don't want a war. Webster doesn't want a war and I sure as hell don't want a war. So nobody wants a war. Things are good at the moment for us. Business is good. Every time we have a war we attract unwanted attention. We get the Feds on our backs. They start poking about. The papers run stories about us and everything has to shut down for a while. No, I don't want a war. It's unprofitable and inconvenient.

"Maybe I can give you something to take to Webster. But I'll need something from you, Jonjo. If Webster found it came from me, then, well, the war might start anyway. One day I may come to you for help."

"That goes without saying, Leo."

"No it fucking don't. Like I said, one day I might come to you for your help."

"Sure. You got it."

"Oh, I know I have. You ever heard of a limey called Eric Wynter?"

"He's the retired boss of Wynter Farmer Management Consultants based in London. W.F.M.C. is the outfit that stitched up Webster with this gun thing."

"I see that people speak to you as well. Okay. Eric Wynter's people acquired some computer disks. Wynter has them now. They contain some sensitive information about Webster family business. Webster knows Wynter has the disks. Here's the bottom line. Hahn is in no position to get the disks back. He wants them back but he can't get to them. Wynter don't want to use them 'cause they might bring all kinds of shit down on him. He's got all the shit he can handle at the moment. If you could get your hands on those disks you might find they'll help when you talk to Webster."

Salmon reached behind him and pulled a heavy coat across his shoulders. "I gotta go now."

"What about your coffee?"

"You drink it. One last thing. If your negotiations fail, if a war breaks out, I'm gonna hold you responsible. If this thing goes wrong, Jonjo, I'm going to have to look you up. Now I'm sure we understand each other. See you around, Doctor."

Julie arrived back at her Filton flat at lunchtime on Friday. The pebble had not rolled off the door. She made herself an omelette after which she quickly checked her food cupboards. There was little to excite even the most easily pleased palette. She committed a shopping list to memory and left for the nearest supermarket. She had no car now and shopping without a car was one worse than shopping with a car. It was ninety minutes later she returned to the flat, laden with groceries. She checked the pebble again and found it on top of the door as expected. When she had stowed the packs and tins in the cupboards and the fridge, she busied herself tidying the flat. It was half past five before she was able to take a much needed shower.

She stood in the shower and found the hot water and soap relaxed her. Letting the water play down her body, she replayed the last few hours in her mind. She felt confident now, that all tracks had been covered. Julie could think of nothing that would link her to Wells or the death of the two unfortunate police officers in Cheltenham. Even the most perceptive sleuth would not be able to pick up her trail back to Bristol even if that remarkable detective knew exactly what to look for. No, she was safe now. She vigorously rubbed herself down with a hard towel, a strange habit she had acquired in early childhood. Before dressing she sat in front of the mirror on the rather shabby dressing table and applied her makeup. In this she was restrained. She was well aware of her own beauty, a beauty that was little enhanced with large quantities of cosmetics.

Before getting dressed, she took some care in selecting underclothes and a simple black dress. The plain black shoes completed the picture she wanted to portray. She stood in front of the mirror and admired her efforts. She was pleased with what she saw.

In the kitchen she unwrapped the duck pate she had bought. She laid out the ingredients for the peppered steak and inspected the marbling on the two Aberdeen Angus steaks. Quickly the salad came together and she smiled as she thought how inappropriate salads were for this time of the year. A good, nourishing casserole might be more fitting. Finally she prepared the pudding, a gooseberry fool which was a favourite of hers since being introduced to it by Harry many years before.

Again Julie looked in the mirror to check herself. Nothing was out of place and the time had arrived to put on the nail varnish. She chose a pale pink. There was nothing left to do now but to sit in front of the television and watch the early evening news. At 7.45 there was a knock on her door and immediately a thrill went through her body. She was delighted to find Chris Latcham standing there wearing a broad grin. As he stepped into the flat he handed Julie a bunch of red roses.

"For me?" she asked in mock amazement.

"For you," replied Latcham as he pulled her towards him. They kissed long and hard.

"I've missed you, Mr Latcham."

"And I you. Have you had a good week?"

"How could I? I've spent most of it thinking about you."

"You say the nicest things," said Latcham.

"Yes, I do, don't I? What about you? You had a good week?"

"When all things are considered, it has not been the best I've known. In fact the only bright spot has been the thought of seeing you this weekend."

Julie smiled her best coy smile. "I thought we might eat in tonight. That's providing you trust my cooking. It's too cold and miserable to go out anyway."

"Sounds perfect. Where shall I put my bag?"

"Oh, let me," said Julie, grabbing the bag from his hand. "I think the bedroom might be a good place for it, don't you?"

Latcham laughed. "Sounds like a good plan. I've had a long day and a long drive. Can I go and freshen up?"

Julie led him by the hand to the bathroom. "You go in there and I'll get you a drink. What do you fancy?"

"You'll find a bottle of bubbly in the bag. Might be a bit warm now, but who cares?"

"Actually I do. I'll put it in the freezer for a minute or two. How about a G and T while we're waiting?"

"Great," shouted Latcham through the bathroom door.

When he had finished in the bathroom he sat next to her on the settee. He took one sip of his gin and tonic and replaced the glass on the coffee table. Drawing her to him again, he kissed her with passion.

"Hungry are we?" asked Julie with mock innocence.

"Don't you think we should take a trip to the bedroom before we eat?"

"Yes, I do think."

Again she grabbed his hand and led him, this time to the bedroom. Their lovemaking was ferocious and exhausting and it was an hour before they emerged back in the sitting room.

"Look, you've ruined my makeup," said Julie. "Let me go and repair my face and then I'll finish dinner off."

After they had finished eating their meal, Julie began to clear the table. As she was walking to the kitchen with her back to Latcham she asked her question with an innocence suggesting interest. It would be unnatural if she did not show an interest in her lover's profession.

"Just what is it you do? Newton and all that is a bit confusing."

Latcham chuckled. "My company is retained by large and usually wealthy organisations in a consultancy role. We only come into our own when they have a problem. We provide a range of services which might be accountancy, legal, marketing, research, in fact, just about anything they need doing for them, providing it's legal of course."

"Of course."

"Anyway that's enough of me. What about you? When are you going to sort your future out? What are you going to do with the rest of your life?"

"My trouble is, I was born with a silver spoon in my mouth. Well, nearly silver anyway. I've never had to get down to anything seriously because there's always been someone there to bale me out. I guess I've had it too easy. The safety net is great while it's there but when someone takes it away, life can be very difficult."

"Has someone taken it away?" asked Latcham with genuine concern.

"No, no. But I sometimes wonder if it did disappear, how well equipped would I be to cope on my own?"

"I think you would be very well equipped. You probably don't know just how many strengths you have," Latcham reassured her.

"That's very sweet of you. You really are a gallant knight, aren't you? It's just that I don't know what I can do because I've never had to do anything seriously. One day I might have to find out."

"Well, maybe you don't have to worry about it right now."

"Certainly not. My concern now is how good a time we can have this weekend."

Latcham helped Julie by drying the dishes. Julie then poured two large brandies and they returned to the settee.

"Do you want the television on?"

"Not really. I'd rather go back to bed," replied Latcham.

"Another of your good ideas?" said Julie putting her head to one side and raising her eyebrows.

"One of my best."

Their lovemaking went on until the early hours of Saturday morning by which time they both fell into an exhausted sleep. One of Julie's extraordinary talents was her ability to programme herself to wake at a certain time. On this occasion she selected eight o'clock. When she awoke she opened her eyes immediately. Within two seconds she was wide awake. Latcham still slept and was breathing heavily.

Carefully, to avoid disturbing him, Julie reached under the bed. Her hand fell onto a box which she opened using a wrist action only. She removed the contents. Gently she rubbed the back of Latcham's left hand. Slowly the veins stood proud. Julie inserted the hypodermic needle into a vein and gently depressed the plunger into the syringe. Ten millilitres of potassium chloride entered Latcham's body. As she withdrew the needle, Latcham stirred and rubbed the back of his hand as if to brush off a crumb. He opened his eyes and looked up at Julie, whose face was now directly above his own. He smiled, closed his eyes again and died.

At ten minutes before eleven there was a knock at the door. Charles Weaver looked remarkably smart for a slob, Julie thought.

"Mr Weaver. How nice of you to come. Do come in." Julie's smile reached from ear to ear.

"Thank you, Miss Noble, and please call me Charles."

"Then do come in, Charles. I'm Claire."

Julie led the estate agent into the sitting room. Weaver looked around.

"You've made this look really nice," he said.

Julie knew that his words were empty. She had done very little to the flat. His small talk and flattery irritated immediately.

"Please sit down, Charles. May I offer you a coffee, or perhaps you would like something a little stronger?"

"I think the sun is over the yardarm. Do you have Scotch?"

Julie didn't answer. Instead she smiled and went into the kitchen. Weaver could hear the clattering of coffee cups and the opening and closing of cupboard doors. He was soon rejoined by his host who carried a tray bearing two coffee cups, a cafetiere, sugar bowl and two glasses. Julie set the tray on the coffee table and crossed the room to a cupboard from which she took a bottle.

"I think I have just the thing," she said.

She poured the whisky into the two glasses and then depressed the plunger on the cafetiere. As she poured the coffee she looked up at Weaver.

"Sugar, Charles?"

"Just one, please."

"Charles, I realise you're not at work at the moment and it's very nice to see you, but I wonder if I might impose upon your good nature?"

"Impose away, Claire."

"I have a problem in the bedroom."

Weaver laughed. "I can't imagine a woman like you having a problem in the bedroom."

Julie did not find it too difficult to maintain the smile. What a charmer, she thought.

"Not that kind of problem, Charles. There's something nasty in there. Perhaps you will be good enough to help me with it."

"Of course. Forgive my little indiscretion. Let's see what we can do."

Weaver rose and followed Julie into the bedroom. He immediately saw the mound under the bedclothes but he kept walking. He stopped when Julie reached the headboard. He was aware she had bent down quickly. She straightened and turned to face him raising her arms at the same time. Weaver was vaguely aware that a gun was being pointed in his direction but he had no time to react before Julie pulled the trigger.

The bullet entered the centre of his chest throwing him backwards against the wall, slightly to the left of the door through which he had just entered. There was a tiny entry wound but no exit wound. Julie knew there was little point in examining the body. The hollow bullet would have fragmented soon after entering the chest. The damage to the internal organs would be horrifying and the chance of surviving the injuries were nil.

Julie put on gloves and thoroughly wiped the Ginsberg Special with a soft cloth. She then placed it in the right hand of the corpse lying in her bed after having first ensured that Latcham's prints were spread over the gun. She smiled at the thought of the confusion this would be likely to cause. The gun would link Latcham to the slaying of Wells. In turn the slaying of Wells would be linked to W.F.M.C. Best of all, it would take away any heat she might have received from Harry and goodness knows who else. If it placed Latcham in Cheltenham when Wells was shot with this very gun, there would be no reason for Harry to suspect that Julie was in Cheltenham at the same time. Harry already knew that Latcham controlled Wells and the hit could realistically be attributed to Latcham, at least for a while.

Now she had a tedious chore. She started to place her belongings into black plastic bin liners. In went her clothes and makeup. She emptied all the food from the fridge and cupboards and placed the packs into the plastic bags. Next she started on the kitchen itself. Filling the washing up bowl from the kitchen with hot, soapy water, she wiped down all the surfaces, shelves, unit doors, appliances, the oven and its knobs. After wiping the electric plugs and their sockets she turned to the door handles on the cupboards and the kitchen door itself.

She thoroughly vacuumed the bedroom, pausing for a moment while she considered vacuuming under the estate agent's body. Good sense prevailed and she decided she should leave Mr Weaver where he had fallen. Forensics might get imaginative if they discovered the body had been moved post mortem. With fresh, warm, soapy water she wiped all the surfaces in the bedroom and then checked that everything she had moved into it was removed and put in the black bags. The sitting room took longer. She vacuumed the furniture as well as the floor. There were also more surfaces, handles and knobs to wipe here. When she was satisfied she had vacuumed all that could be vacuumed and wiped everything that could be wiped, she carried one of the bags to the bathroom door. She tipped the contents of the bowl into the basin and replaced it with fresh hot water and a squirt of washing-up liquid. She took off her clothes and threw them all into the bag.

She showered and dried. Before getting dressed, Julie washed the shower walls and the shower curtain with the water and detergent in the bowl. She picked out the hairs in the plug hole. Special attention was paid to the shower control knobs. Using the cloth as a barrier she pulled the shower curtain across for the last time. Next she wiped down the tiled walls and the towel rails. The lavatory also demanded special attention. The light cord, taps and wash basin were all wiped. Next she got on her hands and knees and wiped the floor thoroughly, leaving an unwashed space by the basin. Julie washed her hands in the basin for the last time and dried them. She finished wiping the floor and then threw the towels, the cloth she had used for wiping, the soap, shampoo, flannel, toothpaste and toothbrush into the bag. She tossed the washing up bowl into the bag and this was followed by the dust bag from the vacuum cleaner. Clarion smiled at the irony of it all. Here she was making an effort to clear away all residue of her presence. On the other hand, there was enough of her genetic material left on Latcham's body for the scientists to have a field day. It would be the simplest matter for them to obtain a genetic fingerprint, but what then? The chances of them achieving a DNA match were so remote as to be inconceivable, hardly worth another thought.

Reaching round the door into the sitting room, she found the pile of clothes she had left there. Quickly she dressed in tight-fitting jeans, blouse and leather flying jacket. She wore brown leather boots that had no tread pattern. Her large shoulder bag had been filled with only the items she needed with her. For one last time she walked through the flat, the back of which she would be very pleased to see. She remembered to wipe the light switches with a tissue. Now she was satisfied she had left nothing behind. She locked the flat door and went to the steak house. It was teatime but, since she had not eaten all day, she ordered a steak. She ate it quickly and returned to the flat when it was dark.

By nine that evening she had finished carrying the plastic bin liners, two at a time, to the commercial rubbish skip at the back of the steak house. She returned to the flat for the last time and collected her shoulder bag. She started the last walk back to the steak house, from where she phoned a taxi. One hour later she was on the last train of the evening bound for Cheltenham.

Harsh Words

Julie picked up a call from Harry on her answering service and, in response, made her way to the Isle of Wight. She usually found the trip relaxing with the drive across Salisbury Plain and the short sea crossing to the island. On this occasion, however, she was not looking forward to the encounter. Harry might well choose to make things extremely difficult for her and, in any case, she wanted the next few days off. This, she knew, was a fruitless wish and unrealistic in the extreme. With the limited information at her disposal, she knew there could be trouble around the corner. One of the key individuals had disappeared. It was to be expected and, had she been allowed to pursue the plan she had devised, this inconvenience might well not have happened. Worse still, the missing target knew Julie's face; the two women had been in the same room and had shared a conversation. This was another example of sloppiness. Contractors should never allow themselves to be compromised in such a sloppy way.

Harry and Julie followed the usual routine in Shanklin. By the time she entered the hotel Harry was already pouring the teas. The two hugged and Julie was relieved that Harry showed no sign of tension. The conversation opened with inconsequential matters, the journey, the weather and each other's health. Harry lied at this point, telling his protégé that he was in the pink. Julie didn't think he looked particularly well but let the matter pass.

"I see the police are linking Latcham with the assassination of Stephen Wells," Harry said. "A gun has provided the link apparently. Might lead back further to W.F.M.C. I dare say."

"What do you know about it? How close are the police?"

"Difficult to say. Pretty close by all accounts. Problem is, I daren't ask for the official angle. It would merely draw attention to the fact that Section P has an interest. I feel that would not be at all wise. Like you, I have to rely on the press reports. In any event Latcham is being put in the frame for the Wells' murder. What do you know about the two policemen who were murdered in Cheltenham around the time of Wells' murder?"

This was the moment Julie had been waiting for with apprehension.

"Saw it in the papers. Nobody's safe anymore. Appalling business."

"Yes, quite. Tell me about Miss Coleman-Burns then, poppet."

"Precious little to tell, I'm sorry to say. She is the sole survivor from your shopping list and I can't find her."

"I'm afraid you must find her, my dear. She is remarkably dangerous to all of us. She operated in Latcham's cell and knows more than I care to think. Find her, Julie."

"She was not at her office yesterday afternoon or this morning. She may have gone in first thing Monday but I wasn't there to see her. She will have seen the papers but, as yet, she won't know that the dead man in Filton is Latcham. Sooner or later, though, they're going to release his name and the proverbial will hit the fan. She can only guess at the moment and I suspect she is not in the guessing game. Normally I would watch the Latcham place and expect her to turn up. Can't do that though."

"Why?" said Harry.

"The goons are staking it out. I've seen the same suits sitting in a car outside that I saw in Wells' road. Clearly Wells was as indiscreet as we suspected. Which department are they, Harry?"

"No idea. Frankly I don't see that it makes any difference."

"Don't you now? Harry, this is your fault. I wanted to get Latcham and Coleman-Burns together. You put the skids under me and it was you who demanded I should act prematurely."

"There's not much profit in going over that again. You know full well that I had no choice and, in any case, you wouldn't have acted unless you agreed with the necessity. So please, poppet, let's not keep going over that old ground. The fact remains that our bird has flown. I can't set up a tracking net, either officially or unofficially. My section is not involved and cannot be seen to be. Find her and find her very quickly. Much depends on it. Now hear me, Clarion. This is not the avuncular Harry speaking now. This is the director of Section P. Find this woman and deal with her very fast."

Harry sighed and looked genuinely concerned as he stared at Clarion. "There's more I'm afraid. You recall there was a target on the original shopping list at which I asked you to look but not touch. Yes?"

Julie nodded. "Plans are in place. I merely need the go-ahead."

"Then now you have it. That provisional target has just reached the list, so now there's two to go, not one."

On the previous day, Monday, Melanie Coleman-Burns had sat in Chris Latcham's office awaiting his arrival for the usual Monday briefing. Latcham was a punctual man and so, when he had not shown by 9.25, she knew something was not right. A call to his PA advised her that there had been no messages. Coleman-Burns further learned that Latcham had not been working over the weekend. It was customary to advise the PA if work was to be conducted over a weekend. Latcham had left no such information. She checked his desk and found no clue there. None of her colleagues could shed any light on his whereabouts. By 10.30 she decided to leave the office and return to her flat. This, she felt, would give her room to think.

At around the time Melanie Coleman-Burns left the office, Julie Martin drove through the village of Little Appleton. She was driving her own Range Rover and kept within the speed limit of 30 miles per hour. One hundred yards from the drive of Latcham's house, she saw the same car she had seen watching Wells' house just a few days before.

Coleman-Burns made herself an espresso coffee and sat in her study to think.

Martin Garstang was dead. Police had made no arrests and, Melanie thought, they were unlikely to. Harvey Walsh was dead. Had Harvey killed Garstang? If he had, then who had killed Harvey? Where the hell was Latcham? Was he dead too? There were only questions now and she had no one to whom she could turn for answers. Walsh and Latcham had always been there before and now she had no one. Perhaps there was another possibility, but she hesitated to contact Eric Wynter. Yet why did she hesitate? He was still in overall control of the W.F.M.C. empire. He had trusted her in the very recent past, so he must have some regard for her.

And who was this girl, Claire Noble? Where had she sprung from? Why had Latcham been so bewitched by her? It was out of character for him. Her mind went back to the conversation she had had with Noble in the sitting room at Latcham's home. What had she learned? Precious little. The car, a Renault Clio, wasn't hers. She didn't work or so she said. She lived on a private income she claimed. And that was it, the sum total of the information she had gained during that conversation. There was absolutely nothing there to give her a clue or a lead to follow. Noble had talked but said nothing.

Chris had told her that Claire had a flat in Bristol and, surprise surprise, the flat was rented temporarily while Noble decided what she was going to do next. The more Coleman-Burns thought about Claire Noble the more she suspected her. She was not sure of what she suspected her but how could anyone pass on so little information? Melanie picked up her telephone. When she spoke to her office she learned that there was still no sign of Latcham.

"I think you had better tell Mr Wynter. Chris should really be there by now."

Latcham's PA told her that Wynter had been advised.

"I want you to do something," Coleman-Burns said. "Check out a Claire, that's C-L-A-I-R-E, Noble. I only know she lives in Bristol. Use the usual channels and be sure not to attract any attention. Call me back at my flat."

When she replaced the handset she already knew that there would be no trace. If Noble was telling the truth and she was renting temporary accommodation, there would probably be nothing if she had only been there for a few weeks. The Bristol people might strike lucky but she doubted it. She also doubted that Claire Noble was this woman's real name. If this was the case then there was no point whatsoever in putting a trace on her. In fact she may not even live in Bristol, but if Noble was not the right name, the matter of location was entirely academic. She cursed herself now. If only she had taken more interest in the hire car she might have had something to go on. All she knew was the make and model. She had no index number and she had no idea from where it was hired. That was another dead end.

The phone rang in the late afternoon.

"We have four Claire Nobles in Bristol spelt in the way you require. Want the addresses?"

"No. What I want is a photograph of each. Fortunately tomorrow is a weekday. Probably best to shoot them when they leave for work in the morning. Leave that with you."

"Okay. When do you want the photographs?"

"Wednesday morning latest. As a matter of interest were there any C-L-A-R-E's or C-L-A-I-R's?"

"Seven apparently."

"Shots of them too, please."

"Fine. Whose account?"

"Put it on my operational budget for now, please."

"You've got it. Anything else?"

"No. I think that'll do for now. Call me if there's any news." With that Melanie put the phone down and cursed.

So now the great Dr Jonjo Grey wanted to meet Eric Wynter. The concept of retirement had long been attractive to Wynter and he resented all the intrusions into his life of leisure. He put the blame wholly on the plate of Harvey Walsh and he cursed his rotten hide most days.

He had gone to eat humble pie with Webster Hahn. He had been brought to the attention of Sir Harry Buchanan and this was extremely disconcerting. It would have been difficult to choose two people in all the world he would rather stay clear of. Walsh had been a bastard of the first order. Wynter should have kept closer tabs on him and he certainly should have vetoed the contract with the Hahn family. At least for the time being, Hahn was off his back. In any event, a solution was forming in his mind, a solution which would put an end to any potential risk from Hahn or the family. But now Dr Jonjo Grey wanted to see him. Normally Wynter would have declined a meeting with courtesy and dignity, but he knew that if Grey wanted to see him it had to be connected with all this trouble he had at the moment.

Part of the problem was that the obvious successor to Walsh was missing. It did not take a great imagination for a suggestion to present itself. Wynter knew, not just suspected, that Latcham was dead. He also knew that Harry Buchanan would not be far from the cause of Latcham's absence. Sooner or later the body would show. Walsh, under Wynter's guidance, had groomed Latcham for the last two years to take over the general management of W.F.M.C. should there be any unforeseen emergency. Now it was a further irritation that this plan would not come to fruition. Because there was no one who could take over immediately, Wynter was still having to work full time.

Jonjo Grey would want something for sure. What had Wynter that Grey could possibly covet? Grey was arriving this day and Wynter had agreed to meet him at his home. This was a considerable risk and he, of all people, knew never to take unnecessary risks. But now he felt too tired to go traipsing up to London or, worse still, to accept Grey's invitation to cross the Atlantic. He had not yet recovered from the exertions of his last trip to the States.

By the time the manservant announced the arrival of Dr Grey, Wynter was feeling some excitement. He asked that Grey be shown to the library. When the two men met for the first time they shook hands. Each had heard much about the other's activities, and it was clear from the outset that each would be respectful and courteous. Wynter made Grey feel welcome and ensured he had been offered a range of beverages, hot and alcoholic. He made sure Grey was comfortably settled in a vast leather chair close to a roaring log fire. This, thought Wynter, would be exactly the ambience expected by an American. This would be entirely in line with the American's perception of the old country. A dusty old man surrounded by dry and dusty old books in a wood-panelled library with a real roaring fire. Here he would feel safe and secure. He would feel able to converse without any undue sense of threat.

"Mr Wynter, I'm very glad you felt able to see me at such short notice," said Grey. "I appreciate the courtesy."

"You're most welcome, Dr Grey. I've heard much about you and I'm delighted to have the opportunity to meet you." Here Wynter paused. "I am bound to say, however, that I am a little surprised that the great captain of industry, Dr Jonjo Grey, needs to see me so urgently. I am a retired businessman. It is difficult to imagine how I can help you. I feel extremely honoured, though, that I might be in a position to assist."

"I come to you on a very delicate matter. You are indeed in a position to help me. You have in your possession some items which are, to me, of considerable value. Like you, I find myself embroiled with the family of Webster Hahn. Perhaps you should be advised that Webster and I have been acquaintances for many years and we can truthfully call each other friends. I find myself in an embarrassing and difficult situation with a member of the family and I think you can help me."

Grey paused to allow Wynter to speak. He wanted Wynter to speak because he had no idea how Wynter would react. In turn, Wynter was far too wily an old bird to show his colours at this stage.

Grey cleared his throat. "As I said, you have something which would be of considerable value to me. I have to risk insulting you by asking you to name your price. By selling me the items, I feel that any pressure you are experiencing from the Hahns will go away. It will focus on me instead. In addition, by selling to me, you will have gained a lifelong friend and ally. A time might come when you will need my help. You would be in a position where you would only have to ask."

Grey paused again. He was aware he had not mentioned the items he sought. He wanted to hold onto this until he could gauge Wynter's position. Wynter however, was aware of the technique and was not going to let Grey get away with it.

"It is difficult for me to assess whether or not I am in a position to help you since you have not told me what I own that is so important to you. It would save us both time if you would unburden yourself of this information."

Grey smiled. He had to admire the old man. It was becoming clear to Grey why Wynter had built such a large and powerful empire in such a difficult and dangerous field.

"You have a series of computer floppy disks. These disks, I know, contain sensitive information relating to the Hahn family business. It is these disks I would like to buy from you. Please tell me your price."

Wynter sat motionless for several minutes, in fact for so long that Grey became concerned for his health.

"Mr Wynter?" he said quietly.

Wynter looked up. "I wonder how it is you came by the knowledge that I have these disks in my possession? This is a matter that concerns me greatly. However we will not pursue this now. At this time I do not have a market price for the disks."

Shit, thought Grey. This old buzzard is going to run an auction.

"In any event, it may be that I will not sell them at any price. I may find I have a use for them myself."

"It's difficult to imagine what use you could have for them, Mr Wynter. You are a retired businessman, you told me. You are retired, living in this beautiful old house in England. My interests and those of Mr Hahn are in America."

Wynter went on as if he had not heard a word Grey had spoken. "However, in fairness to you because you are the first to ask, when I reach a decision I will advise you immediately and you will be in a position to make your offer. I warn you though, Dr Grey, should I decide to sell, the price will be high. Very high indeed."

Julie had found herself the ideal tube station entrance. If she had been able to design one specifically for her purpose, it would have looked much like the one in which she now found herself. The tube station was busy and so it was no great feat to lose oneself. It was spacious and contained a number of kiosks, a coffee shop and a fast food franchise situated around the main concourse. This enabled Julie to move around and still have sight of the building. She could see the comings and goings of passengers and commuters, and just opposite was the main entrance of the head office of Wynter Farmer Management Consultants.

Julie first arrived at the station at seven on Wednesday morning. In truth she expected that the exercise would bring forth no positive result but she had to go through the textbook processes. The time might come when she would be asked to list the steps she had taken to locate Melanie Coleman-Burns. If she ignored this first and most obvious step, she would inevitably open herself to criticism.

She felt uncomfortable on this Wednesday morning and not just because she felt that this observation exercise was a waste of time. She was uncomfortable about the untidiness of the operation. There was a trail of bodies and one extraordinarily important target was wandering around. She was unhappy about how easily Harry had been able to make her change her plans. It was partly her planning ability that had made her such a success in the past, and it was the planning which had kept her alive. Harry had been able to make her discard her plans as if they were some empty packaging. Why had she allowed it? Harry had made her bring forward the killings, to execute the assassinations out of the carefully planned order and in the wrong places. Latcham and Coleman-Burns were to have died within seconds of each other, and Julie had taken considerable risks to set this up. She had allowed herself to meet Latcham and Coleman-Burns. Both could have identified her. Now she was left with Coleman-Burns, who could not only identify her but who was bound to be suspicious of the mysterious woman, Claire Noble.

Her uneasiness turned to resentment. There was a time when she would not have allowed Harry to contact her during an operation still less allow him to make her change her plans. For years she had been aware of burnout but she had assumed it only happened to others. She thought she was not subject to the rules that affected everyone else. But it was happening now. The Clarion Resource was losing her edge, she was burning out. Now was the time to retire or at least take a long holiday. The consequences seemed most unattractive. These were the unsettling thoughts which darted through her mind as she waited and watched from various points in the tube station.

It was while she was drinking her third cup of coffee that Julie saw her. She saw a head she recognised just before it passed behind another and became hidden from view. Julie stood slowly and moved two paces to her right. She now had a three quarters view of the head of Melanie Coleman-Burns. Well I never. Our bird has landed, Julie said to herself. Julie watched her target enter the front door of W.F.M.C. at 10.50 that morning.

Melanie Coleman-Burns felt relief as she entered the secure and familiar surroundings of her office. She called Latcham's PA, who joined her within one minute. She entered carrying a brown wallet folder.

"Any news?"

"Nothing," replied the PA, who looked resigned to the loss of Latcham. She shook her head gently. "I've got the photographs you ordered."

"Good-oh. Let's have a look then, shall we?"

The PA laid out the shots on Melanie's desk. When they had been organised into three rows, the PA started her commentary.

"Right, Mel. The address of each subject is on the back of the shot. These four at the top were all taken as the subjects left or entered their homes. These are the C-L-A-I-R-Es. As I said, there are four of them. The two underneath are the C-L-A-I-Rs and the bottom five are the C-L-A-R-Es. Here's the purchase requisition. Sorry it was so expensive but we had to use a team rather than one photographer. You wanted all the shots by this a.m."

"Not a problem. Thanks for sorting all this. Let me sign that for you." Melanie held out her hand for the purchase requisition. She glanced at it and grimaced. "Bloody hell. You're not wrong. Clearly we're in the wrong business."

She waited until the PA had left the office before studying the photographs carefully. She was impressed by their clarity. Most shots appeared as if the subject had been looking directly into the camera. Several could have been posed, studio shots. Melanie was disappointed but not at all surprised not to find the likeness of the Claire Noble she had met at Latcham's place among the shots on her desk.

She gathered up the photographs and placed them in a file, which she placed in her security cabinet. She left the office bound for her home again.

Julie saw her target leave the front door of her employer's office and head back to the station. She followed her down two long flights of escalators and watched her on the platform. Julie was confident she would not be seen. The platform was crowded and it appeared as if the subject was mentally elsewhere. She felt the wall of air hit her as the train compressed the air in front of it, sending it blasting onto the platform. Next she heard the clatter and rumble and within a few seconds the train stopped. She watched the target press the button to open the door and step into the carriage. Julie counted three before entering the carriage in front. She knew that tails have a habit of coming unstuck when their subjects appear to entrain. It's the easiest thing in the world to step back off again just as the door closes. This leaves the tail with no option but to stay where they are. If they follow suit and jump off, assuming there is time, they are assured their cover will be broken. This was not one of those embarrassing occasions. Melanie Coleman-Burns had no thoughts of throwing her tail. Her mind was elsewhere.

Likewise, detraining is a sensitive part of a tail. Again, this provided no difficulty and Julie followed her target. She watched her walk down the steps to her basement flat. With her safe inside the flat, Julie had time to look around at the buildings in the street. She would give the target ten minutes to settle before she knocked the door and carried out her commission. During the wait she made a note of alleys, high windows, pubs and shop doors. She checked the vehicles and was relieved not to recognise any of the cars which where parked on both sides of the road. As the ten-minute point approached, Julie involuntarily tapped her shoulder bag. She was about to cross the road when her target walked back up the steps.

She followed her to the end of the road where she turned right into another road running at right angles. It was here that Julie spotted the big BMW which, from her briefing, she already knew to be the target's company car. As the car pulled away, she realised she was stuck. She had no transport and the chances of a black cab pulling down the street at this moment were not good.

Before finding her Range Rover and driving back to Tewkesbury, Julie had one more task to complete. It was unfortunate it had to be done now but that was the way of it. Tomorrow would be no good. She needed to find her old friend Dennis Mann. Mann had retired from the army, having achieved the rank of regimental sergeant major. Julie Martin had had the opportunity of working with Mann on a small number of operations and felt safer with him than anyone else in the world. She considered him to be an operational wizard. His practicality and reliability were remarkable and she viewed him as a towering genius. Not for Mann, the status of commissioned officer. His rank of RSM and the life it offered suited him perfectly. He would have liked to have continued longer in the service but he did have one small shortcoming. Whisky was his Achilles heel and so he left the army rather earlier than expected and set himself up as a private detective. He specialised in surveillance and the serving of summonses.

Julie worked alone but once again Harry had placed impossible requirements upon her. He had broken more rules than she could be bothered to count and now it was her turn to break a rule or two.

Eventually she found a black taxi and asked to be dropped at the Prince Consort public house in Camden. When she entered the pub it didn't take her long to find her man. Dennis Mann stood at the bar surrounded by a group of other lounge lizards. These people gave Mann the perfect audience for his tales and enabled him to remain the centre of attention for as long as it suited him. Julie was pleased that he stopped in mid flow within two seconds of her coming into the crowded pub. He had spotted her. "Excuse me," he said pushing aside two of his friends and made for a corner of the bar. This too pleased Julie. He hadn't lost his edge entirely. For most people the natural reaction would have been to approach her immediately. Instead, Mann isolated himself, watched and waited.

Julie walked to the bar and ordered a designer water. She paid and then turned and leaned on the bar in such a way as to afford her a view of the entire pub. For two minutes the two people watched and then Julie looked directly at Mann. He smiled and nodded and walked to a table close to the corner in which he had been standing. Julie joined him and kissed him on the cheek before sitting.

"Well, this is a surprise, Julie. Or is it Julie at the moment?"

"Julie will do very nicely. How are you, Dennis?"

"Mustn't grumble. You know how it is. Do a bit here and a bit there. What about you? I guess you must be working or we wouldn't be talking, would we?"

"What's your going rate now, Dennis?"

"Always to the point. For you let's say two hundred a day plus expenses."

Julie laughed. "You've been watching too many low budget movies. Two hundred a day plus expenses," she mimicked. "Look, I've got an open-ended job, minimum four days but possibly longer. I'll pay you a thousand a week with a guaranteed minimum of two thousand. You look after your own expenses." Julie cocked her head and raised an eyebrow as if waiting for an answer.

"When do I start?"

"No rush, now will do nicely."

The two talked for another hour before Julie left to find her car for the drive back to Gloucestershire.

News from Erifia

Foreigners derive pleasure from laughing at the British preoccupation with the weather. They do it because they haven't experienced it. In their own countries they are likely to be accustomed to a climate. There are parts of the British Isles which don't enjoy a climate, they merely have weather.

Thursday morning was another of those miserable winter experiences so bemoaned by the English. Many had learned at school that the colder the air temperature, the less moisture it is able to hold. This rule didn't seem to work. In fact it was as useless a piece of information as another great misconception, "it's too cold to snow." The air temperature this morning was cold enough to make the bones ache. To make life even more miserable, everything was damp to the touch, a cold miserable dampness. Clothes on washing lines failed to dry, even in the howling wind. The inside of car windscreens were covered in condensation, giving them a frosted appearance. If anyone were foolish enough to venture out without a waterproof coat, then soon they would be soaked to the skin even though it wasn't raining.

Julie Martin was pleased to get inside her shop this morning. She went straight to her office, removed her gloves and coat and flicked on the coffee filter machine. She checked the duty roster on her wall. Before going any further she waited for her coffee. When it was ready she savoured the warmth of the liquid. As she sipped her way down the third cup the clock ticked over to nine a.m. The moment it did so, Julie picked up her phone.

"Gable, Creasey and Stock. Good morning."

"Tim Stock, please."

"I'm afraid Mr Stock is not in yet. May I take a message?"

"Oh, do try for me, will you? It's Julie Martin here."

"Just a moment, Miss Martin. I'll try again for you."

A male voice came on the line. "Julie! How nice to hear from you. It's been a long while."

"I lead an uneventful life, Tim. Little need for a lawyer." Julie often wondered how the partners at her firm of solicitors would view her if they knew of her other identity. Naturally they had no idea that she had another means of acquiring wealth far removed from her tea shop and deli. "However, with your help it's about to become a lot less boring."

"How so, Julie?"

"Simple. I want you to sell the business for me." It was Claire Noble who had put the idea into her head. If Claire could take time out to decide what to do with the rest of her life, then why couldn't Julie Martin?

"What?" This came as a real surprise to the lawyer. "But it's doing really well, isn't it?"

"Absolutely. Just the right time to quit, wouldn't you say? Quit while I'm ahead. It's all getting a bit tedious. I need a change of scene, something new to get my teeth into."

"Like what?" said the lawyer.

"Well, that rather depends on how good a deal you get for me, doesn't it? I want you to keep this under your hat for the time being. I don't want the staff to get wind of it. I think you should talk to my accountants first. They're bang up-to-date and I'm showing a good position."

"Okay. I'll set things in motion immediately. Anything else?"

"Plenty. I won't be putting this with local agents so I want you to deal with all of it at your end. That okay?"

"Of course. Perhaps we ought to meet for lunch and go over the finer points."

"Soon, but there's more. I also want you to sell my cottage."

"Julie, is there anything wrong?"

"No, no. Not at all." Julie laughed. "I really am ready for a change. Now jump to it and get it valued and moving for me. I don't expect I will want to hear from your valuers unless they come up with a figure in excess of seven hundred and fifty thousand for the business and cottage. Now getting hold of me is a bit difficult. I'm having an extended break at the moment. Out and about a lot, you know? Best you leave a message on my answering service at the cottage. I'll get back to you as soon as I pick up your message. Anyway, you shouldn't need to talk for a bit. Just start the ball rolling and don't start at a figure lower than three quarters of a million. Nice to talk to you again, Tim, and I'll take you up on the lunch soon. Bye."

Julie replaced the handset.

On the following Wednesday the press made the world aware that Red Pasqualle, the hero of Erifia, was dead. He had been found hanging from a balcony at his hotel a few miles south of Erifi. There were apparently no suspicious circumstances and police were not looking for anyone in connection with the death, or so the press said. Most of the broadsheet newspapers in Western Europe and the United States ran extensive obituaries on Pasqualle. This was especially true in Britain. The Telegraph, Times, Guardian and Independent each ran Pasqualle's picture and a brief report of his death on their front pages. This they followed with editorial comment inside.

As occasionally happens when an international figure dies, it was difficult to pick up any negative comment at all. Negative stuff tends to follow in later years, but for now he appeared to be a pillar of society, a hardworking and successful man of business. He was not only a friend of President Sandriano but his saviour. The president owed his restoration to Red Pasqualle.

Red Pasqualle was a hero at home and abroad, and while his nation mourned, the world watched with sadness and passing interest. As the week wore on, however, the tone of the press began to change. The world had been told that Pasqualle had committed suicide. Now it seemed as if there was more to it.

The president's solicitor general who, like President Sandriano, had known Pasqualle well, was uncomfortable. Neither he nor the president wished to influence a police investigation, but they urged the inspector general, Erifia's most senior police officer, to take another look at the circumstances surrounding the death. This he did after receiving the official report from the coroner.

At midday on the Thursday, President Jacques Sandriano broadcast to the nation. A transcript of his words appeared in the following day's Examiner. Most of the people of Erifia listened to their radios on this occasion and they heard their president's genuine grief. They heard his voice waver and, on two occasions, crack. Sandriano took time on both of these occasions to regain his composure.

"People of Erifia. This is your president speaking to you at this very sad time. By now all of you will have heard of the death of Red Pasqualle. He died on Monday. All of you know that Red was a dear friend to me and a dear friend to our country.

"During the recent events, it was Red who stood for us and for what we believe, our freedom and our democracy. Each one of us owes much to Red Pasqualle and I, probably more than most. To accept that Red is no longer with us is difficult. To learn that he may have been taken from us is almost too painful to bear. I cannot believe that anyone would want Red dead, but someone did. Red was murdered.

"My solicitor general and the inspector general will stop at nothing to identify and apprehend the person responsible for this heinous act. They will use all their resources, they will leave no stone unturned, they will take whatever action they believe will help them to find this evil killer. Inevitably this might cause some of you, the good people of Erifia, some inconvenience. I hope you will help the authorities in every way possible.

"Now I ask that you pray for our dear, departed friend. God bless you all."

Red's body was found hanging from the rail of the balcony of his apartment. It was found at first light on Tuesday. The first thoughts were suicide. There was no sign of a struggle and it looked as if Red had placed the loop around his own neck, stood on the rail and jumped. Almost immediately, though, there were those who had known Red well and found the circumstances odd. There was no note, not that that was a cast iron indicator. It is not inevitable that the deceased wants the world to know why he has taken his own life or that he has to offer a justification for killing himself. Red was fit, happy and making plans for the future of his prosperous business, plans for holidays, plans for a major expansion and refurbishment of the hotel and restaurant.

Nevertheless, it looked as if Red had indeed killed himself. The feelings of his friends were subjective. Dr Anderson was head of the Public Medical Office, which conducted post mortems and forensic medical examinations. When he arrived at Pasqualle's apartment late on Tuesday afternoon, he took one look and said "Murder." Those present looked at him in amazement.

"It's very simple. He weighs better than two hundred and thirty pounds. How far is it from the rail to his neck. Measure it for me someone, will you? I bet it's a good five metres. Add to that the height of his shoulders above the rail. Five feet would you say? So we're talking well over six metres his neck travelled before it was brought to a halt by the rope. Rate of acceleration is fourteen feet per second per second. By the time the rope stopped his fall he would be travelling at a hell of a lick. That, along with his weight. I'll do all the calculations later but I know that if that's what happened, Red's body would not be intact. His head and body would have parted company. But what do we have here? A neat corpse with what looks like a little bruise on the side of the neck. I don't think so, people. He was murdered."

The report was sent to the inspector general and the solicitor general on Wednesday afternoon. It left little doubt that Red had indeed been murdered. Within a short time the inspector general had set up a task force to investigate the death. Slowly a picture emerged but it was soon realised that it was too late.

Members of the task force, each of which had to report directly to the inspector general, interviewed scores of people, and gradually the pieces began to fit together. The process was hampered by politics, however. Because of the huge public interest and the specific interest of the president, the inspector general tried to demonstrate his commitment by making everyone involved report to him. The Police Department's normal line management structure was bypassed. This made the process unwieldy and cumbersome. It prevented vital evidence being quickly linked and much later would become a case study for police forces and management consultants throughout the world. It showed that, in a democracy, there was no place for political pressure and involvement with the investigation process and it showed the value of a clear line management structure. It clearly demonstrated to future students what could happen if these basic principles were ignored.

Despite the mismanagement, a suspect began to emerge from the interviews. A woman reporter became the focus of the investigation. Unfortunately, there was little agreement about what this reporter looked like. There was considerable agreement among male witnesses that she was beautiful, gorgeous, lovely, stunning, breathtaking. Some of the female witnesses thought she wasn't really up to much. She was variously described as slim, a little plump, blonde, brunette, dark, hourglass figure. Some claimed she wore spectacles, others thought she did not. Two people said she smoked. But everyone agreed that this stranger smiled a lot and was charming.

The task force discovered that a woman calling herself Caitlin Docherty arrived from Paris aboard the Saturday morning Air France flight. By that evening she had booked into Pasqualle's hotel. She had let it be known to staff that she wanted to interview Red and eventually this news reached him. As she ate Sunday lunch in the hotel restaurant Red had joined her at her table. Observers reported that they seemed to be getting on very well. There was much laughing and apparently pleasant conversation. They spent most of the evening in each other's company and when Red left her she ordered another drink, which she drank alone in the bar.

Next morning she ate breakfast alone. The next time Docherty and Pasqualle were seen together was Monday lunchtime. They dined together and again there seemed to be much jollity. At around five p.m. they left the coffee lounge together, and this was the last time Pasqualle was seen alive. Or rather, police could find no one who admitted seeing him after this time.

There was one event that later became the subject of an investigation. Sometime during Monday night a four-wheel-drive vehicle was stolen from the hotel's car park. Car theft was not common in Erifia. Surprisingly this reported crime was not linked to Red's murder until the vehicle was found at the airport late on Wednesday evening.

Passenger lists were only inspected on Wednesday afternoon and evening. There had been four international flights since midnight Monday and four possible women were highlighted from the passenger lists. The name of Caitlin Docherty showed nowhere. It was a simple matter to check with the authorities, immigration and police at the destinations of the four suspects. Three were eliminated quickly but one posed a problem. A woman had arrived at London Heathrow at 1320 on Tuesday. It was determined that this woman passenger, travelling on a passport in the name of Danielle Lambert, was a suspect. In fact, Danielle Lambert was the only suspect.

The name of Danielle Lambert meant nothing to anyone in Erifia. Equally important, absolutely no trace could be found of Caitlin Docherty. There was no evidence that Docherty had left the country by any of the border crossings. No airlines could demonstrate her name on a passenger list. The masters of all ships, which had left the port of Erifi since Monday, were contacted and searches were instigated. No stowaway was found. All that was left was the name of Danielle Lambert, and just who was she? It was not long before the inspector general had to admit that his bird had flown and any chance of an arrest was all but gone.

Surprise Offer

During the afternoon of the Wednesday following the death of Red Pasqualle, Julie knew where she could find Dennis Mann. It gave her some satisfaction that, despite knowing what he was doing, she could not find him. Her satisfaction turned to a show of good-humoured irritation when she heard Mann's voice from behind a van.

"Bang bang. You're dead." Mann emerged from behind the van. He was wearing a big grin.

"Just because you're using me for your eyes it doesn't mean you can afford to wander around with your own eyes closed. Obviously you're getting old and careless."

"Very droll," replied Julie. "I've spotted several of your surveillance spots. There's the basement next door and it's rather fortunate for you there are still hedges around. There's two handy ones where you can see the target's door and the householders are out at the moment. Now tell me, how many cars have you in the road?"

Mann laughed. "Good girl. As a matter of fact two, at the moment. Had three yesterday. Had none on Monday. Had a lorry instead. Actually dug up the road on Sunday. Waste of time that was."

"So what have we got?"

"Not what you're expecting. No sign of the target. Looks like she's sent a runner. Young fellow, 'bout twenty, maybe older. I guess hundred eighty pounds, no less. Dark hair, fairly handsome I should think, but then I expect you'd be a better judge than me. No taller than six feet one inch. Dresses smart casual. He's clean, tidy and well groomed. Know him?"

"No. I don't think so."

"Our boy hasn't shown today. First saw him 1030 hours on Friday. Then 1045 Monday and 1020 yesterday. Like I said, no sign today."

"Nor on Saturday or Sunday?"

"Nope. Just Friday, Monday and Tuesday."

"Okay. She can afford not to send him over the weekend. Likewise she can afford not to send him today. Her boy may not be available to run errands over the weekend. At least let's make that assumption for now. She won't want to let post stack up for too long. She might be expecting important news. Chances are then, our laddo may be here tomorrow. You say each visit was between 1020 and 1045?" Mann nodded. "This runner is not as free as a bird, is he? His life is ordered in some way. Perhaps he's on his way to or from work."

"If you'd let me leave this bloody street I could have had an answer to that."

Julie ignored the interruption. "It's my guess that we'll be seeing our clean-cut friend tomorrow. How long does he spend there?"

"Four or five minutes only."

"Okay, Dennis. You're relieved, for the time being at least." Clarion handed Mann an envelope. "Here's two thousand. I don't think I'll need you again on this, but, just in case, make sure you're in your boozer tomorrow evening, let's say 1800. Just in case, old friend."

"Aren't you going to let me in on the job?"

"Dennis, dear Dennis."

"Oh, well. You can't blame me for trying, can you?"

"You should know better at your age. Now clear away all your equipment, vehicles, campfires and stuff and return this street to proper order."

Julie's first thought was to get herself inside the basement flat. There was every chance, however, that there would be an intruder system over and above the usual. She was not prepared to take the risk. There was a much safer way to achieve her ends. So it was that Julie Martin sat in yet another hire car on this Thursday morning. She could clearly see the top of the steps that led down to Melanie Coleman-Burns' basement flat door. Julie felt waves of confidence wash over her as she waited. She felt she was, by and large, doing a good job despite the irritations along the way. In any case they were not of her doing. It was her client who was making things difficult, but she had the added satisfaction of knowing she had successfully responded to the changing environment into which she had been thrown. Her instinct was telling her now that she was reaching the end of this operation and it was all downhill from now on. She was soon to find that her sixth sense had let her down.

At 1040 she saw the young man so accurately described by Dennis Mann. She saw him descend the steps and then disappear from view. She looked at her watch and waited for three and a half minutes before she got out of the car. Knocking confidently on the door, she waited. There was no reply. Julie knew there was no back entrance and that, at this moment, the young man was puzzling over what he should do. She knocked on the door again, louder this time. There was still no response. She knocked a third time and lowered her head to the letterbox.

"Come on. Open up. This is the police."

Finally there was a response. The young man, who Julie guessed was a little older than twenty, opened the door. He looked frightened. Without waiting for an invitation, Julie pushed past him into the flat. The first impression was extremely favourable. She was surprised at the opulence of the furnishings and the quality of the art on the walls. For some reason she had put Miss Coleman-Burns down as a something of a Spartan. She had expected that everything would have been utilitarian. She now knew that her target was a woman of taste and a high discretionary spending power. She turned round abruptly to face the man.

"Come in and shut the door." She gestured with her hands for him to come closer to her. "And you are?"

"May I see your identification please?" he said.

This was the second time Julie had been surprised in less than one minute. She had expected him to be a little timid. He had regained his composure well and was, quite properly, standing his ground.

"Of course. I'm so sorry." Julie took out a police warrant card and held it up so it could be read. She made no attempt to remove it quickly. Indeed there was no reason for her to do so since the card was genuine. The resources, which Harry made available to her, could make her job such a pleasure. "Detective Inspector Donna Pritchard. Now will you tell me who you are, please?"

"Jon Thorpe. Is there something wrong?"

Julie ignored the question. "Is this your flat?"

"Uh, well, no."

"So what are you doing here?"

It was plain to Julie that Jon Thorpe had been briefed. He was unsure of what to do now. He had probably been told that someone was after Coleman-Burns but he would not have been advised that it was the police. Now here he was, face to face with an inspector from the Metropolitan Police Force. It would have been an uncomfortable position.

"I'm collecting something for the owner."

"Like what, for instance?"

"Like the post."

"Find any?"

"No, there wasn't any this morning."

"This morning? Does that mean you have been here before?"

The was a pause. "No. Only today."

"I don't think you're telling me the truth, Jon, but we'll let it pass for now. What is the name of the owner?"

"But surely you know that, or why are you here?"

"Yes, I know it. I want to know if you know it. I'll ask you again. What is the name of the owner?"

"Miss Coleman-Burns. Melanie Coleman-Burns. Now will you tell me why you're here?"

"Jon, I don't feel you quite grasp how these things work. It is I who ask the questions. It is your place to answer them quickly and truthfully. Have you got it now? To continue, it is unclear to me why you are here collecting the post. Why is Miss Coleman-Burns not collecting her own post?"

"She can't."

"What do you mean, she can't."

"She can't come here."

"I think we'd better go down to the station, don't you? I don't think we're getting anywhere here."

"No, it's just that..." He stopped and appeared to be struggling with the next sentence.

"Just what, Jon? Come on, please. This is getting tedious. Either you tell me what's going on or you and I take a trip to the fun factory."

"Melanie is scared."

"Scared of what?"

"She thinks someone is after her." Julie looked Thorpe in the eyes. It was a cold disarming stare that was well practised.

"She thinks she's in danger. She thinks someone wants to kill her."

"Why would someone want to kill her, Jon?"

"I don't know."

"Guess."

He shook his head.

"Okay. Who are you?"

"I told you. My name is Jon Thorpe."

"Yes, you told me your name. I want to know what you are. How do you know Melanie? How does Melanie know you?"

"I'm just a friend."

"Well, Jon, you give me a problem. Let me put it like this. If you think Melanie's life is in danger you must be a very good friend to get mixed up in her life like this. Coming to her flat, collecting her post."

For the first time there was a slight smile on Jon's face. "I didn't say I think her life's in danger. I said she thinks her life is in danger. I think she has an overactive imagination." He paused again. "Or rather I thought she had an overactive imagination."

"What's changed?"

"You. Why are you here? Is Melanie in trouble with the police?"

"Could be. Trouble is, it looks like she's dragged you in as well."

"No. Everything I've told you is true. I only collect her post for her. There's no law against that, is there?"

"Don't be silly," Julie replied coldly. Then her tone softened. "Well, let's see if we can get to the bottom of this. Where is Melanie now?"

"She's staying with me." Another surprise. This left a trail that was ridiculously easy to follow. In fact, so easy, that Julie thought it rather unlikely to be true. She now had to take a risk.

"What's your address, Jon?" Julie wrote it down as Jon spoke. "I'm going to have to trust you. What I'm going to tell you now must go no further. Is that absolutely clear?" The young man nodded. "Okay. It's like this. Melanie is correct. Her life may be at risk. It is my job to ensure she stays safe and sound. She is in danger through no fault of her own. One of her colleagues got himself mixed up with some very nasty types, one of which is a senior police officer at the Yard. Her colleague thinks Melanie knows too much of his business and wants to quieten her permanently. Trouble is, Melanie lost herself before we could get to her. Now we can't protect her. Do you think she'll be at your place now?"

"I expect so. She doesn't go out much at the moment."

"Now listen very carefully. You must say nothing. It is imperative you act as if nothing has happened. We haven't met here. You have never heard of Detective Inspector Donna Pritchard. Is that absolutely crystal clear? Do you understand how important it is that you remain quiet? You have found yourself involved with a major internal investigation. At this time we don't know how far this penetrates the police force. We only know it does.

"As I said, you are now involved. I will do my best to keep you out of it but I can make no promises. Now go about your business and be sure you keep your routine normal. Melanie must not get a whiff of any of this. Clear?"

Thorpe nodded. "Yes. What else should I do?"

"Absolutely nothing. I will want to talk to you again very soon, but I know where to contact you now. Off you go, Jon. See you soon."

When he had left, Julie breathed deeply. She had managed to buy herself some time. There was every chance that, after much thought, Thorpe would analyse the story and find it wanting. But that would take time. At the moment he would be shell-shocked by it all and he would accept it. This would give Julie all the time she would need.

"Sit down, Melanie." Eric Wynter pointed to the large, leather wing chair as he spoke. The atmosphere in his study gave the impression of Dickensian opulence. Rows of hidebound volumes covered two walls. The vast desk was littered with trinkets collected during half a century and more. There was an astrolabe, pens, and ancient blotter. The impression could be at once comfortable and unsettling. Melanie Coleman-Burns felt unsettled.

"I'm sorry to trouble you, sir."

"Not at all, young lady. In fact I'm glad you've come. We have what I believe they call unfinished business." Wynter opened a drawer in his desk and withdrew a newspaper. He walked to where Coleman-Burns was sitting and handed it to her. "Have you seen this? It's the piece ringed in red."

It was the previous day's edition of the Western Daily Press. The woman read it a first time, looked up at Wynter and then down again to read once more. When she had finished there was a tear in her eye.

Mystery victim identified, ran the headline. The copy was of particular interest. Police have identified the second body in the Filton death mystery. It is that of 44-year-old business analyst, Christopher Latcham. His body, along with that of local estate agent Charles Weaver, was discovered in a Filton flat early last week. Police are looking for the tenant, a Miss Claire Noble. Neighbours have not seen her since before the bodies were discovered. At this time police are not saying if they suspect foul play.

Mr Latcham was a senior representative of leading London business house, Wynter Farmer Management Consultants. A spokesman for the company said today, 'We had no idea anything was wrong until last Monday when Chris failed to turn up at his office. He was well liked and respected by his colleagues and by the company's many clients.'

Our correspondent has discovered that this is not the first death to hit Wynter Farmer recently. The managing director, Harvey Walsh (45) was found murdered near Cheltenham just a few weeks ago. Police are not linking the two deaths.

Wynter handed a tissue to Coleman-Burns. She was clearly distressed. She dried her eyes and blew her nose. Her usually perfect makeup was looking a little jaded.

"Why aren't the police linking the two? Chris was murdered too, wasn't he?"

"The police don't seem to think so."

"What was he doing in that flat with that man, what's his name?"

"His name was Charles Weaver. I was rather hoping you could shed some light on that."

"Shed some light on what?" snapped Melanie.

"What he was doing naked in a flat with another man."

Melanie's forehead creased. "What are you saying, sir?"

"Merely that I find it odd that a very senior member of our firm should be found dead in a flat. He was naked, in bed and in the presence of the corpse of another man. Don't you find that a bit bizarre? Or do you have some knowledge about Latcham's habits to which I am not privy?"

"I can't believe this. Are you saying Chris was gay?"

"I'm asking you what you know. I don't know if Chris was gay. What I do know is that his naked body was found in a flat with the body of another man. Now just what do you think I should be thinking, eh?"

"Look, sir. Chris wasn't gay. He had introduced me to a girlfriend, Claire Noble. I met her at Chris's place. She lived in Bristol. I've run a check on her and come up with nothing. There's a chance the identity she sold Chris doesn't exist."

"All right, Melanie. Calm yourself."

"That's fucking easy for you to say. Walsh is dead and Latcham is fucking dead and all you can say is fucking calm yourself."

"Your outbursts and histrionics won't help. Calm down and tell me why you wanted to come here to talk to me."

Melanie was shaking. Whether it was with temper or fear, Wynter did not know. He was concerned that here was an expensively trained and experienced member of the operations team and she was falling apart. He watched her as she struggled to regain control. Eventually she stopped sobbing and the shaking subsided. Wynter waited with patience until she was ready to speak.

"I'm sorry, sir. I think this thing is getting to me."

"That's all right. I think it's understandable. You've been under considerable pressure recently. Now what is it you want to talk to me about?"

"Well, yes. It's your advice. I need your advice. I want to know what's going on. I want to know what to do."

"You want to know what's going on. I should have thought that was clear. Mr Walsh decided to accept a commission. It was not just the wrong commission, it was also the wrong client. The commission went belly-up. The client was faced with more than irritation, embarrassment and inconvenience. He was faced with the need to save face. More important, he thought there was a chance that Walsh would cover his failure by striking back at the client. I assume you don't know who the client was?"

Melanie shook her head.

"No. Quite. Well it looks as if the client is striking a blow at Walsh and W.F.M.C. Now does all that have a ring of truth to it?"

Melanie nodded. "So this client assassinated Harvey and Chris. I do know that Stephen Wells was Chris's man and he's been killed hasn't he?" She paused here to wait for a response. In this she was disappointed. "Okay. I don't expect you to answer that. It seems logical then that if this client is mopping up then I'll be on the list. I was a big player in the operation and Chris was my boss. I'm next, aren't I?"

"I have no way of telling. However, it would seem likely."

"So what should I do?"

"What are your standing orders in circumstances such as these? You have trained for an eventuality such as this and you know what the operational procedure is, don't you?"

"Yes, but it's not as easy as that. Normally I would go walkabout. Standing orders make it clear. Standing orders also say I don't lose myself before getting approval from my team leader or, if that's not possible, from the managing director. Now I'm sure you'll see my fucking problem."

Wynter winced. While he had no problem with profanity as a rule it seemed so unbecoming when it came from the lips of Miss Coleman-Burns.

"I'm sorry. You are, of course, entirely correct. Okay." Wynter thought for a moment. "Okay," he said again very slowly. "Go and get yourself lost. I authorise it. You will need to contact me when you have found your bolt hole. You know the procedure. Tell no one except me. When you contact me, do not use the phone. Simply write. Plain language is fine. Mail is not censored. Just send me your address and a telephone number. "How are you off for cash?"

"I have about a hundred and fifty pounds. But I've got my company credit cards."

"I assume they are not in our name?"

"Of course not." This was the first time she had smiled during the meeting.

"You'll need more cash. Wait here a minute." Wynter left the study. From the phone in the kitchen he made a call which lasted several minutes. Then he went upstairs before returning to his guest. He handed her a small parcel.

"Here's a few thousand in cash. Leave your car here." Melanie raised her eyebrows and her jaw dropped so slightly most would not have spotted it. Wynter was observant and did not miss the expression of panic, fear and uncertainty. "Your car is a giveaway. Go and buy yourself something small and inconspicuous. The sort of car a young woman would seem at home in. Probably something French and secondhand. Forgive the sexism but it will do you for the next day or two. Use cash for everything you can. When I know where you are I will send you some more. Now you mustn't worry about money. This is all covered by the very comprehensive internal insurance arrangements we have for our people. Remember, no phone calls and do not turn up here in person. Only communicate by letter. Now then, am I correct in assuming you are still staying with your young friend, what's his name?"

"Thorpe. Jon Thorpe."

"Yes. That's the fellow."

"Yes, I am."

"Then you should make haste to put some distance between Mr Thorpe and yourself."

"Why? Is there a problem I don't know about?"

"Not as far as I am aware. It is merely that Mr Thorpe is a student with a few bob in the bank. He is not one of us. He is not a professional. He doesn't know the rules of our game and he could inadvertently compromise you."

"How do you know he's a student? How do you know he's got a few bob?"

"Oh, Melanie. We always look after our own. Do you think we would just cut you adrift, lose all interest in you? Is that really what you think?"

"You've had Jon checked out?"

"What do you think? He may be a problem for you."

"How so?"

"You're sleeping with him, aren't you?" Melanie's mouth opened to respond but Wynter held his hand up to stop her. "You are old enough to know how these things work. What will you tell him? How will you explain to him that you are leaving and why? He will get all macho about it and tell you he can protect you. He will say you are safest with him and all that kind of bullshit. He may put unwelcome pressure on you. I advise you simply disappear while he's out. That will be safest for you. The reality of the situation is that you cannot, under any circumstances, leave him with information. You can't tell him anything. If he gets all soppy with you you may find yourself tempted to throw him a crumb of comfort in the form of information which could come back and get you killed. Mr Thorpe must not be allowed to know anything. Am I being fair?"

Melanie thought for several seconds. "Of course you're right. I'll do a moonlight flit."

By the time Julie reached Jon Thorpe's comfortable 1930s semi-detached home in leafy suburbia, Melanie Coleman-Burns had fled. It was an easy matter for Julie to break in through the kitchen door at the back. She checked the bedrooms and found nothing to suggest the presence of a woman. None of the drawers or wardrobes contained anything the least bit feminine. Last she checked the bathroom and lavatory. The only toiletries were most definitely masculine. She stood at the top of the stairs and swore.

When Thorpe returned home in the late afternoon he had no idea there was anyone waiting for him in his sitting room. He was humming gently to himself as he unlocked his front door and turned the light on in the hall. He hung his jacket over a peg and entered the sitting room. He turned the light on and was startled to see Inspector Donna Pritchard sitting in his favourite chair.

"What are you doing here? Surely you can't just walk in here?"

"Where's Melanie?" Julie said without the slightest hint of friendliness.

"I don't know. Now please answer my question."

She stood and walked across the sitting room towards Thorpe. With no warning she slapped him on his cheek. While he was recovering from the shock she drove her clenched fist into his solar plexus. He folded forward. Even before he had finished doubling, she grabbed his hair and yanked his head upwards. While still holding his head upright by pulling his hair, she slapped his face again, the flat of her hand to his left cheek followed by the back of her hand to his right cheek. She repeated this action twice.

"Now I'll ask you again, Mr Thorpe. Where is Melanie?"

"I don't know," he replied haltingly. "Who are you?"

His back hit the floor hard as he fell backwards after a straight arm punch to his jaw. Julie's right knee hit the centre of his chest.

"This is the last chance you get. Where is Melanie?"

"I told you. I don't know. I thought she was here." Thorpe spoke haltingly. It was evident he was finding it difficult to speak with Julie's weight pressing down on his chest.

It was also clear that he didn't know of the target's whereabouts. If he had known he would have told her by now. This was one of the many positive points when dealing with amateurs. When they are subjected to pressure such as this, they always talk. Julie lifted her knee from Thorpe's chest. As she walked through the sitting room door she looked back.

"You have no idea how lucky you are today, Mr Thorpe."

Mr Thorpe could see no reason why this was his lucky day at all. He had quite a different perspective on his fortunes this day.

Back To The Island

Julie was preoccupied as she drove back to the ferry at Yarmouth. Harry had been angry and unsupportive, which she felt was a bit unfair since it was he who had caused the problem in the first place. She knew now she should never have agreed to alter her plans. Plans were the key, they should be flexible but not abandoned completely. Harry had made her do just that and now she felt that Harry was making her take the blame for the problem it had caused.

When she had told him that Miss Coleman-Burns had disappeared, Harry had been rude and unfair. He tried to lay the blame on her and she wasn't going to have it. Harry had told her she should have struck when she had the chance. It was her failure to act that had caused the upset now, he had said. Julie had told him that she stood not the slightest chance of finding Melanie quickly. Harry had exploded. His outburst caused other guests in the Shanklin hotel to look over at them. He had apologised, but Julie felt the damage was done. Harry calmed down and told her he would sort things. The operation was only a search and destroy variety. There were now no other considerations. Harry would visit Eric Wynter and put the pressure on him. He would make him tell of the whereabouts of Melanie. Gradually an unprofessional hatred of Coleman-Burns entered Julie's soul. She knew this was unreasonable and rather unfair. Coleman-Burns was doing what came naturally; she was trying to save her ass. She wasn't supposed to make it easy for her assassin. But this objectivity didn't help. Julie hated Coleman-Burns and that was all there was to it. She wasn't too sure, at this moment, that she didn't hate Harry as well.

Her mind was wandering and she wasn't concentrating on her driving and so it was she failed to give way at a "Give Way" sign. Fortunately the driver of the van she carved up was awake. He slammed on his brakes and stopped not more than two feet from her driver's door. Unfortunately for the van driver, he chose to wind down his window and shout abuse at the "bloody woman driver who shouldn't be allowed on the road." There was just enough room for Julie to open her door, which she did. Her face bore no expression as she approached the van driver. He was surprised to see her getting nearer but he kept up his monologue regarding women drivers. He only stopped when Julie delivered a backhander to his right cheek.

Before he could react, she grabbed the key in the ignition, turned the engine off and withdrew the key. She walked to the kerb just to the front of the van. Here she found the grill of a drain. Down this she dropped the key while the driver looked on aghast. His jaw dropped and as Julie walked back to her MGF, she stuck the middle finger of her right hand upwards and mouthed, "swivel." This was entirely out of keeping with her normal behaviour, but she had to admit that it made her feel better. It was with lighter heart she drove the rest of the way to Yarmouth.

The hired limousine pulled to a halt on Eric Wynter's drive. A suit jumped out of the front seat, scurried round the back of the car and opened the rear door. At the same time another suit knocked on the mighty brass door-knocker. Webster Hahn and two of his employees were ushered into Wynter's study, where they were asked to take a seat. Wynter joined them within a minute. Hahn rose to shake Wynter's hand.

"How nice to see you again, Mr Hahn. Thanks for coming to England to meet me," said Wynter.

"You made your invitation so intriguing it was difficult for me to refuse, Mr Wynter."

Wynter smiled a charming smile. "Now if you'll ask your friends to leave us, we'll talk some business."

Hahn turned to his men and nodded. As they left the study, Wynter's butler collected them at the door and escorted them away.

The men talked until well into the evening. Only twice did Wynter emerge to order coffees from the butler. And it was only once that Hahn was seen when he asked one of his suits to cancel their seats on the return aeroplane. He also requested a reservation in a local hotel for himself and his boys. His final instruction was to dismiss his men for the evening, telling them to take their dinners in the hotel. He would not be joining them. He would be dining with Mr Wynter.

By the time Hahn arrived at the hotel it was late and his men were jittery. Their relief was evident when they saw their employer enter the bar. He took one drink with them and excused himself. When he reached his room, he found his overnight case had been placed on his bed. Before unpacking he phoned America and quickly found his son, Joseph. Their conversation was long and at times heated.

It was noted that Webster Hahn was in a good humour during breakfast the following morning. He loved a cooked English breakfast and this particular one was especially good. His employees knew, though, that the breakfast was not the reason for his mood. Something big was going down and they were intrigued. Having savoured the breakfast, Hahn hurried his men to the car. As they drove to Eric Wynter's house he issued them with instructions.

Wynter himself opened the door to Hahn's knock and the two greeted each other like old friends. Dismissing his suits, Hahn followed Wynter to his study. It was lunchtime when the two men stood and shook hands.

"Of course, one way to look at it is that you are paying fourteen million pounds for a few computer disks," said Wynter. Both men laughed heartily.

"Yes. The question is," said Hahn, "am I paying fourteen million for the company and getting some free disks or am I paying fourteen million for some disks and getting a free company with them?" The two men laughed again.

"I'll get my financial and legal people to contact yours as soon as I get back to the States," Hahn said. "Let them work out the seamless takeover. I have to say, Eric, it has been a great pleasure doing business with you. It remains for you to advise me about this Coleman-Burns woman. We'll need her out of the picture quickly. You're sure you don't want any help with the matter?"

"No. No. It's in hand."

"Then I suggest we return to my hotel and you allow me to buy you lunch."

When he last met with Melanie Coleman-Burns it had occurred to him that there was a chance she might start to put two and two together and come up with an answer close to four. It was for this reason that he had phoned the office before handing the woman the cash. He had instigated a surveillance operation whereby she would be tailed around the clock. Wynter wanted to know of her every move.

Within hours he was to learn that she had taken his advice and flown without leaving an open trail. There was no forwarding address and she had spoken to no one. She had resisted any temptation to speak to Jon Thorpe.

He was also to learn that Melanie had purchased a small and battered Peugeot with cash. She had driven to Kent to visit an old school friend called Penny Mount. It took the tail several hours to discover that the Mount family owned the holiday apartment in Cornwall to which Melanie had driven.

Millendreath is a small holiday complex which boasts a beach at the foot of a valley on the south coast of Cornwall. Out of season it is very quiet with just a few stalwarts taking advantage of their seaside investments. Almost all the apartments are owned by people from afar who keep them as holiday homes. A few are owned by the developer, who offers them for short-term holiday lets. What attracts people to these properties is the scenery, the fact that it is less than an hour's walk to Looe, that it is handy to the main route into Cornwall and the layout of the apartments themselves. The hills on the west side of the valley are covered in these terraced and tiered apartments. Each has a vast patio that is on top of the roof of the apartment beneath. Each patio is separated from the neighbours by a low wrought iron railing. From the patio it is possible to see not just the beach and the sea but also the single approach road into the valley. It was here, in this quiet valley, that Melanie felt she could lose herself for months, or at least until Easter when the holiday season would start proper.

For two days she spoilt herself. She tried to unwind, she enjoyed the quiet, she cooked and read and, for the first time in days, felt secure. She kept a large handgun in the drawer under the dining table that was situated by the only door into the flat. She was confident she would not need it. Melanie surprised herself when she found she enjoyed sitting with her feet up watching daytime television. By and large it was superficial and banal, but maybe this was why she enjoyed it. She was amazed by the people off the street who were prepared to reveal their innermost secrets on national television. She was staggered by the plethora of chat shows from around the world and was delighted with reruns of old cop series, many of which she had forgotten about years earlier.

On the evening of the third day she cooked herself dinner. Opening a bottle of claret, she laid a place at the table. On the table she placed the Times and turned the television on. This, she felt, was the height of indulgence and by God she was going to enjoy it. She had found she had regained her appetite and she tucked into her meal with relish. As she ate, something began to niggle at her and before she finished the main course she put down her knife and fork. Her brow furrowed. She stood and walked around the apartment. She returned to her place at the table and pushed the unfinished meal away from her. She was asking herself a question and she could come up with only one answer.

W.F.M.C. had operated successfully for many years. It had survived and flourished because of the cell system it maintained. It had the need-to-know principle down to a fine art. Yet Walsh's disappointed clients had discovered Latcham. She could understand how Walsh had been identified, located and killed, but how had they discovered Latcham?

What was it that Wynter had said? They had been talking about mopping up. She had asked if it wouldn't be possible that she was on the list as well as the dead men. Wynter had said, "It would seem likely." He had told them about Latcham. It had to be him, who else was there? She hadn't said anything and so it had to be Wynter. But then again, if that was the case, why had he told her to run? False sense of security. He had also told her to let him know where she was when she was sorted. She had to tell him and him alone; well, that figured. But she had to use the post only. That was what he had said.

Melanie shuddered. Suddenly it felt cold despite the heating inside this holiday apartment. Was Wynter throwing her to the wolves, and if so why? No matter which way she looked at it, she kept coming up with the same answer. For reasons best known to himself, and she knew enough to realise they would be commercial reasons, Wynter had betrayed Latcham. And then there was another thing; they knew about Walsh but how did they know where he was hiding? That had to be Wynter also. He had gone this far and now it was inevitable he would betray her. He probably had no choice. Well, if he was expecting her to write to him with her whereabouts, he was sadly mistaken.

As these thoughts developed in her mind she became aware that she was feeling rather more cheerful than she had for some time. Ah, the perversity of humankind, she thought. The truth was that she felt relief. The confusing thoughts, which had been troubling her, now started to make some sense. Now she had some notion of what she was up against. Wynter was every bit as much an enemy as the hidden assassin or assassins who worked for the mysterious client. Could she prove her theory? Perhaps she could give Wynter a fake location. If she staked it out and someone then showed, she would know for sure. Soon she rejected this. It made sense that she disappear for a while and gave herself time to think, plan and rest. That was it. She would be safe for a day or two then she would move on. She would put some distance between herself and Wynter and W.F.M.C. Her life could be built again, she had some money, resources and considerable abilities.

That night Melanie Coleman-Burns slept well.

Webster Hahn waited in his library. After the cold of England he was pleased to be home. The cold and damp had got into his bones and made him feel the aches and pains of his years. To balance this, however, he was delighted with the deal he had struck with Eric Wynter. Now, for the first time, he had the opportunity to develop business in Britain.

He would be in a position of huge strength. The resources he was in the process of buying were awe-inspiring, the contacts priceless. It put him in touch with major European business and American industry operating throughout Europe. It enlarged his existing contacts with American business and this delighted him. Webster Hahn thought that £14,000,000 was a small price to pay.

To ensure the transfer worked, there were clauses battled out between him and Wynter so that it was in everyone's best interests that the acquisition went smoothly. All in all Hahn was in buoyant mood while he sat in his library waiting for Dr Jonjo Grey. When Grey arrived, Hahn could see that he was a troubled man. Drinks were poured and the two men found themselves alone.

"Webster, I was under the impression we had reached an arrangement. Then I find that I'm being threatened by your son, Joseph. I ask myself, "Why do I receive so much grief from Webster Hahn's boys?' Do you know the answer, Webster?"

"How is Joseph unsettling you, Jonjo?"

"He hasn't forgiven me for Ricky's death. He tells me you've called him off but also tells me that when he takes over as head of the family business, he'll come looking for me. Not a comfortable thought, Webster. I'm left with little choice. Is it your wish that we go to war? Tell me now and we'll get this thing settled."

Webster pondered before speaking. "Joseph was close to his brother. He finds it difficult to forgive. Remember, Jonjo, he's not so much older than Ricky. But I'm sorry he put the squeeze on you. I'll ensure that you never hear from Joseph again.

"Now, Jonjo, I have to ask myself a question. I believe you wanted something that belongs to me. Something to threaten me with. Perhaps it was to offer me a bargain in return for calling Joseph off. This I understand. My question is this. How did you get to know that Eric Wynter had some disks of mine? This has been troubling me."

For a moment Grey was taken off guard. The question took him totally by surprise. He did not reply, instead he smiled at Hahn, who continued.

"Let me tell you that Eric Wynter no longer has the disks. They've been returned to me. I've purchased Wynter Farmer Management Consultants. I tell you this as a gesture of good faith. You will not repeat it, I trust. Now who told you about the disks?"

"Sorry, Webster. No can do." Grey stood and sauntered to a floor to ceiling window. "Can I leave here today knowing that there will be no more bad feeling between us? Can I leave here with the prospect of continuing peace?"

"I've given you my word, Jonjo. Joseph will be no threat to you now or in the future."

"I'm pleased, Webster. A war I don't need, and I guess you don't either." Grey paused. "Wynter told you I enquired about the disks, I guess?"

"Goodbye, old friend. I hope we'll meet again soon in an atmosphere of peace and trust."

The men shook hands and Grey walked to the door. As he opened it Hahn shouted across the library, "It was Leo Salmon wasn't it, Jonjo? Salmon told you, didn't he?"

Without turning, Grey raised his arm to wave. Hahn could not see the smile on Grey's face.

Eric Wynter was surprised when his butler announced the arrival of Sir Harry Buchanan. When the two men met in the study, Wynter said, "I had thought our business together was concluded, Sir Harry."

"As had I. It is with some embarrassment I have to tell you we seem to have mislaid Miss Coleman-Burns."

"How very careless of you. I am bound to say, I'm a mite surprised. Your efficiency so far has been commendable. How do you think I can help you?"

"The whereabouts of Miss Coleman-Burns, if you please."

Wynter made the pretence of resistance. Harry knew that the old crook had no choice but to tell. What Harry did not know was that the last thing Wynter wanted now was inconvenience, exposure to the authorities or trouble of any kind. He wanted nothing that would rattle Webster Hahn.

"If I tell you the whereabouts of Miss Coleman-Burns, am I safe in the assumption you and I will have no further business together?"

"Assuming the information you give is correct, then your assumption is absolutely safe." Harry was hating this interview. It irritated and embarrassed him. He felt it demonstrated weakness to Wynter. This whole operation should have been wrapped up days ago. Harry was also aware that Wynter was enjoying this. It probably gave him a feeling of power and control. Harry felt vulnerable and knowing that Wynter was enjoying it only served to make matters worse. The sooner he was out of here the better.

Wynter wrote an address on a slip of paper that he handed to Harry.

It took Julie more than two and a half hours to find Millendreath and its car park at the foot of the valley and just inland of the deserted beach. Her first thought was for coffee, which she found in the café. This, to her surprise and delight, she found to be open in this otherwise closed season. The only customer, she sat at a table in the window as she drank the coffee. From this point she could see most of the car park and some of the narrow lanes between the rows of holiday apartments. It also surprised her that there were holiday makers at this time of the year. She would rather have been in California or maybe South Africa, indeed anywhere where the sun shone and was hot.

While she could see traffic, the car parks and pedestrians from the café, she could not see many patios and none of the insides of the apartments. Each had large panoramic windows and, she had noticed when she had driven down the valley, few were screened by net curtains. She also noticed that if she sat in her car in the car park she would have a view of the front of nearly all the apartments. This meant she would have sight of the patios and the interior of the apartments through the patio windows.

She walked back to the car and drove back up the hill for fifty yards to the car park. At this time of the year it was possible to choose any spot. She reversed her hired Renault Laguna into a spot at the far side of the park. Here she sat for several hours pretending to read the day's broadsheets that she had purchased on the motorway service area. Every now and then she picked up her binoculars and scanned the rows of terraces. It was starting to get dark as she wandered across the car park, more to stretch her legs than anything else. It was then that she saw the Mercedes. The grey car was parked away from the car park and on a pull-in on one of the tiny roads between the terraces of apartments. It was partially hidden on three sides by trees. Inside Julie could just make out the shape of two occupants. She could not tell their sex. She dismissed the thought of them being a courting couple. This was an expensive car. It would be seen as being out of place at this site. It would draw attention to itself. In any case, if the occupants wanted sex and could afford a car like this, then other arrangements of a more comfortable, safe and salubrious nature could be made. These people were here because they had no alternative. They were here because they had not had the time or perhaps the opportunity to make other arrangements. It was just the sort of situation in which a tail a long way from home might find itself. She returned to her car and was mildly irritated to discover she could actually see the Mercedes from it. Her irritation was due to the fact she had failed to see it before.

One by one the lights of the few occupied apartments came on as the light began to fail. Julie was able to count just seven cars in the car park and a similar number dotted around the complex. Among them however, there was no sign of a BMW. This did not surprise her. If her target was hiding down here in Cornwall she would most likely change her car. So the absence of the BMW did not worry her. What worried her was the fact that there was no sign of life in the apartment. Perhaps Harry had given her the wrong number. In case it was the wrong number, Julie did not concentrate exclusively on the one location. Instead she trained her glasses around the whole complex.

It was pitch black and nearly eight o'clock before she saw Melanie Coleman-Burns. She saw her stretching up to draw the curtains across the ceiling to floor panorama windows. A quick look through the binoculars confirmed the target's presence.

The presence of the Mercedes did nothing to help. From its vantage point, the occupants had a clear view of all the approaches to the apartment. Since Julie did not know who was inside the car she was not prepared to take any chances. She had no intention of being identified. It seemed for a moment as if her problem was going to be solved for her. The Mercedes moved off. Julie slid down in her seat as the big car passed less than fifty yards away. It was not that they would be able to see much, it was dark. More, she did not want them to become aware that there was someone else sitting in a car with nothing better to do with their life. It was in her experience that watchers did not like being watched. It made them feel uneasy and fear the worst.

She considered it would be prudent to wait for a short while just in case something else happened. It did. The Mercedes was replaced by a Rover Sterling. As the new car passed her, she could make out the profile of a man and a woman as the car came between her and a streetlight. These people, she thought, don't seem to mind drawing attention to themselves. She wondered if they had any purpose in making themselves so conspicuous. In any event, the problem still remained. How was she to get to the apartment unseen. There were dim streetlights interspersed throughout the complex that provided enough light to prevent her making her way unobserved. She toyed with the idea of interrupting the electrical supply. This thought she dismissed quickly because she didn't have the first idea how to do it. She considered shooting the occupiers of the Sterling. This she dismissed also. It was not part of her contract, it was not essential and it could cause the kind of furore she relished not one bit. Julie was still smarting from her killing of the two police officers in Cheltenham. This seemed to have gone away but she was still not certain for how long it would stay away. On the other hand, if she could be sure the two in the car were hoods, then she wouldn't hesitate to kill them. The problem was, how could she make an identification from here? She would have to think of something else.

Clearly there was going to be no profit by sitting in her car. This she had done for hours and had so far gained little. She got out and locked the Renault. For an hour she carefully made her way around the site as if to explore. She had still not found a solution until she found steps behind the café in which she had earlier taken her coffee. The steps took her up the hill, behind and above the apartments. Here she found mainly evergreen trees and bushes. Julie felt a thrill as she realised she could pick her way through this scrub to a spot behind the target's apartment. There were no windows in the back of any of the apartments, it was dark because the moon was covered with cloud and because it was so cold there would be few people out and about who might see her. The Sterling would never be closer than three hundred yards and for nearly all of the way the buildings would shield her.

It took her rather longer than she expected to progress through the shrub. Old supermarket trolleys, prams and rubbish made the passage hazardous. But she made it. Her target was not on the highest terrace but at the end of the terrace below. With care she picked her way down the side. There was a high side window through which a light was shining. When she reached it she stood under it and realised there was not a hope of seeing through it. It was simply too high. This led her to suspect it was a lavatory or bathroom. As she pressed her back against the wall she tilted her head up and backwards to enable her to look up at the window. The clouds of steam now passing through it confirmed her theory. This was a bathroom. But now what? She could not reach.

Silently she made her way to the patio. It contained nothing of use to her. The patio of the apartment below likewise contained nothing. Her pulse quickened as she thought of the consequence of failure. It was with a slight sensation of desperation she checked the patio above the target's. She cursed herself for not having noticed before. She saw a white plastic picnic table and four matching chairs. She calculated that the chairs would still not give her enough height. The table, on the other hand, would. She jumped over the low railing and collected the table. It was light and presented no great problem in being lifted over the rails. As she descended to the terrace below she heard voices. Below, on the road, a couple was walking towards the beach or towards the Sterling. She had no time to hide so, still carrying the table, she stood stock still. She hardly dared to breathe. It was a relief when the two disappeared from sight.

Steam was still billowing through the window as Julie gently placed the table against the wall. It did not provide the stablest of platforms but it would do. Carefully she climbed onto the table. Now she could see inside the bathroom. Melanie Coleman-Burns was taking a shower. Julie could not see her because she was obscured by a shower curtain. She had to wait a minute during which time she felt exposed and vulnerable. Not only would she have some difficulty explaining what she was doing acting like a Peeping Tom but, more to the point, if a public spirited somebody shouted "Hey, You!" it would have the effect of advertising her presence to the target. It was with relief she heard the water stop as the tap was turned off. The curtain was pulled to one side and Melanie Coleman-Burns stepped out. As she reached for the towel she looked up and saw Julie.

For part of one second Julie stared at her victim. She was struck by her youth and beauty. For that tiniest moment she thought what a shame it was to destroy something as beautiful as this. Her thought pattern was broken by Melanie.

"Cla-!"

Julie pulled the Type 67's trigger twice. Both the bullets entered the body between the breasts, just two inches apart, flinging the victim across the bathroom. The corpse hit the wall hard and immediately crumpled to the floor.

As she replaced the table where she had found it, she pondered. The target had uttered a single syllable. Had she been allowed to finish the word what would she have said? Was she going to say "Claire" or was she about to say "Clarion?" Julie dismissed such valueless thoughts from her mind. Maybe the recent pressure was making her paranoid. Melanie could not possibly have known her code name. She stood for less than ten seconds to check for suspicious sights or sounds. There was nothing, and why should there be? She had made no sound. It took her another hour to regain her car and it was with relief she started it and drove away. She would be pleased to get back to Gloucestershire.

Completion

Sir Gordon Melville was not pleased. Despite having made the usual appointment, it took him over twenty minutes before he found himself in Harry's office. His irritation was diffused a little when he set eyes on the knight. He looked distinctly unwell, he was sagging. He appeared exhausted and pale.

"My dear Harry. You're not looking your usual self. Feeling unwell, old boy?"

Harry smiled. "Burning the candle at both ends, I suspect. You're right, I do feel a little under the weather. Time for a holiday."

"I rather hope you're going to tell me you're in a position to take a break. I have told the P.M. that the job is complete. Was I correct in my assurance?"

"Yes. The final piece was put into place only last night. It's over, Gordon."

The cabinet secretary beamed and his shoulders relaxed. His relief was obvious. "Harry, my congratulations. I am extremely grateful and I know the Prime Minister will consider himself to be in your debt."

Yeah. I bet, thought Harry.

"That sounds comfortable. Well, Gordon, if there's nothing else I'm going to take a few days R and R. If you need anything in my absence I suggest you contact Vanessa Stone. She will know what to do."

The two knights shook hands and as Melville was leaving he turned to face Harry.

"You look as if you need to take care of yourself, Harry. Make sure you enjoy your rest."

That evening Harry felt nothing but relief. He felt as if the pressure had been lifted after a very long time and now he could get away. He was going to Scotland the next day, take time out and decide what to do about the wretched aortic aneurysm. The only downside to going to

Scotland was the packing. He was not a good packer and it was a chore he hated. It was for this reason he had organised himself so that most of what he needed was already north of the border. By fully equipping and provisioning both homes he could get away with the minimum amount of packing. On this occasion he was not taking any files with him. His laptop was going to remain in Marlow along with his mobile phone. He had told his three deputy directors, Vanessa Stone, John Morgan and Sam Marchant, they were only to contact him in the gravest of emergencies and only then if they could not think of an alternative course of action.

While he was throwing a few of the essentials into his case he heard the knock at the door. He knew this was Julie Martin, who was here to collect her final payment for successfully completing the contract. She had done a great job in spite of his interference. He had shot her plans to pieces and still the commission was successfully fulfilled. This was why the Clarion Resource existed as a contractor to and asset of Section P. The Clarion Resource was remarkable, but then it should be. It had had the finest training spread over many years. The training had cost the taxpayer a vast amount of money. Its supervision had been the most stringent.

Harry slowly walked downstairs. He peered through the peephole in his front door. Sure enough, it was Julie. When he opened the door they hugged each other. Before closing the door, Harry stepped out and looked down his long curved drive. He stared at the laurel trees and across the lawns. Just an oversensitive precaution or perhaps it was a silly habit he had developed over the years. Back inside he couldn't help noticing that Julie looked great. She was dressed in a black leather blousson jacket and tight black leather jeans. She wore flat-soled black boots and carried a black leather handbag.

Harry escorted her into his grand sitting room where she was pleased to see a blazing log fire.

"Sit down," said Harry, pointing to a huge settee. "You'll find that envelope is for you." This time Harry pointed to the coffee table in front of the settee. "Cognac do you?" Without waiting for an answer he poured two drinks. "You've done a brilliant and sparkling piece of work, despite my interference."

"I know you couldn't help it, Harry dear."

"Nevertheless it put you at risk along with the entire project. But, as usual, you came through. I am grateful and so are my masters. Here's to the Clarion Resource." Harry raised his glass. "Where's your car?"

"I left it down the road a way. I'm not happy about us turning up on each other's doorstep. Not a good habit."

"Of course you're right as ever. So now it's over, all the loose ends nicely tidied up. I don't suppose it's any good asking you what's next."

Julie laughed. Harry turned away and bent over a Tudor oak chest on which sat his cigar humidor. This called for a celebration. One of his best Havanas would do very nicely.

"Not a bit of good, Harry. Unfortunately there is still one loose end."

Harry stopped just as his hand reached the humidor. For a second he remained leaning over the sideboard as if in suspended animation. One more loose end. Car parked down the road. Black leather, so no residue, no fibre traces. Flat shoes. She hadn't touched anything other than the brandy balloon. Harry realised that the aneurysm would not be the cause of his death. He straightened, turned and faced Clarion. He saw she was now standing facing him, her legs apart. Both arms were outstretched and in her hands she gripped the Glock. Harry knew he was about to die and would have liked to have said something now to the young woman he had always viewed as a daughter. She gave him no chance.

The bullet hit Harry in the centre of his forehead. The impact made his neck snap backwards but, because he was such a big, heavy man, it did not propel his body back with any great force. He fell backwards surprisingly slowly. His body hit the oak chest and he nearly assumed a sitting position before collapsing onto the carpet.

Julie dropped the gun into her handbag. She picked up the envelope and dropped it into her bag. Finally she lifted the brandy balloon to her lips and swallowed what remained of the warming drink. She dropped the glass into her bag. Without looking to left or right she reached the door, removed a handkerchief from her pocket, which she used to ensure her hand did not touch the knob when she turned it to open the door. Closing the door behind her she walked briskly down the long, curved gravel drive. When she gained the main road she turned left and walked towards Marlow.

It was some five minutes later that a car pulled up at her side. Even before the car had come to a rest the back door swung open. Without the slightest delay Julie jumped into the back seat and slammed the door behind her. The powerful engine in the big Jaguar roared and the bonnet rose into the air. The car was such a dark green that, in some lights, it appeared to be black.

Epilogue

Sir Harry Buchanan. The world heard about Harry's death in the obituary columns of the quality press. He had died, readers were told, when his aortic aneurysm burst. On the day of the funeral, which, as expected, was well attended, it appeared as if spring had come early. It was the first day of the year when it was possible not to wear a coat without freezing. The sky was blue and there was not even a hint of frost, snow or rain. Many of the mourners were civil servants. There were also some politicians from both sides of the House, many of whom were senior. Friends and neighbours were plentiful. No one recognised the attractive, dark-haired woman who stood alone at the back of the church and later, away from the rest, in the churchyard. There was some speculation afterwards as to her identity but her presence was not seen as being especially significant.

Julie Martin. Julie's business was sold as a going concern. The new owner took on all the staff and so there were no unwelcome redundancies. Julie told her staff she was going to disappear for a few months and backpack around the world. Despite the fact that no one knew much about Julie's personal habits, there was some doubt that backpacking was quite her thing. Nevertheless she reassured them that they would receive cards from all around the world. The cottage was sold at exactly the right time. Property prices were to peak just a few weeks after the sale. The selling price exceeded her expectations by over £35,000.

The Clarion Resource. The existence of Section P's asset, or rather Harry's own asset, was never proved. After Harry's death the deputy directors of Section P mounted an unofficial audit and search trail to find documentary evidence to prove that the Clarion Resource actually existed. The team was unable to come up with anything except the payment of large sums of money. Unfortunately for the researchers, the money was drawn from the special contingency fund, in cash. This was indeed its purpose, so that Harry could take whatever steps he deemed necessary without involving anyone else. It became clear by the total silence from above that whatever the problem had been, it had been sorted by Harry and, very probably by the mysterious man known to Harry as the Clarion Resource. Shortly before retiring, Gordon Melville, with apparent innocence, suggested that Harry himself might have been the Clarion Resource. He said that Harry may have invented the asset so that he always had a scapegoat to hand. At the same time he would have been able to enrich himself by pocketing the monies supposedly paid to Clarion. This theory gained little support within the Section.

James Bailey. At the next general election, Bailey's government was brought down by a narrow majority. There was never any hint of impropriety in Bailey's dealings with Erifia. The election was primarily lost because the great British electorate fancied a change. Bailey, his government and his policies, while competent, were now a little jaded. In less than eighteen months, the new government went to the country again after suffering a devastating vote of no confidence in the House. The country disliked the tax-and-spend policy and slung the new government out. However, Bailey did not seek re-election and when he told his local constituency party of his decision to stand down as their candidate there was considerable disappointment. Bailey and his family retired to Erifia, where the bond with President Sandriano was cemented further.

President Jacques Sandriano. Erifia held its election every four years. For many years, the government of President Sandriano was returned by a huge majority. Sandriano enjoyed huge popularity in his own country and in others. He remained fit and well and Erifia prospered due, in no small part, to the influence and wise counsel of Sandriano's dear friend, James Bailey.

Webster Hahn. He remained as head of the family business for years longer than he had anticipated. His trust in his son, Joseph, wavered. Joseph never quite lived up to his expectation. In the United States the business continued to prosper. The acquisition of W.F.M.C. never totally delivered the promise. Hahn installed his own management style, which did not go down perfectly in Britain and Europe. Nevertheless, the business was always in profit and its existence was often of considerable use to Hahn.

Joseph Hahn. Joseph was competent but he could, on rare occasions, be inappropriately unpredictable. Some of his decisions conflicted with those of his father. Twelve years his senior, it was Michael Charlton who succeeded to the head of the family business. This slight was intolerable to Joseph and he was given permission by the other directors, Charlton along with Knight and Goldstein, to leave and set up his own operation based in Atlantic City.

Dr Jonjo Grey. His fortunes continued to rise. The success of his car launches and the strength of the Ribbon Motor Corporation put Grey in the spotlight. He was courted by the opposition with offers that by any standards could be viewed as extremely generous. These were always resisted because of his loyalty to RMC.

Eric Wynter. Wynter died just two months after Harry's funeral. Cause of death was uncertain because the post mortem found nothing of interest. In fact, Wynter appeared to be very well for someone of his age. Inevitably there was some speculation because the business had, just days earlier, been transferred to the Hahn family. But it was only talk.

Sir Gordon Melville. There was the surprise resignation of the cabinet secretary. No reasons were ever made public, but there was the inevitable speculation.

Dennis Mann. Dennis spent less and less time in the pub. As every month passed he appeared busier and better off. Occasionally he was seen around in the presence of an attractive woman but if he was questioned about it, in the pub on a Sunday lunchtime, he would always pass it off. It was an irritation to his friends that he would disappear without notice. He would break appointments and the drinking circle at the Prince Consort seemed to be disintegrating.